The Year of the Frog

A Novel by MARTIN M. ŠIMEČKA

Translated by PETER PETRO
Foreword by VÁCLAV HAVEL

SCRIBNER PAPERBACK FICTION
PUBLISHED BY SIMON & SCHUSTER

SCRIBNER PAPERBACK FICTION
Simon & Schuster Inc.
Rockefeller Center
1230 Avenue of the Americas
New York, New York 10020

First Scribner Paperback Fiction Edition 1996
Published by arrangement with Louisiana State University Press

Manufactured in the United States of America

10 9 8 7 6 5 4 3 2 1

Library of Congress Cataloging-in-Publication Data is available.

ISBN 0-684-81367-X

Originally published as *Džin* by Archa, Bratislava

Foreword

Literature: The Indivisible Domain
by Václav Havel

In this time of political and territorial division, I am pleased to have an opportunity to mention briefly that domain of human thought and activity which is indivisible. For if I am to introduce in a few sentences this English translation of the novel written by Martin M. Šimečka, the outstanding young novelist and political commentator from Bratislava, then I must talk about the domain of literature.

With Martin Šimečka, the theme of the indivisibility of Slovak and Czech literature offers itself with a humorous ease. His mother is of Czech birth, and it was the same with his father, the late Milan Šimečka, who, unfortunately, died in 1990 as one of the world's renowned interpreters of the totalitarian system of the last twenty years—and an active member of the resistance to it.

Young Šimečka, like his father, moves in his utterances from Slovak to Czech and back without any effort or hesitation. As far as I may be allowed to judge, or may follow the judgment of my Slovak friends, Martin Šimečka's Slovak is one of the most attractive and natural among Slovak writers of the last two or even three generations.

He made a conscious decision to become a Slovak writer, and having decided, he did not distance himself by even an inch from his primordial Czech origin. This language decision, however, may also be connected with his resolve to consider his own existential experience, which determines the nature of his work, from the vantage point of Bratislava and, more generally, Slovakia.

For those who cannot sufficiently appreciate the difference between Czech and Slovak, be it as linguists, or as participants in the everyday life of these two communities, it is difficult to grasp how intimately close and mutually enriching these two languages really are. Without any doubt, this closeness springs from the fact that these two communities, however divided in history by the bigger powers, experienced both an oppression and a self-liberation that were fundamentally very similar.

Martin M. Šimečka's novel reaffirms that as long as the interest of literature in the realities of the world and human nature is directed by a "soft," compassionate heart and a rigorously rational and analytical logic, literature cannot be divided and quartered. It will always speak on a higher level in wonderful tongues about individual experience transformed into art.

Publisher's Note

The Pegasus Prize for Literature was established by Mobil Corporation to introduce American readers to distinguished works from countries whose literature is rarely translated into English. *The Year of the Frog*, by Martin M. Šimečka, was awarded the Pegasus Prize in Prague in May, 1992, after an independent jury selected it from among the best novels written in Czechoslovakia in the preceding ten years. The novel, which first appeared in Slovak underground *samizdat* as a series of three novellas during the 1980s and was re-published in one volume in 1990, joins short stories, articles, and essays that Mr. Šimečka has published in his home country and elsewhere in Europe. In 1987 the author won the Jiří Orten Award for young Czechoslovak writers. Mr. Šimečka is also active as a political essayist and commentator, and was an advocate of continued Czech and Slovak union even as the two nations were moving toward their split finalized on January 1, 1993.

The chairman of the Pegasus selection committee was Ludvík Vaculík, veteran Czech essayist, critic, and, with Václav Havel, a founding member of the Charter '77 human rights group in Czechoslovakia. Other committee members were Milan Jungmann, critic, former editor of the journal *Literární Listy*, and chairman of the Czech Writers' Community in Prague; Miloš Žiak, Slovak writer, publisher, and contributor to the underground publication *Fragment K*; Vladimír Karfík, critic and editor of the journal *Literární Noviny*; and Fedor Matejov, critic and member of the Slovak Academy of Sciences' Institute for Literature.

The Year of the Frog narrates the coming of age of Milan, a young former track star prevented by the communist authorities from university enrollment because of the dissident activities of his father.

But while political oppression is indeed an important element in the book, it serves more as a backdrop to Milan's maturation as he progresses through menial jobs, first as a hospital orderly and next as a clerk in a hardware store; finally he returns to the same hospital to work in the maternity ward. More central is Milan's love for the aristocratic but bohemian Tania, and the way that love evolves from the first blush of youthful passion to the hard lessons of responsibility and pain. And all these experiences—operating room tedium, medical tragedy, pushing one's body to the limit on solitary runs, the bliss and sorrow of love, and the sometimes horrible cycle of birth, fertility, and death—serve as fuel for Milan's ever-reflective mind, which always tries to extract philosophical truth from the confusion of events around him.

Mr. Šimečka's novel was translated by Peter Petro, a critic, academic, and translator of Czech and Slovak into English. Dr. Petro is associate professor of Russian, Slovak, Czech, and comparative literature at the University of British Columbia in Vancouver, Canada.

On behalf of the author, we wish to express our appreciation to Mobil Corporation, which established the Pegasus Prize and provided for the translation of this volume into English.

Notice

I stood in front of the payroll office, waiting for a signature on the form. Next to me stood a wizened grandpa in a baggy suit, with an identical form in his hand.

"So you're giving notice too, Gramps?" I asked.

"Yup. I don't want to see them anymore."

"You don't like it here at the Slovnaft Refinery?"

"My boy, I've been working here for twenty-five years. I just can't take it anymore. I've lost thirty pounds in the last three months, as you see."

"I see."

"It's the gas, my boy, the gas that's leaking from the pipes."

"Sue them, Gramps!"

"Oh no. I don't have a brother high up in the Ministry. That's how it is. How could I sue them?" He placed his ear against the mat glass on the door, peeked through the keyhole, and walked a few steps down the hall. Soon he returned and whispered: "They screwed me, my boy. So there!"

The door opened, and they asked me in.

"What will be your next job?" the office girl asked me.

"I don't know."

"What do you mean you don't know?"

"I simply don't know."

"But we have to know."

"I'm very sorry."

"You have to do something!"

"Naturally."

"But that's no answer!"

So I need advice, I mumbled to myself when, two hours later, I jogged in my white shorts and a blue T-shirt past the President's

1

villa, which had been purchased before he became President. It stood above our house, on a hill.

As I started my stopwatch, a German shepherd barked and rubbed his snout against the fence. The President had moved to Prague, but the guard box remained here, to be used when, occasionally, he thought of visiting Bratislava.

Before I began to sweat, I ran through all of Mountain Park and the residential section. I breathed in the hot air with difficulty; my body was tense and my eyes burned so much that I had to look at my own shadow. I began to feel sweat on my brow and my chest as I passed the Red Bridge. I was finally running in earnest. I lengthened my step and watched my thighs. They had gotten thinner since I stopped racing, but otherwise seemed all right. I slid by a dachshund who forgot to argue with his old mistress about the direction of their outing, his brown eyes observing me in astonishment. I also met a young couple connected by the lips. It seemed awkward to warn them that I was coming, so I just flew by in a long jump, grazing the girl and mumbling an apology from a distance. Farther along, the path cleared and all I met were squirrels. As the hillside narrows and dips into the valley, two paths cross. In the distance I spied a runner flashing between the trees down by a brook.

"Hi!" I shouted.

"Hi! Where are you off to?"

"I don't care."

"So come along. I heard you quit. Did you?"

"I did."

We ran and talked about running. They all still run and dream, travel to competitions, win or lose, and talk about running. It all came back to me, and I felt a tingling sensation down my spine. My legs felt as if they had waked up, and I sensed a pleasant tension in my groin. The trees flashed by faster. I passed by my partner as the path narrowed and we stopped talking. The terrain changed, and sharp turns forced me to change my rhythm as well. I started to breathe on each fourth step of my left foot. It worked like a Swiss watch. I stretched my torso, and from somewhere inside, the velocity increased like an unstoppable pleasure. A long, dark alley

2

lined itself up ahead. I turned around, but there was no need to, as my opponent was suddenly at my shoulder. We both took off like airplanes, and I could hear his spasmodic breathing through the pounding of blood in my ears. At that moment, he became my friend and opponent in life and death. We were connected by the dark alley and the insane speed. We had found a common pace. It was a dance of two runners.

"You're still good," he said at the end.

"You don't lose it that fast."

"Come to the stadium."

"I can't."

"Why?"

From the Red Bridge I ran alone again, feeling sad. Water was flooding the pavement, and two men in overalls were gazing at a fountain of water spouting from a hole they'd just dug. I continued running. I was sad that eventually I would have to stop and then remember it all: the water on the pavement and the fact that I did not know what I was going to do. At last I got tired and quit. A bit later I left my house relaxed and ran up to the bus with pleasure, because I love fatigue. It makes my legs hot and pliant like over-heated rubber.

Tania was waiting for me in front of the school; she placed the report of grades in her purse and offered me her mouth. Tania's mouth radiates heat and is full of jewellike teeth. Her sky-blue eyes peered at me closely, and she had to turn her head up. I pressed her body against mine to feel her breasts. She understood, because I caught that particular smile on her lips that communicates approval.

We walked through the city where we had both been born, went to a terrace cafe, and ordered coffee.

"So I'm unemployed as of today," I said.

"And I have vacations."

I didn't mean it that way, but she was right: if we wanted to, we could make good use of that time.

"Do you know what you're going to do?"

"No idea. A man should do something to earn his woman's respect. Maybe he should build a house or chop down a tree."

"That wouldn't impress me."

"You never can tell."

"I don't want you to build a house or chop down any trees. I know that."

Then what do you want? I wanted to ask.

Her head looked beautiful against the background of narrow lanes. It reflected itself in empty faces passing by her and gazing nowhere in particular.

My parents were gone on holiday, and my brother had disappeared for five weeks into some military barracks. They left Lisa in my care, and as soon as I opened the door, she meowed and rubbed herself against my leg. I could not remember if I had fed her that morning, but Tania picked her up and they both asked me for food.

"You'll spoil her," I said.

"And you'd starve her to death."

We continued our game by feeding Lisa. Tania was sitting by me, watching the feline elegance present even while the cat was eating. In the background, the legendary Beatles were playing, though they were as alien to me as Beethoven. But I love them equally.

Finally, Tania got up. She helped me to join the beds together, move the table, open the door to the balcony, and draw the blinds. Ten minutes later, the room where I spent twenty-two years with my brother looked like the master bedroom of a married couple. A room never before disturbed.

When we lay down on the marriage bed, her body smelled of wind and of summer. It was the same fragrance I had breathed in while running, when the crowns of trees arched over me. I dipped my face into her tanned belly, and when I found Tania's mouth, she accepted it as a liberation and gratefully greeted me with her tongue.

Then came the opening. The language of the smooth thighs always confuses me, as they open up like an embrace. She did not invite me with a smile, but with her shy humility. Enter quickly, please, don't leave me like this in front of the whole world, she seemed to say. And so I hurried, moved to tears.

4

"What's happening to us?" she asked when we rested side by side, looking at the ceiling.

How would I know? I thought. I love you. The way a tick loves its host, because I am the same kind of parasite. Through you, I address Nature, and in return, I get a feeling of life. But how should I know what's going on with you?

"I don't know," I said aloud.

She turned her head and observed my profile. She had a glass of red wine in her hand, and it colored the corners of her mouth. I licked my lips.

How should I know what goes on inside a woman? Nature forms her in her image, and I just watch in astonishment. We look at women, build homes for them, play and sing for them, create household inventions for them, force them to work, divide them into states, and keep them in fear that one day we'll get tired of it and wreck it all. Because we mourn our own purposelessness. And what does it matter if I'm wrong?

Tania whispered something in my ear, and behind the blind a bee that had dared to fly up to the fifth floor kept buzzing.

"Don't talk about that," I begged.

But she did it again, even more beautifully.

The fact that she loves me will not make me change my mind.

Lisa jumped up to the door handle and noisily let herself in. She worriedly looked at me, but Tania pressed her to her chest. Lisa started to purr, and the Beatles tune stopped.

A week later, at a railway station, I was saying good-by to Tania. She wanted to come with me, but I wouldn't let her. Certain things have to be experienced alone.

I got off in Pardubice and, following the directions included in the invitation to the entrance examination, found the dormitory without a hitch. In my room I found a person who was just in the process of opening a bottle of beer with his knife.

"Hi there! I'm Michael. Wanna beer?" he asked.

I did want it, for I liked that young man. Behind his thick glasses his eyes looked so small that it seemed he did not move them at all;

they were like little balls centered inside the lenses. We went downtown for more beer, because the one I drank was his last.

"Milan, I see you bought some new Marathon running shoes. That's great. I run, too," he put in enthusiastically. We were sitting in a pub. I liked him more and more.

"But I'm not just an ordinary runner," I said, trying to impress him.

"No matter. We'll run together, and I'll hold on to you like a tick."

We walked around the square, with its Plague Column, and I thought how beautiful life is when you can just walk into a store and buy a pair of Marathon running shoes the first time you go in.

The following morning we finished the beer and went to school. The lecture hall was soon filled with a strong charge of tension. We were all looking up hard at the blackboard, where a bearded, angry man wrote mathematical problems for us. I solved them in half an hour and showed my paper to Michael. It was the third time I was doing such calculations at the exams, and so I felt sure of myself, like a winner. I don't like to take entrance examinations, but I always find it pleasant to sit and watch the others after I've already proved myself. That was my only victory. Suddenly I felt bad that Michael did not suspect that we would never really run together. Maybe he would find another runner, but I would have to make do with the Bratislava woods and loneliness.

Then everything was over, and we were waiting for the train.

"I'll tell you something, Milan," Michael started. "At home I have a beautiful pair of Adidas shoes. Brand new. But I've decided not to use them, and when we meet here in September I'll give them to you."

"Adidas?"

"Brand new ones. Light as a feather."

To run in Adidas shoes is pure pleasure. It's like swimming naked, or playing tennis on a freshly sprayed court on a summer evening using new tennis balls.

"Except that we'll never run together, Mike, because I'm leaving for Bratislava and I'll never come back here. I know it," I said.

"Come off it!"

I shrugged my shoulders.

My train came first, and Michael looked at me with displeasure.

"You really piss me off! The truth is the Adidas are from my dad, who's been living in Munich the past twenty years. You got that? I'm trying for the second time, and I, too, know it won't work. But why spoil it? We were having such a good time."

Then we said our farewells and I watched him from the window.

"Still, I'm glad to have met you," he went on. "It makes a fellow feel a bit better, bumping into someone like himself. You know, it really pisses me off to work in a factory."

He stood there with a briefcase in his hand, and his eyes behind those thick lenses were sad. He stood tall, in his gray pullover and with his red hair. Railway stations always move me. I felt very sorry that we'd never meet again and I would never run in his beautiful Adidas shoes. They must be gorgeously soft and would surely last much longer than the locally produced ones, which I wear out in two months. I felt like cursing horribly—seeing how desperately he wanted to get into that stupid school and knowing that it was in vain and that he knew that. It was so idiotic. When you see your own bad luck in the eyes of someone else, you always feel like vomiting.

He will work in a factory, I reflected, because he must work, and next year he will try again to get into this college, because he will think that perhaps something has changed. But nothing will change, because his father emigrated to Munich, and the son can never be pardoned for that. So he will keep working until he gets tired and only a memory will be left in him. He will always remember: I'm not just any ordinary laborer. Once upon a time I did try to get into college, but my father had emigrated and I wasn't accepted. And the more tired he is, the stronger the memory will be, and he will live for the rest of his life seeing himself as a man who was not accepted into university.

I stretched my hand out of the window, but the train moved out.

When I opened the door, Tania sent Lisa to rub against my feet while she herself waited for me in blue pajamas on our marriage bed. She was lying on her belly, supporting her head on her hands. The world suddenly, painlessly healed itself.

"Hi, traveler," she said, smiling, when I joined her in bed, and she caressed my face with her magic fingers.

I forgot to tell Michael that they can stick their university up their ass. That's what I should have told him, for there is no point in holding on to illusions. Because later on, nothing else would remain. I remembered it all only when I laid my head on Tania's round breasts. I bounced on the milky waves and listened to the thumping of her heart. My thoughts slowly ceased to circle around mine and other people's destinies, and my hand stopped on a curly, hairy promontory that resisted through the pajamas.

This is beauty, I reflected. And Tania understood, because she just opened up in order to endow that beauty with a meaning and to sanctify it. Maybe I should have told Michael about this.

She tickled my belly, as if to revenge herself for almost dying every time I touch her calves.

"Nothing?" she asked.

"Nothing."

She sighed, disappointed.

"You have beautiful medals," she said later, staring at the wall.

"What do you think they are for?"

"For victories, I guess."

"True, but each win was different. This one is from a competition for apprentices, and that one from the Republican Championship."

"I've never won anything. And I never competed."

"Then you'll never understand it. I'm sorry because otherwise you'd certainly admire me. You'd watch from the stands and try to spot my uniform from the crowd. You'd be terribly nervous because nothing would happen the first kilometer. I would run somewhere in the middle, as if I were not interested in anything. And then it would begin. They would announce the halfway point. The straight section follows. I would move over to the second or third lane, lengthen my step, and feel my groin as a sign, and then you'd see me passing my opponents. Now I'm in third place and moving into the second lane at the approach of the turn. Now I'm waiting and breathing deeply, because soon the last three hundred meters begins. And now I'm lifting myself to my toes, my coach hollers at me, but I don't hear him. I'm beside the second runner, and he doesn't let me pass and is speeding up desperately to make the last turn right next to me, so that I'll have to run the longer turn. But I sense terrible power in my legs and angrily push ahead of him. I hear his raspy breathing, and already I'm trying to stick to the first runner. I can't wait and am moving aside even before the turn ends and finally put everything into my legs. Somewhere in the distance is the checkerboard finish. It's all the same to me now, and I feel shivering in my thighs, so I'm straining my calves. Then I realize somewhere in the corner of my brain—which is not really functioning anymore—that I am first, and then keep running to get to the finish line as soon as possible. I'm interested only in the end of this mad race.

"And then I'd come over to you with wobbly knees but revitalized, because every winner is revitalized. I would kiss you through the fence, and my fatigue would disappear very fast while some would still be finishing the race and others would lie in the grass, and we would all have sunken eyes and bloodless faces.

"And you would have loved me in that moment for my perfection, because every winner is perfect."

Tania stared at the ceiling and kept quiet. Slowly my excitement receded, and I suddenly realized that I am a fanatic and Tania knows it. She could not feel the shivering that went up and down my legs and vibrated my muscles, but she sensed it.

"I'll take these medals off the wall," I promised.

She smiled coquettishly and summoned Lisa, who prowled toward us and now stood with her front paws in the air, staring at me.

That was how the summer started. I stopped working and stopped competing. It doesn't matter now why it happened. I walked downtown in a T-shirt and old jeans, and almost everyone else was wearing the same thing. In the windows of the public buildings paper peace doves could still be seen here and there, but most had been torn off after the last official celebration. As I walked up to the villa district, there were no more. I opened the garden gate of Mr. Bartholomew, if I may call him that, and entered. He was sitting in the smoke-filled room on the second floor and writing. The room had a view of Bratislava from the Castle to Rača. Under his desk I spied a bottle of wine, and though it hurt me, I said nothing.

"Welcome, Milan." He embraced me and pressed me into an armchair. "Tell me, my boy, how are you?"

I'd just come to ask him the same, since he had just returned from the hospital.

"It's not worth talking about, you know," he waved his hand. "Come, come, I'll show you something." He showed me two black trunks. "Lift them up."

"What's in them? Sand?"

"Those are my writings, you know. And now come, come." He led me to the balcony. I inhaled deeply and was delighted with the view of the city spread below us. However, the old gentleman pointed at his garden, at the peach trees that had ceased blossoming, and then at the fire pit. Then he grabbed my hand with his dry hands and said, "I'll burn it all tomorrow."

Full of righteous anger, I solemnly said, "You must not!"

"And why? Nobody needs it."

"That's not up to you to decide. It's literature and cannot be burned!"

Embarrassed, he avoided my gaze, and we returned to his room. We talked for a long time, and Mr. Bartholomew slowly emerged from his sadness. He brought out the hidden bottle, guiltily poured me a glass and searched for his half-full glass under the table. Then he leaned toward me and whispered: "Get out, Milan. Get out while you can."

I shook my head.

"It's all monstrous. It's a monstrous concept that will destroy us all. No one will be able to withstand it, not even you. It will get worse."

I shook my head again.

He peered at me seriously and searchingly. "Watch out, Milan. Think it over, my boy, because I see in your eyes something else."

We finished our wine, and as he followed me downstairs into the garden he grabbed my shoulders and said: "Athlete! What a firm step! You are strong and supple."

I smiled like a woman who's been paid a compliment. "So what?"

"What are you saying? That's everything! Everything in the

world! When you get up in the morning and know that as you walk down the street the women will stare into your eyes . . . ," he said, following me with his eyes as I stepped out with my bouncy walk and took off downtown.

On my way I bumped into a dog and recognized him as Mr. Bartholomew's dog, Nox.

"Hi, Nox," I called out to him, but he ignored me.

Mr. Bartholomew did not really find anything in my eyes. I was sure of that, and I did not like it that he was trying to get at me that way. I was born here and I will stay here, just for the sake of order, I told myself. It's my only free choice, and I will not give it up so easily. But enough!

I was walking toward a tall black-haired girl in a long skirt and black slippers. She passed by without even so much as a glance at me. But when I turned my head, we faced each other.

Downtown the people were shimmering in the overheated air, and the asphalt pavement was losing its color, blinding me. In vain did I try to hold on to the dark T-shirts. The sun would bleach even the funeral parlor operator's tails today, I said to myself. I closed my eyes and waited for the bus. Suddenly, fear gripped me. The kind of fear of which we know only that we have it. We don't know its origin. For a moment I hoped that it would turn out to be the fear of something simple, such as, for example, the realization that I'd forgotten to do the shopping. But that was not it. I reviewed the familiar depressions, but none of them fit. The bus came, I hopped on the steps, and then it hit me. It was the most unpleasant fear, and that is why it took me so long to identify it: the fear of life ahead of me. It annoyed me, but once it is there, you can't do anything about it. Devil take it! With fear like that, one doesn't feel like living. Half-dead, I dragged my body home. I saw my entire future in front of me, and I longed to be on another planet.

In the mailbox I found a form letter from Pardubice, informing me of my rejection. Mr. Bartholomew came to mind. He was right. The monster will gobble us all up. But I may be the mouse that cannot run while the python is already licking her.

In fifteen minutes I was jogging down the Mountain Park alley, waiting for the first drops of sweat to cool me. Up to the Red

Bridge I held on to the idea of turning back; I was dying of fatigue and the hot air was burning me down in my gut. Then I stopped thinking about it as I reflected on my life. I was running by memory and don't remember what the path looked like. Most probably like a couple of days before, but drier.

I found myself by a deserted ski lift five miles from my house, as always. I warmed up under an old maple tree, the sweat suddenly pouring from my entire body, as if I were letting blood. My eyes were burning with salt, and the sweat was dripping off the tip of my nose. Not a leaf moved on the maple. I got ready, inhaled deeply, noisily exhaled, jumped, and as I shot out, I pressed the stopwatch and mumbled, "Now show what you can do."

For the first kilometer the path meandered and was full of stumps. My knees hurt. Then the wooden bridge thundered under me. I checked the watch and noisily exhaled. Then came the plateau. It was like a car ride. I speeded up my breathing, switched exhaling to each third step, stretched myself up from my hips, and lifted my knees, quite automatically, because the runner said, "Faster!"

Obediently I speeded up.

"Good grief," I said, "we'll kill ourselves today."

"Shut up," said the runner. "What are you? An old hag?"

I kept the pace obediently and took the turn by the fish pond full speed. My right thigh began to give out. I had to increase the frequency to relieve it. Shortening the step helped, and I even increased the tempo. A hundred meters of pavement was ahead of me and then the valley by the brook. Two-thirds was behind me, I ran onto the path permanently covered by leaves, and suddenly, quite soberly, I realized that I wouldn't last the final kilometer. I felt it.

"What an idiot," the runner boomed. "Now he is running alone, without an audience, and right away he wants to give up!"

"What do you mean 'now'? I almost always run like this!"

"Shut up!"

I speeded up my breathing, but it seemed too soon.

"Forget about the reserves! You're always afraid that you can't make it! I detest you!"

Madman.

It stopped being simple. I kept changing the pace often. When I stretched the step, it helped the lungs but my thighs hurt. When I put the weight on my heels, my muscles got a break, but my lungs began to pull.

"You scum! Don't hang your head—pull yourself up from your hips! You have to have an audience?"

The first red circles began to form before my eyes. It was too soon. Five hundred meters before the finish. Hard, shitty work.

"The last fish pond! Raise yourself on your toes, you bugger! The old man ahead of you would beat you with his thumb up his ass!"

I gave myself an excuse for another five meters, but then there were no more excuses. Every runner does the last five hundred meters on his toes. Suddenly the wind hit me and everything flew by me. My feet were tearing up the soft, yielding soil. The old man guessed something, turned around, and, when he noticed me, held on to his hat. I flew past him and caught his frozen gasp.

The tingling started in my thighs and went up to my back and shoulders. I couldn't see, because my eyes were closing with fatigue; someone was closing them. Nothing hurt. But I wanted to die.

"Push! Just one hundred meters!"

But I could not go any faster. My legs went soft and turned to lead.

"Goof," said the runner.

"Good Lord, I thank you. It's over." I pressed the stopwatch, supported my upper body by holding on to my knees, bent down, and inhaled tearfully. My whole body pulsated from head to toe; my hands were wet and icy. The stopwatch was showing 9:08.

"Goof," said the runner once more, and went silent.

Three minutes later my breathing was normal and my legs began to work. Only the eyes remained sunken. All of my friends' eyes are sunken like that after such runs.

The remaining four kilometers I jogged with pleasure, as if I had just awakened from a nightmare. The muscles regained their suppleness, and I luxuriated in the realization that I would not see any more red circles today. I was horribly tired, so tired that I didn't want to think about anything. Not even about my life, which I feared so much. I feared my life, but I wanted to live. Somehow I'll muddle through, I thought.

And so it happened that in the evening I got an idea. I liked it even the next morning when I entered the hospital and found the head nurse. I had decided to tell her that I wanted to work as an orderly and, if she asked me why, to tell her that I was fed up with everything else. And that's what happened. She asked me if I had been to prison, saying that she would not like that, and I said I would not like that either. I promised to start a week later.

Across the brook lay broken trees, and underneath them sand was accumulating. I was stepping on the rotten trunks, thinking that my dream had come true. From above, a hawk dove down and glided over our heads into the valley. I watched it grow small, and beyond the next turn I saw the spot I had chosen.

"This is it," I said.

I pitched the tent and went to get wood. Tania was sitting on a rucksack, gazing somewhere below, where the unused road ended. Then she brought two flat stones and placed the bread, the knife, and a can on top of them. She sat down on the rucksack again and probably looked at the water and sand glistening with mica or gold. I dragged two broken spruce trees over and made a fire. I used no paper, but she did not notice and only silently went about making dinner and warming up her back.

At night we looked into the fire and talked. She spoke quietly. "When I was young, it bothered me that I couldn't capture the moments that made me happy. They always somehow slipped through my fingers, and I realized that only later."

"It doesn't bother you now?" I asked her.

"Now I know that it has to be so, because I experience them in motion. I can experience them because they flow. It's a law I can't influence. Still, it bothers me."

That is the kind of discussions we have. The spruce fire shot straight up, and the forest stood still. I, too, was conscious that the moment was slipping through my fingers, but it did not bother me, because I've always thought about the future, and what I have experienced already does not interest me anymore. Tania, on the other hand, was experiencing the present as the most important thing, and that, perhaps, was the reason I was in love with her.

I grabbed her by the hand and played with her fingers, one by one, down to her ring finger, which she was to break three weeks later.

Then we crawled into the tent, where the candle was burning and the sleeping bags were laid out. Tania smelled of smoke. She smiled. When I lay my hands on her soft body, some strange joy always manages to conjure up such a smile. I can't figure it out, because her beauty confuses me and I have no time to smile. Such joy is unfamiliar to me, and that particular smile I once understood as gentle ridicule. I felt my bony frame on her soft and hot body, and my chest rested on her breasts as on pillows with erect little horns. They rubbed me in a rhythm of which I don't know if I am master or follower. I was going crazy and felt a searing sweetness in my heels that would jet forth into Tania, somewhere deep inside where even I cannot reach. There was the little piece of rubber, though, that gorgeous Tania got ready in advance and pulled over me the way she would put a little gown on a baby. Afterward we lay for a long time with our eyes staring into the darkness.

A long time before, I had dreamed that one morning I would wake up next to Tania under the blue canvas of our tent. Because Tania loves to sleep, I would be the first one to stick my head through the opening, just to get a look at the world—from close up, on my knees, smelling the grass, supporting myself against the moist earth. And that was how it happened.

The fire was still smoking, so I sat down by it and blew on the blackened logs. They lit up under my breath and immediately went out. Low clouds flew by above my head, gliding somewhere away, into hillsides that lowered themselves, across, into the valley. The clouds would crash against the hillside and release rain. Silence reigned here. The flaccid trees were waiting for God knows what, and the brook burbled to itself.

From behind, Tania's arms embraced me and locked me in. I closed my eyes and remained motionless for a long while. Tania leaned her head against my back, and that's how we communicated. I was telling her that I was living through a moment that will never return. I forgot about my life that frightened me so much and experienced the clouds above my head. The wood was crackling in the fire and writhing in the transparent flame. Tania was holding me and pouring into me from her body a sense of the present.

Then she made breakfast. She spread jam on the bread and boiled water for the tea, and we ate for an hour. I watched the hawk circling and gliding above the brook as the thick forest covered everything else. Only for the two of us was there a piece of clear land left. The hawk suddenly dived, folded its wings with serrated edges on their tips, and dropped among the trees. Nothing else happened.

Strange days. Tania, a girl with sky-blue eyes introduced me to them, holding me by the hand like a child.

I went to get a drink from the brook, and the icy water tasted sweet after the tea. I took a drink offered by this land, and when I straightened out, my head swam. I returned to the fire.

"I don't want to leave here," I said, because I was thinking ahead again. I saw the streets packed with people whose destinies made them nervous. "I don't want to go back there." I really felt the distaste.

"If you really didn't want to, you wouldn't," Tania said. "But you do, in fact, want to go back. You just don't want to admit it."

She was probably right; it does not matter. She kissed my cheek and then we packed the tent. I love sadness—and I loved the brook that flowed from somewhere above us and carried the gold-bearing sand down. And I also loved the fire that released its last ribbons of smoke from under the rocks, together with the branches with the needles and the rotting wood. All of that was terribly sad. I did not understand the truth, but it seemed to me that sadness resembled it a little bit.

We descended into the valley by the brook, and the gray clouds were still racing above us. That's how it was ending. In the valley we held hands and walked down a deserted road. It followed the brook, and raspberries grew on its sides. Tania understood everything and did not fear silence.

The head nurse did not ask me anything, but simply grabbed me by the arm and dragged me into the interior of the hospital, down the corridors and past the elevator. Patients in blue robes and slippers were everywhere. We passed through several doors, and she always closed them behind us, as if she wanted to keep me there for good. Then we stopped in front of a door with a sign: OPERATING ROOM.

"Maya, take care of him," she told a nurse in a green smock.

I received a green shirt and pants and thus entered the operating room.

I'd never seen anything like it. Like a sacrificial altar, the operating table stood in the middle, and all around were hoses, instruments, drums, and, above the table, a reflecting lamp resembling an eye of a bee. It was sprinkled with circles of many tiny lamps. Everywhere one looked, there were green tiles, white chair legs, and huge milky window panes. Behind them, the summer still reigned. There were three rooms like this one, and I walked in and out of them. I was afraid to touch the walls, to say nothing of the instruments. Maya, however, gave me a green rag and said that I should wipe everything. No operations were scheduled that day, and so I wiped the table and also the lamp above, because someone had sprayed it with black drops. When I realized that the drops were dried blood, I had to sit down and figure out how the blood got up there. Once you looked at the situation in a matter-of-fact way, you realized that it had jetted up from the table: a thin geyser of blood five feet high. I remembered seeing blood when I cut myself while slicing a melon and when my brother fell off his bike. But then the blood flowed only slowly, lazily, unwillingly, until it got tired of flowing after a while. Without thinking, I started to wipe the white chair in which I was sitting, and realized that even there I was wiping dark spots. I felt like opening a window to get a breath of summer and have a look at the sun.

I went to the next operating room, which was as spattered as the first. I was wiping the round spots when I began to swell with the idiotic feeling of a perverted intellectual that I was doing something good, something right. Here it is, I said to myself with satisfaction, and for an hour I worked in full comfort.

It occurred to me that the last time Tania and I made love had been two days earlier, before daybreak, when the birds were singing, and I was banging my head against the dewy canvas.

That had really worked out well. That week we fooled them all, because we were happy and free. We hoodwinked the State for a week, and that made it all worthwhile.

Then the door opened, and Maya shouted at me with the tilelike voice I remembered from the swimming pools, "Milan, bring Mrs. Bohush. We're operating!"

"Where is she?" I asked, terrified.

"In the women's ward. Make it fast!"

I ran into the corridor and oriented myself by the arrows that brought me to the women's ward, where a nurse was already waiting for me. It turned out that Mrs. Bohush was a young woman, unconscious and with fine hair on her chin. I took her in my arms, and she was light as a feather. Her eyes were half-open, and her lips were cracked because she breathed through her mouth. She did not move her tongue. She was completely immobile, and through her gown I felt a body heated by fever. The nurse grabbed her swinging arm, and we put her on a wheeled stretcher.

I brought her into the operating room, the nurse opening the doors for me. Maya was already waiting, and in her hand was a pair of hand clippers, the same kind my barber used when my father and I would visit him after my mother pointed out that our hair was getting too long. And now Maya lifted the clippers to Mrs. Bohush's hair, saying, "Now watch. Next time it'll be your job."

Tufts of hair flew off Mrs. Bohush's head. The clippers were buzzing and leaving behind short stubble, uncovering a nakedness of which I had had no inkling. I saw that a hairless woman was the most naked woman possible and was glad Mrs. Bohush was unaware of what was happening. She was breathing superficially, and her eyes were veiled by unconsciousness. But all that was not enough. It was also necessary to shave her head smooth, and Maya gave me a razor, an Astra Superior blade, with which to do so.

Afterward I took her in my arms and carried her to the altar. I placed her limp body there and in my mind begged her pardon, because who knows if I was doing the right thing? If I were not, I felt that it would be hard for me to go on living. I continued to do what Maya told me, however, step by step. I switched on the instruments, and tied Mrs. Bohush's hands while her fingers seized my index finger. That shocked and frightened me. Maya said it was only a reflex movement that had nothing to do with consciousness, but in my own mind I kept saying that something strange was happening. I became an audience for what was transpiring, waiting for the next event, my attention riveted to the screen where the action would take place. I had no time for anything else—not even for asking questions about what to do and how. I just gazed in astonishment.

From somewhere the surgical team appeared. Two male doctors emerged first, and behind them came three female doctors pulling some kind of instrument. The women stuck needles with hoses into Mrs. Bohush's veins, and liquid from bottles suspended on stands began to drip in. Then they put a red pipe into her mouth and connected it to an instrument that started to wheeze like a tired person and seemed to lift her small breasts with their defiantly raised nipples.

In the meantime both male doctors washed up. Everything went so fast that it seemed like a play or movie. Even the jokes and witty comments they exchanged seemed movielike, because on the altar lay a woman noticed by no one. She lay there like a property on a set, with the red pipe in her mouth. No one glanced at her until, finally, one of the male doctors, the younger one in glasses, approached her and lifted her eyelid. He studied her eye briefly and then said, "Let's wash."

I jumped in and sprayed alcohol on a piece of gauze. The younger doctor cleaned a place at the back of the head, and then both men put on sterile gowns and gloves with their curled wrist hair showing through. I turned on the bee's eye, and Mrs. Bohush's head lit up. Everywhere else it was dark, and in fact it was only through the place where they cut a hole in the sheet that was over her that I could see the skin with its light brown coloring of iodine. The surgeons made themselves comfortable on the chairs. I pushed closer, and the older one, whose gray beard escaped his mask, made the first cut.

I hid behind his back and followed the movement of his hand. He moved the scalpel, which I could not see, as if he were drawing with a piece of chalk on concrete—hard and repeatedly. I fidgeted in my chair with alarm. Something is going on, I kept telling myself. I need to rest; I need a bit of time to understand it! But the bearded doctor went on and on until he finished a half circle. I did not know how, but suddenly I was watching from over his shoulder.

The half circle opened up. The blood silently spilled from the edges and flowed down onto the green sheet, and the younger surgeon collected it in the suction tube that I connected to the vacuum. Then he lifted the half circle of skin and wanted to cut something, but a red jet shot up from there. It was thin like a thread, and at the tip it separated into a thousand drops that stuck to the lamp, though some of them dripped onto my green shirt, where they immediately turned into round dark spots. The jet pulsated in rhythm with Mrs. Bohush's heart, playfully and carelessly, until the doctor clipped and cauterized it with an instrument I connected. I felt something breaking inside me. Luckily I had on a mask that covered my mouth—now gaping—and my tongue, which was sticking out, like Lisa when we took her out of the apartment for the first time and she touched the real ground with her paws. The blood was flowing down more slowly now, and I saw how they were uncovering Mrs. Bohush's skull—scraping it white—and how Maya handed the doctor a drill. Oh no, not this, I thought, and closed my eyes.

I heard the high-pitched whine. Then it became lower, changing into a tired groan, and suddenly I smelled the odor of burning bone. My stomach was turning, because I remembered that that was how the dentist had drilled my teeth. An identical stench had risen from my unfortunate tooth bone, and rivulets of perspiration flowed from me. My head had been clouded with pain, but the dentist had mercilessly kept on drilling. I smelled the odor that spread from under the bearded man's drill, and my teeth started to ache.

Mrs. Bohush had a hole in her head, and white smoke from a second point rose until the whine of the drill became a slow growl and suddenly stopped. There was another hole in Mrs. Bohush's head. It filled up with blood, and that was all. The blood stopped at the edge as if it wanted to provide a veil of chastity. Finally there were six holes, and the room was full of that odor. Maya passed a thin wire to the doctor. It was in fact a saw that he threaded from one opening to another one and cut the bone that separated them.

He continued like that until he removed a toothed wheel, big as the bottom of the cup from which I drink my hot chocolate each morning, and then I saw the brain. Better to say, I saw the membranes under which it was hiding. The doctor moved his finger along its surface, pressing it searchingly.

Under those membranes is your secret, Mrs. Bohush; that's where you're hiding. Your "I," which I did not meet, is there. I've seen only your blind eyes and your nakedness. Yet she had managed to give birth to healthy twins a week before, as someone wrote in her case history. The same person also wrote down a terrible word: *expansion*. A word that I know from our newspapers: I imagined a vanquished enemy. But I could not go on, because the doctor was cutting with little scissors. Why shouldn't he, right? And yet again, my tongue was sticking out, because there, where the little nickel-plated scissors went in, it began to open up. The brain was pressing, it was swelling like rising dough, as if wanting to escape from its owner. Interwoven with blue-violet veins, it was pushing out, all the while pulsating with its own life.

"Look at this," sighed the younger surgeon.

The one with the beard nodded and continued cutting until he arrived at the other side. Then he stopped and looked at the gray matter as it distended itself capriciously, pushing aside the membranes, until an entire little mushroom was visible.

So this is what an expansion looks like, I thought, and I knew that I would never again be able to imagine anything else connected to this word. But they did not give me time to reflect even that much, because at that moment the doctor grabbed two shiny little shovels and dug them into the moist, wrinkled little mushroom, as if it were a pudding.

This was enough for me. I didn't want to see anything more and focused on the remains of Mrs. Bohush's toenail polish as if someone had switched me off.

"This is how you take out a tumor," said the man with the beard. "We have to get at it through the cortex." I realized that he was talking to me. Maya was smiling at me through her slits for eyes and passing to the doctor the "grasping tweezers," a mundane term that woke me up. He stuck them inside Mrs. Bohush's head and tried to grasp something in that bloody stew, sucking it out through a metallic pipe that became clogged. But the vacuum was stronger and swallowed it hungrily.

So this is how it is, I said to myself. They don't kill. Just the opposite. I swiveled happily on my chair, because the truth resides in dialectics and what looks like a murder is actually the saving of a life. My soul trembled with the delight of knowledge while the surgeons finished, stopped the bleeding, poured water in the hole, and, when it did not change color but peacefully pulsated, began to sew. First they did the membranes; then they snapped the toothed wheel into the skull and pulled the skin over it like a cap and sewed everything up.

I ran for the wheeled stretcher, and when I returned, the women doctors were slapping Mrs. Bohush on her face, shouting, "Mrs. Bohush, good morning!" They lifted her eyelids and took the red tube out of her mouth. The woman whose life had just been saved was coughing and spitting, her chest bouncing as if by itself. Her legs spasmodically kicked and got tied up in the bedspread. But in her snow-white cap of bandages she displayed a beautiful childlike face, and when I picked up her sweat-drenched body I quietly mumbled, "We made it, Mrs. Bohush."

"Who are you bringing in here, boy?" asked Annie, the nurse in the intensive care room.

"This is Mrs. Bohush. I saw them take her tumor out, and you'll take good care of her, because she's got week-old twins and she has to return to them, right?" I said.

"That will be all," sighed Annie, pouting her lips, which displeased me.

There was nobody in the operating room. All that was left were the blood spots and a pile of green gowns with large, drying spots. I switched off the suction, still whining and disturbing the surface of the foamy blood in the bottle. I poured the blood into the sink and turned off the lamps. As I washed the floor and turned thousands of spattered drops into red lines, I realized it was time to go. I checked the wall clock: it was half past five.

I was surprised by the dust, the sun, and the people on the bus. I walked down Michalská Street and watched my athletic step in the shop windows. My feet were dying to pound the mountain path, but it would also have been pleasant just to run down the street. Tania had been waiting for me for two hours in the university library, and I found her sitting and staring into a book, though she was not reading. She would lift her head every time the door opened, even as I entered, and her eyes were marked with pity.

"Where were you?" she asked sadly.

"At the hospital," I said, realizing that she'd been waiting for me for two hours and that in her pretty head an idea must have been hatching: for the rest of her days she would sit there, lifting her eyes at each banging of the door.

As we left, her face was sorrowful, madonnalike, and she walked half a step behind me. How familiar it all was!

We entered a cafe and silently sat drinking something, and she kept turning the glass in her hand. We were both waiting for salvation.

"Okay," I said. "You must know why I didn't come. Had you been there, you'd have done the same. We were operating and I had to stay."

She didn't answer, and I could see that she was still thinking about it. There would be operations every day, and I would never come on time. I had no answer to that.

"This won't work, Milan," she said, shaking her head. But it was no threat; the statement communicated only unhappiness and powerlessness. She kept turning the glass in her tiny hand. In her mind she saw the tent and the valley down below, the burbling stream, and the fire from the smokeless spruce wood.

"Look, Tania, I didn't even have time to phone. At two o'clock, they suddenly said there would be an operation, and I had to run to fetch Mrs. Bohush . . ." I kept talking, telling her about the hair that I dumped in the garbage, the red tube taped to the mouth, the head that opened up like a cracked egg. By the time I finished, Tania's love returned to her eyes.

I took her little white hand in mine. It's wonderful when the woman entrusts the man with her hand. She was already smiling.

We walked through the city and approached the Castle. In the courtyard, a few foreigners were strolling while the sun was setting above Austria. A few red clouds were crowding together, but otherwise the sky was green. At such moments, I regret that aliens from another planet do not land. They would gaze in astonishment at the dance of colors. If they could not read our minds, they wouldn't be burdened with the knowledge that I felt like taking a walk in the forest, beyond the mirror of the river Danube, and that I was forbidden to do that. Maybe the thought wouldn't have occurred to me either but for the fact that during the last two years all the trees on our side of the Danube had been cleared.

"Come on, honey," Tania said, "don't look over there."

I listened. Where would I go? To a ranch in America? I believe a person does what he wants, after all, I said to myself. That means that if I stay here and tomorrow go to the hospital to place people on the altar, it must mean I want to do that. Does it mean I don't want to go to America? It probably does.

And so the next morning I said hello to Annie, a big girl in a blue dress and a white apron, and went to get Mr. Palichka, because that was what my schedule said. I sat down on his bed and said, "I've come to get you, Mr. Palichka."

He found my hand by touch, because his eyes were shut. The pus was streaming from them. He took my wrist into his dry, wizened hand and said, "I'm coming, my boy."

"I can wheel you there."

"No need, my boy. I'll walk. You just hold on to me, because I can't see."

We went down the hall, and the old man was walking like a prophet, like an apostle, slowly, solemnly, and humbly. He helped me when I cut his hair, turning his head exactly as I needed it, so my clippers had a clear path. I also shaved his neck, and he liked it.

"You are shaving me so well, my boy, that I can't even feel it."

Then I placed him, blind and humble, on the altar. The bearded surgeon came and asked him, "How are you, Mr. Palichka?"

"Thank you, Doctor."

"We are going to cut you open a bit, but it's not going to hurt, and you need not worry. When we find out what exactly we're dealing with, then we'll put you to sleep. Okay?"

Mr. Palichka then said: "Just go to work, Doctor, go to work. You know what's best for me."

Then the doctor started. He injected the old man's neck with a solution, after which walnut-size bumps appeared on the neck and the doctor made an incision. He entered the opening with his fingers and stuck his index finger somewhere deep, twisting his entire body to reach something. He cut again, and again explored the opening from which the blood oozed silently onto the green sheet.

"Mr. Palichka."

"Yes."

"How are you?"

"Thank you, Doctor."

"I'm asking you, how are you?"

"Fine, Doctor."

"How old are you?"

"Seventy."

And again he explored with his finger. Then he dried the wound with a gauze and stuck a pair of tweezers inside, and suddenly I saw an artery. It was thick like a mountain climber's rope, pale and pulsating. It was clean and had a piece of rubber attached to it.

"So how is it going, Mr. Palichka?"

"The same, Doctor. Fine."

"Does it still make noise in your head?"

"It does indeed, Doctor. Since three months ago. Loud as hell."

I was holding the old man's hand, a large and dry hand with broken nails, and he was cheerfully pressing mine in return. The doctor then took a clip and squeezed the rope the way you step on a water hose.

"Now Mr. Palichka, how do you feel?"

"Thanks . . . Doctor."

"Can you hear me, Mr. Palichka?"

. . .

"Mr. Palichka, can you hear me?"

. . .

"Mr. Palichka!!"

. . .

Maya was winking at me from above her mask. The doctor released the clip and looked at us helplessly. I felt sorry for him.

"Mr. Palichka!!"

"What is it?"

"Gosh, Mr. Palichka, you scared the heck out of me."

"Don't you worry about a thing, Doctor. You just go right ahead."

"How old are you?"

"Seventy."

"We'll try it again." Again he squeezed the beautiful, pulsating artery on his neck. "Breathe deeply."

In the meantime, I was pressing Mr. Palichka's hand, bursting with sympathy for this old man, and his hand answered me with the cheerful play of his fingers.

"The noise is gone, Doctor."

"Great, Mr. Palichka. How are you?"

"Thank you, fine, Doctor."

"And now we'll put you to sleep. Okay?"

"You just go right ahead, Doctor. You know best what I need."

The women doctors from Anesthesiology arrived and put him to sleep.

"What's coming up?" I asked.

"Now we'll open his head. That noise is caused by bleeding into the brain, which happens sometimes. We'll just clip the vessel."

"And the eyes?"

"They're connected."

"And won't something happen when you clip it?"

"You just saw what happened. He got used to it. He's got one on the left side as well."

Full of doubt, I looked at Mr. Palichka. He, too, had a red tube in his mouth, holding it like a pipe. They stuck the tape across the moustache, which I had not shaved off. The machine pumped air into him and lifted his bony chest. It seemed too slow. It would not have been enough for me.

"His pressure is dropping," the anesthesiologists announced as they infused him.

"We'll wait," said the bearded one, and went to read the paper.

Just hold on, Grandpa. You are so close to victory. You won't have to put up with the hell in your head. Just don't lose it now, I thought.

But the pressure was dropping, and old Mr. Palichka was losing hope. He could not help it. They put him to sleep, and his will went to sleep, too. The doctor sewed up the incision, the silver clip still showing. The anesthesiologists pulled the tube out and slapped his cheek.

"He won't make it," said Maya, the surgical nurse. "He's old."

I was wheeling him through the corridors. His hands were crossed on his chest, and the pus was flowing from his inflamed eyelids, down his temples, but he did not care. He was listening to the thunder that, like a tide, would arrive with each heartbeat and scatter his thoughts. I don't know, but I think I would dash my head or stab my heart—just for a moment of silence.

As I returned to the room, Annie called me. "Come help me with this little old lady, boy."

"Why do you keep calling me 'boy'? I may be older than you."

"Because you are a boy."

She moved her hand under the old woman's back, I grabbed her big pink hand, and we turned the grandma on her side. Her name was Mrs. Kiss, and a transparent tube was sticking out of her nose. There was another tube between the poor thing's legs, but it was a different one, red. It led to a bag of bloody urine. And Annie was sticking yet another tube, a green one, into Mrs. Kiss's mouth.

"What are you doing, Annie? If she had some other holes in her body, would you put some more tubes there?"

"Oh, shut your face. You don't understand."

I obeyed. Annie's hair was falling into her eyes, and when she stepped toward the washbasin, I saw how tall and strong she was.

"Grandma, what are you doing?" she suddenly shouted, and ran toward me.

Grandma, who I thought wasn't conscious of anything, was pulling the tube from her nose with her eyes closed and an expression of concentration. I grabbed her hand and pried away her fingers.

"You must not do that, Grandma," I told her.

"She is stone deaf."

"But you were shouting at her just now."

"So what?"

She was smiling, but not at me. God knows what she was thinking. I was thinking that if she had not turned up her lips yesterday, today they would look very nice.

At three I was sprinting in the air full of light to the bus stop. I walked through the old town to the square, where Tania, sitting on a bench, was expecting me. I was looking someplace . . .

Suddenly I saw Mr. Palichka and the hole gaping in his neck. A wide-open mouth full of blood, and clear-red blood on the green sheet. I looked closer, and it was no wound. On the ground, on the pavement, a torn red rose was lying, with red petals strewn around.

I told Tania, who really was waiting for me on the bench, about it. She closed my eyes with her childlike hand and said, "Don't think about it now."

We held hands, passed under the new bridge, and hid from the city behind huge billboards that I had never noticed before. They were covering up the ruins of the gypsy homes. Tania was walking ahead of me up the hill where the Castle stood.

She was struggling through the underbrush covering the old path, and soon we stood in a clearing from which a view of the embankment loomed. Below us the street was rattling and the Danube flowed quietly, but we lay down on a small plot of grass, because we did not care to look down. We were protected by the waist-high bushes, and the blue sky was smudged with contrails left by a jet plane. It would have been a sin if we had not made love then and there.

Soon I again realized that we could see the embankment, and I heard the buzzing of a bee. The sunlight reached us through the crown of a tree. Lovemaking is nice, I reflected. Afterward, I can just lie next to my woman, and rabid Nature does not push me into her lap. I placed my head on Tania's chest and experienced fatigue as a gift. I wanted to be dead tired, to fear death, and thus approach closer to life. Mr. Palichka is an unusual man because of how he suffers. Such noise in one's head can turn life into a diabolically authentic experience.

Tania was playing with my hair; she embodied all women. She was lying naked on the grass amid the rattling of the streetcars, and God knows what she was thinking. I thought that for Mr. Palichka there was only one truth today: that he would get rid of the noise in his head or die.

And what about us? How many truths shall we invent?

"How beautiful and quiet is the sky compared with the street-cars," said Tania. "Down there is hell, up above is paradise, and we lie somewhere in the middle."

Tania and I were walking back through the old town, and we stopped at a fountain, sat down on a bench, and looked at the stars. People here go to bed at nine and leave the streets to the care of cats. They illuminate their apartments with blue light. The cats' only enemy is the yellow-white Zhiguli police car that slowly floats across the square. Tania hid herself in my embrace.

When I got home it was midnight and I could hear my mother turning in her bed. She could not sleep, but maybe only because my father snored. When I lay down, my legs started to kick spasmodically and the muscles hurt. I got angry at my body, which used this method to demand fatigue. I hadn't run for two days. There was no time. But you can't explain that to your legs, and I fell asleep only at daybreak.

School began and summer was over. It was September 10, the air was clearer, it penetrated deeper into the lungs than in August, and I could feel autumn in my legs. The calendar can't fool me.

Before noon only a few old men and a mother with a child came to the Iron Fountain. I ran into the forest. There wasn't a single leaf lying on the path, but the leaves were beginning to yellow at the edges. I was running fast, because I wasn't clocking myself. The body takes advantage of this sort of thing. I remembered my victories, and that made my feet feel good. Sometimes I would dream about the victories I had not experienced, and that made my feet feel even better. They sped up by themselves, reliving the final three hundred meters, passing others again and again. It is true, though, that I never won a really great race. And now I don't know what in fact did happen. Why did I leave the track when my legs so loved that red oval? And why will I never again put on the spiked running shoes that awakened the devil in me? They gave me wings!

For life is strange. There are people who cannot make any sense of it, and I belong with them. Two hours before the competition I would lie on my bed with my feet up on the radiator to relieve them. A week before the race I would not eat any sweets and would even use saccharine in my tea, in order to eat five pastries the night before and pack my muscle cells with extra sugar for the race. I would do that just to beat my opponents, who, as a result, would become sad. And I would do a hundred different things and so ignore life.

I worked for a company that pollutes Bratislava's underground water. Not only the water, however; it pollutes the soil, air, animals, and people as well. While at work, I would go out to practice. I could run twenty kilometers along the canal into which the damned company disgorged its effluent, and for fully ten kilometers the dead water even the rats rejected would meander next to me. But nothing except my legs was of interest to me then.

Then one day I realized that I had never won a great race before and that maybe I never would. Five years of training for nothing. A few medals. And it felt as if your lover has let you down.

I really don't know how it came about. I didn't know it then either.

Two young trees were lying across the path. I had to jump over them, and that interrupted my rhythm. I realized I was running too fast. My head wanted to stop me from thinking.

I have no idea how many more times I'll find I've been wrong, and it's not pleasant to contemplate that.

I passed a girl who was perspiring heavily and whose head rocked from side to side. She did not have enough energy even to say hello, poor thing. She probably hates me. I stretched my step and disappeared from her view. In vain did Nature pretend that it was summer. The air betrayed her. My lungs were sucking the stormy catalyst in, and if I permitted it, the air would completely dry me up and destroy me.

I turned home, facing the sun. At the last fish pond, there sat a man in a hat holding a fishing rod. As always, I felt like calling to him, Which of us is crazy? As always, I did not call out.

I knew the hospital mornings already. I looked in Intensive Care and said, "Good morning." Annie was on duty, but she was washing something, so I couldn't see her.

"Hi," she said. "Did you shave?"

"Oh, Annie, not again! I wouldn't want you for a wife."

I hadn't shaved, for heaven's sake. I had no time for such things. She peeked from behind the door and did not smile at all.

I looked at the schedule. EMMA HOLAN, 1961. TUMOR, CRANIAL OPENING.

She looked seventeen, had black eyes and hair, a pale face, pretty, with an aristocratic pallor. I pushed the stretcher into the room and said, "Hi, Emma."

"Hi."

Her voice was faint, her lips colorless. I gathered her in my arms, and she held me around the neck. I felt her in my arms, a pleasant, hot burden. She was holding my neck as if we were dancing; she even put her head on my chest. I could have carried her like that all the way to the operating room. When I put her on the stretcher, she looked at the ceiling as if in reproach.

"Outside it is a beautiful Indian summer day, Emma," I said as I picked up the clippers. She was watching my hands, and so I sat down on the stretcher next to her and put the clippers down.

"I wish I were walking around Bratislava," she whispered.

"Except that you'd have to be in school anyway."

"I wouldn't go to school."

My God, she was right, I thought. Neither would I.

Emma turned on her side so that I could cut her hair. The jaws of the clippers chewed through her girlish hair. Then I took off her pink pajamas. She was helping me, but she was bashful when her little white breasts were uncovered. I covered her with a gown.

"How did you sleep?"

"Sleep?" she asked quietly. "How could I sleep?"

"And why not?"

"I was so afraid I couldn't close my eyes."

"Afraid of what?"

"That I will not survive."

"Come on, Emma!"

She did not want to say anymore, and just looked around. When I moved her to the altar, she held me around the neck as before and pressed her head against me.

The anesthesiologists came in and put Emma to sleep. Then I

adjusted the table so that she would sit and lean with her forehead against a support I had prepared unknown to her. I did not want her to know that she would sit taped to a frame. I got everything ready. I sat behind the bearded doctor, focused the bee eye on Emma's neck, and waited.

It started quickly. He made a deep incision and drew the scalpel along the clean skin. In its wake followed the flood that he wiped off with gauze. Then he inserted pliers, which he squeezed with all his force to make a fist-size hole in her. But that was not enough for him. He continued cutting, and the tissue became unglued as he approached it. First it looked white, and then it started to bleed, flowing down the sheets in darkening streams. Then he hit the bottom of the skull. He could feel it under his knife, and I touched the same spot on my head in the depression above my nap. He began to chip at Emma's bone with another pair of pliers. It crunched the way Lisa crunches when she eats chicken, and sometimes it cracked loudly, as when you break a branch.

And then I saw the spinal cord: a white rope with plenty of little strings that spread themselves somewhere into the body. It was covered with a network of red veins, and it looked so naked that my hands started to sweat.

Suddenly the man with a beard stopped. Then he cut the crown of her head, and before I could gather my wits, he was already drilling into the skull.

"What's going on?" I asked a doctor standing behind me and watching.

"Nothing. He's got to drain the liquid that normally flows through the spinal cord."

Nothing? They'll drill a hole into your head wherever they like and that's supposed to be nothing? Oh, my dear God, I'd love to be a guardian angel, but now I just gazed in astonishment and prayed. The most impossible sentences would occur to me, and I was in despair of being a heathen, for the madman picked up a four-inch needle thick like a shoemaker's needle and fear gripped me. I saw that tool enter Emma: the devil was pushing it in with two fingers until it completely disappeared from view, with only an attachment sticking out. Then a stream of clear water came out, a pulsating fountain. He hit the chamber. Everyone was happy, and so even I sighed with relief. He pulled out the needle and instead inserted a little white tube that hung from Emma's head like a jolly ribbon.

Then he returned to the wound in the nap and uncovered the cerebellum. It sat there gray and serious. I knew that much: it was the gray eminence of all thought.

Somewhere in there, there was something wrong. A tumor was supposed to be there. It turned Emma into a beautiful but limp girl with the eyes of a doe. A month ago she had fallen face down on the street, and when she came around she vomited. It passed, but the X ray showed a pinched blood vessel behind the cerebellum, and that was where the problem was supposed to be. I'd seen the picture, I attached it to the glass, and everybody was pointing to that vessel.

The man with the beard was at home now. He was pushing the cerebellum aside with a shiny little shovel and mumbling something in displeasure. He was twisting his body every which way to see from below, from the side, and exploring with his gloved finger. His expression was rather dreamy.

I wasn't praying anymore. Do something, bearded man! I am sitting behind you and watching!

However, he just went on mumbling, illuminating the red tunnel, at the bottom of which blood glistened. As soon as it was suctioned, more gathered: the blood was constantly flowing from some source. Under those green sheets Emma was certainly growing paler, despite the steady supply of foamy plasma.

"I can't see anything there," he spat out, and pinched a bit of tissue with his tweezers.

Don't poke it if you can't see anything.

Two more doctors looked in, and they didn't see anything either.

"We are sewing up," the bearded doctor announced. And the wound was closing. He punched the needles into the flesh so hard that blood spurted out of the punctured skin under high pressure, tearing the suture. But that was not Emma's fault!

Soon almost everyone was gone. Only the red footprints were left behind. Two doctors from Anesthesiology and I remained. I leveled the table. Emma was paler than before, but her pulse was strong. I was holding her slender wrist and looked forward to her awakening. I would tell her that they did not find anything and that her hair will grow back. And that she is beautiful.

They took the tube out of her mouth, and she breathed on her own. She opened her moist lips like a child, and the bee eye reflected itself in her teeth.

"Emma, wake up!" the anesthesiologist called, slapping her cheek. Traces of her fingers remained on the cheek, but Emma did not open her eyes.

"That's all right. The main thing is she's breathing on her own, so she can go to Intensive Care." And she turned the stubbornly wheezing instrument off.

I took her into my arms, and she was wet with perspiration, though shivering with cold. I put her on a stretcher.

Annie turned up her lips and said, "Who are you bringing in here, Milan?"

"Emma. She's a good girl, Annie. Take good care of her."

She said nothing, but took a clean shirt and dressed Emma as soon as I placed her on the bed. She changed her IV and the drip bottle, checked her pressure, released the oxygen, and kept trying to push me out with her big, firm, resilient body.

Annie had a sad frown on her face, but she worked eagerly. I couldn't read anything in her face. She let me stand by the bed and call: "Emma, can you hear me?"

Emma lifted her right arm, half-opened her right eye, and absentmindedly made circles with her right hand above her face. That was no answer. When I took her wrist, she stopped, but only because of exhaustion.

I left to pick up the bloodied gowns. The room looked like a battleground. Rags and sheets were lying all over the place. Red tampons and gauze were strewn on the floor, and wherever one looked, there was drying blood.

That's all right, I'll clean up, but what was the battle all about?

As I was leaving for home, Annie was sitting in my little closet with a view of Intensive Care, smoking. She was staring at me now, and I could see she was tired. Actually she was not smoking; the cigarette was burning out by itself in the ash tray.

"You've had enough," I said.

Silently she pointed her head toward Intensive Care. The bearded man was pressing the sensitive spots below Emma's ears, calling out: "Emma, can you hear me?"

I could find no compassion in Annie's eyes, however. I saw only fatigue and wisdom: fatigue from wisdom, such as occurs with philosophers. She stubbed out her cigarette, gathered her strength, and then got up.

She was standing within my reach, and involuntarily I put my hand on her hip. I touched her firm body, and it did not resist, but neither did it soften under my hand. She smiled and tousled my hair, but then I gently patted her behind and said: "Go see your patients. They need your smile more than I do."

"They don't need it at all, Milan," she said seriously, and left.

I stepped out into the transparent autumnal air, and the world looked like a giant circus full of life and colors. I jumped onto a bus painted yellow and red.

In the university library I sat far in the back and took a book on anatomy and one on neurology out of the stacks. I learned to read books a long time before I even attempted to learn how to live. That is why, alas, I still need the aid of literature. And so I was reading and looking at pictures in which the arteries were red, the veins blue, and the nerves yellow. I was looking at a picture of the rear cranial opening, and suddenly it started to click. When you see something with your very own eyes, you don't have to believe it, but here was a picture! In a book! Exactly as I'd seen it, only without blood and in color: red, blue, yellow. Suddenly I was seized by a feeling that everything really did look like that.

I did not perceive any sounds, though occasionally someone would pass by and the unmuffled noise of the street would penetrate through the open window. Only once did I raise my head—when the door banged shut and I saw Tania. There was something unusual about her. She approached me smiling. And as she walked she rocked her head a little from side to side, as she used to do. She raised her eyebrows as if to say: You don't recognize me? She even lifted her left hand and moved her fingers, perplexed, as if trying to awaken me from a daydream. Then I noticed that her right hand was in a cast. I did not see it at first, because she carried her hand as if it did not belong to her, like a briefcase or a piece of wood. The cast was shining with fresh whiteness, and from the bottom of it her pink fingertips showed.

"What happened to you?" I asked.

She looked at the cast.

"This? I broke a finger. We were throwing the medicine ball during PE."

"And?"

"And I didn't catch it."

"But not catching it still couldn't break your finger!"

"Well I *did* catch it, but not properly."

"And?"

"And it crushed my hand against the floor," Tania said guiltily. Again she looked at her hand with an expression full of surprise about the world of things that so willfully hurt her.

We went outside, and Tania walked half a step behind me. How familiar it was. Tania feels guilt for everything, perhaps even for the famine in Biafra. Perhaps she is right and we all are guilty. But she broke her own finger! It is all the same to her, however, whether she hurt herself or somebody else, or if somebody else hurt her. She feels guilt the way a police dog sniffs heroin, and this perplexes her to the point that the world around her stops functioning.

The stumplike cast swung at her side like a police stick, but she refused to notice it. Yet I saw it only too well.

We entered a cafe and I ordered coffee. We had no choice; we had to stay together. It was impossible to say, There's no point to it today, so let's go home. There was a threat that we would never see each other again.

Finally, they brought coffee. I picked up the spoon and felt relief that entered through my fingers. Empty hands will drive me crazy one of these days.

You could say, after all, that a broken finger is nothing. I should have felt sorry for Tania. It must have really hurt her, and it is no fun to walk around with a cast. However, Tania did not let me behave naturally. I felt that she was blaming me, and I did not know why. Maybe because I could not free her from her guilt complex.

I reflected for a moment, and then I concluded that I could not figure it out. And I didn't really care one bit. I saw Emma lying on her stretcher, and she let me take off her pajamas, under which she had nothing but her tiny, tender little breasts on her white chest. She looked at me helplessly, and I covered her with a green gown. A doe has black eyes like those: equally terrified and equally wise.

"You are unbearable, Milan," said Tania.

"And what do you want me to do?"

"Stop hinting that I am an idiot."

I shrugged my shoulders.

"What is it you want? You want me to leave?" she asked, looking at me as if she could not believe her eyes, as if my cruelty surpassed all conceivable limits, as if my body had become covered with thick fur.

I did not want her to leave. I did not want her to become an unreachable idol. I'd rather suffer now until it passes, I told myself.

"Are we going to sit here and look at the ground?"

"We can leave. It's still nice outside," I said.

As we got up, I realized what fools we were; we had suffered there for an entire hour.

Giant chestnut trees packed with spiky balls were shedding leaves with yellow edges. I watched their pendular descent. Could it be true, I reflected, that only the day before yesterday we were making love in Tania's room when her mother was out?

I felt the body sitting next to me, and I thought it was going to drive me crazy. If Tania places my head on her breast just one more time, I thought, something will break inside and I will collapse into a pile of fragile limbs. She will carry me to her cellar in her silk scarf, like a scalp.

What happened to that love? Now I would rather crush a spider in my hand than touch her. And she felt the same. We were sitting next to each other and yet flying apart like stars after the Big Bang. With increasing speed.

We suffered through another hour; the sun went red and peered at us through the chestnuts as if through fingers. I was getting cold, my pulse slowed, and the blood pressure went down. This happens when I sit for a long time. The body sleeps, because its form of life is running. My legs began to ache.

"Let's go home."

Tania said nothing. She just sat for a while and then got up, as if getting up in a movie theater after the feature. She was leaving the park, and this time it was I who walked half a step behind her. I didn't want to lose her, but she turned to me and said, "Bye."

She left while I stood there stunned, wondering what was it that had struck me. I discovered it was her eyes. They had hardened somehow. I watched her back until she turned the corner. The cast stump was swinging by her side, but her walk had changed. It was more serious somehow.

I ran across the street and jogged to the villa district. It got dark, and I could have taken off my jeans, but I was happy just skipping home.

Those eyes let me know that I'd lost it. They embarrassed me with their hardness. I did not have enough energy even for peace-making, while she could have easily made love, so much energy radiated from those eyes!

I was slowly warming myself up. Beside me floated yet another yellow and white Zhiguli police car. It slowed down to keep pace with me, and the hats inside turned my way. They disturbed me, as always.

Only after the driver stepped on the gas and the red lights vanished around the corner did my thoughts return to Tania. And I stopped in astonishment. Again I saw her hand in the cast, and she was obviously giving me the cold shoulder. She was carrying that burden so unself-consciously, like a turtle its shell. However, now I knew that she did so not from shame, but because I really wasn't worth noticing. That was because she saw in my eyes something that interested her far more. Something I'd experienced and should have shared with her. But I had refused to talk and so offended our love.

So she had felt guilt, but not for herself. For me! I leaned against the railing and looked at the stars. So that's how it was. Already in the library Tania had felt that I should have told her something. She knew it before I did and waited for me to tell her. But fool that I was, I thought only about her broken finger. It provoked me because I, too, sensed that something more important stood between us.

I started to jog again. Slowly, so that my thoughts wouldn't scatter. I should have talked. I should have said that Emma was now making circles with her hand above her forehead trying to wake up. And that I would exchange ten broken fingers for Emma's health. My own fingers. That was what Tania wanted to hear. She wanted to experience it with me!

What was the reason I didn't tell her? Because I was a fool. I was offended that she dared to break her finger at the time when Emma was looking at me with her doelike eyes, when she was looking into the barrel of a rifle.

I woke up late and the apartment was empty. They had all gone somewhere. If only I had a headache, I said to myself, so that I would know I was in mourning. But my head never aches. My legs ache, and I know the medicine to cure that.

I slowly increased my speed past the Red Bridge. The slower one speeds up, the better. The body needs to adjust; you have to give it some time. Then you can wring from it the kind of energy you only dream about.

As I was running back, a dog started after me, but I laughed at him. The path was uphill, and he gave up after two hundred meters.

I arrived at work in the afternoon. They were all just leaving. The hospital was emptying out, leaving only the sick and a few resolute saints inside.

In Intensive Care, I found Annie changing the dressing on Mrs. Kiss's side. I held up the old body and let Grandma's hands clutch my cotton shirt.

"Hi, Annie."

"Hi," she said, and frowned.

"I don't have time to shave constantly," I said mildly.

"And I don't like hairy men."

"What kind of a man am I?"

Annie uncovered a wound the size of a fist and removed the pus from the pink walls of Grandma's flesh. The body was moving its legs and sighed. At the bottom of the wound, one could make out the pelvis bone.

"What will you do about that?" I asked.

"Nothing. What would you do?"

"I'm not a nurse," I countered.

"And I'm not God. Nobody can help this grandma!"

"Why?"

"Because she has a similar wound in her head. My God, she is ulcerating all over. One more week and instead of Grandma, there will be a pile of pus." She stuffed the rosy tunnel with gauze.

With her big hands, she changed the dressing. Those were the kind of hands Alberto Moravia wrote about. All the women he loved had hands like those and were themselves massive and strong. I looked over Annie's shoulders and hips. They were wide and firm. She leaned over my hand while taping, and I could feel her hard breasts on my forearm. Red cheeks and hands like shovels, Mr. Moravia!

She looked into my eyes, and her full lips relaxed a bit in a smile. She stood so close that I could have kissed her forehead. I breathed into her hair, and we turned Grandma on her back. She found my hand under the body, and suddenly the three of us stood connected against the world. Grandma sighed and checked us out with her sky-blue eyes.

"How did you get to do this?" I asked when we finished.

"There were no jobs back east where I come from."

"Do you want to stay here?"

"Yes."

She walked between the beds like a queen in her blue dress and her paper crown. Her thighs filled the soft fabric of her dress, and her calves were stuffed into white knee socks.

"You're beautiful," I said.

She looked at me seriously, but I did not believe that she understood me.

We approached Emma. She wanted to touch her forehead, but it did not work. She just circled with her hand. Annie touched the arch of her foot with her finger, the way one tickles little children to make them laugh. I couldn't see any reflex. Annie then buried her pencil in the skin. Emma moaned, and her hand circled higher, as if to shoo away bad dreams.

"Well?" I asked.

But Annie just moved silently over to Mrs. Bohush.

For a while I observed Emma's troubled chest. Her tender breasts were forced to move, and her nipples were quite hidden in the brown aureoles. I placed my hand on her forehead, which was hot and smooth, and closed her eyes. What are you thinking about, Emma?

Then I covered her up to the chin with a sheet. A minute later the circular motion of her hand uncovered her again.

Mrs. Bohush was in the next bed. Nothing was happening. She had been sleeping for three weeks, and on her head grew fine dark hair. Her wound had healed, and in the stubble one could see a pink scar. The intravenous solution was dripping into her arm, the oxygen was blowing into her nose, but Mrs. Bohush just slept on. The twins were already a month old.

"What do you think, Annie?"

"What can I say?" She pursed her lips, checked the needle in the arm, and went to her desk to write something.

The violet light blinked in the operating rooms, and there was a smell of ozone. The altars stood ready on elephant legs. I lay down on a stretcher in the hall. I had a view of a residential subdivision and a section of illuminated highway. The phone was at arm's length.

Tania, I imagined, is probably in her bed, surrounded by plush teddy bears and black rubber dolls, reading Dostoevsky. The corners of her mouth are drawn down, and every once in a while she combs her hair with her hand. Or she is studying and listening to Beethoven. Or she just lies there and watches the ceiling, breaking off her toenails, her toes being (as she revealed to me once) childishly pink and without calluses.

A month before, I had been feeding the fire with spruce wood while Tania cooked using dry spirits. All the food and dishes were spread around her on the grass. She was like a child who was playing with thirty different toys at the same time and wanted to have all of them handy.

"You'd never make a cavewoman," I said.

"Just be quiet, old man, and take care of the fire," she said, slicing the bread while supporting it by pressing it to her breasts. She stirred the beans with a wooden spoon or a piece of branch with its bark removed, and yet she sometimes thrust her hands into the pot up to her wrists. To distract myself, I looked up, watching a hawk as it flew overhead peering into the valley. The clouds hurried across the sky like angry faces of Nature.

"What can you do with a woman who can't even cook dinner for her man on time?"

"Hold on, honey."

"How is it with the seizing of the moment? You didn't mention whether the person was supposed to get the food before or . . ."

"It's coming." She ladled up some beans and spread them all over her mouth.

The hawk still circled. Perhaps he was not searching for mice; maybe he just liked it up there.

"You wouldn't believe what catastrophes can happen as a result of too much intelligence," I said.

"In a moment, honey . . ." she said calmly.

Well, I concluded, Tania is certainly not sleeping, and if she is not reading Dostoevsky, then she is breaking off her toenails. Preparing to test my musings, I placed my hand on the phone.

At that moment the door opened and Annie called out: "Milan, come quickly!"

I ran into the corridor and pushed open the doors as a stretcher rolled toward me. One of the wheels was locked, and it made a whistling noise as it left behind a whistling black smudge on the floor. Beside the stretcher, a doctor was running along pressing a black rubber ball that breathed for the old man who lay there. He was grimacing in his sleep, probably because of the red tube that distorted the corner of his mouth. There was blood on the pillow.

I shoved the altar aside and pushed the stretcher into its place. The doctor put away the ball and connected the old man to the machine. Everyone relaxed. His chest was soon rising in the same rhythm as the respirator. The surgeon was washing up, and the surgical nurse was readying the instruments.

But I was moving around the room like crazy, making big jumps from place to place, switching on instruments, untangling the hoses, turning on the light, feeling that my hour had come. It was just like after the firing of the starter's pistol. Energy was exploding inside me, and I vibrated with surging force. Before the four minutes were up, a distance of less than fifteen hundred meters, I was ready. I tried to shave the temples, but some of the hair was matted with blood and hard to cut, so I used scissors for most of it, then removed the rest with the razor. It had to hurt, but the old man was just frowning, his eyelids quickly swelling and turning violet.

Only four of us were left: the anesthesiologist, a surgeon, a surgical nurse, and me. I had gotten everything ready. My moment had passed.

Over the man's head, the surgeon placed the sterile sheet with a hole in the middle. He cut into the temple, and the blood flowed into the man's hair and ear. The doctor opened the wound and dried the opening with a tampon. Then he picked up the drill, a little spinning wheel with a nickel-plated pyramid at its tip.

Suddenly he said: "Milan, hold his head, please."

God, I grabbed the old man's forehead and crown under the sheet with great pleasure. I would love to take my friends' heads into my hands instead of shaking their hands. I would close my eyes and experience the nearness of their thoughts so very close to my fingers. Or I would touch Tania's smooth forehead with my bumpy one and confess my love to her.

I felt a sort of thundering through my hands. I remembered the feeling when, as an apprentice, I had to drill thousands of little holes into tin. The tin vibrated in my thumb, producing a pleasant shiver. Now, however, as I closed my eyes, I felt that it was not the old man but I who was the recipient of the nickel tip, and I heard the fragments of my skull as they shot away from the angles of the pyramid bit. I was holding my own head, and it was my head under the drill, my body in the straitjacket.

My hands started to sweat and slip along his forehead. The more I pressed them, the faster they slipped. It was not necessary, though, to press anymore. The surgeon took a thick needle with a blunt end on its side.

I felt that cold needle enter my brain, felt it brush against my blood vessel just so and push through a lobe, moving through the universe of white matter, stopping only when it reached the chamber. A stream of pink water jetted out from the needle, and when it stopped, the doctor attached a syringe and slowly suctioned off the liquid, pulling the needle out. The syringe filled with a black mush.

He was finished. He took out the old man's congealed blood, and that was all. He dried the wound and sutured it with a bent needle that punctured the skin with difficulty. The old man almost woke up from the pain, and he bent his right leg. Then the doctor got up, took off his gown and gloves, and invited the women for a cup of coffee.

The anesthesiologist checked the pulse and lifted the violet eyelids, and then they all left. It was up to me to wheel the old man to Intensive Care. When we were all alone, I felt like talking to someone.

So how are you, Grandpa? I asked him in my mind. What happened to you? Did you fall down the stairs? Did a car hit you? Or did you get drunk and fall on the sidewalk? How did you come to be lying on a blood-filled bed with a hole in your head?

I poured the blood in the sink and cleaned the tubes. I collected the gowns and sheets and swept the bloody tampons. Then I wiped the floor, put the instruments back, and sat down. It was half past two in the morning.

So that's how it is, I said to myself. Why go to America, when I can find my freedom in Bratislava? Is it not an expression of freedom when you help save someone's life? What do you think, Gramps? Who would hold your head if I were hanging out somewhere in America? I turned off the bee's eye. Only the white light bulbs were still on. They wreck your eyes: when you look at them from the side, you can see how they flicker. They invest everything with paleness and shake my image on the milky glass.

Soon I was sitting on a swivel chair, listening to the breathing of a respirator. In that light, the old man's face became unpleasantly yellow, as if he had a liver ailment. I took him by the hand. After a while I felt his pulse. It was slow and regular, the same as mine. I lifted his eyelids, but I didn't know how his eyes were supposed to react. His chin fell. Still, he breathed regularly.

I walked around his bed, studying his body. It carried traces of a long life. It was a little dried out. His feet were bent, and instead of toenails, there seemed to be claws growing. I touched the arch with my finger, the way I saw Annie do it. Nothing happened. Then I remembered something.

I took his wrist again and pressed my thumb on the artery. But this time I touched his neck with the other hand and waited. And I clearly felt it: boom . . . boom . . . boom . . . both on the thumb and the neck. Slowly and regularly, the same as mine. Shit, I was feeling my own pulse with my thumb!

Annie was suctioning off Emma's phlegm.

"Annie, come and have a look at him," I said.

She came to his bed, had a look, and said: "Call the doctor. Tell him to come here and turn the respirator off."

And that was all. Grandpa was dead. Now I saw that his lips had turned completely blue and that the only thing acting alive was the respirator. It kept lifting his chest, it hissed, it rattled the valves, and it couldn't care less for whom it was providing the oxygen. It tricked me, the bugger.

Annie returned to Emma. I felt tired. The stupid machine kept working. It was disturbing both the dead and the living. But I did not feel like fetching the doctor. I wanted to have a chat with the old man.

So how is it going, Gramps? Can you hear me? Who are you? I don't feel anything. Not even sadness. Only fatigue. I understand that you died, but it does not mean anything to me, you know? I did not know you when you lived, walked, talked, and did all those things that living people do. If you had said just one word, just looked at me, or made a gesture. But this . . . Were you alive at all?

I went to get the doctor, but he just phoned Annie, listened for a moment, and said to me: "You can turn it off. I'm not surprised." Then he turned to one of the anesthesiologists, who stubbed out her cigarette.

So I pressed the button, and when the cylinder folded like an accordion with a sigh, I sat by the bed and waited. What do those doctors know? Maybe my old man will come back to life. The taut skin on his belly will slowly start to pulsate, his mouth will open, he'll inhale, maybe he'll move his arm . . .

Then I took the bed out of the room, and with a brush Annie painted on his yellow thigh: IVAN ROYKO, 1918. So that was his name. He was sixty-two. So he had lived, after all. Who would have thought that? He could as well have been a wax figurine.

She was dipping her brush into the ink so calmly and painting so nicely, that I asked: "How many times have you painted names on a thigh, Annie?"

"Many times. They die often here," she said.

"Why?"

"I don't know."

"Maybe you attract death."

"People die before morning, and I'm often on duty at night. It's not over yet tonight, you'll see."

"Come on, Annie!"

"So what? Do you think I'm going to harm them by talking about it? It's true after all. Others will die today and I know who."

Behind the window, the city slept. The dark residential quarter was lost in the black hills. Occasionally the night bus's headlights would shine. Annie sat by the desk lamp and rolled tampons.

So Mr. Royko is dead, I thought. Why am I not surprised? I've never seen a real corpse before, yet I'm not touched. What does it mean? That death is so natural that one does not have to get used to it? I don't know.

Annie interrupted my thoughts: "Milan, come and give me a hand." She was standing beside Mrs. Bohush, and we washed her and turned her on her side. We passed from bed to bed, turned the bodies, holding our hands under their backs. I always firmly pressed her big, manly hand.

"Who are the ones who will die today, Annie? You don't have to change them."

"You are silly."

"Hmm."

"And anyway, have you ever washed a corpse?"

"No."

"So you don't know anything. I'd rather wash ten living than one dead."

Then we sat down, and Annie continued rolling the tampons. I could have gone to bed; my work was finished. I don't know what I was waiting for. Annie's huge shadow on the wall slowly paled, the stars disappeared in the east, and soon I saw the horizon. Then she got up, put the tampons away, scanned the room, and went over to Mrs. Bohush.

She touched Mrs. Bohush's wrist, held her own hand over her mouth, and said: "See, I told you."

We stood over Mrs. Bohush, and I was thinking what could be done when one stops breathing.

"There was no point. The surgery gave her one more week of sleep," Annie said.

"Then why did they operate?"

She did not answer, but turned up her lips. She got her bandages ready, together with her brush and ink, and waited. Nevertheless, Mrs. Bohush did not breathe even when day broke and when the eastern sky turned red. Annie bound up Mrs. Bohush's arms and legs and tied her chin. She was bound the way toothache sufferers once were: a piece of cloth under the chin with a bow on the crown of the head. She then painted the thigh with her brush: VIERA BOHUSH, 1948. We pushed her bed out into the corridor, behind Mr. Royko.

So that's how one leaves this world, I thought. She waited until she gave birth to her twins and then fell asleep as if she were tired. They'll push you out into the corridor and let you reminisce about your life.

The sun came out over the residential quarter, and perhaps the birds sang as well, but the sound did not reach the ninth floor. Only the crying of a child reached us from some other wing. It was crying in helplessness and rage, the way I used to cry as a child. I would shake the wooden bars of my crib. My throat hurt, my parents stood above me, and I had no idea to whom this shouting was supposed to be addressed.

Annie turned the light off. Her cheeks were still red, I saw clearly against the sunlight. She turned to the window and looked outside, squinting. Her shoulders and hips were wide, and yet she stood there as a woman and not a wrestler.

Suddenly something made me nervous. Something had changed, maybe inside me, maybe around me. I began searching for it the way you search for something you can't recall but nevertheless know that you should eventually find. I could not come up with anything. I did not need anything, I did not feel thirsty, my sleepiness was gone, and my head seemed empty. I seemed to have no idea, yet I did not look for one. Something else struck me. I scanned the intensive care room twice, and then all of a sudden I had it—Emma had stopped circling with her hand.

I took her wrist and tried to see if she was breathing. It seemed that her mouth and nose shook, and on her neck I noticed the pulse of her artery. Then she suddenly inhaled. Hungrily, deeply, like after a run. Her chest rose sharply and then fell. Annie was already by her side, holding her other hand.

Nothing was happening. I concentrated on her neck, but I could not see anything. Nothing was happening even in the girlish dimple between her collar bones. Only her mouth was half-opened, as if ready to take another breath. And then it came again. One heart-beat and a small explosion of the artery. Emma was drawing the air hungrily in, she was all bent as she did it, but it did not help her. She got stuck in the middle, and it did not work anymore. She now fell back, lifeless.

As the minutes passed she turned more and more yellow. Beautiful only an hour before, her moist teeth soon looked gray, and the features of her face seemed sharpened as in a sculptor's relief. I held her hand; it was getting colder and I could not keep it warm. Her nose got thinner, the skin of her cheek became taut, but her forehead remained gorgeous. It was round and marblelike, the same as it had been when I carried her in my arms. She had pressed it against my chest, and I had been happy that it was muscular and bulging. That was how Tania did it, and if they both were looking for protection, then I loved them because I was able to offer them this illusion.

I loved Emma in the last moment in her life, I know now. At that moment she lived more than anyone else I knew. Even when she looked at me with her black eyes from the operating table, I loved her because she sensed that she was going to die. That made her a real human being, an infinitely wiser being than I and all the rest, because that sort of wisdom can be bought only at the price of death.

I also loved her because she was beautiful and young, and I wanted her to live, wanted her to leave the hospital with a smile. I wanted her to come to me and shake my hand or give me a kiss, and then I would say: "Go, Emma, make some young man happy. Let him put his head on your tender breasts, accept him into yourself, and give him your wisdom."

But those tender breasts were turning a marble color, the little blue veins disappearing as the blood drained from them, and I was looking at the brown aureoles, wondering whether Emma ever felt the touch of boy's hands on her body.

Annie took the brush and ink and painted: EMMA HOLAN, 1961.

"Why did this girl die, Annie?" I asked.

"I don't know exactly why. She had to die; she was sick. Today or next month, what's the difference? She had cancer, and they couldn't help her."

"They did not find the tumor, though."

"Because it was deeper than they could go."

"But why did she have cancer?"

"How am I supposed to know, Milan?" Annie looked at me, upset, and moved to the window.

"That's nature," she added after a while.

Yes, I understand. We are all nature. But what the hell is that supposed to mean? When do I see nature? When it draws me to Tania like a magnet, then I see its power and strength. But otherwise it does not concern me.

Should it happen, however, that my body were to contain a defect, that a faulty cell would be born in my brain and give birth to other defects, and my head would start to hurt, then I would realize that there is Nature inside me and that she had sentenced me to death.

She made herself known to Emma each second. She made herself known to her with pain, with fear, and did not let her relax for a moment. She forced Emma to accept her as a deity. Emma felt Nature in her body, I saw that in her black eyes. The rest of us were different. She pressed her forehead against my firm chest, but it was merely an attempt to approach something that would never be hers. I don't know what. Maybe the right to live.

In the morning the hospital filled with people in blue and white gowns. Annie did get black circles under her eyes after all. She moved ghostlike through Intensive Care, wiping dust. I was sitting on the windowsill, watching her. There were three beds in the hall, now empty. I was so tired I almost fell out of the window.

Others arrived and we changed shifts. I took the elevator down to the basement. At the end of Pathology was the entrance to the dissection room.

It had the same flickering light bulbs as the operating room. Four men in black rubber aprons quietly worked around four tables. They paid no attention to me. There were people lying on the tables. The first three had their insides placed by their legs, and someone had stuffed their chests with paper wadding. The last one was Emma.

On her face was the same expression: a slightly open mouth that had not finished her last inhalation, and inside, the dull-gray teeth. One of those gorgeous eyes Annie did not manage to close.

One of the men was getting ready to work on Emma. He took a big knife in his hand and cut the skin around her head. He left the forehead untouched, and casually rolled the skin over. Then he took a saw, the kind I used to cut branches from trees when my grandfather grew old. He told me what to cut and what to keep, and then I sawed.

So the man used such a saw to cut off the top of Emma's head, and I could see her brain. Then he took big garden shears and cut open her chest. He continued cutting through the neck and then stuck his hand with the big kitchen knife in it into her chest. Soon Emma's tongue disappeared from her mouth and reemerged from the hole in her chest. He brought out the lungs and pleura, the heart, the liver, and all the intestines, until she lay there like the others, with paper wadding in her body.

The pathologist came, and I watched as he picked up the lungs, cut into them, and explored the pink depressions with his thumb. He did the same with the heart and liver. Good God! How young and how pink was Emma's body inside! The pathologist didn't say a word as he put the dissected pieces aside. It was a long time before he picked up the brain: a soft, gray ball. He cut it in two and looked at the right half. I saw a dark point where the needle had gone in. I relived how it had entered Emma's head and how the doctor with the beard kept pushing it in with his thumb and index finger until only the attachment remained outside. My heart started pounding as the pathologist slipped his knife inside the brain and cut across. The two parts separated and lay in his hands.

There were spotted white-gray fields with chamber lakes, and in the middle was a big red spot smudged at the edges. He studied the spot for some time and then looked at me, saying: "You're from Neurosurgery?"

"Yes," I said.

"There are traces of a brain hemorrhage. That could have been the cause of death."

I nodded and left. I could not make it out of the maze. I kept opening doors to stairways leading only down, it seemed, and then I burst into a lab where I startled a girl sitting over a microscope. Finally I collided with a huge cleaning lady who showed me the way out.

At the bus stop, people stood waiting, and the sun was shining on them, I think.

"I was so afraid I couldn't close my eyes."

"Afraid of what?"

"That I will not survive."

"Come on, Emma!"

How could I say something like that? Are you allowed to say such things? But Emma was not affected; she was right. Maybe she didn't know that they would kill her, but nevertheless, she knew infinitely more. She knew everything there was to know about this world, and then it hit me. There at the bus stop I became Emma, and I knew that I would die. Then the people around me began to disappear, flying away at great speed, as if my eye had become a camera lens, and I remained alone. Euphoria was flooding me, because the sun was shining for the last time. My throat contracted, and bursting cells appeared in front of my eyes. They grew inside my head and now were rolling in the blood that issued from the broken vessel flooding my clean, white brain. I felt my pupils enlarged by terror until it all suddenly passed away as abruptly as it had seized me. Only my heart was still pounding unpleasantly.

The bus had not arrived, or perhaps it had arrived and new people were waiting. I don't know.

I was trying to understand, so I reflected again. I really would accept it, Mother Nature. I was a good pupil, and when I happened not to understand something, I would bow my head before authority. But tell me, why did you make her a woman? Why did you let her bleed once a month from the age of twelve, as her medical chart said, "without problems"? Why did you let her eat, dream, understand? And why the hell did you make her in the first place?

I didn't make it onto the next bus, because people were hanging out the doors, but later another one came. I found the apartment clean, tidy, and abandoned. My father was messing with cement on some construction site, my brother was doing math in some school, and my mother—I don't know—she had gone downtown.

I ran into the sun, among the trees, to feel the soft soil under my feet. I ran through the park to the Red Bridge and across the brook, and then I went berserk. Why should I save myself? For whom? Do I want to live a long time? I flew down the narrow path and counted the wooden bridges. They ached under my furious pounding and jumping, buckling the old logs, but I had no time to turn and see if they were broken. I rushed on to the short ascents, looking forward to them because there I could become completely spent. I could torture my thighs into working despite the searing pain and then let them quickly relax on the way down, as I punished my hips. I sprinted with long jumps and refused to soften the impact; the sunrays blinded me, and the faster I ran, the more often the rays would shine through the leaves. I ran after them, closing my eyes. I realized that I felt like sleeping and dozed off for two or three seconds, but then came the curve. I flew by its edge, but the centrifugal force pushed me into the hill, and half-asleep I ran through the big loop that returned me to the road home. Only then did I realize that I was at full speed. I knew that I was going back, or rather, my body knew, because it dashed ahead without reserve. My head was pointlessly rocking on my neck, and that weight bothered me. I could not keep it straight, all my energy was spent on the legs. My hands were growing cold; my shoulders were hardening. I was slowly dying, but my legs were coping. They continued angrily moving forward. It occurred to me that I was kind of light because I had not eaten ever since time immemorial. There was no food inside me. I burned my own body for energy, and that made me happy as I gunned up the last hill. Still, the wind blew on my cold forehead, and I ran fast.

I saw the finish through a red mist, my eyes were falling shut. My legs, though, felt the asphalt, and thus I knew I was standing by the President's villa above the city. If I had the strength to look, I would see in the mist thousands of houses and the bent strip of the shiny Danube.

I took a cold shower, because there was no hot water, and rolled myself into a ball on my bed and went to sleep.

Thirst and cold woke me up. Lisa was still wandering around the apartment alone. She rubbed herself against my legs and marched to the kitchen. There she kept sticking her snout inside a bowl and looking at me significantly. I put on my jeans and T-shirt and went down into the blistering city.

I avoided the shade, but it did not help much. Gooseflesh was breaking out on my skin, I shook with cold, my head was swimming, and my body seemed drained of blood. The cold passed through my insides, twisting my stomach, and I had the feeling that if I did not eat, I would die of cold.

I had a bowl of soup in the cafeteria on Michalskà Street and then bought a bag of bread rolls. I wanted to eat them on a bench near the fountain, but I could not wait and chewed a hard, dry roll on my way there.

I used to spend a thousand crowns a month on food on top of what I got at home. At track meets I would eat three helpings of steak and eggs with extra bread. Now I had only twenty halers in my pockets because I still had not received my hospital wages. I looked in puzzlement at an old lady as she fed the pigeons with bread. They hopped around and stupidly rolled their eyes.

People sat everywhere and looked as if they knew everything. They were not looking at anything in particular, only passing the time. Some of them ate, and others held in their hands open books or newspapers, turning their faces to the sun—the sun that would not tan them through the Bratislava smog. I, too, faced the sun, digesting the rolls and thinking of Emma's black eyes. They were looking at the ceiling when the anesthesiologist was searching for the vein with the needle. It seemed to me that she waited for that injection as if for salvation, because she slowly started to close her eyes. I could have sworn then that I caught relief in her eyes. However, now I knew that her pupils were drawn by anesthesia.

I took a look around the square. The crowd was streaming along the promenade. It entered the stores or just rolled on. Suddenly, I jumped up and started running, knocking the bread out of the old woman's hand, the pigeon wings flapping around my head. In front of me a threesome of girls filled the sidewalk. So I stepped on the flowers planted in the dry soil and threw myself into the crowd. Weaving among the people, I hit a shopping bag and heard the crunch of eggs; somewhere ahead of me the crowd was opening up. The yellow and white Zhiguli police car floated before me. I bounced off its hood to get away and realized that I was making myself conspicuous. But I could not help it. Ahead of me I saw a golden head and a waddling walk. I was already right behind her; she was wearing a blue skirt and blouse. I passed by and saw a made-up face and black pencil over the plucked eyebrows.

Astonished, I stood on the cobblestones, I had no idea that I'd been pursuing her in the streets. I entered the public library where we used to meet, and picked up a newspaper. I sat down at the closest table and put my head on a pile of papers . . .

It was about two o'clock in the morning, and I was sitting in a chalet near a dying fire. I saw in the faces of others an unwillingness to keep the fire going. That year they had moved the athletic season because of the Olympics. May was not over yet, and running was already in full swing. I was thinking about the finals of the Slovak championship, in which I was supposed to have run that day at eleven in the morning. But in the qualifying run I had finished fourth. All I had needed to do was move to the second lane, stretch myself up from the hips, shed the tow, and pass the two runners who fought each other, ghostlike, ahead of me. Had I finished in front of of them, I would have run in the finals and would not have been sitting there next to Tania and looking into the blue flames. I had been watching my opponents' heels, and I don't know what it was I had been thinking. But when we passed the checkered flag, I was happy that it was over.

Tania and I remained alone by what was left of the fire. Upstairs the beds were still creaking, but otherwise everything was silent. Outside day was breaking.

"Let's go for a walk," I said.

We climbed to the top of the hill and walked through beech woods and talked about something, probably about life—about what sort of life it is and what sort of people we were. The sun was rising in front of us, and we reached places where the woods thinned out and there were grassy meadows. I wanted to stop in each of them.

Tania's hands fascinated me. They were so small that I could hide her entire fist in the palm of my hand. I let her talk and touched her tiny fingers.

At first they went limp, as if all energy had left them, though they were radiating warmth, but then, as if accustomed to it, they comfortably settled in my hand. She did not let me know in any other way that something had occurred. She kept on walking, and if I stopped, she would take one more step and turn with surprise. What's keeping her back? I wondered. Oh yes, the hand!

We were holding hands, I was touching her, and she kept on talking. When we were returning home by bus, I kissed her mouth for the first time. When I got off, she smiled and waved to me from the window.

I found myself in the shade, and gooseflesh appeared on my hands. I left the newspaper on the table and went downtown. There were even more people now in the streets, and the smell of sausages and hamburgers wafted from the restaurants. I had an attack of hunger that drove me home.

Now it was clear to me that to live I needed Tania. She needed to know that Emma had lived and died in front of my eyes. She needed to know of that experience I had had; otherwise everything would become pointless. Without Tania my world would lose its dimensions, and the space would be empty. I would move in it aimlessly, like a fish in an aquarium. I discovered that when I dashed after her through the crowd after I'd seen merely a shock of blond hair. I should have realized it a long time ago. That was how I reasoned as I was in the elevator.

As soon as my mother opened the door, I inhaled the smell of meat.

"Tania called," she said.

I was hanging around the phone. Every ten minutes I would get up for a drink to get closer to the phone, and once I put my hand on the receiver. I even lifted it up, but someone else was talking on the party line, and I felt great relief. I did not really want to call her. Now that I knew that we would see each other again, I wished to get to know that empty space, to experience that short moment without dimensions.

The next afternoon I went back to the hospital. It was a thirteen-floor building with wide balconies. They say that about twice a year a patient jumps from one of them.

As soon as I changed into the whites, a doctor came in and said: "We're going to operate, Milan."

I pushed the stretcher down to the men's ward, but Mr. Tomko was standing on the balcony. It turned out that he was mobile.

"You see, Mr. Tomko, I came to fetch you with the stretcher, but you are in excellent shape," I said with a waiterlike smile on my face.

He turned around and looked at me sadly. He was fifty-three years old, with a gaping mouth and about half his hair left. I took him by his arm, and we walked toward the operating room.

In the hall, I set him down on a chair and got the clippers ready.

"Well, Mr. Tomko, I'll cut your hair now, all right?"

He looked at me sadly and said: "Cut my hair? Why?"

"Because you are going to an operation."

"An operation?"

I browsed through his chart. It said: "Suspicion of expansion: left temporal." Mr. Tomko had no idea that he had a full right to that sad look of his.

"Yes," I said.

"What kind of operation?"

"An operation on your head."

"Will you put me to sleep?"

I was pleasantly surprised by the logic of that question.

"Yes, we shall, Mr. Tomko. But have no fear. You won't feel a thing."

I waded with my clippers into his graying hair, and Mr. Tomko was helping me, turning his head the right way and looking out the window.

"Why are you cutting my hair?" he asked suddenly.

"Please, don't move. I have to cut your hair, because you are going to have an operation."

"An operation?"

"Yes."

"What sort of an operation?"

"Head operation."

"My head?"

"Yes."

"Will you put me to sleep?"

"Yes, we shall."

He nodded his head and let me finish the haircut. Then I got the water ready and squeezed out shaving cream in some pretty shapes on top of Mr. Tomko's nicely formed skull.

Mr. Tomko stopped looking out the window. "What are you doing?" he asked.

"I have to shave you."

"Why?"

"It does not work otherwise, Mr. Tomko. Because of the disinfecting."

"Disinfecting?"

"Yes, so that you don't start to fester after the operation."

"What operation?"

I could not hold myself back anymore. "Mr. Tomko, you have a tumor in your head, and it causes you to forget things. Two minutes ago I told you that you were about to be operated on, and now you're asking me about it again. In a couple of minutes you'll forget and ask yet another time. And so on in a circle."

He went quiet and let me shave the stubble. I had begun to like bald people. It seemed to me that I was unveiling their final likeness. They became interesting. The faces lost their priority and became only a part of the skull. The head sat on the neck like a real crown, without the false frame of the hair.

The green gown in which I dressed him instead of his pajamas reached only down to his knees, and I led him—barefoot and poorly dressed—into the operating room.

"Where are we going?"

"To the operating room, Mr. Tomko."

"To the operating room?"

"Yes."

"What are we going to do there?"

"They'll operate on you."

"Operate?"

"Yes."

"What will they operate on?"

"Your head."

"My head?"

"Yes."

"Will they put me to sleep?"

"Yes."

He lay down on the altar with his hands crossed on his chest and watched me as I tied his legs. Then he let me tie his arms and held them fast by his sides, like a soldier, and when the doctor told him to exercise his hand, he exercised for a whole minute until he forgot.

Later he watched us with an inquisitive look until they released the drug into his veins and his eyes rolled up. The surgeon started drawing his big U on Mr. Tomko's head and beneath the scalpel opened a red abyss. It filled up with blood that spilled over its edges and flowed onto the sheets, was absorbed there, and turned dark. The blood also sprayed out in thin geysers and dripped on the tiles.

Then came the odor of the burning bone and the whine of the drill. I was familiar with that already. I watched the surgeon's hands as one watches a woodcutter at work. In half an hour he lifted the toothed wheel and uncovered the hard membrane below which pulsated the brain of Mr. Tomko.

The small sharp scissors cut into the fairyland domain, where no one had ever entered. However, under pressure from the tumor, dark little bulges covered with a network of veins pushed out from the edges as if trying to escape. That doomed them, because they would never get back under the membrane. The surgeon did not hesitate. He dug into the brain with his shiny shovel and sliced a piece the size of a plum, threw it into a bowl, and started to suction the dark blood that streamed into the opening. He was suctioning off the white brain as well, as he increased the opening until he hit something that he could not suction off. The metallic pipe kept getting clogged, and I saw that it was not the light pudding of the nerve fiber, but something firmer, and grainier, though it was hard to distinguish in the flood of blood and white mush. The blood started to flow faster. It was clear from the X ray that the tumor was overgrown by veins. They branched out to feed the tumor. It was as if you wanted to fall on a sword and, just to be sure you achieved your object, sharpened it like a razor. When Nature decides to destroy, she does it thoroughly.

The torn veins were releasing blood with frightening speed. The opening was filled in two seconds. The surgeon was looking for the veins to cauterize them with coagulation tweezers, but new ones were constantly appearing. The blood was spilling from who knows where; it rose from the dark mush, from all sides. The doctor was jabbing the tweezers in blindly, burning everything, until it started to bubble.

I had to change the suction bottle because one was already full: a liter of dark blood with violet foam on top. It took three seconds to change the hoses, but in just that short time the opening filled up. The doctor was eyeing me with despair.

The pipe was almost insufficient for the flood: a big vein had burst somewhere. The woman doctor from Anesthesiology was signaling to me with her eyes that his pressure was dropping, but I just shrugged my shoulders. Let her tell him herself.

Suddenly I jumped up on my chair. I spotted for a second in that flood a thick thread, almost a thin tube. But the doctor, too, noticed it, grabbed it with his tweezers, and zapped it with electricity. The vein crackled, the fiber contracted, and a black knot appeared on it.

Only now did I realize that my entire body was hurting from the tension. But Mr. Tomko's veins were being supplied with new blood from infusion bottles, so everything was straightened out and the surgeon continued working. He was ripping out pieces of a tumor that was as hardy as a mushroom, and cauterizing the veins. Mr. Tomko's tumor was slowly disappearing, but so was his brain, until the doctor stopped and said: "I can't go any farther. The tumor has spread somewhere below."

He was finished.

"There, it's done," I said when I moved Mr. Tomko to the stretcher. His body was covered by the green gown, and he was now wearing a white hat that looked like a turban. "Now we'll leave you in peace, Mr. Tomko." I took him to Intensive Care, away from that bloodied room where a piece of his life and death remained.

"Who are you bringing me, Milan?" Annie asked. She had just arrived for her night duty and was trying to insert in her hair a hairpin I did not like.

"Mr. Tomko," I called out, "this is Annie! A good and beautiful girl who will take good care of you tonight."

"Oh, come on, Milan," she laughed.

"Well, what about it? Isn't it true?"

But Mr. Tomko was sleeping and did not see her blush. I carried him to his bed and stood by as Annie took his blood pressure, pulse, and temperature. She then dressed him in a shirt. While she did those things, I was experiencing an irresistible yearning to touch her big body, the way a child involuntarily reaches for a toy behind the shop window, to feel in my hands the divine purity reflected in her movements. I gazed like a child on her nurse's uniform—all blue, with a white apron—which reminded me of the beautiful dress worn by Snow White. I felt joy from this beauty and from the realization that I liked Annie as a gorgeous treasure that you discover, yet at the same time do not desire to take home with you. She may have noticed my ogling her, but she did not show it.

When she covered Mr. Tomko up to his chin, because he was shivering with cold, I left to clean up the operating room. I spent an hour, hosing down and wiping off everything covered by Mr. Tomko's blood. When I returned, Annie was sitting in my place, drinking coffee and watching the intensive care room through the open door.

"Do you want some coffee?" she asked.

"Yes." I wanted to drink coffee with her. I think I wanted to evoke the act of communion by doing that. And indeed it appeared that I was communing by drinking that beverage given to me by the hands of Nature, because I suddenly realized that Annie embodies Nature. She never asked questions, never wondered about anything, because she felt the immutability in the way things work, the same as a cat never wonders about anything but just acts according to its essence. So I drank the coffee from her cup and felt as if I were lying in the embrace of her wide lap.

"Annie, how did you get the idea to become a nurse?" I asked, and handed her the cup.

"I didn't get any idea. I always wanted to be a nurse."

"You never wanted to be anything else? Say, go to the university?"

"I can't remember."

"Every girl wishes at least once in her life to be a teacher."

"I didn't like school."

"But there are so many things to do in life . . ."

She shrugged her shoulders and turned up her lips. She was holding the cup in her hand and watching Intensive Care, and one of her legs was folded under her in such a manner that just looking at it hurt my knees. She raised her head and asked, "And what about you?"

"What about me?"

"Why did you come here?"

Now it was my turn to shrug my shoulders. Did I know why? What did I expect to find—human tragedy? I think I hoped to find its meaning rather than its real face. Instead I discovered helplessness and not a trace of meaning. Perhaps I also wanted to help, or live in the illusion that I was really helping. Instead I was seeing people out of this life.

"I would love to be like you, Annie, at least for a while," I said. "To be born in a village, in the dark woods, to have gone to the kind of school from which you could see your little house and a few nearby shacks, to have had parents who worked in the fields, and to have known from childhood what I would do when I grew up."

"That's not funny," Annie said. "Our village is not that small. And it's not my fault that I was born there."

"I am not making fun of you," I countered, wanting to continue. But I was interrupted by some movement. We both ran into the intensive care room.

By the window stood a barefoot man. His shirt covered barely half his behind, and he was looking at the illuminated subdivision and the headlights as they reflected themselves on the asphalt, for it was raining.

"Have you gone mad, Mr. Tomko?" Annie shouted in anger. He turned around and calmly observed us from below his turban, which pressed down on his eyelids.

"I have a headache. I must go home," he said.

"You've just had an operation, and you must stay in bed," said Annie.

"An operation?"

"On your head."

He touched the bandage on one side, where a red spot was growing, and let himself be taken to bed.

"Why are you tying me down?"

"So you don't get the idea to get up."

"That's not nice," he said.

He lay with his arms outstretched, as if he were crucified, and looked at the ceiling.

Annie sat down by the window, placed a wicker basket on her knees, and tore off a piece of cotton wool. She wrapped it around her index finger and sealed the ends of the little roll she made with a peculiar play of fingers. She dropped the finished tampon in a basket. The lamp was shining on her fingers, and her hair was falling on her forehead.

"Irma!"

"For heaven's sake, what is it, Mr. Tomko?" I said, startled.

"I'll shout."

62

"Let him," said Annie without even raising her head.

"Irma!"

"Who is Irma?" I asked him.

"My wife."

"But she is at home. She can't hear you."

"Irma!" He drew the last vowel out in a wailing cry.

Annie ignored him.

"Can't you sedate him?"

"No," she said.

She worked steadily, moving her lips to the words of a tune that she silently sang to herself. She kept dropping the tampons in the basket and reaching blindly for the cotton wool on the table. The edge of the lamp illuminated her profile, her full cheeks, her mouth, her lowered eyes, and also the exposed pale skin below her neck. This is what my wife would look like if I had lived in the last century, I told myself. I would come home from working in the fields to find her mending my socks by the kerosene lamp. I would sit down and watch all evening long those big hands and the face illuminated from below by the flickering light.

"Irma!" The yelling sounded throughout the clinic. I heard the echo rebound all the way from the children's ward.

"Are we going to let him shout until he wakes up the entire hospital?" I asked.

"And what am I to do? He can't have an injection. He just had brain surgery."

She radiated such certainty that I calmed down. She persevered in making the tampons and did not change her position for an hour. She did not even raise her eyes, though she had to know that I was observing her.

Then Mr. Tomko made himself known again, as if remembering his duty. He arched his whole body as he screamed: "Irma! Irma! Iaaa!"

Annie turned on her chair and asked: "Why are you screaming?"

"Because I am tied down."

"And if I untie you, will you be quiet?"

"No."

63

"There, you see."

It was quiet for a while. Mr. Tomko was thinking. Then he said: "I'll help you."

"You're not going to scream?"

"No."

I let him sit on my chair and was rewarded by a touching scene. He sat opposite Annie with a blanket over his lap, because his shirt was too short. He took the tampons from her hands and threw them in the basket. On the white turban the red spot was the size of a fist, and his ears stood out under the pressure of the bandages. His expression was serious, and Annie behaved the same way. It seemed both were completely immersed in their work.

I realized that I envied him. I, too, wanted to sit across from Annie and take the tampons from her fingers.

"Annie, I'm going to take a nap," I said, swallowing a malicious comment.

"Good night," she answered. Mr. Tomko did not even acknowledge me.

I dreamed about blood. For a month there had been no dreams of anything else. Nothing but blood. Around me lay dozens of people bleeding profusely, and I jumped from one to the other, tying their arteries with rope. The arteries crawled out from the wounds like worms, and there was more and more blood, until I was wading in it and the people were drowning, their bodies floating in red streams.

I was awakened by some noise. I had just opened my eyes when the doors flew open and Annie burst in. She was screaming about something, and then she sat down crying, hiding her face in her hands, her shoulders shaking hysterically. I ran into the corridor. Mr. Tomko was walking up and down, rocking from side to side, holding in his hand an oxygen hose.

"What have you done to the nurse?" I asked him.

"The nurse?"

I took the hose from him and walked him to the bed. He let me tie him down without resistance and fixed a vacant stare at the ceiling. As I was about to leave, he said: "I am going to yell."

Annie was sobbing on my bed. Her big body was shaking as she cried, and her hair was spread on the pillow. I sat down and touched her shoulder.

"There, there, Annie . . . ," I said.

She shook her head. She became a little girl or a real woman, I don't know which. I simply felt a need to take her in my arms.

"Irma!"

She suddenly sat up and wiped her tears.

"He followed me like a ghost. Wherever I'd go, he would be behind me. I asked him to go to bed, but he didn't seem to understand. I got scared, because he wouldn't say anything. Then he ripped the hose off the wall and started to beat me!"

"There, there, Annie . . ." I did not know what to say. I felt guilty for leaving her alone with him, and at the same time, I was overtaken by happiness at seeing her cry, at tears flowing from those round eyes, and at seeing her face become more beautiful.

"Irma!"

"My God, he'll drive me crazy!" shouted Annie, and ran out.

I found her leaning against the wall, her eyes lifted to God.

"I'm sorry, Annie. It was my fault," I said.

She shook her head again and placed her hands on my shoulders. She leaned her forehead against my collarbone, and I smelled her fragrant hair. I pressed her closer to me and felt the tender resistance of her bosom on my chest. When she lifted her head, before I could kiss her, I saw the sheen of her teeth. Her lips were salty from her tears, and I licked that salt like a believer drinking holy water.

"Irma!"

Screams separated the night into a series of one-minute intervals. We sat by the window. In front of us lay five patients, including four unconscious ones and one who lived in his own world, where he desired Irma and nothing else interested him.

"Milan?" Annie said.

"Yeah?"

"Sorry that I woke you up so abruptly."

"Oh, come now. On the contrary, I'm happy that it happened. You're beautiful when you're crying."

"Really?"

"Really. A woman's crying is like the sudden awakening of the whole world. Everything is suddenly real because it is reflected in your crying and I can finally see it, I can touch it. You know what I mean?"

"You say it beautifully. But I don't quite understand."

Annie, it's as if the whole world is behind glass, I said to myself. People don't notice it, or they are embarrassed to show that they do notice it. I don't know why it is like that. Sometimes I fear that the reason for it is that the world actually does not exist. Thus, there is nothing to perceive. But when a woman starts to cry, it is like giving me the proof that something is happening. And not only inside my head.

Out there, day was breaking again. The same as when Emma was dying. The sun came up over the same building and reflected itself in the glass of the medication cabinet. The night slowly assumed its final shape. That night Mr. Tomko inevitably entered my life through the blood that flowed from his brain, through the madness to which he was sentenced, through the surgeon's pipe that suctioned the white mush, or through the tumor that would grow one day into the size of an orange and later a coconut. For Annie, it was through the hose that Mr. Tomko used on her behind. With his tragedy he had attached Annie and me to each other and to himself. It was foolish of us to think that we would get rid of him by strapping him down to his bed.

The morning was joyful, however, because of Annie's smile and her red cheeks.

"I'll take a hot shower and I'll hop in my bed," she intoned, and kissed my lips.

Mr. Tomko was moving his tired wrists, trying to free himself. He was no longer screaming, because he had lost his voice. When I approached him, he followed me with his dim eyes and smiled.

"How is he?" Annie asked, standing by the sink.

"I don't know. He's smiling," I said.

I found the apartment full of down-filled comforters and dishes from breakfast. Through the open windows came the racket from the street, and Lisa, with her spotted fur coat, rubbed herself against my legs.

"Scram," I said.

She took a leak on the cotton wool in the bathroom before I could manage to brush my teeth. I changed the cotton wool and sliced the meat. She wagged her tail in excitement.

I slept through the entire morning and spent the rest of the day lazing about.

The phone did not work.

Next day was Saturday. The blinds were drawn and the street empty. I was waiting for the bus, and I could see steam coming out of my mouth. The autumnal mornings were beginning. Again I entered the hospital, breathing in the heavy odor of antiseptic, and walked down the hall with a feeling of oppressive sadness from fatigue.

In front of Intensive Care I found a bed. Yellow legs were showing from under a clean sheet. I uncovered the sheet on the other side and saw Mr. Tomko's face. His chin was tied and his nose suddenly stuck out toward me, big and pointy. Stubble had covered his face during the night, and he was still wearing the now unnecessary white turban.

Annie had arrived before me and was already bustling about the room.

"Hi," I said.

She smiled at me: "Hi, boy!"

"Why are you smiling?"

"I'm happy to see you, boy!"

"Because Mr. Tomko has died?"

"No, he left us at three. We were still sleeping then, weren't we?"

"How did he die?"

"I don't know," she intoned, drawing the words out, dancing between the beds.

"Then why do you feel so good?"

She stopped and looked at me.

"And why are you questioning me?"

"You feel good because Mr. Tomko has died and you have one less patient to take care of?"

"How can you, Milan?" Tears welled up in her eyes.

"I'm sorry," I mumbled, but I did not approach her.

"Then why did you say that?"

"I don't know. I didn't expect it to happen so soon."

"But surely that's not my fault. I didn't kill him!"

"I know. I'm sorry."

And who killed him? Can I say that the doctor killed him? After all, I'd seen with my very own eyes how the doctor managed to stop the bleeding and how he took out half of the tumor.

We washed all those who were still alive, holding our hands in a conciliatory way when we turned the patients. Mrs. Kiss was surprisingly improved. Her eyes were running up and down the room. She took the bandages off her head, took out the tampon that filled the festering hole in her head, and popped it into her mouth. She sucked on it as if it were a candy and did not want to let go when Annie tried to take it out.

"That doesn't taste good, Mrs. Kiss," she said, and smiled at me so cheerfully that she took my breath away.

"Annie, when did he see his Irma for the last time?"

"A day before the surgery. I was on duty in the men's ward and saw her. She talked to the boss."

"What did she look like?"

"Pretty. Dressed in a fur coat."

"How did she behave?"

"She was crying and squeezing the old man's hands. The boss was blabbering that they'd fix everything and her hubby would be all right."

"That's not possible, Annie. Even I knew from the picture that he had no chance!"

Annie eyed me cheerfully. "Boy, oh boy. Did you fall down here from the moon? What do you think would happen if they told everyone that there was no point to surgery?" And Annie rubbed her thumb and index finger together.

"Don't be disgusting, Annie," I quickly said.

"Why? Isn't it true?" she asked stubbornly.

"You could be mistaken."

"I've been here for a year, boy!" And the cheerfulness slowly vanished from her face. She wrinkled her brow, and her eyes filled with—not quite hate, but with a blasé distaste for this world. She seemed tired of what she had seen and known: I am here to take care of the patients that you send to me, doctors, she seemed to say. I'll take care of them till the last moment. I'll fight for their life until their last breath, and I will be there with them in that moment. But don't expect me to cry over them—there's no more strength for that left.

"You're beautiful now, Annie," I said.

She slapped Mrs. Kiss on her behind and laughed: "That was for you. If you don't smarten up, you'll get one for real."

I felt joy from her dark hair and the red ladybug in it, from her wide shoulders, from her big hands that Moravia would like, and from her round brown eyes. I felt so happy that I didn't quite understand right away what she was talking about: "You know, it doesn't matter whether you have money or not. The only difference is that when you pay well, you'll be operated on more times," she said, smiling happily.

"If I were to die, Annie, I'd come to you, to this intensive care room. I would lie in bed and wait until you'd say, get ready. I envy those who breathe their last when you're on duty."

"So you won't behave? You are a bad boy and I won't talk to you," she said, laughing, and her cheeks went red.

"Hello."

"Tania? Hi, it's me."

"Hi."

The operating room is usually cold and empty on Saturdays. I was sitting on a side table, holding the phone on my knees.

"I would like to see you tomorrow. May I?"

"Come on over. Mom is going on a trip. How are you?"

"Fine. Well, no, I'm not fine. You know."

She laughed quietly and said: "I called you, but you weren't home."

"That's all right. It's better like this. Girls shouldn't call first."

"An orthodox man . . ."

"I'm an idiot and not an orthodox man."

"So we'll see each other tomorrow."

"I'll come around eleven, all right?"

"Fine. See you."

"See you."

She was waiting for me in old jeans and a faded T-shirt she had taken from me on our camping trip. She smiled, embraced my waist in a lustful and playful way, unloverlike, and did not let me go for several minutes until we told each other all sorts of things in our minds. When we finished, she made coffee, as if my arrival had exhausted her.

In the garden in front of the quiet house plums were falling on the grass, and the leaves of the oak tree were slowly changing color. One day about two months before, while Tania's mother was away on another trip, we had picked apricots. I threw some at Tania, and she tried to catch them like a bear cub, in her mouth. When she succeeded and the apricot vanished into her mouth, she was still for a while, her cheeks stuffed, and then she threw the pit at me. In the mornings she would take cream of wheat and chocolate powder out on the lawn, and when I wanted to eat, I had to get out of the bed, go outside, and sit in the morning sun, crossing my legs in a lotus position. Then she would place the plate in my lap and sprinkle cinnamon on my cream of wheat. When we were finished, we would leave everything there and lie down embracing in the garden, hiding from the passersby.

Tania played records and drank the wine I'd brought. She also poured some of it into my mouth, but it flowed out of the corners down my neck onto the white feather quilt. So she placed a towel under my head—the same towel that, once upon a time when she was about to lose her virginity, she placed under her beautiful behind in hopes that the blood would flow on it. It did not work out then, perhaps because of that stupid towel. Finally, two weeks later a dark stream did flow down her thigh, and she dashed into the bathroom, laughing with happiness. Then we drank the champagne that she had saved for the occasion.

Now, with all that wine spilling, I felt as if the seriousness of my life were also dripping from me.

"Why don't you want any more wine?" she asked me, offended.

"Because I am lying down. Do you have a straw?"

"Won't you sit up?"

"You have no heart."

70

"And it's all right for me to sit?"

"After the lovemaking, the woman becomes silly, while the man prefers to lie with dignity and reflect."

She hit me on the head with the pillow, and then I felt her smooth, soft body on top of me. I realized that she was again summoning that hot sweetness that gradually grows and grows and passes throughout the whole body until it takes off in salvos. I remembered everything from the first time, and it was just the same this time except that the sweetness penetrated more slowly and more intensely.

"Tell me about the hospital," she then suggested.

On the wardrobe opposite, Tania had pinned a photograph of Picasso, and next to it I saw the wallpaper, which had a brick pattern. Over her bed she had a bookcase, and in one corner of the room was a deep wing chair that I had wanted for a long time. I imagined sitting in it as an old man with a pipe in my mouth. Next to the chair was a table, above which was another bookcase filled with books, half of them in French and Russian. On the table there was a mess of papers in Tania's perturbed hand.

In that room I talked about Emma, about Mr. Tomko, and about the grandpa whose respirator I had turned off. Sadness was growing in my soul, though only slightly, because Tania was playing with my head, combing my hair with her small fingers. She confused me for a while. I could hear myself say in a lazy voice: "I believe they all experienced happiness more than we do. Even Emma, who never made love. Because happiness comes only when you can experience things deeply. And she experienced so much that it was shining in her eyes. I could see that. We only bum around in the world, talking about where we'll go tomorrow or what we did yesterday and telling someone that tennis balls are on sale at the Prior department store. Once in a while, when we get drunk or make love, it seems to us for a moment that right then we should stop, because we are really experiencing something. Maybe we live as we do because we are saving our energy for happiness, making sure that when it comes it will last. But Emma did not save it, and neither did Mr. Tomko. He managed to yell for his wife all night long."

Tania sneaked out from under the cover and brought back some mandarin oranges. She was standing above me, and when I stretched out my arms, begging, she kneeled down and dropped them on my chest, smiling as they fell on the pillow.

The sun circled the whole house and shined into the window of the room where we lay. Tania was leaning against a rag doll, and I spilled wine on myself.

"You see," she said. Then she just waved her hand. Just a few drops of wine on the quilt!

She walked me to the bus, but then I sent her home, and when she waved at me and turned the corner, I remained as alone as I had ever been.

November began, and with it another year of my life, because I was born on All Souls' Day, or, as my mother says, a few minutes after midnight of the next day, because she was holding me back as much as she could. I don't know why I should not have been born on All Souls' Day. Be that as it may, I passed my birthday and didn't care a bit about reflecting on it. Why spoil a birthday?

The wind was blowing away the leaves. The wood was thinning out like the fur coat of an old dog and storing its treasure under the trees. It rustled beautifully under one's feet, covering all the roots and holes, so that I had to run by memory and my ankles were protected by the spongy surface.

In the hospital people continued to die. But something did change after all. One day I went to work and, as always, peeked in Intensive Care and called out: "Good morning, Annie!"

Instead of Annie, a woman named Helen was washing the syringes.

"Hi," she said.

"Hi. Where's Annie?"

"In the operating room."

"Why?"

"They offered her the surgical nurse's job."

"And she accepted?"

"Of course."

When I went into the operating room, Annie greeted me in a sterile gown. She was laughing and gave me a firm hug: "Hi, boy!"

"Hi. Your gown is no longer sterile," I reminded her.

"And I like you so much that I don't care!" she playfully shouted, and ran off, taking her surgical gloves and gown off.

I did not have time to think. I brought in patients and accompanied them to the operating table. I held one lady's hand while in terror she watched the instruments I dragged in all around her until her grip at last relaxed and her eyes closed. And so it went all day. There was the same blood flowing down onto the sheets and spraying in thin fountains on the tiles. And again the tissue came unglued under the surgeon's scalpel, and each skull gave off the same odor under the drill. Even brains resemble each other like eggs, it seems.

As I washed the last spots away, I told myself that no one would leave behind red footprints that day. I was assembling the suction unit and almost blacking out from hunger when Annie kneeled down beside me and put her hand on my shoulder.

"What's wrong, Milan? Has anything happened?" she asked.

"No. Nothing's happened," I replied mechanically.

"You look strange, so lost in thought."

"Nothing's happened, really. I'm hungry."

She left, and I continued messing around with the hoses.

When I passed through Intensive Care on my way to change into my jeans at half past three, Helen was sitting there, smoking. In the ashtray were a few cigarette butts that she had colored red with her lipstick. I went out into the hall and signed out. From the surgical nurse's room came the sound of Annie's deep laughter.

Outside the cold made me shiver, but in my stomach I felt a peculiar warmth. I imagined that my stomach acid, because of my hunger, was burning everything that came in contact with it. While my head was pleasantly swimming and my hunger was passing, the acid was eating up my stomach rather than go without food.

I took the bus downtown and fed it. I stuffed myself with a sausage and salad, bread rolls and pastry, a soft drink and poppy-seed crescents. Then I went outside, and small drops fell on my coat. The sidewalk grew dark with wet spots, until it went black and started to shine. I was climbing toward Slavín. It felt good to walk on a full stomach.

Mr. Bartholomew opened the door, and Nox jumped up next to

him. The dog pressed me with his snout, and wagged his tail when I massaged his head.

"Welcome, my boy," the old man greeted me. "Come in, just come in."

From his typewriter grew a piece of paper, but I did not take a peek.

"Haven't seen you for a long time, my boy. Tell me about yourself," he said when we sat down. Again he wore the black woolen cap. Winter had begun.

"I just dropped in," I apologized.

"Good you did, you know," he said, leaning toward me. "Nobody comes here anymore." And he just waved his hand. "So I started to think, you know," he began. "A story of a man and a woman . . . You know?"

And so he talked, all the while smoking and coughing. He opened the window; he poured the tea from a thermos bottle, because he knew that I would not appreciate it if he poured himself the wine that he kept under his desk. Nox scratched on the door from the other side, and when I opened it, he lay on the doormat and whined.

"And so that's how it is, you know?" he said as we descended the steps. Outside in the dark it was still raining. "Women are devastating."

I did not let him walk me to the gate, and so he waved good-by from the door, petting Nox on the head.

Neon lights were showering the street, thousands of them, and so I had to put on my hood. I thought about all sorts of things on my way home. The rain got thicker, slowing down, and when I took my hand out of my pocket, I felt the first wet snowflake.

Annie had judged my mood right, but I didn't know it then. I thought I was sad because of hunger or fatigue. Had I sensed in the morning that women were devastating, as Mr. Bartholomew said, I would have told her: "You know, Annie, you betrayed yourself."

I went home and called Tania. I listened to her voice and her laughter, which sparkled like the wind in a dry shell.

"When shall we see each other?" I asked.

"Wait a minute. You have nothing else to say?"

"What else can one say on the phone?"

"All right, then."

"I'll wait for you at the Slovan Hotel tomorrow at six."

"Fine. See you," she said in a pampered tone.

When I put down the phone, it occurred to me that I had not seen her golden head for two days and that I yearned to know what thoughts had been born in that head in the meantime.

Next morning I opened my eyes, and no matter what dream I had been having, it was forgotten in a moment because I was blinded by some radiance, white like a welding arch. So I just drank my hot chocolate and sat around in my pajamas for a while, reading a day-old newspaper the way you read when you're waiting for something—just looking at the words on the page in order not to think about what's coming up. For it is something pleasant for which you don't have to prepare yourself.

So then I ran outside through the Mountain Park, baffled by an old memory. I was running and trying to recall the silence that sprinkles down from the sky, gathers on the leaves, muffling one's steps. The landscape froze from surprise and let itself be painted white without resistance. It did not even raise a breeze to protest. This was my birthday. Now I celebrated the beginning of my twenty-third year pressing the seal of my Marathon runners into the first snow.

I ran under the Red Bridge and took off up the hill along a traverse route. I looked back at my footprints and saw a perfect chain, which makes athletes crazy. I really screwed them, I said to myself. Nobody else will run up this route first, and anyone who follows will only step angrily into my footprints. And they won't be able to make it, ha, ha! Only three people in Bratislava have such a long step! And the other two run on different hills. So just get into it, stretch those joints, ha, ha, and speed up!

I flew through the winter landscape. The snow had surprised it, and it could not move under that cover. If someone had been standing on the other hill, they would have seen me. They would have seen the red warm-up pants and patterned cap gunning it on the white canvas, high above the road in the valley.

Something always begins or ends with the first snow, doesn't it?

I got that feeling in the morning when I drank my hot chocolate, looking out of the window. I was remembering Annie. She would sit by the window when, behind her back, people whose consciousness was foggy and whose wounded brains were searching for the way to think were silently breathing. I always imagined that in some lobe they knew about her and sensed the proximity of her big body. She talked to them as if they understood her. She touched them as if they could feel those strong fingers. She also said good-by to them as if they were still alive. The way she painted the names on the thigh made me expect to hear a child's cry come from her. I don't think she believed in death, though she always sensed it a few days ahead. But that's not important.

I remembered Emma in her pink pajamas, as she lay in my hands, smelling of shampoo, and I thought of her black hair, which I had cut. It fell in a green washbasin and it did not occur to me to save it.

Annie stood by her when she was dying, searching for her pulse with her fingers. Now she held her wrist, now she felt her groin, looking somewhere off in the distance in concentration. Two women were saying good-by to each other. One of them was lying down, the other standing, and it was only an accident that things were not the other way around.

Others had also died. Mrs. Bohush, Grandpa, Mr. Tomko—they had all seemed to wait for me to come to the hospital. Only Mr. Palichka is still alive somewhere in Slovakia, if he has not jumped out of a window. He listens to the noise in his old head and sometimes touches his festering eyelids.

Did these people exist at all? If I had found a job as a boiler stoker or a manager of tennis courts, would they have died just the same? Then what the shit is going on with reality?

I ran down into the valley and passed by the old ski lift where I usually made the turn to go back. Farther on I could run only on the pavement. It was lost under the snow, which was clean, without any car tracks. I stopped by the abandoned quarry where we used to go with my parents to roast sausages and where I used to fence with my brother using hazel switches for swords. Only a few big boulders were left there, together with a couple of old tires, and an old pot in the stream, probably left by people who also came here to roast their sausages.

I shook my head, and the first snow of this year fell on my shoulders. Annie was a devastating woman, but she did not know it, and that's why she left to become a surgical nurse. Well, would you want to be beaten with an oxygen hose if you could avoid it?

I returned home at a comfortable jog. In the Mountain Park, the new snow was already covering my footprints. There were five black limousines by the President's villa, and yellow and white Zhiguli and Volga cars were blocking the access roads. The President had come to have a look at his native city. I ran between the cars, and no one stopped me.

The city turned the snow into a brown-black mush, and one could slosh in it to his heart's content. In the crowd rolling down the Slovak National Uprising Square, fear seized me again.

This time I did not have to search for the reason. I knew right away what kind of fear this was, and at the same time I realized that it had been with me for a long time. Had I lived at all since I said good-by to Michael at the station in Pardubice? How could I find out when everybody around me seemed to be dying?

I entered the Slovan and sat on a bar stool, something Tania does not like to do, because her legs hang in the air. At the corner of the bar an informer was sitting, drinking a glass of white wine. He was scanning the room in a disinterested way and playing with his cigarette lighter, but one was not allowed to smoke there. Maybe he was not on duty. Maybe he was not an informer at all.

Tania's coffee was getting cold. She likes cold coffee, though. When the doors creaked for the hundredth time, her golden head peeked in. She smiled in the distance, and her wondrously brilliant teeth that sometimes make her dentist gasp, shined in the weak light. When she kissed me, I noticed that she honored me with a fragrance of lemon with which she rubbed her lips at home.

"Hi," she said, wrapping her legs around the bar stool leg like a rope climber.

"Hi."

She took a sip of the cold coffee and kept smiling. Had she found out something? When I find out something, I look like a martyr. Maybe she was merely smiling.

She let me have her hot, living hand, the way you give a finger to a child to play with, and she was all smiles. I kissed the spot where little blue veins showed through, joining into a little knot.

The informer was not showing any interest in us, because he was openly studying Tania's profile. It's beautiful, that profile, by the way.

Tania expected me to say something, but I did not feel like it. With each new snow I feel like a newborn. That does not mean I am happy. Just the contrary. Something is finished, and something else has to start. That is tiresome.

We walked through the wet city, and I listened to Tania's child-like voice, with which she was telling me such wise things that I could not fail to love her. Women are devastating, old Mr. Bartholomew had said.

And so she helped me to get over the end and the beginning in that quiet house from where her mother had left an hour before to go to the theater. Inside a room crammed with plush teddy bears and other animals. I don't even know how.

The next day at eight in the morning I stood outside an office in a pleasantly heated hall and peered through a little window. On the other side of a wall lined with filing cabinets, someone was hiding, rustling, dragging his feet. But when I knocked at the window, the person became quiet and did not make any more noise.

"Hello. . . . Good morning," I began uncertainly. I did not get an answer, so I sat down in the armchair in the hall. After an hour of delicious waiting, the door opened and a woman came out of the office.

"Good morning," I said quickly. "I would like to make a submission."

She mumbled something, and I followed her into her office.

"What do you have there?"

"Notice."

She took the piece of paper out of my hands, banged a stamp on it, and put it away somewhere. I left satisfied. It was snowing heavily outside.

The Year of the Frog

"How beautifully bony you are," said Tania, "and hard." We were standing waist-deep in the water, and she was holding me by the shoulders with her tiny hands. She bashfully felt my chest and then hit it with her little fist. I had been relieved, then elated, when she arrived at the swimming pool in her two-piece swimsuit, for she had a surprisingly womanly figure and smooth, cream-white skin. She had always dressed so poorly that I could never have guessed what was hiding under those wide pants and loose shirts.

"Most men my age are like that," I said, but she only smiled, as if to say that this sort of lie is not worth an answer. I was happily ogling a girl who in the next few years was going to become a part of my destiny, because a few minutes before, on the bench by the pool, she had looked me in the eye and said, incredibly seriously, "It seems to me that you are afraid of something."

That was true: I was afraid of her. But in that moment she removed the enchantment, and then we stood waist-deep in the water. I could wonder all I wanted that a girl that I was about to love for her mind and soul had a creamy body, breasts with a deep cleavage between them, and round hips that I just fleetingly touched.

"I'm getting gooseflesh," I said, and started for the other side with a magnificent front crawl, finely honed by thousands of kilometers of training. I wanted to show her my gratitude somehow for all that beauty. She was swimming behind me, calmly and elegantly, I could see. Nothing depresses me more than watching hysterical nonswimmers. It now seemed to me that nothing else could threaten our love.

This is how it had been three years before the events I will relate. I was ready to love her for her penetrating intelligence and talent, for the intimations of wisdom that her spirit wasted to such a degree that it took my breath away. When I held in my hand her dainty fingers with chewed-up nails, I let her body heat flow into my cold body. Had it occurred to me then to search for feelings, I would have found in myself a certitude stemming from the immutability of the way things are.

Now I am sitting in my room, and behind me is a long portion of my life. Outside, spring is beginning again, and it would be fitting to rest in wonder, because when I engage in wonder, I have certitude. I am sincerely surprised at my insufficient ability to understand the essence of what is taking place. That is, if I *can* understand it. Just a few years ago I had the impression that I was quite clever, or that I was at least showing promise. Today I regretfully note that wisdom does not consist in remembering what has happened, but in its analysis and repeated synthesis (that is not original with me), and that I am far from accomplishing that effectively. Ordinary people like to say, "I don't have the mind for something like that." I used to consider that an affectation—making a virtue out of necessity. But what can I do if it really is like that? If I really don't have the mind for that?

It all began approximately a year ago, if one can talk about the beginning, when they arrested my father. I happened to be in Warsaw then. As Adam and I were getting off the train, he said: "This is that Polish rain that I told you about. When it rains here, it blows and erupts and comes down for at least a week."

We had heard that there was freedom in Poland, and we wanted to see it. We strolled downtown, scanning the posters with texts like DOWN WITH CENSORSHIP! We tasted sophisticated meatless dishes in the bars. In the evening it stopped raining. We entered the Old City, which the Poles had rebuilt. There was peace and a feeling of someone's quiet work going on. The Old City felt like a dark forest: the sky is high above the crowns of the trees, and you feel that the trees are watching you. The cobblestones that flew into the air like flocks of sparrows during the war were again set in the ground. One doesn't feel good walking on the cobblestones in tennis shoes, but we went on. Some sound, some tone was tempting us. The closer we got, the more distinct it became, as we turned one corner after another. There were more tones, louder ones, and then, as when you open the door to a disco, the music overwhelmed me. Beautiful trumpet and saxophone, drums and bass. I stopped in the corner of a square and gazed in astonishment: in the middle a band was playing, and around it the people danced. We hurried because we, too, wanted to dance. As I ran, my rucksack jumped up and down, and the boys were playing like crazy. They did not see anything; it was as if they didn't care if anyone listened. They were just playing in the middle of the square. In the light of the stylized lamps, I saw that their cheeks were puffed up and their veins bulging.

When I returned home, instead of my father I found a male kitten with a pink nose and a silly face. He had peed on my slippers. I went outside into the courtyard, and we drank coffee there—my mom, Peter, and I. Mother's eyes often were red in those days, and occasionally she would use an obscenity. I was glad that she did not refer to father's books or his guilt. I felt that resignation was taking me over, that I was speedily becoming resigned to everything. After all, we all had expected it to happen, and in that moment only that which had remained unfulfilled was fulfilling itself. Lilac fragrance wafted above our heads, and I turned my face with delight toward the May sun, closing my sleepy eyes.

"I managed to pack only his toothbrush and comb for him," she said. "He took nothing with him. Doesn't have a single crown."

"Don't worry about that now," I answered. "We should rather prepare ourselves for not seeing him for some . . . three or four years," I carefully concluded.

"That's what I think, too." Peter said.

Our neighbor was watering her balcony plants. It was already dry and hot, and the summer dry spell would break long-standing records. By the end of June, the trees turned gray-green, and the water level of the lakes as well as the Danube dropped.

What will Tania and I do today? I asked myself one morning. The sun was shining into the apartment, and Mother was sitting in the kitchen, reading, as if waiting for me to get up. Peter left for work, but I didn't work in the summertime. I had quit the day before, and for that kind of relief I would have been glad to starve.

"Let's go for a swim," I told Mother.

We stopped to get Tania and then went to pick up Adam and Dana. He was typing something on his rickety machine, and Dana was sleeping. I announced to them that the sun was shining and that it was daytime.

It was Thursday, and we were walking down a dusty acacia alley toward the lake. We were talking, as was our habit, about serious issues.

"The sun and the water are all man needs to live in summer," said Adam. I knew he meant it. He could lie all day on the hot gravel, like a yogi, and gamble that he wouldn't have a minor heart attack when he dived, overheated, into the water. A moment later he would get out and again assume his motionless position. He did not eat or drink, and that day I had told Mother not to prepare anything for me. Beside his black eyes and hair and tanned skin, Dana chose what seemed the only beautiful option—virginity and facial purity. Hers was a face that I liked to look at, because it was hiding a suppressed sin, and in the blue eyes behind her spectacles, there lived a desire for primordial innocence. She walked calmly beside her man, and her blonde hair was done up so I could see her high, smooth forehead.

"I wonder if Milan"—my father's name is also Milan—"will see the lake this summer," said my mother bravely. I knew how difficult it was for her to say that, but I supposed that she said it to become more reconciled to her fate.

"Hardly," I supported her. "But maybe they will let him use the shower occasionally."

"I feel so guilty when I swim here. What he would have done to be able to plunge in for a minute!" she said. The water was unusually clean. I dived very deep, floated above the gravel bottom of the lake, carefully swallowed some water, and released air bubbles.

"I wouldn't say that," Adam joined in. "On the contrary, it is your duty to live happily precisely now, to experience life in a transcendental way. Then your pleasure from the sun and water will become a source of joy for your husband."

"How can he be happy when he sits alone in a dark hole and even may be cold? And anyway, I stopped believing in the meaning of anything a long time ago. If he did not have to write, he could be here swimming with us. But . . . he thought he would save somebody with his ideas!"

"Bullshit," I could not resist.

We became quiet and spread the blankets on the gravel. The lake was surrounded by cleared sections of the alluvial forest, and in the distance, on the other side of the lake, stood an abandoned bulldozer with its shovel in the ground. My mother entered the water. Her figure was full and beautiful, exhibiting harmony and grace. It was as if she purposefully maintained that perfection of form out of her passionate desire to defeat diabetes, the disease that wanted to destroy her from inside. I hoped I was observing her discreetly, but when I looked at the others, I noticed that we were all looking at her.

"That mother of yours . . . ," said Tania, shaking her head.

If it is possible to enter the water from a steep shore in a dignified manner, my mother had demonstrated it.

"A masterpiece," Adam noted.

"Let's swim to the island," I suggested.

"You are also beautiful," I whispered to Tania, and she kissed me behind my ear. Her beauty was different, in her innocently hidden sensuality, which always so surprised me when I saw her in her swimsuit. Where did she learn to transform that childish waddling walk into an undulating rocking of the hips? I wondered, troubled. Not so long ago she walked like a duckling, rocking her head from side to side, like the little bulldogs sitting in car rear windows. Who knows if it is not only a question of time before that beauty bursts through her clothes and I'll definitely lose my precious secret?

On the island we lay down on the gravel, absorbed the heat of the smooth stones and continued talking—seriously, unnaturally, and at length. In our discussion we seemed to find ourselves in a better, more interesting world where named things acquired shape. We surrounded ourselves with them until I got the feeling that I was being buried under them. Then we jumped in the cool, diaphanous water that sucked everything from me. Even today I fear the quantity of named things. They are on the increase, and I don't know how to get rid of them.

My sad mother came ashore to eat. You can get joy from observing a person eat. It seems that such a person radiates optimism.

"I hate food," my mother would say if she had an audience.

"But you must eat," I would tell her. "You have diabetes."

I was attacked by hunger of the cruel and aggressive kind. I swam across to my mother, and she gave me a slice of bread with cheese and green pepper.

At four o'clock, clouds started to gather at the edge of the sky. At five they covered it almost entirely, and only by accident did the sun just happen to shine through a hole, right on that spot of this stupid globe where we were lying, roasted and juicy.

Downtown we met Vincent. He had an angelic face, and his yellow hair fell down to his shoulders. After all, he had been a priest, but the authorities did not allow him to preach and so he got married. Now he was dragging along two demijohns of Pezinok wine.

"What are you doing here? Aren't you supposed to be in Prague?" I asked him.

"I came for the wine. I'm going over to Julia's place now, and tonight I'm traveling back."

We carried the demijohns to Julia's. In her small room with arches above the window and an irregularly designed ground, we sat down on the floor.

"Pour out two liters of the wine," Adam said.

Julia brought bread with double-smoked bacon and onion, and we drank a toast under the stucco ceiling while the oppressive darkness entered through the window. The wine tasted like a divine handshake. I dipped my tongue in it and saw that the others had done the same.

"What's new in Prague?" I asked.

"New? Well, they've released Richard."

They had released Richard! That bearded Richard to whom we had said good-by last autumn, because he insulted or did not insult—who can be the judge now?—some policeman or customs officer? And who cares about it now?

We walked Vincent to the train station and, dazed by the hot

Bratislava night, strolled downtown. Somewhere there, in the empty streets under the black sky, Adam told me that Dana was expecting his child.

The sun woke me up, or rather its reflection from the windows of the nearby houses did. The tireless August sun seemed to have gone crazy that year. It heated the streets, and the white roofs of the houses were undulating in the thick air. July had already dripped down between my fingers. I had avoided the touch of sweaty bodies then. I spent the month lying by the lake, whose water became so hot that I swam in it as if I were doing laps in a pool. The feeling that I could swim forever returned to me. My lungs and muscles adjusted to the heat. They remembered those long, tormenting hours when I used to swim from edge to edge of the pool, crazy from counting the laps. Now I was getting a payoff in the form of relaxation and obedient power.

But vanity kept its hold over me even in the blue water: I could not avoid it even in exhaustion. The first of the two months that I stole from the State by refusing to work went by, and I saw that the time was not mine at all. It did not belong to me, as I had hoped. I distributed it among others in a way that did not suit me. I couldn't remember what it was I had wanted to do. I was puzzled when I looked at my sad mother, when the sun that thawed my determination and turned it into a sleepy languidness touched me, and by two pieces of news about my father: first, that he had lost his front tooth, which he left in a piece of bread, and second, that he had lost thirty pounds. There was all of this, and, in addition, shiny circles of suntan lotion on the surface of the water. Tania was accepted by the university, and new life unmistakably sprouted inside Dana. But both events happened despite me, and so I was happy only on their behalf, and something like that demoralizes you terribly.

I got up, drank a bit of hot chocolate, bummed around the apartment in sleepy expectation, sat for a while in the bathroom, and then put on my white shorts and blue T-shirt. Mother raised her eyes from her book and said: "You can't run outside dressed like that! Those shorts are full of holes! Someone could see your asshole. I won't let you."

She was right. The shorts were full of holes. She had already mended them three times, but I had run at least five thousand kilo-meters in them, and even Adidas would not last that long. But I didn't have money for new ones. Besides, one couldn't buy them. Only red shorts were available.

Slowly, very slowly I set out for the Mountain Park. It was Tues-day and people were stuck at work. At first I jogged languidly, as if sitting in an armchair. I shook it off past the Red Bridge, for in the shade of the forest I could breathe easier. I did not meet anyone, and my lonely craze in that stifling morning made me think of my father. He was sitting in his cell and trembling with horror, even more alone than I, because he perceived the factual essence of time in such a space. He saw ahead of him a mountain of days, and he felt every one of them already because they would all be the same. As if they buried you under a mountain of clay and you could feel it with your whole body. You must feel each ounce of it.

Apparently my head was not the same as other people's, for now it seems that it could only have been lunacy that suggested in the emptiness the thought that I could redeem a little bit of my dad's suffering. A day like that was not suitable for redemption of the kind I meant to give him.

One kilometer before the ski lift, where I usually turned around, my lungs were getting warmed up. I could feel the oxygen gather-ing in my legs and filling my thighs with disquiet, and I wanted to stretch them a bit. Then suddenly I saw black spots all over the path. The spots were jumping before me, dispersing right in front of my Marathon shoes. Astonished, I stopped: I was looking at thousands of tiny frogs. They jumped inch by inch ahead, all in the same direction, as if to spite me—toward the ski lift. They were moving with dreadful decisiveness from one brook to another along this highway of death. I ran on past them, angry at the meaning-lessness of life and cruelty of Nature.

At the ski lift, I peed against a tree, walked around, washed my face in a brook, and waited until my stopwatch said five minutes. I was afraid. A presentiment of physical suffering always calls out fear in me. I used to have it before each race, but after the starting shot it disappeared as if by a miracle, because I was always surprised how easily and effortlessly I ran.

I jogged in place for a moment to assure myself that my legs were springy, then I noisily exhaled, and when I passed the sign reading ATTENTION! SKI LIFT! I started my stopwatch. I ran up the hill, and from there I darted with big jumps to the footbridge. I should have softened their impact, because they often hurt my stomach, but that day was an exception. I decided that I would not save myself. I slipped on something on the footbridge, and when I looked under my feet, I saw the frogs swirling and scattering in a deranged ecstasy. They were popping under my shoes like tiny balloons, but I refused to stop and lengthened my stride, feeling my stomach turning. My face grimaced with disgust, and I let out a helpless cry. I was flying away demented, shaking my head, not wanting to see or hear a thing. When I hit the gravel it was over. The disgust propelled me away from that place, but I had to watch out, because I felt a slight shiver in my thighs and was afraid of exhaustion. I shortened my stride and speeded up my pace, so that it felt like I was galloping in a rotating drum. With minced meat on my shoe soles, I hurtled down a road covered by foliage. It changed to hard cobblestones at a highway crossing, and on the other side was a meadow that opened out onto an endless plain. I was gasping for air that entered my lungs hot, as if I were inhaling in front of the open grate of a stove filled with red-hot coal. As I passed an oak, I desperately sought to help myself with my arms, trying to use them to improve the rhythm of my legs. I felt with disappointment that my legs were dying.

The blood was rebelling. It could not push through the veins; it circulated in the body in confusion, as if on a crazy merry-go-round, thundering in my temples, sweeping out all my thoughts and feelings except for fatigue and one and only one image. The deafening thunder projected itself into bright red flames and dancing circles in front of my eyes. They rushed against me and tried to embrace me, and suddenly from among them floated up a picture that lazily turned and hung about as if unwilling to enter this flickering world. It slowly grew, and the more painfully my thighs hurt and the more urgently my insides wanted to leave my stupid body, the more emphatically did the image stay in my consciousness. It forced me to raise myself onto my toes, it gnawed through my thundering brain, turning me into a tangle of painful and pushy tissue. It burned into me its outline, and the faster I ran, the slower my father moved. Now he was merely sitting on the bed in his cell with a window under the ceiling, staring directly ahead, supporting his chin with his hand. He was looking at me through the fiery curtain. He sensed me, sensed my fatigue! I tried to lift myself again to my toes and fire my knees ahead of me, and then came the end.

I wanted to cry out because of the spasmodic weakness inside my body, and I wanted to sit down or lean against the tree. But I can't, daddy, I thought. I can't do a thing. I'm afraid that something will burst in my head, for it thunders so much in there and presses against my forehead. At least I've suffered enough to get through to you, because I have never felt so bad before. And if I had had strength to look at my stopwatch, I would have seen that I had never run that fast before.

I forced myself to walk about in the shade of the trees, because I feared I might burst like a bubble. My legs were shaking and gave way under me, but were starting to obey, and I could distinguish the green color of the trees that pushed through the red mist. A few minutes later only a painless emptiness remained: Father hid himself behind the motionless trees and dusty leaves that rustled under my Marathon shoes as I jogged home.

Mother went downtown, and Peter was sleeping off his night shift. I took a cold shower, but my body was breaking out in a constant sweat. I ran a tub full of cold water and lay in it, sizzling like a red-hot piece of iron. After leaving the tub, I felt the inner fever burning me up.

This sort of fatigue usually clarifies one's mind, I reflected, and decided to take full advantage of it. I sat down by my typewriter and asked myself a fundamental question: "What am I?"

SHIT, the fingers punched out. Oh, this won't do, I told myself. Let's not pretend that we've discovered something new. We don't really think I am shit. The problem merely consists of proving that I am something. Proving it to whom? To Tania, understandably, because in her head mysterious ideas reside and from her sky-blue eyes radiates a confidence of which even she might not be aware: the certainty of predestination. And she expects the same from me.

But how will you manage without an education, without dreams, and—oh, my God, what if?—without intelligence? Yes, yes indeed, I thought. Do not stray from the unpleasant topic: What if you are stupid?

I sighed audibly, went into the kitchen, and drank a bottle of soda. The sweat broke out with a renewed force. When I went out, I shook with fever. I returned for a couple of bread rolls and ate them on my way.

Dita was playing with her little daughter, who was dropping her toys all over their apartment with unalloyed pleasure. I stuck my head into the window and said, "Hi, Dita."

I gave little Barbara my finger, and we went out into the garden. She walked with her legs spread out, as little children do, and observed the world in a well-meaning way. Dita brought steamed dumplings with jam.

"These are great," I said. "Where did you learn this?"

"Nowhere. I don't really know how to cook."

"Then you're a genius. Does it come from being a Slovak woman?"

"Get out of here," she laughed.

In the meantime, Barbara was playing with a hammock. She even climbed into it, and Dita swung her around like an astronaut. It occurred to me that such a child is better than a kitten. But do I have the right to bring a child into this world? Yes, I do, I answered myself, and moreover, it's not at all a question of right. Of what, then? Of desire, I answered. Yes, I would like to have a child with Tania.

That same day I walked downtown. I saw many women there, breathing uneasily in the blistering streets and wearing colorful dresses. They seemed to me fresh and clean, and I felt like touching them. Some of them reminded me of Tania, and those I wanted to touch most of all. Some of the women also had fresh faces, and I felt that they must be intelligent since they looked so pretty.

When I walked down Post Street, an idea came into my mind: In the final analysis, it is not important what I am, but what kind of person I am, or better still, what kind of person I appear to be. If

I were able to appear until the end of my life as good, wise, and handsome, would that not mean that I had indeed been good, wise, and handsome?

Tania insists that I am beautiful like Michelangelo's David. It seems to me, however, that she has merely learned to parrot my belief that she is beautiful like Venus. Basically, it is all the same to me what I am, I continued reflecting. It is important how Tania sees me. Or is it? Be that as it may, is there any other way to see myself than through myself? Hardly.

That makes my reflections unnecessary, I concluded with relief. I did not suspect, fool that I was, that a harsh revision of this idea was in store for me.

Tania was waiting for me by the statue of Roland. She was sitting on a bench and lifted her head for me to touch her lips. She was reading something in French.

"Hi."

"Hi, my love," she whispered.

Her hair smelled of shampoo, and she was wearing the white dress I brought her from Poland. Judging by the French book, she could pass for a tourist from Paris.

"I called you in the morning, but you weren't home," she said without suspicion.

"I was running. Then I dropped in at Dita's to return a book and have a look at Barbara."

"Running!" she exclaimed. "In this hothouse! Oh, you exhausted yourself again, and you are white as a sheet, you unfortunate man," she sighed.

I shrugged it off. "How about you?"

"I slept in." She stretched herself with pleasure. "Then I had breakfast, and so on. Then I went on a date."

"Is that all?" I asked her in a threatening way.

"All," she intoned.

I kissed her behind her ear and whispered, "You lazy witch."

I envied her that ability. She could dawdle through an entire day without doing anything.

"Mother told me that somebody was looking for me last night," she said.

"Who?"

"One of my cousins three times—or how many times—removed." Tania had many relatives that she was unaware of. I have already met several cousins, and bunches of others were to be found dispersed in the intellectual communities of Bratislava.

"This one is a philosopher," she said. "He walks around in jeans and rides a bike."

"What did he want?"

"I don't know, but Mom invited him to dinner tonight, and we are supposed to go, too."

"Good," I said. "At least we'll meet another human being."

We still had a lot of time left, and we strolled down the streets. We were holding each other by the little fingers, because our hands were perspiring, as the heat rose along the walls.

Adam and Dana were home, and she greeted us with her pained smile. "Hi," she said in a singsong voice.

"Ah, the young ones," Adam said. "Come in."

We were sitting in their eternally cool room, and I couldn't take my eyes off Dana. She wore a long, loose dress, and Nature was modeling her slowly and lovingly.

"Bratislava is Hungary," Adam used to say, "and this is a Hungarian life." He poured red wine, which always leaves red rouge on Tania's lips because she drinks like a barbarian, dipping her lips in the glass.

"How is the old man?"

"I don't know," I answered. "He lost thirty pounds and one of his front teeth."

"That's horrible," Dana whispered.

What was horrible was that along with the wine, joy and happiness entered me. It's always like that when I sit down with people I like. My father's plight could not change that and he would not have wanted to change it. I find happiness and joy when I know I am secure. And I am secure when I am with people who I believe like me. It's very simple, I thought with certainty.

We finished the bottle, and Tania pulled on my T-shirt.

"Well, we are invited to a dinner with a philosopher," I said. "We'll have to go."

"With a philosopher?" Adam asked, raising his eyebrows. "Have fun."

We walked to Tania's part of town, and I had to think about Dana, because I wanted to know what it would be like once new life started to germinate in Tania.

"Children, where have you been wandering?" exclaimed Viera (Tania's mother). "The dinner is almost on the table, and the guest about to arrive any minute!" From the kitchen issued an aroma which put me in an euphoric mood.

"Long live the guest!"

At that moment a bell rang out, and in came a slim, bearded man in round glasses, really dressed in jeans.

"Welcome. We just mentioned you," said Viera in a deep voice that she reserved for interesting men. She leaned her head forward and shook his hand.

We sat down at the table. The philosopher was helping himself with his slender hands, and the meat disappeared somewhere into the beard. I liked the way it vanished into that growth, which for a moment would uncover a dark opening and then immediately close it. Wow, I'd love to be a philosopher and have a beard like that, I said to myself.

"You work in the Academy?" I asked him.

"Yes."

"You like it?"

He smiled again and then quickly shook his head: "No."

"Why not?"

"Can you tell us," Viera interrupted me with the same deep voice and a smile that I dislike, "to what are we indebted for your kind—and how nice, after all—family visit?"

"Yes, I can tell you," answered Eman (for that was his name). "It may happen, because anything can happen, that one day I'll find myself abroad. Maybe, say, in England. Because we can never know how our destiny will unfold itself, we cannot afford to miss an opportunity. I want to prevent the eventuality that, when I am in England, someone might ask me, 'Are you from Czechoslovakia? Do you know Tania L.?' and I would have to answer, 'I do not.' Therefore I came to meet her."

"That's marvelous!" Viera cried out, laughing heartily. "Did you hear that, Tania?"

"I must add," Eman continued, "that I have read Tania's work, and that was also one of the reasons why I wanted to meet her." Tania had entered some school competition that year and had written an excellent essay about the boredom that accompanies every hour of instruction in the schools.

It grew dark outside. Hot air was streaming in through the windows, and we were drinking chilled wine that slowly entangled our thoughts. The discussion continued, and the topic turned to literature or something like that. Eman had just paid Viera a compliment: "I believe you were studying Nabokov, and you were even intending to publish one of his books?"

"Yes, yes, that was in 1970. But we did not make it in time."

"I have recently read his *Lolita*."

"Is that the one about the guy who falls in love with a thirteen-year-old girl and then kills her?" I asked.

"He kills her mother, whom he first marries to get to Lolita," said Eman. "It's the best novel I have ever read."

"Aha!" I exclaimed, looking eastward out over the city, where I could see light from the flames of the Slovnaft Refinery, as if the sun were setting on that horizon. I had not been home since morning, and a familiar oppressive feeling seized me. Ever since my father had left, my fear for my mother had been growing in me proportionally with the growth of my knowledge of how screwed up the world is.

"I mention it because I have the book in English and in Russian, and I was wondering if Tania could help me with the translation," Eman went on.

The empty place after the faith in the goodness of the world left me was filled by my relationship with Tania. Today I would say that this faith had moved to another picture. She was sitting on crossed legs in such a manner that my joints began to hurt.

"I don't know if I'll have the time," she said calmly.

"It's a great book," Eman repeated.

I'll read *Lolita*, I thought. I know that much English.

"I'm glad I have seen you, but my mother is at home alone," I said. "See you, Viera. See you, Eman." I nodded to Tania. She was sitting in such a spot that to reach her I would have to bend over him.

Mother got up and turned on the light to see what time I had come in. That angered me, and I went straight into the room I shared with Peter, my good brother Peter, who would leave in a month to do his military service. He had made my bed, and I thanked him in my mind. I picked up some detective novel in English, one that I did not really want to read. I could understand the first two pages, but when on the third page I came to a description of a murder, full of unknown words, I turned off my light, and in a world rocking with alcohol, I somehow fell asleep.

Next day I found Tania sleeping on the lakeshore with her face turned up to the sun. I wanted to go into the water alone, but she heard me and came after me, throwing herself into the water in a typically female way. I sat down at the bottom to see her above me. At the moment she started to swim, I would have forgiven her anything in the world. In the water I felt better than I did on the dry land, and I liked everything about her, most of all her body, which was swimming indifferently on the shiny surface above me. I swam upward and grabbed her by her foot.

"Get away from me, you water creature!" she erupted.

I was dying of laughter, and she almost drowned me, because she pressed my head against her breasts. She did not realize they were underwater and that I liked that, because for me love and water are connected. When I was younger, after endless kilometers of swimming, I would play water polo with my friends Suzy and Kate. Seeing Suzy's firm, soft body was a great reward to me for the tears of fatigue and anger poured into the pool during those tiresome kilometers. Tania could not have known it, but besides everything else that was worth loving in her, I also loved her because she swam beautifully and her body underwater looked flexible and smooth.

"What do you think about Eman?" she asked after a while.

"He's okay," I said. "He's frightfully educated. And I loved how he ate. Did you notice? How did you spend the rest of the evening?" But she could not hear the last question, because she had dipped her head underwater.

She lay on the shore with her eyes closed, and the drops on her belly were drying out. In the past year she had learned how to be silent. She used to be afraid of silence. She was afraid that love would disappear in silence, and therefore she constantly called to it with her stream of words. Those words were a bridge to everything, they were even a substitute for lovemaking when we were afraid of it.

I must have dozed off, because when I opened my eyes Tania had gotten up and was going into the water again. The water was hot as hell, and half-asleep, I swam up to her, and she asked: "Do you know what time it is? Shouldn't we go to the railway station to pick Sam up?"

Oh, Sam. I'd quite forgotten him. He was an American Tania met in Moscow. He was studying there, and she was taking part in some school competition. That's Tania all right. Even in Moscow she would meet only an American.

We got there late. The train had already left, and we were standing helplessly on the hot platform. That's Tania for you. She never makes it on time. A few sweaty travelers and a drunken railway worker were sitting on the benches. Only one man was heading for the exit. He was carrying a violin case in one hand, and on his back bounced a small backpack with a pair of tennis shoes hanging from it.

"Look over there," I said, pointing him out to Tania. "Doesn't that guy look like an American?"

"Hey, Sam!" she called out. He turned around, bearded, curly-haired, and funny-looking.

"Taniushka," he laughed, and kissed her forehead: a giant American with big feet and a beaked nose.

"And this is Milan! Hello, Milan. I know everything about you."
I smiled stupidly. I was glad Tania owned up to me.

"Would you like to have a swim, Sam?" I asked. I wanted terribly to go back into the water. I felt I would dry up and crack.

"Oh, yes, *kharasho*, *ochen priyatno*, good," he laughed. He looked older than I, but that was only because he was an American: big, healthy, and cheerful.

We returned to the lake, and he swam as funny as he walked—in a scattered, clownish, and extremely winning manner.

"You swim very well," he told me.

"Yes," I nodded indifferently. Sometimes I wish I could forget my stylish stroke, I said to myself, but I did not translate it into English and tell Sam.

Tania was far ahead of us, waving and shouting: "Where are you, lazy boys?"

Sam darted ahead, splashing beautifully, and when he was about halfway there, I followed him in my perfect sad crawl. Then Tania and I dried ourselves in the sun, as we had that morning, except that beside us lay a bearded man radiating a natural attitude that I had to admit burned me as much as the sun. Between us lay Tania, already tanned brown. Through the blades of grass I looked at the intimately known curve of her thigh, and it occurred to me that it was impossible for a man not to fall in love with Tania once he got to know her.

In the evening we went up to the Castle. The sun, as always, was setting over Austria, and I got the obligatory feeling. "Can you see that?" I said, pointing toward the other side.

"Oh, yes, very nice," said Sam. The sky turned red-gold.

"I know, *ya znayu*," he said, sounding serious for the first time.

It had to be Monday, for the Castle restaurant was closed. We sat down on a wall from which we could see St. Martin's Cathedral, Michael's Tower, and the fires of Slovnaft.

Sam opened his violin case. Only there was no violin, but a saxophone. "What do you want to hear?"

"Play what you want," Tania said, and I nodded.

So he played. I heard a saxophone up close for the first time, and so did Tania. She sat between us, and the city was spread out below. Sam was blowing into that brass so hard that his wail flew over the roofs toward City Hall and the Manderla Building, and all the way to the Danube. The American was broadcasting it with his brass spout in all directions. The roofs cowered under that bombardment, or so it seemed to me, because for a moment the high-rises collapsed—including the ministries and the hotel built for the police. He breathed like a marathon runner, and when he finished, with his saliva still flowing down his beard, he quickly asked: "Did you like that?"

Tania said nothing, just looking at him in disbelief from below with her head at an angle. I had often felt that look: she used it to raise me to heaven, among the gods.

"It was very nice, Sam, really," I said quietly.

"Now . . . I'll play . . . hmm . . . okay." He crossed his legs, touched the brass with his lips, anchored his look somewhere below, and continued the miracle, which sent shivers down my spine. A searchlight was turned on below us, but it was aimed at the stars. Surrounding grass lit up green, and fireflies flickered. We remained in the dark, and Sam was releasing his magic, his brow shining with sweat.

"So," he said when he finished. "Oh well," he laughed. "*Poydem,* let's go."

I jumped off the wall and held the sax for him.

"Come on, Taniushka, *ya tebya.* I'll help you," he said, and approached the wall to give her support with his hands.

"*Nu,* Sam, I need no help," she answered. Yet she slipped into his hands in the white dress I brought her from Poland. He had giant hands, the American.

"*I teper ty.* Now you, Milan." He put her back up on the wall. I shook my head.

"She doesn't need any help." She always jumped off the wall by herself. She wanted it so. But he pushed me, and so I offered her my hands. She slipped into them and grabbed me around my neck. I could feel everything through that light dress.

"Very well," he said cheerfully.

By the time Sam arrived, the sun had already for several weeks been beating down harder and harder with each passing day. The water in the lakes heated up to the temperature of mineral hot springs, and it was not much fun to swim in it. But, there was nothing else to do, and so we would bathe day and night in it. It seemed that I was melting in the stifling city heat, and with me was melting also my will and my interest in life. Tania and I were happy only that we could walk around the city barefoot, enjoying the warm cobblestones on the squares. I managed not to think much about the fact that it was August and that in September I would have to start working somewhere or they would arrest me. I managed not to think about anything as I read three pages in the sun before dozing off. We used to meet Mother at the lake. She would be in the company of one or two lady friends who also had to live without their husbands, though not because they were sitting in jail but because they had somehow disappeared God knows where. I would see Mother's face at home, still untouched by wrinkles despite the streams of tears. They would flow from her eyes without ceremony, like a child's runny nose. And just like a child, she had learned to behave as if they did not flow, as if it were all an accident, an oversight. Peter and I got used to it, behaving as if we did not see the tears, and we tried to watch over her. She liked to forget to eat, perhaps enjoying the insulin shocks, since she smiled and caressed our faces when they came. In vain did we try to stuff sugar into her mouth. She would turn her head, keeping her mouth closed. There was nothing to do except wait for the saving spark when her consciousness realized that perhaps she should eat that sugar after all. Then she started to cry again.

Tania shared my fear for her. When we walked around the city at night, or made love on the freshly mowed lawn in the old cemetery, or walked about naked in Tania's apartment when her mother was away, or ate breakfast in the garden, it was always with the feeling that I should really be home.

This was how things were when Sam found us with his saxophone.

The next day at noon we had breakfast at Tania's. Viera was very animated, discussing politics with Sam, as if something like that were a normal thing to do with an American. When I arrived, Tania welcomed me with a private kiss, pressing herself to me to let me know that I had nothing to fear.

"Good morning," I greeted them.

"Hello," they both answered, and continued their dialogue.

Oh well, I sighed inwardly, everything is screwed up, so what's the point of discussing it, especially in English?

"Eman called," said Tania. "He suggested we join him in his mountain chalet. He has a log cabin up there."

"This is it! This is our salvation! Hey, Sam, stop talking! We're going to the mountains!" I exclaimed. Suddenly I knew exactly what I needed. We had to get out of the city at least for a couple of days. We had to run away from this kettle where Tania and I were roasting in helpless waiting for God knows what. Most probably for my father, who could show up one day, but at that moment I saw that it was all nonsense and that one more day of it would have driven me mad.

We set out the very next morning. Sam was singing. Tania was sleeping next to me in the front seat, and Eman was calmly smiling through his *muzhik* beard. I saw them both in the rearview mirror: two bearded men—great guys, both of them.

Since that moment when Tania, up to her waist in the water, told me that I was bony and hard, three years had passed. Much had happened in our lives during that time. Most of it we experienced together, and it happened somehow that we stopped perceiving the world individually and each added to his or her observation the spirit of the other. Thus the presence of the other became, apart from desire, quite a normal need. Without it, the day lost a part of its meaning. Sometime later I noticed that, with Tania around, I was losing my restraining watchfulness toward the world. I discovered in myself the same feeling of security I had known in my home—which I enjoyed, for example, when I unconsciously left the bathroom door unlocked or when I delighted in being quiet for hours on end. Under those circumstances it was quite natural that a conviction took hold of me: that just as Tania was for me a unique being and a part of myself, I too was for Tania a unique man, living in her and representing the entire male world. I accepted this conviction so unreservedly that I believed that, not only for myself but for everyone who knew Tania and me, the interconnectedness of our lives was quite evident. That is why I could not seriously entertain the thought that some other man could be interested in Tania, or some other woman in me. They could be interested only in both of us, I felt.

Besides, on the day we departed for the mountains, I was not really concerned about anything like that. I was sure that only I could uncover the beauty of Tania's body and the attractiveness of her personality. No, at that time I wasn't thinking about anything at all. I was just driving along in the car with Tania, who slept next to me, and two bearded men in the back seat.

I stopped at the end of a narrow valley by a white wooden house and a burbling stream. The others went inside with the baggage, and I locked the car and walked around it, listening to the engine as it made crackling sounds while cooling. I badly wanted to cool myself in the stream, to submerge my head in it and lie down on the stones. I don't know why I didn't do it, for there was nothing stopping me. I joined the others, and the August sky was terribly blue.

Tania and I got a room of our own with windows on the yard. Tania spread the sleeping bags on the beds and put the T-shirts on the shelves. She had lost weight in the tropical heat. I could surround her waist with my two hands.

"What are you doing?" she whispered.

"Taniushka," Sam shouted from the kitchen, "*poshli!* Let's go!"

We went outside into the heat. I had hoped at home to cool myself in the mountains. Eman turned up in shorts. He had thin, healthy legs, and his round glasses reflected the sun.

We arrived at the ski lift, which was operating. There were single seats, and I placed myself between Tania and the others. I did so unconsciously, but I managed to catch Eman's smile. Tania waved at me and cheerfully kicked her legs.

"Sam dislikes heights," I called to Tania.

Eman was last, and his glasses flashed in the distance.

Only grass grew on the summit, and I could see the peaks of the Low Tatras range where Tania and I had hiked the year before. Sharp points of gray rock were visible farther in the distance.

"Let's go," said Eman.

"Yes," Sam nodded. "Taniushka, hmm, *poydi, ya tebya,* come on!"

He squatted and offered to let her climb onto his shoulders: "Here."

"No, Sam," she laughed, "I don't want to."

"Taniushka," he begged, "please."

And suddenly she was high in the air and with her tiny fingers held on to Sam by his curly hair.

"I'm afraid, Sam."

"Don't worry," Eman smiled. "Sam is strong. He is American."

"I can see a lot. The whole globe!" she enthusiastically shouted.

And so we hiked up the range. Tania was holding on to his neck, and he held her by her ankles with his huge American hands. I walked last, looking at Slovakia: mountains, mountains, and more mountains. Out of boredom I remembered the day a long time before when I had sat on one of those mountains. I knew people used to do that, and I wanted to try it. At the time I thought that something important had entered my mind, but now I doubted it. Nothing important has ever come to my mind, I said to myself. If it did, it did too late.

"Sam," she said, pulling his hair, "stop. I don't want to ride anymore."

"Don't worry about him," said Eman with a smile. "He can endure like a horse."

"Isn't it nice? I am okay," Sam insisted, and jumped.

"Don't! Oh, Sam!"

We took a turn down the hillside through sharp grass. Sam galloped with Tania on his shoulders, and Eman threw himself on the ground and rolled down the hill like a little boy except that he remembered to put his glasses away. I stayed behind, baffled by a sudden loneliness. A big American was carrying my Tania away, and I suddenly realized that I was not able to do anything to prevent it. I could not fight for her love; that would have meant that I did not believe her. But I could take a look at myself, and I did so. I appeared ridiculous, abandoned, helpless, and awkward. Mainly and above all awkward—something that I never wanted to be.

Finally he let her go. Suddenly she was so small that she could hardly see a short distance ahead. The three of them sat down by the edge of the dwarf-pine zone. Sam was placing a grass crown on her head, and Eman was handing her bluebells with a smile. She attached them all to her hair like a princess. I had no idea that she could do it so easily, as if she had not done anything else all her life. I had never given her flowers.

We entered the forest, and the road we expected to take us down to the valley suddenly went upward and narrowed, so we walked in a file. Tania was between them, and I was last. The sun was shining at an angle through the trees and turning red. I felt like lying by the lake, feeling Tania's body next to mine, and putting my hand from time to time on her smooth belly.

"Where are we?" she asked.

We stopped on a hill, but because of the trees, we could not see anything. Sam leaned against a beautiful tree woven from two trunks. Its crown was high in the foliage, and the branches forked out wildly. In my childhood I had climbed every tree in my neighborhood.

"I'll take a look," I said. I went up with my feet first and head down, and for a moment I was afraid I had forgotten how to do it. Then I suddenly found myself on the first branch and knew I could climb higher, to the thinning crown, where I thought I would have a good view of the countryside. It would be a place away from the three of them, a dignified, lonely place where the awkwardness would lose its power.

"What can you see?" Tania shouted.

"Not a hell of a lot. Just more hills."

When I climbed down, she still had a bunch of grass and flowers sticking out of her hair.

"Okay, I'll try it," Sam said suddenly, reaching for the branch.

While Sam clumsily climbed to the crown, Eman touched the trunk with a smile, looked up, took hold of a branch a few times, but then shook his head and stepped away. There was no doubt about it. Now all three of us were awkward and ridiculous. I felt somewhat relieved.

In the meantime, Sam started to climb down. He had not managed to make it to the thinner branches.

"Very difficult," he mumbled. He stopped to think about how to make it the rest of the way down, then jumped, scratching his knee and banging his wrist. We moved on.

It was dark when we arrived at the chalet. In the huge wedge of the sky, stars were crowding each other, and some cosmic wind swept them into the Milky Way. It was the first time I had seen it in a year, because in Bratislava you can't see it. You won't find that gorgeous ribbon blown all over the heavens.

That evening I saw Tania for the first time near a red-hot stove where the logs were bursting. She was cooking dinner, and Eman was showing her, with some embarrassment, where he kept the salt, tea, plates, and spoons. He was smiling slightly, and when her rice boiled over, he shook his head and said, "That doesn't matter."

In the meantime Sam was singing, accompanying himself on the guitar. His fingers danced on the frets with dizzying speed. Shit, how was all this possible? Studying history at Yale and Moscow, he was the son of an American corporate executive. Huge, healthy, and curly-haired, he traveled around Europe on a scholarship, playing the saxophone and the guitar.

"Taniushka, sing with me," he asked her, and Tania, who never sang, sat down by him and with her high voice intoned as best she could.

"Very well, Taniushka," he said, and played, the devil, in key with her singing. Eman was smiling, and I knew why.

That was how the evening went. Tania sang and Sam played. Then we drank tea, and Eman and Sam talked philosophy. I was too embarrassed to go out, and so I sat silently, feeling how terribly sleepy I became, how I wanted to sleep under the night sky, watching the stars and listening to the stream, and finally also how badly I wanted to pee. After midnight, when their discussion stopped at Kierkegaard and the guitar was silent, we slowly went our separate ways.

When Tania came to our room, I was searching for matches so that I could have light to find the towel.

"Are you going to wash yourself in the stream?" she asked.

"Yes," I answered.

"Hmm," she sighed, and followed me. On the way, she took my hand and tickled the palm.

"What is it?" I asked.

She kept quiet; only her little fingers were moving. She has many childish habits that certainly attract men.

I stopped and squatted down.

"Come on, climb aboard," I urged.

She put her hand on my head.

"But Milan," she said, "don't be silly."

"Come, come. I'll give you a ride, too."

She sat down on my shoulders, locked her feet under my armpits, and put her hands on my head. We walked down into the valley by the stream. She was squeezing my neck and tousling my hair under the Milky Way while the forest road grated under my tennis shoes.

"Stop now," she begged me. "You must be exhausted."

"Not at all."

"Don't you think I'm heavy?"

"No."

She was heavier than I suspected. I could feel her solid weight with my entire body, and I held her by her ankles. When I was small, my father carried me like that on May Day, and it was clear to me then that life with my head at such an altitude is completely different. When I put her down and she had to raise herself on her toes to kiss me, I remembered that once upon a time almost everybody had been taller than I and that I had found this humiliating. It was a fleeting kiss. Tania offered me her lips, and so I touched them.

The stream rolled over the flat stones with a familiar roar, and when I stepped in, the icy cold of the surrounding mountain peaks entered me through my feet. Tania undressed with a quiet sigh and followed me. On her tanned body glowed the white negative of her black swimsuit, and the moon that shone through the forest showed more of her than I liked. I thought that a sleepless Sam and Eman might be walking along the stream, and the idea turned my stomach.

There was nobody on the road as we returned home. The moon turned us into funny long shadows.

It was only when we lay next to each other and I could feel the proximity of her body and smell the fragrance of her wet hair that I understood that everything I had experienced that day was directed toward this moment. It was quite clear to me right then that I was losing Tania. The longer we lay motionless the faster we flew away from each other. I knew it for certain, the same as I knew that if I reached out with my hand, we would be back together. But a hundred-pound boulder rested on my hand. I myself had placed it there, putting a spell of immobility on both of us, hopelessly expecting the spell to break.

I was afraid of sleep, because that thing would crawl over me, and—spell or no spell—that would be something for which Tania would never forgive me. My eyes wandered in the darkness, and I listened to the sounds of the night until suddenly Tania's breathing changed and I noticed that she was breathing through her mouth. Either her nose was stuffed up or she was resisting the impulse to cry. I lay there for a long time listening closely until I heard a short sob. It was so quiet that I thought I might be mistaken, since I didn't know whether she had a reason to cry. But perhaps she, too, had had a bad day. I knew that she had laughed too often.

But somehow my hand began to move. It slowly crawled on the blanket toward Tania's face. It felt her hair and found her ear, and past the cheek it reached her eyes. I was trying to find out if they were dry; when I felt wetness, I quickly licked my fingers. They were salty.

"Why are you crying?" I asked.

"You're up?"

"How can I sleep?"

"I'm afraid."

"Afraid?"

"I can't help it if somebody gives me flowers. Was that so great a crime that you wouldn't even look at me?"

"You looked so happy," I said. Tania had the ability to be in a good mood at any time. That frequently confused me, and I suspected that she didn't herself know how she felt, that she was often happy only because she was supposed to be. She was not faking it, or if she was, then she faked it from the bottom of her heart.

When I was small and would fall out of a tree or hurt myself in some other way, the other boys would laugh uncontrollably and I would join them. I laughed until I realized that I was supposed to cry. It was only then that I started to cry, and to this day I remember the relief I felt.

"And why are you crying?" I asked.

"Because I am afraid that you do not want me," she quietly answered. "Anyway, this day was so sad."

Our hands had already found themselves, regaining their freedom, but I wanted to say something. Those two guys wanted Tania. I wanted to continue having her in the way only I knew her. They had showed an interest in her, and I was an obstacle, a necessary evil. They had separated us with their attitude, and we were no longer a couple. They divided us into a beautiful woman and an undesirable man. I cannot stand the feeling I get when someone wants me not to exist. I don't know how to handle that. And I cannot tolerate it when Tania and I separate. Then I am quite alone, helpless and terribly bored all the while.

That's what I would have said then if I had known how. Instead I just lay there silently, and while Tania caressed my face with her fingers, a wave of sadness came over me. Mechanically I bit her index finger when she tried to open my mouth. When she squealed in pain, I let it go, my sadness leaving with it. And so I explored with my hand under Tania's blanket and found again what I wanted. A moment later a wave of terrible laughter welled up from somewhere inside me. I wanted to jump out the window into the yard, gallop with a victorious yell up the valley, and thump my chest and head like a gorilla. As we lay peacefully next to each other and I could see only a gray rectangle cut into the wall and in it my hand with fingers spread out, Tania whispered: "Eman told me yesterday that he wants to go out with me."

Well, I'd like to know how a normal man is supposed to react to something like that. I shook with disgust, and my saliva began to flow. When I imagined Eman touching the same Tania who lay next to me, I felt worse than if I imagined he were touching me. Not because he was ugly or loathsome; on the contrary he had a pleasantly hairy head and face, and his slender figure inspired no revulsion. However, he was a man from a different world, and such people terrify me. He simply did not perceive me. And he refused to take me into consideration, and obviously I did not exist for him even during those moments when he spoke to me. Otherwise I couldn't understand his declaration to Tania.

"What did you say to him?"

"What can one say? I told him it would be a mistake."

"He would be a bit too old for you too, don't you think?"

"If he really is so crazy about that *Lolita*, then he would not mind."

"He wouldn't mind? Shit! But you are my wife!"

"Am I?" she asked me, smiling.

"Oh! And what about Sam?"

"But Milan," she answered, chiding, "Sam is just a crazy American. Why don't you like him?"

"I do like him," I mumbled. Sam was leaving the next day by train to catch a plane to America, back to his university, his freedom. He will leave us, I told myself, wailing for weeks on end, remembering his saxophone, dumbfounded by his American normality, possessed with an inferiority complex.

"Did you tell Eman that you are dating me?"

"He said that was your bad luck and he felt sorry for you."

The light through the window was getting brighter, and I could see the outline of Tania's figure. She lay there uncovered, and her knees were sticking up.

"It's getting light," I said.

"I gotta go pee."

And so we climbed out of the window and ran naked to the stream, with Tania's behind shining comically in the morning mist. I thought back to a certain morning when we had been camping and the sun woke us up, burning its way into our tent. For a time, we slept on, exhausted by a rainstorm that had kept us up, threatening to wash us out into the woods below the meadow. It had washed the kettle clean and filled it to the rim. Its sound had echoed in our ears as we dozed. The sun must have gone mad from the storm and lost its sense of proportion, for the extreme heat expelled us from the tent. Barefoot, we stood in the wet grass and then set out for the woods. Tall beeches grew there, and hundreds of fallen trees were strewn about the ground plowed by the rain. I had seen such a forest in school pictures of the Tertiary Period. Striped wild boars and a little doe were walking about, but no people. "Come on, let's take off our clothes," I said to Tania, "in the forest where people do not belong." I unhitched her swimsuit and her white breasts shone on me. We walked toward the fallen timber, a man and a woman, and she was smiling, because my roguish penis was becoming erect.

As the path narrowed, she walked ahead of me—beautiful, striped like those wild boars—and I felt she belonged there after all. Let her know ten languages, read the history of philosophy, and win all kinds of competitions, I said to myself. Here and now walks a woman with strong legs, ridiculously small feet, swinging hips, whose figure is narrow around the waist but widens beautifully around the shoulders. I felt under my toes the cold mud from the night storm, the wet foliage torn off by the wind, the slippery branches, and the thin grass. All of it was new to me. I finally walked on earth and worshiped it through my humble feet. If only that silly rogue of mine did not stand to attention, so awkward and undignified. Why do I want to screw immediately everything that I happen to like?

We entered a clearing that was probably very old, because thin branches of other trees were growing from the stumps and the fallen trees were overgrown with raspberries. It was deep, and its walls ran down steep. As we stood on its edge, we could not see the bottom of it. We held hands and faced the gray mountains across from us. They paled in layers in front of our eyes until they became blue and merged with the sky. We stood on a hot trunk, and the sun was roasting us. I was quickly scanning the surroundings because I wanted to see it all with Tania in the middle. If I had been able to, I would have gone to the edge of the forest and watched her as she stood there in the sun: her head, breasts, crotch, all shining. I felt like shouting with joy.

On the way back, we picked up our swimsuits and tennis shoes left on the wet path, and when we arrived at our tent, Tania took out a blanket and spread it in tall grass in the shade of a huge oak. I probably had had an erection all that time, but I remembered it only when she put me inside her. I was grateful that through it I, too, became Tania, that beautiful woman who just now had stood in the middle of an old forest and prayed to the sun. As I peed into the thorns, I understood why I was thinking about that particular morning. Eman and Sam wanted Tania, and it was all the same to them whether or not she was my wife. And I was afraid of them because I did not know how to defend myself and did not even know whether I had the right to do so. And only now do I realize that I carry that right within me. That morning in the old forest had been our wedding day, though I had not told Tania.

I waited for her, and when she arrived all covered in dew, I pushed her into the room while holding that cute little bum. Then I climbed in, and she kissed me in the window frame and said: "Now we'll go to sleep, and tomorrow we'll go home. All right?"

In the afternoon, we drove Sam to the railway station. He played his saxophone for us until the arrival of the train. Then we helped him load his belongings into the train car. So much for the American. We said good-by to Eman and let him stay in his chalet to read. So much for the philosopher.

The tin monster was hot as the devil as we set out on our way home. Tania tied a knot on her shirt and took off her jeans. I reached for her smooth thigh.

"You can sleep," I told her.

So I drove her through Slovakia while she slept. We passed through the gray country around an aluminum smelting plant that belched white smoke into the overheated sky. It hid all the colors along the river Hron and the adjacent road that leads to Košice, a road I knew well. Tania also knows the road to Košice. She came to see me there in the military barracks that I still hate. In those days she terrified me with the way she dressed and by wearing her hair cut like a boy's. Still, I had been flattered that my attitude did not prevent her from coming. We had changed during those three years, and she had become a woman. Now I was dreading the moment when this woman that she had been hiding inside would become visible to others, and I hoped that she would see her first. But she had not yet noticed, and so I worried about what was to befall me.

Sometimes I didn't feel like going on when I thought about that. She still does not know that she is beautiful, I said to myself, though I have told her a hundred times. One day she'll find out, and she'll also see that she is surrounded by a lot of hard and bony men.

I may have made a mistake somewhere in being the kind of man I am, I reflected. One day she will stop and realize that. She will realize it and never forget it. She will be afraid that she might be in it with me. It may be madness to build a love relationship on the illusion that we belong to each other. However, Tania thought otherwise. She hadn't figured it out yet, and even I did not really know it. I had just guessed it, the way you know that no matter what, your teeth will hurt and yet, when you feel the first stab of pain under the toothbrush, you shiver. You realize that you could not have truly known it until then. But she simply thought differently.

Alas, a bony man will come, and I wonder where will I go.

Bratislava had not changed. Driving into the city, I gasped for air. Tania opened her dazed eyes, and I saw that she was not well. She had lain in the sun and had a rather bad case of sunburn.

"We'll go for a swim in the evening," I said.

She looked at me uncomprehending, rolled her eyes, and under the kind protection of sleep permitted herself to ask, "Are we home already?"

Her mother had gone somewhere, and we knew where and with whom and were glad to be alone. Tania took a shower, and in the meantime I called home. Mother answered right away.

"Hi, how are you?" I asked, relieved.

"Hmm. So-so. How about you? Where are you calling from?" She switched to the sad tone of voice that she reserved for the family.

"From Tania's. I'll be home in the morning, all right?"

"You returned very quickly."

"Yeah. How is Father?"

"Nothing new. I don't know anything."

I knew that her lips had started to tremble, and so I quickly finished talking. But I remained seated by the phone, because suddenly I felt so sorry for her that I could not move. She had an unbelievable ability to be despondent, and I dreaded the thought that I could have inherited that trait. If evil exists, then its most nutritious food is the unhappiness of such people.

When it got dark, we drove to the lake. The surface reflected the neon lights, and a few anglers sat by the water.

"Come on," Tania said, dipping her toe in the water.

I jumped in, releasing into the water a long sigh of relief. It is a miracle how the body suddenly remembers the kilometers it has swum. The muscles, preheated by a full day of sweltering heat, perfectly propel it through the peaceful water. When I stopped, my momentum continued to disturb the surface, and then I dived down into the dark depths, in order to be able to look up, where the light was diffused in tiny waves, as if the city was lit by tiny bulbs. I stopped, utterly devoid of worry, at the bottom, up to my ankles in mud, alone in the middle of the lake. I was tasting that precious moment when you feel that you don't need a thing, not even oxygen, and all you have to do is to stand, deep down, in silence.

When I surfaced, the lake was deserted and smooth, vanishing in the black spaces between shiny belts of lights. I swam back to the shore, but Tania was not there. Her white dress was lying where she had dropped it when she invited me to follow her into the water.

"Tania!" I shouted into the lake. "Tania!"

The summer before, I had sometimes dived from a rock near a dam, only slightly missing the rocks that I knew were hiding in the water. Once, before I could say a word, Tania jumped after me. She got a nasty wound on her instep as a result. Afterward I had tried to make her understand that I don't want her to be an Amazon. However, Tania's ambitions are often stronger than logic.

At the lake, there were also steep shores full of sharp rocks.

"Tania!" I called.

Not far away from me sat one of the fishermen, a little piece of hot coal shining in his mouth.

"Sir, have you seen the girl I came with, by any chance?" I asked him.

"I saw her. She jumped in the water," he nodded.

"Was she swimming? Did she come up?"

"A fish was just biting, you know? I wasn't paying attention."

His voice was full of compassion. It can't be! I shouted inwardly. Evil cannot be that pernicious. Nothing would make any sense!

"Tania!"

Then I heard from the lake: "Milan!"

"Tania!"

"I'm here!"

She appeared in one of the belts of neon light, turned it wavy, vibrating the light, and raised her head. I felt like sitting down, placing my head between my knees, covering it with my hands, and staying there until the weakness should pass. I jumped in the lake again, and anger and terror pushed me until I approached her wet head.

I did not have to recollect that banal event at all, but I did so for two reasons. First of all, it did take place. Second, there was a moment when I lived believing that Tania had drowned. During those few seconds I lost my mind. I know it for certain today. In the moment when I realized that I would have to continue living without Tania, I surrendered to madness, and that feeling, of your mind turning upside down, remains with me as a present from Tania.

The next morning we saw that the sky had turned dark, and a cold wind was blowing. Summer was ending.

August went as quickly as the preceding months, and I welcomed September as any other month, surprised when it arrived. Once upon a time school began in the fall, and it still seemed to hold true, for Tania was registering at the university.

With the last of my money I bought myself a bike. It was beautiful, black, Russian, and cheap. I hopped on it and rode around looking for a job. I didn't really feel like it. But there was only the last hundred crowns in my pocket, and I was also tired of watching out for the police. To live without a stamp is tiresome. The police who arrested my father were waiting for me to make a mistake anyway, and my mother worried, thinking that the police would come back again. Had she known how afraid I was of them, she would probably have shed fewer tears.

Why I found this particular job and not some other, I don't quite know. Maybe because it did not oblige me to work every day and partly because, after all, I had to do something, so why not this? I inquired at a hardware store, and the supervisor gave me his businesslike look and said, "You can start tomorrow."

I managed to find Tania at the university. She was in the cafeteria, sitting at a long table together with friends who had gone there for years as to a soup kitchen for the poor. Now I saw for myself that one could meet everyone there. There were dozens of familiar faces whose names I did not know. However, Adam and Dana were there, too. I was happy to see them, because I had just decided to go to lunch there every day. I would meet friends, talk with them, and find out what was going on. In other words, I would get closer to these people, this community on the edge of which Tania and I moved. Next to Adam sat Richard, who had let his beard grow since he returned from prison. The same policemen who arrested my father had arrested him. His face was vanishing in the thick stubble, and he was forgetting to eat, because he was talking intently. I watched him with sympathy, because he had just come back from prison, from where my dad would also appear one day. Adam joined the discussion, and Dana was helping herself to a piece of meat with some disgust. At other tables a few typical students were sitting, though among these thirty-year-olds they looked quite out of place.

"Hi," I greeted them. Next to Tania was a vacant spot, and she offered me her lips.

"Hi, university woman," I whispered in her mouth.

"Hi, love."

She was sitting among them like a child, her blue-gray eyes radiating innocence and trust, making her virginally beautiful. Her eyes shone with enthusiasm when I announced, "I have a job."

"What kind of job?"

"Sales clerk."

"Sales clerk? Where?"

"Hardware and stuff."

We left together with Adam, Dana, and Richard and went over to the Danubius Cafe for coffee. Gulls were floating on their fluffy feathers down the Danube to the old bridge, and from there some of them flew back, landing under our terrace. The sun was shining but for some reason gave off no heat, and the hair on Dana's forearm stood up. I imagined that a child was radiating heat into her insides, substituting for the little daughter who had died sometime ago. They had started dating when Dana was fourteen and Adam seventeen. Now, twelve years later, they were sitting here with us, and the unfathomable mystery of their love hovered above the table. I sensed it and rejoiced in its existence. The presence of love is a terribly pleasant thing.

"Well, one day," Richard was saying, "they called me into the officers' room and told me that my application was accepted and I was to go home the next day."

"Did you suspect they would pardon you half the sentence?" I asked.

"No," Richard laughed. First, the police kicked him out of school, and then they waited awhile and finally arrested him.

"How was it when they were releasing you?" I asked.

"Fine," he said, mangling the paper from a sugar packet.

The gulls were cawing, probably out of joy. Why else? The Danube rolled by the embankment and reminded me of Europe. The fact that we lived in Europe seemed to me beautiful, even though it had to be in a screwed-up country where I felt happy when someone was finally released from prison. It was strange.

Tania took me by the hand, and I remembered my father. I called him up to this cafe on the Danube to let him feel the quiet joy from the gulls in the water and from the friendship that I shared with people at this table.

I would like to describe our conversation, because I know that its content was wise. The problem is, I can't remember it. That happens to me often. I like Adam for his wisdom and his long monologues. I feel bad that practically all that remains in my memory are his serious eyes and the hidden energy that he wants to imprison in his controlled mimicry, which always thickens the atmosphere with a pleasant tension. I'd rather not think how wise I would be had I been able to remember a fraction of what people have told me in my life. In a word, I hope I won't be too mistaken if I mention that we were talking about something serious, such as truth, freedom, art, or life. I certainly liked that. I like topics like those most of all.

114

When Tania and I said good-by to them and walked up the hill along the cemetery where we once made love at night on a freshly mowed lawn—not out of perverseness, but because of a lack of privacy anywhere else—she said, by way of an introduction, "So you're going to be a sales clerk."

"Yeah," I nodded.

"And do you think that's good?"

"What is good today?"

"That's a good point," she answered without conviction.

"The supervisor seemed pleasant. And I don't have to work full-time. He'll pay me for as many days as I work."

"They won't like that."

"Probably not. But they can't arrest me."

"Perhaps not."

Sometimes she is as slippery as an eel, and you can't catch what she means. It seemed to me, though, that she meant to tell me something. I had no idea myself whether I had made a good decision. Selling hardware suggested boredom, but did Tania have a better idea?

She unlocked the empty apartment (her mother was working) and started to make coffee. I waited for her in her room. I was sitting in the old wing chair, pulling out books according to how far I could reach. There was a mixture of *War and Peace*, *Angelica*, something in French, dictionaries; there were also fairy tales, which was highly appropriate. On the floor were mattresses from old beds placed together in a huge square; on the wall was a picture of a beetle in a clown's hat and with an electric lantern in his hand. And next to a big box of condoms was a wooden bowl with children's beads.

She brought the coffee in ugly cups that would not hold an ounce of rum, and instead of plates she used salad bowls. Whenever something like this happens, it's clear to me that I love her to death; otherwise I could not stand such a morbid hybrid.

"How was registration?" I asked. She put the monstrosity on the table and waved her hand.

"There were an incredible number of people there." And only when she sat down on my knees and pressed her head against my

115

chest did my uncertainty leave me or, if it did not leave, I forgot about it. She took me to that grotesque square of mattresses, undressed us both, opened herself up, and, I felt, pulled me in like an anemone.

When we lay next to each other and Tania lazily stretched her arm to get her cold coffee, she asked, "Do you love me?"

"I love you," I answered, "even if now you are a university student."

"Get away from me, you monster," she whispered lovingly. "Is that my fault?"

"No. Just your bad luck." She rolled into a ball and let me pass my hand over the calming curves of her body.

"Do you know what I am looking forward to?" she asked.

"No."

"When we get old. You will be a beautiful old man, slender and white-haired."

"Great."

"You're not looking forward to it?"

"I am."

I left two hours later. Until then we remained naked (Tania pulled on her socks, because after the lovemaking her feet were like ice), talking about serious topics that, for unknown reasons, I cannot recall. It is a paradox that, even though I love her brain, for me her ideas—if my goofy theory that they are stored in my unconscious does not hold—escape hopelessly into forgetfulness.

As I was walking down the street, in my mind a merry-go-round started to spin, as always when I'm alone. My father's pall of love and suffering descended on my shoulder until my knees sank. Prisoner's slippers thumped inside me, running from one window to another, and in addition, my mother, blinded by insulin, walked into a busy intersection, or she lay on the floor in the hall, the cat wailing next to her. Tania was hiding her tear-drenched eyes, because I am an insensitive man unable to love, and I myself . . . Look here, Tania doesn't even suspect how gladly I would like to be that white-haired old man, I thought.

Mother was reading in the kitchen and, with her glasses on, she looked pleasantly domestic. Vienna was just chiming five o'clock.

Ever since my father had been in prison, Mother had fanatically listened to the radio. But I think that with all the evil in the world, even if they had twenty-four hours to catalog its victims, my mother would still not hear Father's name. And they set aside only five minutes each hour for news.

"Hi," I greeted her.

"Hi. How come you're home so soon? Don't tell me you've argued!"

Shit, that made me mad! My mother is the only person in the world who can make my blood boil in a second. I went into my room, which now belonged only to me, since Peter had left for his military service. The cat was resting on the pillow and observed me as I sat down at the typewriter. In his spotted face, green color shone because he had clear, beautiful eyes. He remained there, unlike my brother and my father: beautifully hairy, with a pink nose and paws.

"Hi, Dad," I wrote to him. "Mother is sitting in the kitchen and Tomas is lounging on my bed. This day would be under different circumstances a very pleasant one. The gulls are giggling on the Danube. Have you ever noticed them? I listened to them from the Danubius Cafe, where we were drinking coffee. The pain in the ass is that you are there, and I cannot forget that. It simply changes my perspective on the world. I feel that I am smarter than others, though facts show the opposite. Anyway, all wisdom is nothing but shoulder straps that help us carry our cross. If I judged wisdom according to how a person carries one's misfortune out in the street, Mother would be as wise as Solomon. Outside she looks better than ever. However, I don't have to tell you how that picture changes at home . . ."

When I finished, it was dark outside, and I could hear from the kitchen the oscillating Voice of America.

"Are you going to eat?" I asked.

"I'm not hungry," she answered, and I had to bite my tongue. After all, I am not a nanny, and Mother is supposed to be responsible for herself.

The cat pulled down my towel from a hanger and lounged on it in the bath tub.

"How am I supposed to dry myself, you thief?" I asked him, but he just observed me silently with his green-bead eyes. I brushed my teeth and dried my wet face in the pillow.

Emptiness stole into my bed and crammed my head full of nonsense that then mockingly marched under my eyelids, each idea dumber than the one before. I fell asleep before I managed to shoo them away, because shortly before I woke up, I dreamed about an owl with a broken wing. It climbed to the top of a mud hill, screeched terribly, and looked like a monkey. And it even behaved like one, because it was banging with its healthy wing on a tin drum. The banging in the hall woke me up.

I found my mother bent over a cabinet, banging her head against the wood. She knocked down a platter hanging on the wall and was about to slide to the floor. Trembling, I grabbed her by her shoulders. Her pajamas were wet with perspiration.

"Go to bed, Mom," I said. Before she could come up with a defense, I pushed her into her room, and she slipped into her bed by herself. I ran into the kitchen for sugar and managed to stuff two cubes in her mouth before she closed it shut and rolled up her eyes.

"You can't do that, Mom," I said pointlessly. "You can't just lie there, you'll suffocate!" I sat her up, and suddenly she seemed awfully heavy. I dragged the limp body of my beautiful mother toward the wall so she could lean against it, while saliva dribbled from her tight mouth.

"Mom, don't do this to me," I mumbled, because her head fell back and banged against the wall. "You must sit up, Mom." I managed to support her so that she lowered her chin to her chest, and again I ran into the kitchen to get a slice of bread and butter. The butter was hard as a rock, impossible to spread. I was swearing aloud and tore up the slice of bread.

Mother was lying on her side, shaking in spasms. I wrapped her in a blanket and drew her closer to me in a sitting position. I stuffed another piece of sugar into her tightly closed mouth with my free hand. Her teeth relaxed reflexively for a moment, and I managed to pour in a little water.

"Swallow that, Mom," I said.

But she just stared at me goggle-eyed, opened her mouth, and spat out the water. She stretched out in a spasm and lurched back so vehemently that the blanket flew out of my hands and she landed on her bed with a long sigh and her eyes wide open.

"That's enough!" I said. I wanted to shout, slap her face, do something that would penetrate her blunted consciousness. I knew too well the futility of such a gesture: she would answer with dilated pupils and a tightly closed mouth. I went into the kitchen. A few minutes later the sugar would start to take effect.

When I returned, she lay as I had left her. I drew her to me by pulling her blanket. She opened her eyes, rolled them, and then broke into a wide smile and threw herself on her bed before I could catch her. I had to use all my strength to keep her in a sitting position. She was jerking her body and turning her head, but I managed to tie her hands and body in the down comforter. During the moments when she was resting, I fed pieces of bread into her mouth. A few times she obediently opened her mouth, but she was forgetting to chew and I moved her jaw with my free hand in vain. But the sugar began to work. Her eyes, blind until then, looked at objects, her expression cleared, and her spasms relaxed.

"Eat, Mom," I said, and it seemed that she nodded.

Ten minutes later she asked, exhausted: "What's going on? Have I done it again?"

I silently gave her a piece of bread and changed her bed.

"Forgive me," she said.

"You should take a shower and change your pajamas," I answered.

It was half past four, the sun was rising, and the first buses were roaring down the street. Her consciousness was coming back quickly, tears were flowing from her eyes, and her chin was shaking. What point is there, I reflected, for a child to see the nakedness of his mother? If that were proper, would Nature not arrange it so that I would remember my birth? If there is some good in every evil, where should I look now for that good?

"I'm all right now," she said. "Go to bed."

The cat was lying on my bed. He had meowed sorrowfully near my mother when I started wrestling with her, and then he had probably gone to my room. Now he was observing me with sleepy eyes.

I got up at eight, because I heard Vienna on the kitchen radio announcing dispassionately that the world was all screwed up. Then it stated the same in English, and I was gratified that I could understand it. In the meantime I drank my hot chocolate. My mother sat opposite me and injected herself in the thigh with insulin. Her eyes were sunken, and she watched the syringe as the milky liquid disappeared from it. It was chilly in the apartment, and the air was so thick with sadness you could slice it.

I rode my bike downtown and stopped in front of my store.

"Here is your new colleague," said the supervisor, and gave me a push in the direction of ten girls and two guys. "Ellen, take care of him."

Twelve names were said, and then the radio announced nine o'clock and we opened the store.

Ellen showed me to the counter. She walked ahead of me, tall and slender, or rather thin and a bit hunched over—obviously because she had small breasts. But many girls are hunched over, no matter whether their breasts are big or small. I couldn't understand that. She lowered her eyes when I stood next to her and turned her pretty face away.

"What am I supposed to do, Ellen?"

"Nothing. Just stand by me and listen to what I say."

Streams of people rolled into the store; they walked in front of us and looked at the shelves lost in thought. A woman in a blue coat and humble eyes stopped by.

"Do you have a strainer?" she inquired.

"No, we don't," Ellen said.

"And when will you have it, please?"

"We'll get new stock next week."

The woman sighed, searched the shelves with her eyes, and left.

I looked around Alice's Wonderland and read the names on the price tags. Pasta machine, vegetable slicer, french fry cutter, lemon press, water spout, special bottle opener, stopper. And so on and on, row after row. I did not understand anything, and the point of all those objects escaped me. I picked them up and felt them like a gorilla, I was so astonished. Could it be that the world consists of so many incomprehensible things?

At one o'clock I hopped on my bike and sprinted toward the

university. Tania was waiting for me in a small circle of our friends, and a penetrating joy seized me when I saw her. An innocent beauty that I loved so much radiated from her and illuminated the surrounding people. It issued from the shiny, toothy smile and from each gesture in which naïveté turned to naturalness, because Tania did not suspect that a hand movement could have aesthetic significance and this lack of knowledge excluded any sophistication. She was standing there, waving to me, and my inward smile changed into an idiotic grimace, because it suddenly seemed stupid to me to be standing with my bicycle at an intersection smiling while being covered with truck exhaust.

We met downtown often, and sometimes I would see her first as she was walking toward me. I would hide and secretly observe her. I etched into my memory the way her walk was when I was not around her, and the capricious rocking of her head, because I had no other opportunity to do so. If she noticed me too soon and waved at me from a distance, we could not control ourselves but would make faces at each other for the full hundred yards that separated us. With an inward sigh of my soul I would then feel my comfortable dignity departing from me.

Our store closed at seven, but all the other stores closed at six and people refused to change their habits. I enjoyed that extra hour, because in that silent world I could examine with my hands the inanimate objects. Bunched up in front of me was the world of artificial things. They were lying on the shelves crowded together and bereft of their sense. The absurdity of manufactured things used to terrify me: for example, a bottle left in the forest by a stream that mockingly exhibited for our admiration its lost essence. But now I touched with interest the transparent bowls, cups, and trays and smelled the weak odor of plastic.

I heard a sound, and in came a man in overalls.

"Did you get the enamel cups?" he asked me from the door.

"Enameled cups?"

"Yeah. I have six kids, and they break the ordinary ones all the time, you know?"

"Aha, let me see," I said, and went to the storage room after Marika.

"We don't have any," she scoffed. "Only a few pieces, and I

won't give him those. He's been pestering us for a month."

"Shit," I said, losing control. "What the hell am I going to tell him?"

"Tell him we'll get new stock next week," Marika piped up hatefully, and mumbled something to herself.

When I went back, he was waiting for me by the door with his hands joined, looking at me from below like a dog.

"We didn't get them, Sir. And I don't think we'll be getting any anytime soon either."

"Oh no," he said, twisting himself in a bow. Then he added, "But I'll come tomorrow, if you don't mind?"

Leaving, he seemed smaller than he had been before, and I spat with disgust.

Tania came around seven.

"We are closing, Miss," said my supervisor, who had suddenly showed up.

"She's mine," I blurted out. "She isn't shopping."

"Am I yours?" she asked me outside with a smile, and pressed herself to me. In the cafe she embraced the coffee cup with her hands, and the coffee colored her lips dark brown.

"What did you do this afternoon?" I asked.

"When you left, Richard invited me to tea and told me about prison and so on. Then I sat in the library, waiting for you to finish working, so that I could come for you. How about you?"

"I was lying all day long. It seems to be my work assignment from now on. I say, 'We don't have it,' even though the warehouse is full of it. If my tongue and my whole face does not turn black in a week, then I will have learned how to do it perfectly. Then I'll fool everyone, even you," I whispered in her ear.

She smiled and licked my nose. Her beautiful golden hair was washed, and it fell into her eyes, making her look like the ponies in the zoo, the ones that carry around little children on their backs for ten crowns a turn. She looked at me from behind it, the university student.

"You'll freeze," she said outside, and buttoned my sweater at the neck. Then she got on the trolley bus, and I got on my bike.

The trolley gathered speed around the Palace of Justice, and

Tania was standing at the rear, waving at me. I stepped on my creaking monster and sprinted after her. But the bus suspected something and took her away ever faster, passing by Avion without stopping even as the light flashed amber. I flew after it, hoping to catch up near the next stop, but only a handful of people got on, and it continued. I got as close to it as a hundred feet, even though I had to jump over the rain-soaked rails at an intersection. Then she escaped from me into the distance, and I almost blacked out on Kollar Square Hill. That Russian tormentor weighed half a ton, it creaked and jerked under my hands, and the electric vehicle playfully escaped from me with its cosmic music. Helpless pain was entering my thighs when I remembered the bus stop behind Tatra, and so I climbed that disgusting hill and saw the red lights of the brakes. I was catching up and already saw Tania's face behind the dirty window, but the bus lurched ahead and wove through the road. At the square it turned right sharply and so had to slow down while I just angled my mount.

Now I caught up with her. I could have touched the rear of that machine, and Tania was laughing and waving while I grimaced and stuck out my tongue victoriously. Then the bus turned toward the Palisades and up to the Red Cross. I let them go.

Mother and the cat waited for me with dinner. The cat's pink mouth was salivating. He was lying on the table and looking at our plates. The hopeless silence of the apartment was broken by the droning of the elevator, which stopped on our floor. The door banged, the key jingled in the neighbors' lock, and mother started to cry reflexively, her tears falling on the pork steak that had caught the cat's attention.

"Please, eat. You can't cry every time you hear the elevator," I said carefully.

"I can't eat." She shook her head, put away her silver as she sobbed, and took out her handkerchief.

"That's no argument. You simply must. Wasn't last night enough?"

"My stomach is turning. What am I supposed to do?"

"Eat," I said firmly.

I left her in tears alone in the kitchen; I didn't know what to say.

My mother had no use for the kind of consolation with which I doped myself.

"Nothing makes sense," she said. "I simply don't want to live. For what? I can't see any joy in my life. To suffer? What's it all for? What sense does it make to put your father in prison? You tell me."

"It makes no sense," I answered. "But you should be happy that he is alive, and that you are alive, even when you suffer. What right do you have to say that you don't want to live? Anything is better than death. Anything is better than nothing."

"No. To hold on to life at any price? Blind, deaf, without legs, without arms—that's ridiculous. People celebrate it as heroic, while in fact it's cowardice."

She did not know what she was saying. She was still beautiful, but in the last few months fear had made her eyes look more ethereal and pushed them deeply into her face.

The telephone rang.

"You were good!" Tania said.

"I was," I confirmed. "And if I had a better bike, you would really see something. I can't do much with that monster."

"That was enough for me."

"It's great that you are so undemanding."

"Yeah. Good night then," she said, purring.

Tania has a great influence on me. That night, for example, I slept without disturbance. That's how I like it. She also influences me in other ways. During those three years since she first took me into her life, I had changed a lot. I stopped sniffling and learned to use a handkerchief. I stopped whistling in her presence and grew a beard. I liked that change. I started to think of myself as a bearded young man who did not whistle or sniffle and who would never put a checkered pullover over a checkered shirt. But otherwise, I did not change. Tania did not dare and did not want to touch my essence. I continued to appear to myself the man I imagined myself to be, and she confirmed that.

It took Eman and Sam to make me feel a certain conflict that showed signs of wear: the colors somehow did not quite match the outline of the figure.

I came to realize this a few days later, one morning when I entered the back room of the store to put on my work gown. Ellen was sitting in the corner, smoking and weeping bitterly.

"What happened?" I asked.

"It's Marika, that stupid cunt," Jane answered.

Marika used to say, "I have a great husband," but in reality the man was the ugliest brute imaginable. She made no secret that she wanted to become the supervisor, but we all knew that she could not write even a price tag right, to say nothing of keeping accounts. She kept bragging how popular she was with the customers, but I found out from the girls that there were written complaints against her. She declared that she did not want children, but a few days before, she had arrived with a victorious smile on her lips and announced, "I'm three days late." But the next day she came in gloomy, and the girls laughed: "Tough shit. She got her period."

We were not open yet, and I found her behind the counter—small, gloomy, and with two lower teeth missing for some reason.

"Ellen is crying," I said.

She frowned even more and looked nowhere in particular. "I haven't done anything to her," she said. "I just asked her if she knew the price of that blue bowl. She didn't know it. Can I help it?"

Poor Marika. She believed that she had a handsome husband, that she would become the supervisor, that people loved her, and that she would have a child. At the same time, her husband was a clumsy and crude elephant; it was obvious she would never become a supervisor, because she was such a blockhead, poor thing; people hated her; and she would probably never have a child, because she was either infertile or had never really slept with that jerk.

So, what sort of a person was Marika?

"A stupid cunt," Jane would have said, and all the other girls would have agreed. That was what she was like in reality, or at least how she appeared to the others. Her good fortune was that she did not suspect the terrible gulf that separated her from those around her, a gulf that she would probably never cross.

These were my reflections as Marika stubbornly looked at the floor, scratching her calf with her foot. How do I appear in the eyes of the others? I wondered. Who am I really, and who decides about that?

I walked unhappily past the crammed shelves, and outside, in front of the store window, people were gathering and waiting, observing me and pointing to their watches. I barked angrily and placed myself behind the counter, because the supervisor was just opening the store. How would I find out by how much and in what direction my image of myself differed from my image in the minds of others? I did not want to think what it was I represented in the minds of Eman or Sam, for example, or how I appeared at that moment in my work gown when a fat man who had nicked himself shaving that morning asked me for a poppy-seed grinder.

"We don't have it," I said.

My God, how terribly ordinary!

"How come you don't have it?"

"We simply don't," I shrugged my shoulders. "That's how it is today."

"What a mess this place is," the fatso declared.

"I agree with you completely. But we don't have the grinder," I answered.

How would you like to appear to the world around you? I asked myself. The answer came soon enough, and there was no sense resisting, though my nose was turning up. The answer was: I wanted to be a romantic young man.

Fall quickly filled up with increasingly chilly mornings, and each of them my mother marked with a flood of tears.

"I constantly think about how cold he is there," she would say as she touched our cold radiators, which started working at nine, though we could turn on the electric heater.

And when the first snowflakes floated down from the sky, she stood for hours on end by the window, tears pouring down as if from the tap in our kitchen that I did not feel like fixing.

I stood behind the counter all morning long and thought about lunchtime, when I would meet Tania. She waited for me at half past twelve, and we went to have lunch with the others, sitting with our backs to the younger students. Richard's beard and hair were growing like tropical vegetation while Adam had a crewcut and others wanted to stop their hair from falling out. And so it went, round and round; after lunch to the Crimea Cafe for coffee, twenty minutes disappearing as I held Tania by the hand, resting.

Well, I was not really resting. One can't manage to do anything in such a short time. Tania's hand lay in my hand just like a sweaty piece of flesh, nothing more.

In the evenings we sometimes made love in her room. She played some record on her awful record player. Afterward we lay in her feather comforters, and I played with her tiny hand, which she rested on my belly. I reflected calmly about why it was that I felt that her beauty was beginning to seem commonplace. She talked to me about her days, about her tiresome struggles with sleep during lectures, about her conflicts with her mother. She filled the empty time with ordinary words. I noticed I was upset. I was missing something in her life. It was as if her life was marked by boredom, and that was unusual. Or was it I who was bored? I thought about it, waiting. But waiting for what? Although I wanted to stay with Tania, because I suspected that we discovered our love in these conversations, I decided to go home. There, my mother might be sitting in the kitchen, perhaps even drugged by insulin, the cat biting her hand to amuse himself. She might entertain the delusion that Father would return and let her eat. When I missed the bus, I would jog a few stops on the sidewalk, in order to get home quicker and find with relief the light in the window.

She would be sitting by the television set with the cat sleeping at her feet.

"Hi. How come you're home so soon?" she would ask. "Did you have an argument?"

Everything seemed rotten somehow. The whole globe was swelling with nervousness, so I stopped reading the papers. I didn't feel like wading through the dirt to find a bit of truth.

Without realizing it, I was glad only because of Adam and Dana. Dana was getting round and often had a mysterious smile on her face, and the pile of children's clothing in their apartment grew larger and larger.

That was how things looked in the middle of December. One day it was snowing heavily, and joyfully I walked past the sighing buses throwing up geysers of snow from under their tires. I stopped at Adam's place on my way to work and the door, usually locked, was open, and so I went in.

"Hello," I shouted, "is anyone home?"

I thought I heard some noise in reply, but nothing moved in the quiet dusk.

"I'm here," I heard more distinctly. It was Adam's voice, coming from the bathroom.

So I opened the bathroom door and found him submerged up to his neck in soapy water, with moisture dripping from the misty mirror. He lifted his hand and waved to me like a Hungarian count.

"Hi, old man," he welcomed me. "I haven't seen you for ages."

"I'm in a hurry, on my way to work. I dropped by to bring you something to read and to ask about Dana. How is she?"

"Fine. She gave birth last night."

"No!"

"Oh yes!"

"And?"

"I have a son," he said, smiling. I sat down on the rim of the tub, unhinged by the surprise.

I left him in the bath and rushed through the city on my bike. The snow was coming down harder, falling into my eyes, nose, and mouth. But I was happy that I could shake my head, spit, and swear—I was wildly overjoyed. I welcomed that feeling as an old friend I had not seen for a long time.

Even behind the counter I could not shake a silly smile. It sat on my face like a spasm, and my soul took joy from everything around me. I welcomed the crowds that pushed in and marched by me with masks of indifference.

"We don't have such valves, Madam," I rejoiced. "It's of Italian make. We haven't had those parts for two years, and we won't be getting them."

"But what am I supposed to do? My water leaks!" she countered, narrowing her big blue eyes framed by black pencil.

"Throw it out and buy one of ours, made in Myjava," I advised her enthusiastically. "It's ugly all right, but it works!"

"No," she stated stubbornly. "I'll go to Italy on holiday and buy the seal there!"

"Hmm," I murmured, defeated, and turned to the next customer. "Can I help you?"

"I would like to talk to you," said a man in a brown suit, with a narrow moustache. He did not carry a shopping basket.

"Hmm," I murmured again, and left the counter.

"You do know who I am, don't you?" He smiled.

"I don't. But it doesn't matter, does it?"

"No," he said, still smiling. "Go get dressed. I'll wait here."

"Joe, the police have come to pick me up," I told the supervisor.

I had to get into a white Zhiguli, where another man with a moustache waited, warming the car for us. I should have realized a long time ago that they would come one day, I thought, and when the driver skidded in the curves full of snowdrifts, I wished from the bottom of my heart that we would hit a pole.

"What are we going to talk about?" one of them asked.

I shrugged my shoulders. It was cold in the office, and my body was shaking. I envied them their body fat and the calm certainty with which they lit their cigarettes. I was freezing, but they didn't seem to notice. Apparently, the cold came from inside my body and was felt only inside me. I closed my mouth to prevent my teeth from chattering, and I breathed slowly, and deeply, as I used to before a race when I had to calm my heart so that it would not exhaust itself by irregular thumping. I was slowly succeeding. The blood was returning to my hands and my muscles were relaxing bit by bit.

"Tell us about your trip to Poland. Who did you meet there?"

I shrugged my shoulders, and so they took everything I had on me, including my shoelaces, and led me down a long corridor.

"I hope you will let my mother know," I said. "She is sick."

"Everything depends on you." Both of them smiled.

The cell surprised me with its cleanness. I received an ironed sheet and a cake of soap in a paper cup.

Well. And what next? I asked myself. The reinforced glass window high above my head was covered with snow. That was where the ground began and where I had walked earlier that day. I asked myself whether I was in a cell where in the 1950s they had sprayed priests with the water hose attached to my wall. Or was this the cell where my father spent his first days of imprisonment? I searched the walls, but none of the few scribbles was his.

I should think, I told myself. Now I have enough time and no distractions.

For a while I honestly tried it, but then I stopped with a sigh and did a hundred squat-thrusts instead. They warmed me up, but I would have to find another source of heat. I remembered the hot radiator in my room, but I quickly shook my head and imagined something colder than this cell. For example, my bicycle in front of the store. It was freezing, and snow was falling on the poor thing.

They came for me the next day at ten. My joints already hurt from constant exercise. If they keep me here six months, I will turn into a regular Hercules, I thought.

"You are not talking, but you would like to go home," one of them said after two hours. "You are not helping us at all."

"You locked up my father, and now you want me to help you?"

"Have it your way. But your mother is worried about you," he said, and they locked me up again.

"What do you want from me, pigs?" I mumbled. "To lock up a person like this . . ."

But they released me two days later, and I was grateful even for that. There was more snow on the streets, and the streetcars were digging deep trenches into it.

My mother's eyes had turned red and sunk more deeply into her face, but I liked how they shined with joy when she threw herself at me in the door.

"Oh, those pigs, those pigs," she repeated happily, and hugged me tight.

When she let me go, she stuffed me to the gills with meat. Vienna was announcing that something had gone wrong with the world again. I was surprised that our earth still turned once every twenty-four hours. Then I went to Tania's.

The dark and empty streets confirmed that nothing had changed. The world continued as before; the streets were wrapped in snow that reflected the blue light from the windows. Maybe the change would come sooner than the blue windows might realize. That streetlights still burned here and there and that the trolley bus carrying me would still make its rounds even empty was something I didn't believe anymore. There was no proof.

I suppressed the joy that took hold of me with these gloomy

thoughts. You see, after a long time of doubt I felt once again that I loved Tania and that I belonged wholly to her. I even felt worthy of her and could hardly wait to see her. I could not find in myself a scintilla of the fear of boredom that so recently had beset me. It rarely happens in life that one sees oneself in such a clear light. That day I was sure that I appeared to everyone as good as I wanted to be, and so I did not even try to analyze my image, but just rejoiced in it. Prison is a beautiful thing, I blasphemed.

In Tania's eyes I found a spark that could have been joy or relief, but I interpreted it as admiration.

"Was it bad?" she asked with a trembling voice as she put a record on her horrible record player.

"The worst thing is that you never know how long they'll keep you there. Could be two days or two years," I answered.

We made love surrounded by the croaking of oldies and to the sound of her mother mercifully hammering on her typewriter next door. I was astonished by Tania's beauty. It was as if she had been hiding it for this moment. She took her undershirt off in an unbearably sexy manner, and I shook because a fire entered me suddenly and lit the fuse. That's how I imagined it; I distinctly felt a crazy power coming from outside and hitting me in the groin, burning there, and then pushing me into Tania, who probably knew it, because her eyes went dim and she opened up to me and answered my stroke with a long sigh. The explosion came unexpectedly soon and with such force that I surrendered to it in a fraction of a second. I regretted it, but when I saw all that energy as it victoriously pulsated and poured out onto my abdomen, peace returned to me. It was the peace I had desired for a long time, and it erased from my memory everything except the gentler present.

Our tea got cold. Tania slipped her feet between mine and wiped me with a handkerchief that she would hide under the pillow. Then I placed my head on her warm belly, with only one idea in my mind: Everything is actually incredibly simple—nothing is easier than loving.

Three days later the snow turned into a brown-gray mush that cars sprayed on me, so I had to use the crooked little lanes to bypass the traffic. My breath would freeze on my beard, and my toes were numb. You could see our breath in the store, because it was heated by a single pipe hidden behind the shelves. I was trying to warm myself up with the realization that my father was worse off than I. His lawyer had churlishly remarked that yes, it was quite cold there, which prompted a flood of tears from my mother.

It was dark before I left for work and dark again when I finished, and so by the time I made it to Adam's I was frozen to the bone.

"Hi," I said, and joyfully entered the warm room. Adam was sitting in the armchair. There was not a piece of paper or a book lying around, and it was clean everywhere. On the table was a little pile of baby clothes. "What's the little guy doing?"

"Nothing," said Adam, shrugging his shoulders. "He died yesterday."

"No!"

He just nodded, and I was falling down into terrible depths. I could swear that I was falling with great speed somewhere downward, most probably into the past, and that if I did not sit down, I would feel the same in my stomach as when I jumped off the ten-meter tower. I saw in that depth a crowd of millions; they were waiting to tell Adam: Do you see? This is what it's all about. Remember.

To hell with a world like this! I shouted to myself. What good is it to him, you clowns? *Memento mori*, you jerks? What's the point when all of life is screwed up?

Two hours later I got up from the armchair. Adam remained sitting, and so I just quietly closed the door. Outside it was snowing heavily, and behind me remained a thin track after my bike, the only one in these parts. I felt sick, and I could not make it up the hill, because my wheels were slipping. I pushed my bike home.

At New Year's I made a resolution to reflect on my life, but I soon learned again I should let such moods pass.

Sometime near the end of January, for example, Tania came to see me at the store. She stuck her nose into my blue gown, and I rested in the peaceful presence of her warm hands and soft body, stealing heat from her embrace.

"You're cold here," she said. "We'll go for tea."

It was freezing outside, and snow had accumulated. In front

of the store there was a white ocean of snow relieved only by gray islands of concrete. I nodded in agreement because a desire for warm liquid in my stomach distracted me from the icy melancholy.

We sat by the radiator and dipped our tea bags in the cups. Tania forgot hers, turning her water black, and not even lemon could help. She tasted it with disappointment and then left it alone.

"You see," I said, and we exchanged cups.

"What did you do all day?" she asked me, probably to make me think of something else.

If I had had a free hand, I would have shrugged her question off. I just wanted to sit and listen to her voice, to the words that enabled me to enter into her life while mine was falling apart. I had nothing to tell her about that day or any other day. Life in the store was an illusion; it did not exist. To speak of it with interest was a lie, and I felt that I did not have any energy for that lie or even for the truth. I just wanted to sit until it passed.

"You tell me. What can I say?"

Someone was dropping coins into the jukebox, and Tania was silent. She, too, had nothing to say, or perhaps she was thinking, or observing the jukebox and the people who fed it. Meanwhile, the waiter brought us more tea. The old Bratislava cafe was filling up with noise and smoke. Opposite us a young couple sat down and ordered hot wine. I found a narrow crevice under the marble top of the table and pried it with the aluminum spoon until the spoon bent.

"Quit that, please," she said, grabbing my hand. "Lick it or put it in your mouth, bend it or bang it on the table, but please don't stick it there, and don't lift the marble!"

"I'm sorry," I mumbled.

We finished, the waiter took my spoon, and I walked Tania to the bus stop. There I mechanically petted her, kissed her dry lips, and let her get on the bus.

Around me the buses were rolling, enveloping me in a cloud of blue gas. I had nowhere to escape, so I breathed it in until my eyes watered. I gasped for the air that had suddenly disappeared.

Mother was listening to the news from Vienna, drinking her tea, and reading an old book from the family library.

"Anything new?" I asked.

She shook her head. Radio is a pig. It always announces something new, but in the meantime everything stays the same.

A great advantage of my work was that it now began at ten. I could sleep without an alarm clock and get up with the light. After waking, I lay with my eyes closed while the blackest thoughts passed and I tried to decipher what the kitchen radio was saying. The phone would ring, and mother would drag me out of bed.

"Tania is calling."

"Hi," she said. "Did I wake you up?"

"No."

"Mother is going out tonight. Will you come over?"

"Sure. I'll be there at half past seven. Make something good for dinner."

I was glad, because we had not been alone together for a long time. The day was supposed to have been easier, then, but it was not. The sky remained colorless, and from time to time it dusted the equally colorless city with snow. I was used to the gloom, perhaps had even come to like it, because I suspect that deep down I like a stereotype. That part of my being that likes to suffer was satisfied. I consoled myself that I still had Tania's love, but actually the evidence was inconclusive. Nevertheless,-the evening was to furnish me some proof. That's why the day should have been easier, but when it was not, obviously the problem lay elsewhere. But where? Anyway, I was terribly bored all day long and watched the clock. People asked for snow shovels until I got fed up, for none had been delivered since summer. Occasionally I became rabid and almost threw my hands up to shout: Are you all crazy, or what?

However, at seven we locked up promptly, and I sprinted to the bus stop. Tania would certainly wait for me in her heated room, where on the stove oil would crackle under a piece of meat.

"Hi, Richard," I noticed a figure at the bus stop.

"Hi," he said. His face was covered by a brown bush that disguised his features. I kept forgetting that I, too, out of sheer laziness, had a beard.

"Are you in a hurry? Let's go get a cup of tea," he said.

Tania is waiting for me, I told myself, hesitating.

"Let's go to the Metropole. I am leaving for Prague tonight," he added incoherently.

So we sat down to have tea and he was wringing the wet tea bag in his palm, dipping it, and wringing it again, until he tore it. Then he ordered another cup of tea and did the same thing. All the while he looked into my eyes as if expecting something from me, and that made me nervous. I told him about the books I was reading and played with a cube of sugar wrapped in smooth paper.

When I think today about that half hour I spent with Richard, I shiver and the hair on my hands stands up. That's because I still don't know that I can really be myself when someone looks directly into my eyes. But how Richard saw me I was to find out very soon.

"I'm really sorry," I said when he finished tearing up another bag, "but Tania will kill me if I don't come on time. When does your train leave?"

"In three hours."

"Hmm. So, I'll see you. And give my regards to people in Prague."

At Tania's I opened the door myself and was embraced in the hall by hot air and the penetrating aroma of meat.

"Anybody there?" I shouted. "Hello!" However, I did not find Tania in the kitchen. She was lying in her room, on her mattress, and her moist eyes reflected the table lamp. The alarm clock said half past eight.

"Come now, dearest," I started, soothing her. "You must pardon me. I met Richard at the bus stop, and he forced me to go for tea with him."

Tania was silent, and that put me out a bit.

"I know, you were waiting with dinner, but ever since he returned from prison, I've seen him only a couple of times, and only for lunch."

Again she said nothing, and that seemed to me a trifle theatrical, as she was looking up somewhere, biting her lips, and her eyes were welling with tears.

"But, Tania," I mumbled, perplexed, "surely it's not so bad."

"Milan," she finally whispered. "I have to . . . Richard and I, we . . . There was something . . ." She was overcome with tears.

It's interesting how everything can change so suddenly. Really funny. When I was twelve, I was almost the smallest boy in the class, and my face was so childish, so pure, that the girls in my class dressed me as a girl for a party. The change was enjoyable, and I smiled from the excitement of this mystification. My short hair was hidden under a bonnet, and I sat in an armchair. My male classmates would approach me one by one, and a momentary confusion would turn to cool annoyance: "Come on, Milan, don't be stupid." I would have been a beautiful little girl, but I had ugly teeth, which showed in my excited smile, and was recognized by them. In a word, everything changed for them in an instant. There was no little girl, no mystification. I was an idiot.

The saddest part of all, so sad that I don't even feel like writing about it—and that is perverse, for I write in order to write about my sadness—was the sudden change in me after Tania spoke those few words. The notion of my new "I" oppressed me with such force that I sat motionless with my back to her, watching myself fly back into the past. That past was replaced in that moment by a new past. The man who had tea with Richard an hour before no longer existed. There was no longer a romantic young man. Someone else was there, though I was unwilling to admit to his new status. And Tania's tiny fingers belonged to another Tania, and they did not caress my chest inquisitively. My memories were blasting away from me as from a rocket that opens a door to the cosmos. They flew out in bunches and remained outside, blunt and banal.

I was sitting in a lotus position observing the demolition. I was reading the spines of the books in her childhood library, from *The Count of Monte Cristo*, to Tolstoy and Rolland in the original—*War and Peace, The Enchanted Soul*. This was Tania all right, but now this realization was no longer of any use to me. It was useless as my knowledge of the price of the blue pot with white flowers that arrived in the store that day. I would have stayed quiet even longer, deceived and disgraced, but for my fear that I would awkwardly get up and leave.

"Well, say something," I managed to slip in.

She answered in a quiet little voice that I knew well. She used it seldom, but I remembered it well—from all our other arguments.

"What do you want to hear?"

You know very well, I thought.

"Did I sleep with him?"

Oh, God, not that. I can't bear to think about that.

"I did not. I didn't even kiss him."

"That's not how I meant it," I protested. I really did not think that far.

Now, however, I wanted to know. I wanted to know about each look, each word, to walk where they walked, to sit at tea and listen to their conversation. I wanted to get to know their past that did not belong to me, to trap it into a form that I could absorb into myself. Then I wanted to wring it out, turn it around, dissect it, understand it, because I was sitting there like a plucked chicken, helpless and empty. I wanted to punch it out of her, shake it out of that beautiful body that I suddenly saw with painfully different eyes. However, my energy suddenly evaporated, and the meaning of everything just disappeared. I, too, disappeared. I evaporated, bless my soul; I felt I was turning into jelly.

She did not sleep with him. But she could have, I reflected. She compared him with me, then. She thought about it and weighed the options. No, quit that, you idiot, or else you'll really evaporate.

The notion that in her eyes I did not have to be the only one was crawling up my back, because that's where I shivered. If not the only one, then not even unique. Oh, my God, enough, enough!

"And then?" I asked, exhausted.

"Then what?" she asked coldly.

"What now?"

I looked at her, and she was still lying down with her arms under her head and her eyes swimming in water.

"I told him yesterday that I want to be only with you."

Ah, words. How healing they can be, I said to myself, and waited for relief.

She finally sat up, her golden hair falling into her wet eyes and her mouth mournfully bent. I wanted to be cruel, but I realized again that I have no energy for that. The energy had no one to radiate from, because I had vanished. After all, why did she choose me? Maybe only because I'm taller. In a word, relief was not forthcoming, somehow.

My pasts definitely separated, and two shared my soul: the one who loved Tania and the one who was deceived by her.

But she was no better off. Here was a girl that I loved, and there was some girl who would go for walks with Richard, considering who to choose, who would be better. We were sitting there, multiplied by our worse counterparts, watching the devastation they left.

Why does she want to stay with me and not him? I thought. She must have some reason, and that could be a key to understanding how she sees me, that is, who I am. I had no idea why I had won, if one could talk about a victory.

"Why, you are not my type at all," she used to say at coffee, in a good mood. "You should be a little plumper, with black hair and glasses."

There you go, I thought. I was all muscle and had eyes like an eagle. Shit, I can't make any sense of it, I thought.

"Milan," she started suddenly.

"Hm?"

She lay down on her back again, fixing her eyes on me.

"Don't you want to . . . lie down?"

I joined her, and we lay side by side, motionless, as one lies before getting up in the morning or before a battle. I closed my eyes and gave in to the fatigue. I thought she had turned to the wall to cry, but I was not sure. I touched her shoulder, round and beautiful. She had inherited it from her mother. She became quiet, and I asked her, "Why are you crying?"

She continued crying. I did not see the tears, but I imagined them flowing down her cheeks and then feared that I was mistaken. She is not crying at all, I thought. She is breathing aloud because of a cold. That happened to her often. A cold would attack her, and then she had to use nose drops that I could taste in her mouth as I kissed her good night.

"Say something," I begged her.

She did say something, something that I was supposed to understand, something that apparently did not have to be articulated, because she said it into her pillow, and now she was waiting for an answer while I, distressed, looked at the back of her head.

"I . . . ," I said. "Excuse me, but I did not understand what you said." And I moved closer to her, touching a body that seemingly did not belong to her.

"I'm afraid . . . ," she whispered, "that you don't want me anymore."

When she turned to me, I fell thousands of years into the past. What now? I asked all the men in the world and passed my hand over her wet face. "You have such beautiful big hands," she had told me often, "so big and strong. I enjoy them terribly." And so I was sliding my hand along the wet face that fit into the palm of my hand. I passed over her lips and felt the tip of her tongue. It tempted me. I wanted to feel that tongue in my mouth. Her mouth was wet and salty, and bashfully, it licked me. That elicited memories of all my lovemaking with Tania, like a film going backward at full speed. She lay below me white and beautiful, the way only I knew her. I banished the eyes of all the others, who wanted to watch through me, and bit my tongue, because a cry of excitement was forcing itself out, so irresistibly was I growing.

Then I was flooded by heat, but not a triumphant heat. I was drenched in sweat because of astonishment and fear, and suddenly it no longer seemed to exist. It was as if somebody cut me off, I swear. I was vanishing, and everything was disappearing while despair and revulsion grew inside of me.

Jesus, not that! Not on top of everything else, I thought helplessly.

Tania took my head into her hands, pressed it to her breasts and caressed me mechanically. Silently I hated my body while Tania's hand reached for the comforter to cover my shame.

A moment later she got up, and as she was walking toward the bathroom, I saw that she was stepping very gingerly and unsurely, turning around in an absentminded way. It was as if she were thinking of something else, though she did not quite know what it could be. That happens to her when she knows I am angry. I guess she loses her certainty about me and perhaps about herself as well,

139

though from the outside it looks as if each movement were directed by remote control, though with poor results. Very simply, she looks broken. She does not work.

Well, serves you right, I told myself. I don't work either.

I drank the cold tea from both cups and put on my socks and then the rest of my clothes. Tania walked with me through the darkness in her open robe, and outside the cold wind awaited me. No sooner did I kiss her good-by than the wind grabbed me by the hair and pushed me down the street.

At the bus stop I finally found time to look into my soul, but I found nothing but loneliness. I had it in my hand and observed it with distaste as it was budding.

Everything changed. If I had not been suffering, it could have been entertaining to study the new forms of old things and the notions that connected me to them. Instead, I was trying to stop the collapse of a pyramid of opinions and feelings that was in the dwelling where I happened to live, after I found out how stupidly and hastily it had been erected. I imagined it collapsing like a children's puzzle made of glass beads. Sadly I watched their playful motion. The glass beads rang out as they fell, and it was so painful that I often found myself gnashing my teeth. For example, once I caught myself standing in front of a mirror, considering if I had enough courage to go out in my old boots and torn coat. I used to wear both very gladly. It was only now that I realized I actually looked like a bearded and hairy ruffian (exactly as my mother used to say), and I immediately understood that I had walked around the city like that only because I knew with certainty that Tania liked me like that.

Now I knew nothing and was finding out in horror that this uncertainty was dissolving everything. I would instinctively pull philosophy books out of my father's library and then jeer at their wisdom that told us how to understand the world but did not say what I needed to do for Tania and me to love each other again.

Letters from my father arrived. He had lost another tooth and his eyesight was weakening, but his hand remained unchanged. He pressed the words into the paper so hard that each letter resembled

140

an etching. I worried when I saw how my mother pounced on the envelopes bearing the prison stamp. Their supply could be stopped anytime, and I feared that would finish her off. I was worrying unnecessarily. One day she came home from the city with terror in her eyes, sank into a chair in the kitchen, and, with the cat on her lap, cried while he compassionately nibbled her wrist. Somewhere in the street the insulin attacked her, and she could not remember a thing, did not even know how she had gotten home. That two-hour blackout terrified her so much that the next day she left for the hospital, and it was not even necessary to blackmail her with a letter from Father.

Only the cat was left at home, and all I had to do was change the cotton wool where he peed twice a day, feed him once a day, and pet him some. I ran to the Iron Fountain more often and cursed the bumpy, frozen roads. Nature was solidifying. The wind could not bend trees wrapped in a layer of ice and snow, and I was sorry that Mother was not home. I liked how I amused her with the icicles hanging from my beard and hair after each run. Now only the cat would welcome me, nuzzling with pleasure my sweaty warm-ups.

My brother was writing wise and sad letters from the army, and I was entertaining myself by typing my answers in triplicate: one copy to my father in prison, another to my mother in the hospital, and the last to my brother in the army. I would sit typing in my room and look out the window ever so often and feel afraid because it seemed that I no longer understood my fate but was beginning to understand my meaninglessness and the fact that I had never understood it before. I turned red when I thought about that creature dressed like a girl, and I feared how embarrassed I would be later by the memory of my stupidity during that winter.

I wanted to live with Tania. Her body did not leave my mind, but its curves were suddenly so foreign to me that her plush teddy bear in the corner of her room seemed closer to me. Then the horror of the soft impotence. I tried to exorcise it by long sprints, but I merely gulped down too much freezing air and spent the rest of the day coughing and wheezing.

One day followed another. The movable mist descended from the gray sky, or the sun appeared, melting half of the accumulated snow. Tania would come to meet me in the store and would silently bear the cotton wool with which I revengefully stuffed our conversations. She would slip her hand into mine, and I would reflexively hold it, hoping to feel through it her presence.

The only thing I wanted to hear was her confession about Richard. I wanted to know whether she had held him, too, by the hand. But had she told me, I would have let go of her and and sent her home. I feared that I would ask the question, because that was what connected me to her. When I found five crowns in my pocket, we would go for tea. We would look for a place without a coat check.

"How was school?" I asked.

"Fine. How about the store?"

"So-so." Frightful boredom. People started to buy sprinklers for their gardens, and I had to fetch them, crawling all over the highest shelves, because someone had stored them there. Gardeners are dull shoppers. They stick their noses in the instruments, try every part, observe them with love, and get really upset when I don't show any interest in discussing with them the advantages of this or that nozzle for a spray pistol. I prefer the lisping village grandmas who want a cabbage slicer, because we don't carry them. When these grandmas want to buy garden shears, I talk them out of it, because the shears are no good.

Lately, Tania had been a bit down in the mouth. She was hunched over and seldom washed her hair. Her fingers were stained with ink, and she was quiet, so that I began to doubt whether I would live to see the revival of the love I knew had existed.

We finished our tea, and I suggested we go to Adam's.

"Hi," Dana intoned with a painful Madonna smile. She turned small and slender, and I hugged her and kissed her forehead as if I did not know what confusion and panic that would cause her.

"How is the old man?" Adam asked when we sat down to another mint tea.

"He lost another tooth, and it's awfully cold there."

"And your mother?"

"Mother collapsed and is in the hospital right around the corner."

"Parents are nothing but problems, my friend. And they'll still be, even when your father comes back from prison and your mother returns from the hospital."

"That's true," I said. "And anyway, I never thought that it would be so hard and complicated just to live."

"We didn't think that either, Milan," Dana said. "But maybe it's supposed to be like that."

And so we drank fragrant tea in a common presentiment that something evil awaited us all, and strangely enough, it gave us joy. I looked at Tania and saw that her eyes widened in pleasant musing, as she sat with her legs crossed. I like the presence of destiny. It brings forth a euphoric feeling of kinship with everyone living and everyone who has lived. Had Tania not been sitting so far away from me, I would have caressed her little ink-stained hand, which was twisting the wrapper from a sweet she took with her tea, because at Adam's one does not sugar one's tea. She was sitting opposite me, however, and so I conserved my mood by switching to politics, because this touched all of us equally and vitally.

Out in the street the inky fingers slid into the palm of my hand, and I sighed with surprise when they felt so pleasant. She moved them cheerfully, and I wanted to know how she guessed.

"Well?" I asked in a threatening voice.

"Nothing," she laughed.

"What do you mean, nothing?"

"Just that."

I decided to walk her at least up the stairs.

"Are you making fun of me?" I asked.

"I wouldn't risk that."

"You were laughing at us all evening."

"I beg your pardon!"

Her indignation pleased me. I imagined her room and her soft body under the lamp with the burned shade. I carefully tiptoed around the image of how I would spread the comforters on top of the mattresses, kick aside the plush teddy bear, pull the record player cord out of the socket, and place two coffee cups on solid saucers on the bench. I would place my hand on her white hip and smile in a conciliatory way so she could pardon me. My heart beat faster, because none of it seemed repulsive to me.

"I've seen through you, you wicked heart," she said. "Get out of here, you pig!"

I fled, and she chased me, laughing. I waited for her around the corner. She thundered on the cobblestones and pounced on me with her little blue fists.

"Your vain knocking reminds me of the storm we waited out under the tent," I said.

"But then you were afraid."

"Not because of the raindrops."

"Why?"

"Because of the lightning. Don't you remember how close it was?"

"I wasn't afraid."

"That's because I was afraid for you."

The bus took us above the city, and we walked down to the villa district where she lived. The moon came out, and its light was blending with the red fire of Slovnaft and reflecting itself in the clouds. For the first time since the moment she told me about Richard, the question of who I had been and who I was now did not bother me.

"Tell me something about it," I suggested.

"About what?" she asked quietly, because she knew very well.

"About what you were thinking when you were having tea with him and later when you were alone. Or on the way to my store."

It took a while before she made up her mind. She waited until the moon crawled behind the clouds.

"I don't know. I still don't understand why it developed that way."

"Did you know what you were doing?"

"I think I did. One thing I know for sure. I couldn't be unfaithful to you. I would leave you first."

"Did you consider that?"

"Yeah."

The notion that I had been selling pots without suspecting a thing, and looking forward to the half hour that we would spend having lunch took my breath away again. I was selling nails, hoes, and attachments, while she was holding my fate in her hands like a peeled orange she could toss in the garbage anytime she wished. I had been an idiot placed in her hands.

"Did you know that I didn't suspect a thing?"

"Yeah."

"Do you also know why it couldn't occur to me?"

"Yeah."

"It would be the same thing as if you were to ask me whether it made any sense to breathe, or to eat, you see?"

"I know, Milan."

"Then why, for Christ's sake!"

"I don't know. It scares me. I think I needed to risk our love to be able to enjoy it later."

"Ugh!"

We were silent, and I was trying very hard to understand all of the meaning of our misfortune.

"No matter what, as soon as you started you could finish only by hurting someone. Either me or him," I said.

"But by the time I realized that, it was too late."

"So that in the end, you've hurt us both."

I desperately wanted to ask her why she had decided for me, why she had told him that she wanted to be with me and not with him, but I was afraid.

"I know," she said sadly.

"What now?"

"I don't know."

"You know, Tania, I imagine life as a path with a series of cross-roads. (That's dumb, right?) The problem is, we can't go back. At the same time, there is no longer any such thing as the right path, because it is missing the crossroads that you could have passed. If you choose one route, others remain untried. After each crossroads you change and will never be the same. That's what I'm afraid of."

"That I've changed?"

"No. That I've changed."

I did not want our conversation to lead to such a highly banal point, but once I said it, I realized it was true. I kept silent then, and Tania was stunned. Her walk became uncertain, and I could sense in her brain the little corridors of nerve endings of her natural motion closing one after another: bang, bang, bang. For a few seconds a robot controlled intelligently, but sometimes imprecisely, walked next to me. Ah! I felt like shouting with full force, so angry was I with myself. I'd screwed up again!

We came to her house. Her mother had left the light on in the kitchen and was mumbling something to herself. To get to Tania's room, we had to pass through the kitchen.

I looked at Tania, and she seemed pale. But under the neon light, every face is pale.

"I don't feel good," she said.

"What happened?"

"Nothing. I don't know. My stomach hurts."

"Do you feel sick?"

"Yes." Inwardly I berated myself for my stupidity.

"Did you eat anything?"

"The same as you." It was true; we had had lunch together. (Richard had sat a few feet from us, I was hot from the fast ride on my bike, and I was praying that we would leave quickly.)

"Do you have any Gravol?" I asked.

"We do."

"Take at least three pills."

She nodded and looked at me like a sad doll that had forgotten how to walk. Her hair was falling into her eyes.

"Bye."

Her mouth was like a sponge: pleasantly soft and lifeless. I felt her touch even as I ran to the bus and wiped my lips with my coat sleeve.

On the other hand, my mother was doing fine in the hospital. She was wearing her orange robe, and she would go for a smoke in the doctors' room. She would write hopelessly sad letters to my father, and he would try to comfort her in letters that took a month to arrive.

"Do something, Mom. Do you want to wear yourself out before he comes back?"

146

"And you? What are you doing? How long are you going to bum around? A little bit of this, a little bit of that, and in the summer just bumming around?"

"That's no answer."

"You won't get another one. I don't want to live."

"You don't care about him? Or Peter, or me?"

"That's something else. Besides, you don't give a damn about me."

I had more fun with my mother these days than when the whole family was together, but it cost me more adrenaline. I used to drink coffee with her instead of with my father, and now that I lived at home alone, I realized how I missed the coffee. It occurred to me that I could drink it with Tania in our kitchen, if we did not screw up.

Mother asked me about the cat, and I had only bad news. Tomas could not reconcile himself to the loneliness and, out of despondency, was peeing all over the place. I could not clean the carpets fast enough, and I would growl in anger as he observed me from around the corner. Mother was happy. "He misses me," she said.

Otherwise, I found the empty apartment satisfying. I walked about barefoot trying to think. The cat, meanwhile, kept demanding attention, lying down in front of me on the floor and occasionally batting a tennis ball in my direction. I would kick it under the bed. My brother was in the army, keeping track of laundry and sabotaging proper military behavior. He kept writing level-headed letters. He was bothered by a pimple on his face and by his servitude, but it was clear to him that he was a soldier and that was that. At least for now. Father was stuck in prison, and he, too, was writing level-headed letters. He was bothered by the cold and by Mother's condition. It was harder for him. If he wanted, he could have cursed the day he ever got involved in subversive activities and ended up in prison. But I did not think he was doing that. It was surely clear to him that he was a jailbird, and such an obvious distinction cannot be overlooked. My mother was, then, the wife of my father and the mother of both Peter and myself, though I thought that was not enough for her and that was why she was suffering. In addition, she had diabetes and did not want to live. It is probably hard to carry on with a such a burden. I, originally a romantic young man, was selling kitchen appliances and hardware: a failed swimmer, athlete, and lover. Although I still didn't believe it myself, the facts were speaking loud and clear. If the world had been interested in me, that's how I would have appeared. I did not want to believe it. I thought it would be best to verify it with someone. However, I could not ask my friends, because they would not tell me the truth. Perhaps they didn't even know it, for that was the reason why they were my friends. I could not ask those who did not like me, because I didn't talk to them. And those who had nothing to do with me knew nothing about me.

When I was in the army, they once transferred me right at Christmas to another unit in which, besides the sentry and myself, there wasn't a soul. They gave me a trailer that some other soldiers had just vacated. I was allowed two hours to buy groceries to last me for three days, and then left alone in the trailer. I caught a frightful cold and a sore throat. I lay inside a sleeping bag and cooked with a hot plate. I suspected that it was cold in the trailer, because it was snowing outside. But I did not have a thermometer and could have been shaking just because of fever. I hoped that in reality it was warmer than it felt. I boiled tea, sweetening it from a sugar bowl left by the previous inhabitants. I longed terribly for hot tea, but every time I made it, it tasted like a laxative and I spit it out immediately. My head was cracking, I was breathing through my mouth, and my throat had turned to a painful wound. Again and again I would boil the tea, hoping that my taste buds had come around. And every time I would spit the tea out into the washing bowl. Only on the third day did I stick my finger into the sugar bowl and taste its contents. It was salt. There had been no one else there to drink tea with me and tell me, You idiot, it's salty!

Evidently, there was no one in the world who could tell me what I was like and whom I should believe.

"Tania," I said bitterly, looking out of the window onto the roofs of the buses as they crawled up the hill, vibrating from the effort and spraying the concrete wall with dirty snow. "What have you done to me?"

We continued walking together through the cold city, passing the same little streets a thousand times. Tania would slide her hand into my pocket to warm it there. I would recognize her hand among all the others in the world: a little paw resembling a child's hand ready—because of its immature clumsiness—to get messy with jam, whipping cream, or ink, a hand with bitten nails and round fingertips.

We arrived at the university library, but it was closed.

"What are we going to do? I don't even have money for tea," I said. The past few days I had been rifling through my old jeans to find some forgotten five-crown coins, but I had not found anything that day. I hadn't been so poor for a long time, since I was a little kid.

Tania was leaning against the wall.

We could have gone to my place. It was warm at home, and the cat was bored, but an empty and warm apartment threatens love-making. Ugh!

"I don't feel good," she said.

"Who feels good nowadays?" I mumbled. "In what way?"

"The same as last time."

"Your belly?"

"Yeah."

Suddenly she bit her lip, turned gray, and took a deep breath.

"What happened?"

"I don't know. It hurts," she said after a while, and slid down into a squat.

"Shall we go to the emergency room?" I asked, and was terrified when she nodded.

In the waiting room, heat and antiseptic embraced us. They were wheeling in a paralyzed old woman who reacted to her misfortune with an absent gaze directed to the ground. We were left alone.

"Well, come in," said the doctor, and Tania, bent to her waist, shuffled to him.

"And you?" he asked sarcastically.

"I'm healthy."

When I find myself unexpectedly alone without a book or newspaper, I get nervous. For two minutes I was saved by reading the stupid health regulations displayed on the wall, but then I found myself helplessly standing in the emptiness. In those moments I envy smokers. I tried to think. I was unfair to the members of my family. None of them would agree with my descriptions of them. And I had forgotten their main characteristic: their likeability. I like them. Obviously we like each other, I told myself. Or at least I think we do.

Tania came out even paler than before, but smiling.

"There is nothing wrong with me."

"And the pain?"

"Maybe there was none." Tania had been taught from childhood not to cry, and a family story says that she did not utter a sound even when they sutured six stitches into her head when she was five. They told her it was shameful to cry for such a trifle. Meaning that any pain is only as big as we make it. If they cut off her head, she would merely shrug her shoulders.

I must have looked at her murderously, because she said: "It's really gone."

"And what did they do with you for so long?"

"They asked me, for example, when I last menstruated."

The last time I had worried about her period was after the beautiful lovemaking when I returned from my two-day imprisonment. Since then she had her period twice. That was probably our last beautiful lovemaking, I reflected sadly.

"Last week!" I said.

"Yeah."

"And the appendix?"

"It's on the other side."

"So it did hurt you! Do you know where?"

"No, I don't know for sure." Every time I tried to attack, Tania escaped into a world without logic.

I had trouble falling asleep, and when I succeeded, nightmares and bad air woke me up. I opened the balcony window.

In the morning I could not take it anymore and moved my bed. On the carpet was the cat's shit, directly under the spot where my head lay. He knew it, the bastard. I wanted to tell Tania, but she was not picking up her phone. She sleeps like a drunk.

It was my day off, and in the morning I paced up and down the apartment, marching from one room to another with my head bent over, because that was how I had liked to think when I was on guard duty in the army. My hands were deep in the pockets of my warm-up pants. Understandably, I didn't come up with anything. I didn't have a head for that, it seemed, no matter how much I bent it.

At noon I gave up and went to see her. The little window on her door was opened, and through it I could reach the handle. I found Tania lying on a mattress, in a fetal position. She looked at me without a word.

"You sleep like a log," I told her. "One day someone'll burglarize you."

She shook her head feebly.

"I'm not sleeping. That was you?"

"I wanted to wake you up. The cat dumped his shit under my bed."

"I wasn't sleeping. I just couldn't make it . . . to the phone." She exhaled the last words the way the last bit of air escapes from an air mattress, and her eyes widened.

"For God's sake, what's going on? Is it the pain?"

She did not answer. I saw only how her eyes seemed to empty themselves as she focused wholly inside herself, feeling something that brought sweat to her brow. Anxiety filled the room, and I felt it penetrating me as well.

An hour later an emergency doctor arrived. He felt her and said, "It's a pinched nerve." He gave her an injection and vanished.

In the afternoon, her mother arrived with another doctor. He shook his head and said: "Hmm. Could be kidney colic. Let's wait and see." He gave her another injection and left another one to use if things got worse.

Her mother was on the phone in the next room. I could hear her deep voice as I sat by Tania, my leg falling asleep.

"Can you describe the pain?" I asked again and again. "Where exactly is it?"

She obediently thought about it, her eyes wandering around the room like those of a schoolchild getting ready to answer, but then she closed them, as if she were searching for a monster that was stomping inside her body and she were trying to follow its steps.

"At first, it hurt on the right side. Then . . . now it hurts all over the place," she said, and helplessly looked at me.

"How does it hurt?" I insisted. "Pinches? Bites? Burns? Pushes?"

"Pushes."

It was getting dark outside the window. A greenish pallor appeared on Tania's face, and black semicircles around her eyes became more defined. Because of fatigue or pain she stopped talking and managed to say only one thing: "Give me an injection."

I turned her on her stomach, took off the pajamas drenched in perspiration, rubbed alcohol on her behind that looked as if pain did not concern it at all, tempting and calm as always. I jabbed the needle in and pushed in the useless painkiller.

At night she kept closing her eyes in the childish illusion that this would make her sleep. Her mouth turned down in exhaustion, and some time before dawn it seemed to me she was dozing. I was terrified by her pain, because I could not imagine what it was like.

Jesus Christ, I said to myself, if I had a pain that had turned me green, I would scream, writhe, and crawl in rage. I would struggle even if it tore up my insides. But not this, not this helpless, passive lying, not this surrender that's destroying me because I don't understand it. What have I done to deserve this disaster? I asked myself. Anxiously, I reviewed Tania's illnesses. She would get them suddenly, and I had tolerated with a certain self-conscious stoicism their horrible forms. Once she was so completely swollen after taking penicillin that I had to involuntarily admire the ability of human skin to distend itself on such short notice. Sometime later she got foot-and-mouth disease, and her mouth was completely black because of some lotion, so that she looked like a witch.

It occurred to me that it might be profitable to pray. I didn't have enough imagination to be able to conceive a future better than the present, and therefore I seldom experienced disappointment. But that night I put all of my mental energy into the idea that she would get up in the morning with a smile, spend half an hour in the shower, and wolf down her breakfast in a half-opened robe.

However, the daylight brought with it only a strained face with a look of fear and a powerless silence. I took her into the bathroom. She was bent over like an old woman, and through the house echoed the energetic voice of her mother, burning up the telephone lines. That made me feel apathetic, and it seemed that Tania's pain sucked power from me to feed itself. We tried to pour some tea into her, but she just guiltily shook her head and asked for an injection.

"It does not help you," I said.

"Then a stronger one."

"Only morphine is stronger."

"Then morphine."

"That's enough," her mother announced. "We're going to the hospital."

We loaded her into the car; she was green from exhaustion. As I carried her in my arms into the waiting room, I remembered that the last time I carried her like that was on Sam's orders the summer before at the Castle. Then she had been very tan in her white summer dress and had locked her hands behind my neck.

I was left alone, for she hobbled between her mother and the doctor down the corridor and vanished around the corner. The sun shone on the tiles, revealing the unevenness of the glaze. I recalled that the day before it had also been sunny, and I had arrived in Tania's house with my coat unbuttoned. After all, it was March already, and so it was quite appropriate. Spring would pass, and it would be a year since they had imprisoned my father. His last letters had not passed the censor's sieve-like hand, so that I didn't know how many of his teeth were left. As a result, Mother was nervous and was fainting even in the hospital. Time is accelerating, I thought, perhaps exponentially. One year used to seem like a whole life. And I am only twenty-four. I will die in a moment.

"They're going to cut her up," Viera shouted from a distance. "They were feeling her all over, but she was very brave. They say it's appendicitis, but they will wait till evening." As she finished the last words, she sat down by me, and I saw how fatigue had overtaken her.

She almost fell asleep in the car, and when I stopped in front of the house, she said quietly: "We'll root for her this evening."

* * *

153

In the afternoon I called at Adam's, and Dana opened the door. I liked it when she answered the door, because she always smiled and intoned: "Hi. Come in."

I rested in the corner of the dark room and drank herbal tea from a familiar cup.

"So your woman has joined the ranks of the tin cans? At least she's gonna have that under her belt," Adam said.

"What do you mean?"

"In Europe today, they open up everyone at least once. Especially women. I don't know a single one who isn't cut up. At last Tania will join them."

"Don't worry, Milan," Dana said seriously. "Everything will happen the way it should."

"Exactly," I mumbled. "God knows what's in store for me."

They stood with me for a while in the hall as I put on my coat, and I thought all the way home (how can one say it?) how one is sometimes grateful for merely existing. By the time I got home, I realized that this feeling cannot be expressed in normal terms.

On the hillside behind our house the last snow had melted from atop the previous year's grass. I stood on the balcony and watched the twilight. Spring blasts across Bratislava like a thermonuclear explosion. One day it is suddenly warm, and there is an abundance of light. It makes people drunk; they reel in the streets. It is the only day of the year when you feel that if you were to take a bath in a fountain, the police would not show up and other people would enthusiastically plunge in with you. Such a day is due tomorrow, I told myself. But now the evening was beginning, and in the hall the phone rang.

"Hi, Peter!" Peter was on duty and had managed to cut through the jungle of wires with his military telephone all the way home.

"Hi. What's new?"

"Shit all. Mom is in the hospital, and so is Tania."

"What's happening?"

I gave him an explanation.

"And how are you?"

"I won't talk about that. But now maybe better off than you."

He was sitting in an overheated guardroom. I remembered the silence of those wakeful nights and the transcendent poverty of that life. I, too, had once had such a slow and lugubrious voice on the phone.

At ten, the phone rang for the second time. Maybe that's how it is supposed to be: shock arrives in growing waves, it pleasantly slows down thinking and muffles movement. For example, I sensed its first hot lick only after I put down the receiver.

"Well, hi," said Viera loudly. "It's all over."

"Well, great. Excellent."

"Don't get too happy yet. Do you know what it was?"

"No."

And then Viera spelled it out nice and slow.

"Ectopic pregnancy."

"No!"

"Yes indeed. At three months. It was as big as an orange. That's why there were the pains. Are you there?"

"Yeah."

"Take a pill. And we can visit her tomorrow at lunchtime."

I don't take pills, but I stumbled to my bed as if I had taken five of them. Besides, Mother had taken all of them with her.

I must have fallen asleep the moment I lay down. I just managed to spread my arms and legs, because I sensed the earth's gravity insistently pushing me down through the comforter. It was pushing me down with a childlike stubbornness. I was falling faster and faster, so that by the time sleep arrived, I recognized for a moment a feeling of nonexistence I used to have when I jumped off the diving tower at the Brick Field swimming pool. It always seemed that I'd never reach the pool.

I opened my eyes again when the reflection of the sun from the windows of the houses opposite shone on my eyelids. The cat was lying by my feet and staring at me.

I got up, but I did not go wash, because water washes off the dopiness from one's brain. I took from the radiator my training rags and put them on. The torn outfit was not yet dry, and I shivered from the moist cold.

With my remaining strength, I climbed to the top of a hill above the city, which was covered by a radiant haze and by smog that spread itself far beyond the last subdivisions, wrapping everything in a blinding cover. Only the shiny Danube was wholly visible as it meandered around the remnants of woods and the cranes of the port. I felt like crying because of the heat and my fatigue. My eyes were burning, and a dancing light penetrated into my head. The jog into which I switched was slower than a walk, but my body was rejecting even this compromise and screamed in revulsion. There has to exist a duality, because my soul smiled murderously and prepared its torture instruments.

I started through the Mountain Park, away from the city. In the shade of the hill it was cooler and I could see my breath. Past the Red Bridge I ran onto a traverse above the valley. My pulse and breathing became regular, and it was warm under my windbreaker. If my body had had an instrument panel, all the gauges would show the hands in the green zone of optimum operation. That was how I ran under the motionless ski lift. The countryside seemed abandoned, because the absurdity of the motionless objects left here by the people took the spirit out of Nature and turned it into a theatrical backdrop. I was running up Kamzík Mountain, where the athletes have a circular track. I once lost my way there and ran into the Malé Karpaty range. It was raining then, and I returned home after making a thirty-kilometer detour. Afterward I could not eat all day and shook with fever.

I stopped before the track, and when I stop I get a powerful emotional reaction. I was not ready for it, but warmed myself up with noisy exhalation. The sun was shining on me from above the bare crowns of the trees, and the old grass was warming up, still wet after the morning fog. I could feel it on my hands when I touched the ground as I bowed. I straightened out, and on the hills above the valley lay spots of snow in the shade of several overhangs.

"Enough of that. It's time," I said to myself when my heart slowed down, before the existential monsters entered me with the forest's silence.

"Jump for a little while, like so. Then exhale, hit the stopwatch, and let's go."

With the stream of cold air, the sweat on my brow cooled. I wrinkled my brow because of the chilling pain and concentrated on my breathing and heartbeat, so that I could run those ten kilometers while accelerating. That requires synchronizing the exhalation with every fourth step, collecting all the thoughts from the corners of my brain into the motor center, and harmonizing the movement of my body. It means leaning forward, relaxing the thigh muscles, the tendons around the knees, the ankles, and the fingers. Then you fix your head and gaze. When you feel that everything is running in an ideal fashion, and without disturbing the rhythm, you slowly release all your thoughts but one: accelerate the rhythm.

After three kilometers, a view of Rača and Krasňany opened up. I could not make out the houses, and suddenly understood that my vision was obscured by high blood pressure. I searched for the fatigue, but I realized that my legs were running easily, driven by adrenaline. I became afraid, because I sensed a distinct drumming in my temples, but my body kept accelerating.

At the fifth kilometer I stopped perceiving the calm indifference of Nature. The heretofore motionless trees started to melt into a dancing smudge with an admixture of flashes pounding my pulsating brain into a neurotic knot of spasms. The back of my head was freezing, and my neck was locked. My body probably went insane. It switched the exhalation by itself to every third step, flew down the forest path in a crazy escape, thundered into the ground the thoughts disturbed by pain.

There, where the traverse falls and the path is cluttered by fallen leaves, somewhere into the sixth kilometer, I separated. My legs worked in a murderous tempo and by themselves selected the road, which was mysteriously sketched into my memory; they were overheating and burning while my powerless brain, flooded by the roaring blood, cowered in confused astonishment. And then it stopped struggling. Sometimes I go to sleep. I remember nothing of the next two kilometers except that I met a huge crowd, a line-up of men, all of them looking at me and extending their hands to me in a friendly fashion.

"What do you want from me?" I asked them.

"Nothing. It's just that we . . . ," they said, and then grew serious, even sad.

"But she didn't die!"

"No . . . no," they stressed, but their heads nodded seriously, slower and slower, and then vibrated and smudged until only a spotted stain remained of them against the white light. That stain turned into Tania's smiling face.

"Do you know you could have died?"

"Died?" she laughed. "You little fool. Why?"

"Because of me. I almost killed you."

"Get out of here! Ha, ha, ha!" In my head sounded a rhythmic laughter.

"I really did. First I poured a time bomb into you, and then I walked around the world asking myself idiotic questions such as Who am I? and What am I supposed to be? That's how it is."

"Come now, my dear old man, don't be silly."

"But those are the facts!"

The rest of the dialogue vanished in the delayed echo, as when you pull the plug on a record player.

Silent pictures followed. They rolled over each other lazily, as if projected by a drunken operator. I wanted to know the inner logic of this selection, if there was one. I saw Adam as he ran after me through the square in Warsaw with a rucksack on his back. Right afterward, I was sitting with Peter and my mother in the courtyard, and my father was watching us from behind the table, holding his tooth in his hand. Mother was entering the lake, and Tania was holding me by the hand. Dana had the painful smile of Our Lady on her face, and she blossomed, racing with the time. Then on a radiant summer day I saw the flash of Eman's glasses, and Sam was carrying Tania on his shoulders, and so it went. Ugly flowered sets of pots grimaced from the shelves, I had lunch with Tania, and Richard was sitting across the table. That was how I saw the time that marked the change. That was how I had thought of it until Tania's operation the night before. I had secretly hoped to understand its meaning. But I may have been right when I said at the outset that wisdom not only reflects reality but analyzes it and then synthesizes it again.

I noticed that the circle was finished, because the rhythm of my legs—transmitted to my brain in the form of a wild drum roll—changed to harsh beats, and I understood that I was jumping downhill on a narrow path full of roots and was amazed at this hazard. My exhausted ankles threatened to slip their joints at any instant, and my knees protested with a stabbing pain in the meniscus.

I hit the valley, which was flooded by a penetrating light. I gasped for air, as my lungs were refusing to inhale the heat. My chest was wheezing, and I ran for a terrible ten seconds blind, wrapped in a red mist that steadily thickened. I was missing oxygen and shivering all over my body. Thank God, my legs felt the asphalt: one feels safe on it, as if you're running along a conveyer belt. Slowly, my breath and sight returned to me.

One more kilometer and three minutes and it will be over, whispered my brain to my legs, after it finally came to. Ahead of me glistened the fishing pond. The asphalt road along the pond was strewn with old foliage, reminding me of autumn. My face must have been marked by fatigue and crying. I couldn't tell if I was crying *from* exhaustion or *over* my exhaustion. The same thing would happen to me years ago in the swimming pool when I had used up my last reserve of strength pushing through the heavy water. A stabbing pain was tearing my shoulders apart.

From a distance I must have resembled a man charged with electricity. A spasm of revulsion yanked me out of my rhythm and threw me high into the air. It forced out of me a desperate yelp that lit the fuse of my remaining energy and drove me sprinting through what became a horrible stretch of road. For the old foliage turned to frogs. As I approached them, the horror concentrated my vision, and I saw big toads, green-brown with immovable eyes, as they lazily hopped along the warm asphalt. This time they were double-headed monsters with goggle eyes, because they had made on that fateful day the decision to mate. Each female toad carried on her back her male, who held on to her like a child. They breathed together, shining, glued to each other, hopping into the sun.

Then I saw the car. It approached mercilessly. I had no time to close my eyes or stop my ears: there was the slapping sound of popping under the tires and out flew pink entrails as the glued bodies exploded, slippery flesh quivered, and little tails of intestines stuck to the road.

Before I managed to look under my feet, I slipped on something

soft, and from under my Marathon shoes I heard a loud "Aaah!"
My stomach reacted by spraying my mouth with bile. It sprayed
out, together with saliva that suddenly filled my mouth and flew out
with a shout. Revulsion and horror catapulted me up and ahead; my
eyes flooded with tears, so that I couldn't see a thing. I had never
suspected frogs to be capable of producing such a grievous sigh. I
flew down this horrible zone of sex as one bereft of senses. Again I
fell on a soft mound, and again there was the same sigh. "My God!"
I shouted through the tears. "Enough, enough!"

I was kneeling on a bench, my head and arms suspended over
the back of it. I had seen exhausted horses in the movies. They lay
on the ground, shaking their heads. I understood now that this was
the only possible motion, and I shook my head listlessly about everything that remained in me. I refused to open my eyes, move my
hand, or think about anything, because I felt bad and sensed that
evil was out to poison me.

However, while we are alive, something always goes on, and so
my legs began to shake, demanding relief, and I had to get up and
allow them to walk, even though I still couldn't see a thing and my
head kept falling backward. After a while I opened my eyes with
astonishment and moaned with relief as my furious blood, which
until then had torn away all feeling as it rolled on, settled down,
beginning to flow in the original riverbed. I looked around victoriously, rising from the dead, and walked toward a forested hillside
onto which the sun was pouring out its light. The grass was warming me up from below, but I still saw a bit too much radiant red
and was again playing a corpse with outstretched hands.

Right below my nose grew a snow drop. I removed it and then
collected others as well. On the way home, my body jogged freely.
In my mind I could only guess the delicious laziness with which it
must have brought me to the Mountain Park and to the top of the
hill from which I could have seen the city gone mad with sudden
frenetic activity, had not my thoughts been elsewhere.

The walls of the apartment were not yet warm, and so I crawled
out of it into the street like a bear from his den. I was overwhelmed
by the heat and light, frozen though I was, and stumbled to the bus
stop, weak as a fly that had crawled out of a crack under the window

where it had waited out the winter. People were smiling, surprised by the sun, holding their overcoats in their hands.

On the bare crowns of the few trees in the hospital park, sparrows chirruped noisily, and two ambulant patients in blue robes sat tentatively on a bench. They wore slippers on their feet, and they had on sunglasses. I almost laughed, but then noticed white gauze behind the dark lenses.

Tania was lying on her side, leaning on her elbow. Her pajama top, held together with a single button, was delightfully revealing. I felt a strong desire to stick my nose under that top to get closer to the body underneath, to smell its antiseptic fragrance. I even kneeled down to do it, but I did not and instead kissed her cracked lips, sensing the all-knowing smiles of the thrombotic old ladies behind my back.

"I love you," I whispered in her ear, and she responded by smiling cheerfully, as if, the day before, it had been someone else they had almost severed in half.

Gin

"I'm not going to the concert," Tania said, shaking her head. "I've had it with those bouncers after last night."

She was right. At the jazz festival, the same people always checked the tickets, but they got meaner every year. Not long before, it would happen that around 10 P.M. they would give in to the patient little bunch that had been waiting outside and open the glass doors into the hall of the Cultural Center. But for some reason the bouncers had stopped doing that and had even turned into diehard enemies of us jazz fans. I felt that they hated us, especially those of us who couldn't keep up with the rising price of tickets and depended on their charity or at least their indifference.

The night before, someone had said that you could get inside from the adjacent hall, which was unguarded, and then go through a broken window at the back of the sloping auditorium.

"I'll try it tonight. For at least one last time," I said to Tania, and kissed her good-by.

The Danube rolled noiselessly along in its bed, reflecting the lights of the few neon signs on one of its banks. Sometimes, when I was in the mood, I could sense its aroma and majesty and accept for a moment that the river lends the city some luster—particularly when aided by black jazz musicians.

At the right wing of the building some trees were growing, and they shaded the windows of the neighboring hall. I climbed up the lightning conductor to the gutters and slipped through the toothy hole, obviously produced the previous night at someone's request. I found myself in a huge dark empty space. I was cheered by its respectful silence and sat down in a chair to listen. From the distance, from behind the walls, a bass guitar reached me. My feet and fingertips vibrated with it. But the doors into the hall that connected me to the music were locked. The bouncers had wised up. Disappointed, I sat down on the stairs and resisted with annoyance the temptation to go home. I couldn't care less about the music, but that guitar bothered me. I don't actually understand music, but I react to it the way fish react to a flashlight: I know nothing about it, but it attracts me. I can't tell major from minor, and our music teacher forbade me to sing when my class rehearsed the national anthem. Only once did I ever have a musical instrument in my hands—when they handed me a triangle to keep time. In a sense music is my enemy because it humiliates me, dominates me more than is right, persuades me that I'm better, then stops and leaves me alone.

I went down the aisle to the empty stage in order to try out the boards. Along the sides behind the curtain I found an armature reaching up to the roof, and I climbed it, but the door to the attic had no handle, maybe on purpose.

The bouncers got drunk, their watchfulness declined, but they remained sober enough to block the entrance with their bodies. I was waiting with a little group of fans some thirty feet from the entrance when inside me contempt began to well up. We all looked so proud and indifferent, but our presence and posture displayed humiliation. It started to rain. Enraged, I put on my hood and was getting ready to leave when I noticed that someone was opening a smaller door away from the main entrance. He motioned to us, and we moved silently toward him. I entered the lobby so easily that it felt unnatural. Things like that never happen to me.

The bass guitar was still playing. I couldn't hear it properly, but I could feel it with my whole body and in the roots of my hair. The aggressive saxophone attacked me quite openly, and I had to lean against the column to be able to bear it.

"Hi, how did you get in?" A friend of mine, someone I often bump into at jazz concerts, slapped me on the back.

"By a miracle," I answered.

"I saved the cost of a ticket as well. Let's get a drink instead."

He gave me two drinks, and while I was downing the first, the second paper cup started leaking: the wine drained into my hand and forced me to drink what was left in a gulp.

We stood in a circle of friends. Jazz is a bit like a secret code. It attracts a certain kind of person, including those who have no great knowledge of music, like myself. I always see the same faces as in the film clubs and every other place else that smacks of art. Once recently, my friend Timothy had clutched his head in despair and wailed: "I'm forty, and for the last decade I've wandered all over Bratislava without meeting a single new person. It's monstrous! I know every stone, every face. I know everything about everybody, and everybody knows everything about me. We have nothing to tell one another, nothing to look forward to. I'm going mad!"

That offended me a bit. After all, I was fairly new at jazz festivals, and Timothy and I had known each other barely three years. But I understood him. We didn't have much to say to each other. No one had anything really interesting to say anymore.

The bass and saxophone were replaced by crazy drums. Everyone had been waiting for them, and the lobby emptied in a few seconds except for myself and a few other people. From our circle only a black-haired girl with silver earrings remained.

"I'm Nora," she said.

She looked a bit older than I. I raised my eyebrows.

"I don't think we've met."

"But I know you."

"Me?" I shook my head. "Why would you know me?"

She shrugged her shoulders and lit a cigarette.

"Why did you light up? I want to hear the drums."

"So why don't you go on in?"

"Because a woman shouldn't smoke alone."

"So wait here with me. After this I have to go home. My girl-friend is baby-sitting my kids."

She wore a dark skirt and a blouse with buttons. Her clothes were inappropriate—too proper—but in her elegance there seemed to be more than snobbish defiance. She kept smoking and looking me over with a disquieting sentimental look that I thought appropriate for a fifteen-year-old. They fire all their guns at once, unaware of the destructive power they have.

"If you didn't come to hear the drums, you shouldn't have come at all," I said.

"I'm doing all right." She smiled suddenly and grew astonishingly beautiful.

"Give me your hand."

"What do you mean?"

She took a pen out of her purse, grabbed my hand, and wrote down her telephone number on it.

"This is my office number. Call me."

"What office?"

"I'll tell you later. Go listen to your drums."

Such arrogance, I thought. Nobody was going to offend me with such banalities.

In the washroom a pathetic-looking young man was vomiting, and someone had done the same in the sink. I held my breath and rubbed my scribbled-on hand under the tap.

The drummer's black shoulders glistened with sweat, and I worried that he would collapse with fatigue. He stopped at one o'clock. My legs were hurting from standing so long, and when I realized that I had only four hours left for sleep, I cursed jazz down to its tenth generation.

Down through the skylight flowed a gray light from the heavens, a promise of a new day I didn't want to live through. I wanted to stay in bed even at the price of death. Tania's naked arm began in a roundish shoulder sticking out from the quilt, and I knew that it should have reminded me of the previous night's lovemaking. But it only inspired envy. I envied Tania her immobility at the same time I was glad she was sleeping, because in the morning I was like an animal that, expecting its end, crawls into a corner. I allowed myself only the Viennese news, because it did not come from this world, and the female broadcaster's voice smelled of Colgate toothpaste and hot Nescafé Gold, for which I had neither time nor money.

I melted my congealed blood by walking to my trolley-bus stop, and melancholy cleared my head. I inhaled the fog and smelled the sulfur—my ally against my life. I bought my morning paper, which

I would certainly forget to read, attached myself to a post on the bus, and for a moment looked into Pepina's eyes. She sat on the sidewalk waiting for me to call, though we both knew it would never happen. As the doors began to hiss, she lowered her tail, sniffed my tracks in embarrassment, and followed them home.

My hungry stomach was challenged by well-known brands of perfumes, and I watched with admiration the carefully painted faces of women. I knew that was not allowed: these faces were not painted for me, nor for the bus. They were for carpeted offices with well-shaved men. They bridged the morning transit hour with an immobility as, insectlike, they faked a momentary death. I admired their vitality, their ability to start the day in front of the mirror, and so I peeked at them out of the corner of my eye with respect, so that I wouldn't disturb the illusion of their absence, so that they wouldn't find out that this time, too, belonged in their reality.

At the endloop, the trolley bus began to dance on the rolled-up asphalt, shaking my bones and upsetting a painted lady.

"Is this what we are paying for?" she complained, while fishing with pins for the stray little snakes crawling out of her hairdo.

The building I walked toward had been built in the Art Nouveau style, but the decorative stucco around the windows was knocked off a long time ago. They had patched it up with plaster and tin, and the only thing left of the Art Nouveau was the old elevator, which was regularly out of service, and the wet spots on the fourth floor that burst through the new paint like an indestructible fresco.

The nurses would suntan on the roof in the summertime. Once, when I went up to check for the origin of the water leak, I discovered Judith lying naked on the cracked tiles.

"It's cloudy," I apologized, and slowly she turned over on her stomach.

"What is it with you—one more naked broad?"

"You're right. Nothing," I snapped back, annoyed because I had wanted to take a look at the city but now couldn't. I liked to look at the sculptural ensemble of the chimneys in the distance. There was a burning match in the middle, and yellow-brown smoke rose from them. From a slender waist it would grow mightily in its shoulders to embrace us all lovingly. It was fatally horrible and beautiful—

more beautiful than Judith. The roof was cracked like the bottom of the dry arms of the Danube. Someone had tried to caulk the cracks with asphalt, but he interrupted the job halfway through, and the moss finished it up for him. The water could have chosen any of a thousand paths, but it persistently leaked into the obstetrics ward.

The ceiling of my room on the main floor was slanted, following the stairs. It shared one wall with the elevator and another with the telephone room. My cubicle was noisy like an intersection. I could hear the hurried clicking of heels over my head. From the right, the breakfast trays creaked into the elevator, which dragged them upstairs, catching its breath. From the left came the rattle of the telephones, as if the hospital were calling for help to the end of the world.

I took a deep breath and suspended myself from the heating pipe. I stretched my shoulder joints and twisted my head until I heard my vertebrae crack. Then I jumped down, made a few squats with the oxygen bomb around my neck, and listened to hear if my heart was thumping angrily in my chest. Then I put on my green surgical shirt and tied my waist underneath with a wide belt.

To enter this world in the morning was about as pleasant as jumping in the lake in December. One could train oneself to do it, but to make it really work, you would need gills.

I entered the corridor with the certainty that come evening time I would be half an inch shorter. You see, my job was to lift bodies: slender ones that carefully watched their diets, others wasted by illness, and two-hundred-pound broads who were too big to carry. They had short rhinoceroslike legs, and a sack of flour was a tiny handbag compared with them.

But Pista *bacsi*, Uncle Pista, showed me how to handle them. He would stop with his stretcher next to the victim's bed as she looked at him in horror. In that moment she probably cursed all the pastries and schnitzels she had ever eaten, because now they threatened her life. If only she could have avoided that satyrlike, shrimpy man's embrace! "I'll walk myself," she would blurt out, and try to support herself with her hand. But her sutured belly betrayed her, and she would limply fall back. "Have no fear, my lady. Hold on to me here," Pista *bacsi* would say, and bend to her as if to whisper something confidential. She would take hold of him in resignation, grabbing him around his neck, which he offered her. This gesture was the embodiment of the humility of two ordinary people who did not feel anything toward each other. Yet for a single moment they had no other choice but to get close. I liked that gesture so much that I decided to stay.

Since then I have held in my hands hundreds, even thousands, of women, and I have never tired of that moment. On the contrary, it is like a drug to feel the shiver of absolute closeness, pure and innocent, though with a ticklish realization of transgressing some unknown limit. This strange world, this strange country into which I was born, allowed me that transgression. Otherwise it would have been impossible to put in motion such a fireworks of intimacy, which led the chambers of emotions to explode one after the other in order to submerge, thereafter, into the darkness, the emptiness. The only key to these fireworks was the employment contract. It opened the door to the empire of women, the empire of suffering that, together with chloramine, saturated the air. A person could only sense, with irritation, the presence of destinies hovering in the draft. They flew over the heads of the women in blue robes, and the women, though they sensed them and searched for them, could not catch their odor. No one would reveal their destinies to them, though a few people did know. Even I knew some fragments of the future mosaic. But I forbade myself to interfere by word or action, in part because I did not dare to distinguish good from evil, but mainly because I wanted to stay to one side. I had always stayed to one side, and the only space I truly was completely "in" was Tania.

So I only smiled at them and took their hands into mine, and it worked miraculously. They would squint like cats, and the more sensitive ones would press my hand against their face or breast. Almost all the middle-aged women had a son like me, or a daughter they would immediately have given me to marry. Motherhood was a suppressed passion that broke out in that setting. The women wanted to keep me with them when, the day after the operation, I moved them before daybreak into their beds. They didn't want to stay alone with the pain in their sewed-up belly or with the uncertainty that would emerge in them. I smiled at them and babbled away about recuperation, for which I was not responsible, since I was not a doctor. We could link each other's fingers intimately like the lovers that we did indeed become for a moment when she lay in my hands naked, embracing me around the neck. Before falling to sleep, her eyes would look up at me as if asking for help. What was a touch of fingers compared with what I knew about the body whose insides I had seen in a way her own husband never could?

Later she would stop me in the corridor with a carefree, confidential look, like a girl who, after a declaration of love, throws off her bashfulness with relief. She would look straight into my eyes and perhaps caress my hair. I accepted this game because it was simple and undemanding. I would smile and press their hot hands. Almost all were feverish after the operation. At the same time, their frankness, that echo of the emotion that had jumped between us like an electric arc when I carried them to the table, that echo disturbed me. That was because their faces hardly reminded me of anything; they were merely faces in a crowd of a hundred others. It disturbed me that they remembered and I did not. It led me to think that I was a professional, that maybe I already belonged with those who so much like to "work with people." But I had never wanted work like that. I was always surprised that I was paid. The supervisor did not like me, because on payday I unconsciously avoided her and she had to guard my money until she caught me or until I plucked up enough courage to overcome my embarrassment and ask for payment for work that should not be work.

Maybe I did not remember their faces because they were all in that moment wrapped in the uniform of fear—fear stronger than the perfume or make-up that they were not allowed to use. They were not allowed to paint their nails or eyelids or lips. Everything would be checked by a female anesthesiologist who made sure that those lips, symbols of feminine beauty, originally rosy, did not turn blue after the anesthetic.

The plaintive squeak of my white sandals on the shiny linoleum disturbed the patients at their breakfast. They looked at me so intently that I decided to say hello and wish them a nice breakfast to

169

assure them that the meaning of that squeak would not worry them all day. Faces shining with smiles, they made snide remarks behind me. Every morning I felt like a woman facing a horde of men: suddenly I felt absolutely defenseless against the majority of their sex. Serves me right, I thought, and overcame a sudden urge to run to my room, curl up in a corner of my bed, and bury my head in a pillow.

I pressed the door handle and found myself in an abandoned room. Only the bed by the window was occupied. Mrs. Lukas was lying there, hungrily awaiting my arrival.

"Good morning," I said cheerfully.

"Ah, here you are," she greeted me without smiling. "You've come for me with the stretcher. I'm really glad, because my legs are shaky."

"Mine too," I said, trying to stop her from telling me about her fate. I saw in her feverish black eyes that she had been waiting for me, so as to burden me with it before her operation. I wanted to give her an opportunity to escape into a joke—not because her fate did not interest me, but because I had nothing to give her in return.

"But not from hunger in my case," she said, shaking her head and grabbing the hem of my shirt. "Tell me, will you be with me the whole time? I'm afraid that something's going to happen. Promise me that you'll stay with me!"

"I will," I answered, omitting to say that my presence would make no difference whatever.

She grabbed me by the hand and buried her long nails into my palm. When I sat down on the edge of the bed, I was warmed by the heat radiating from her bedcover. I saw her round dark eyes up close and her surprisingly innocent, thick eyebrows, which had never known the beautician's tweezers.

"Don't think I want to . . . I screwed everything up. My husband has no idea, he doesn't even know I had an abortion, and I won't ever tell him. He always wanted a second child. But I didn't know whether it was his, if you know what I mean. Do you understand? I fell in love with someone else, but he didn't want the child if he couldn't be sure. It was horrible . . . God, I'm so dumb! I could be giving birth today, and instead they're going to gut me. They said that something from the little one stayed in there and, because of that, I'm rotting all over. It's his revenge for my doing this to him, I know it. Oh, I'm so afraid, I really am!"

She spat these words at me as if afraid that I wouldn't hear her out. As I gradually understood what she was saying, my compassion grew, and I was flooded with tenderness, with sweet pity for her lot. When I think about it, I realize I was flooded with love. Under my fingertips I felt the velvety skin of her face. I wanted to convey that I was at that moment entering the depths of her unhappy soul and at the same time to hint at the evanescence of that moment of cosmic intimacy, but she snatched my hand and bit my thumb. We peered intensely into each other's eyes, and in hers I read despair and passion. Passion is a gift, wherever it comes from, and attracts me so strongly perhaps because I have never felt its destructive power. A wave of passion could never wash away those sober thoughts that corrode the brain like poison. Now she was flowing into me through the hot tenderness of her mouth; she was addressing me with the desperate, merciless pressure of her perfect teeth. Desperate, because I was her last witness.

A shiver ran through me, and everything disappeared. She let go of my hand, and her head sunk into the pillow.

My sandals squeaked and the wheelchair squealed as we passed the cafeteria where the women at breakfast were waiting for us. They waved to us, raising their fists, lucky thumbs up. It was strange: the patients changed, but the ritual stayed the same. As always, some arranged themselves in two rows, and as we passed between them, they stroked Mrs. Lukas' wet face as though she were on an assembly line, and whispered incantations.

In the operating room the nurse was banging the instruments, arranging them on a sterile cloth into an abstract pattern whose significance, meaning, function, and even aesthetics were understood only by us. It was strange: the nurses and patients changed, but the picture remained identical; the same instruments spread out on a table according to the same code that had evolved into an absolute functionality.

When the room filled with the sonorous voices of the surgeons and the thunder of running water, her trembling stopped, as she

171

softened in exhaustion and gave herself to me. I felt that I was removing from her life the graceful beauty and radiance that was hidden in her semichildlike body, a body that seemed not to have the time to mature. Her breasts were childish, her belly smooth, and if it had been up to me, I would have forgiven her sins.

But what do I know about sin? Sin is the victory of that mysterious power that suppresses moral will. It is a victory over reason, because morality is naturally rational. My mind tells me that to be moral, to be good, is the only thing in my life that has any significance and meaning in relation to death. Sin and stupidity belong to each other like Siamese twins, and that enables me to feel sorry for evil people because they are stupid. I'm more afraid of stupidity than sin, and when I say that I'm innocent, I also mean that I'm rational. I'm innocent in the sense that I don't have pangs of conscience and I don't sin. But to tell the truth, I'm getting suspicious. I'm beginning to fear that my judgment is faulty. If I start to believe that I'm not innocent, and despite that, have no pangs of conscience or even a latent consciousness of sin, it would necessarily have to mean that I'm simpleminded, even stupid!

If that's really what I'm like, then this unfortunate circumstance has been caused by a fate that has always placed me in the role of the one who has been wronged. Not long ago Tania mentioned that she had run into a certain lady downtown who had known her from childhood. When Tania told her whom she had married, the lady gasped, "You mean that ill-fated boy?" I was offended, but really she was right. Ever since I can remember, everyone has pitied me for the injustices done to me. When they refused to accept me at secondary school, my homeroom teacher burst into tears and asked for early retirement. The more unjust it got, the more innocent and pure I felt, and up to now no one, including myself, has been able to find the tiniest fault with me. Maybe all these people are stupid and the government alone is right. Government employees have always told me that I've gotten what I deserved and that they've seen through me since I was fifteen. Maybe they've seen the future sins of which I'm still unaware.

While I meditated on such matters, Mrs. Lukas became a mannikin handled by window dressers. One of them took forceps with an antiseptic-drenched tampon and inserted it into her crotch. The smooth belly undulated, reacting against this violence, but a few seconds later everything was back to normal. It was as if the Cyclops had opened his deranged eye for a moment and then immediately closed it so that only the elect could see that he had, for an instant, caused the planetary axis to deviate. Alas, I do not belong among them. The undulations seemed normal to me, for I've seen enough evidence that human tissue under anesthesia follows the same physical laws as any other matter.

Besides, perhaps it is the mission that determines the character of an act. It may seem only to me that the surgeon's hand that elegantly wields the scalpel along the warm, smooth skin and leaves behind a gaping abyss in the belly feels a delight it should not feel. But maybe I imagine it, because I, too, would like to trace the line. I even catch myself being envious when I see that hand in a thin rubber glove dip into the hot, red depths and splash around. I, too, would like to transgress the norms of nature and ethics in the name of good.

I waited until they enlarged the hole with clamps, and then I moved a little ladder to the table. I peered down into Mrs. Lukas' belly, but instead of the pink pear of the uterus and the two nutlike ovaries I saw only a black clot.

"All this has got to go," declared the surgeon. "This isn't a uterus, it's mud."

And so Mrs. Lukas' sex appeal was transferred together with her ovaries and uterus into a bowl that I held in my hand and from which some tiny bit would be examined by a pathologist and the rest thrown into the garbage can.

She was exhausted as I wheeled her back; she had lost two pints of blood. Her faded lips were trembling, her shoulders shook with cold, her face was distorted from an intubation tube, and her groin was empty. The women were waiting for us in the hall and silently accompanied us to the intensive care room. They moved along the space between the two sanctuaries that were also waiting for them, but in the meantime these were places as unapproachable and mysterious to them as an Incan temple. I was one of the guardians of these mysteries, and that tickling realization made me nervous. The world is filled with sealed messages and doors with seven locks for one reason only: so that we may forget the mysteries that genuinely exist. One evening I took some patients to the operating room and rejoiced in their rapture as the mystical fear began to leave them, as one after another they tried out the operating table and started to giggle and smell the bomb filled with laughing gas. Unfortunately, they woke up nurse Otilka, who threw them out in a fury and complained to the head doctor, with the result that I lost my bonus and my keys.

I understood Mrs. Lukas when she did not want to regain consciousness. But the anesthesiologist slapped her marked cheeks so that she finally opened her atropinized eyes, looked at me, and probably read from mine what I was supposed to hide, because she soon closed them again, and I decided to leave.

Misfortune has a special odor that excites my nostrils, and I never mistake it for anything else. In contrast, I find happiness suspicious, because I recall its aroma only when it's gone, and so have doubts about its earthly provenance. But misfortune, pain, and horror I recognize without the slightest doubt. If I'm unhappy and afraid, I know I am. These feelings are an umbilical cord connected to sheer existence. I follow misfortune like a hunting dog. I trace its carriers, because they're closer to naked reality. Perhaps I hope that they will lead me there.

It is a mockery of fate that I'm so healthy. My health is like armor, like a diving suit. I cultivate it and keep it running like a good motor. I take it for a spin in the woods and let it run in high gear to circulate the oxidized blood through all the pipes, down to the tiniest capillary. But recently I've somehow been too careful not to black out, and when I feel my fingers going numb and my ear drums popping and the first dose of acid from my upset stomach hitting my mouth and my temples getting the first knock with a hammer, I'm not provoked as before, but just the opposite—I'm warned. So I obey and slow down, and in order not to allow my soul the slightest dissatisfaction at not getting anywhere that day, I immediately spit.

In such health I entered the intensive care room that evening, wanting to take Mrs. Lukas by the hand and descend with her into the depths of her horror, to stay there with her and feel for a moment that we were like the last two people at the end of the world. Her eyes were moist, and she looked at the ceiling. The light bulbs bleached her face, and the liveliest object in the room was the IV bottle, with its bubbles of air climbing one by one to the surface. I was standing by her, wondering whether I should call for Luba, when she finally moved, turning her black eyes to me. If I were more of a romantic, I'd swear I saw them flash.

"You've come to comfort me. That's nice of you. What are you going to say to me? Not to take it so seriously? So what if I'm dry? We've got Vaseline, don't we? Get lost!"

She could have torn her stitches with that shout. I ran out into the hall and heard her stifling her sobs with her fist.

There is one more peripheral area left in Bratislava. All the other suburbs of its bombinating body have been chewed up, pulverized by the big teeth of hungry excavators painted yellow and red. Behind their backs remained artificial hills, burial mounds on which weeds and little trees grow today. Then they spit out cement blocks on the ground and washed their hands. It remained at last to name them. In this country, anything, be it a thing, a city, or a person, begins to exist only after it is named. And here I bow in honor of a grand joke worthy of a king. I will never tire of this joke, and my diaphragm is always vibrating when I pass by on the bus through these new subdivisions with their delightful names redolent of natural tradition: "Meadows," "Marshes," "Corners," "Woods."

That last suburb is called Trnávka, or Dornkappel. It originated in the twenties, when the city gave the land to immigrants, allowing each family to erect a brick shack at the back of a lot with the condition that ten years later, when they were established, they would build a decent house up front, facing the street. But ten years later the war came, and all the contracts were void. The shacks are still standing there, disappearing behind the fruit trees, and in the front, facing the street, are huge bushes of roses full of thorns instead of decent houses. The immigrants grew old; they sit, tired, on the benches and mumble in Hungarian. Their children have vanished to new concrete apartments, and "house for sale" advertisements appear with increasing frequency in the papers.

On a certain Saturday morning I found an advertisement like

that in the papers. I phoned Tania, and we made the trip on bicycles. I had never been to Trnávka before. The children divided the street with chalk lines and played a ball game. A little Gypsy sat on the sidewalk, holding a puppy on her lap. The plum tree alley was just blossoming, and sweet juice sprayed down to the asphalt from the branches. The May sun and fragrances enchanted us, and the factory chimneys were hiding behind the trees. An east wind was blowing, and in the garden the buyers were already standing around, whispering curt comments among themselves. One of them carefully tried to move a fence post, and another was scratching with a nail the cracked stucco of this low house. Water marks trailed down from the windows, and an elderly gentleman was standing on a ladder, checking the gutters and sighing about the roof.

Everyone was overshadowed by the distinguished crown and leathery leaves of a big walnut tree. Its trunk separated right above the ground into two, and both forks leaned away at dangerous angles so that I felt that an acrobatic feat was being performed for our entertainment.

"Look," I said, grabbing Tania by the hand. "Let's buy this tree!"

We entered the house through the kitchen and went on into a single room where a woman in black, her lower lip extended, stood ready to cry.

"Are you selling the house?" I asked.

"Yes," she said sadly. "Do you want to buy it?"

Tania pressed my hand, and I just nodded, dumbfounded with terror, as I knew we had no money.

In the end our house seemed unbelievably big compared with the little package of borrowed money for which we exchanged it. I walked around the garden and measured how many steps I could make on my own land. I settled into the crown of the walnut tree, amazed that even that height was ours, that we had bought space that extended upward and actually now belonged to Tania and me.

Because of the heat Tania went barefoot, wearing only my T-shirt, which reached down to her behind. It was enough for her to stop under the tree for me to climb down like a trained gorilla.

Then we would make love on a wooden floor smelling of wax. From a framed wedding photograph that we found in the woodshed and hung on the wall, a man and a woman from the 1930s looked at us. They had built the house and spent their entire life in it. The woman was beautiful and tender, and the man looked a bit like a soldier or a civil servant. But they say he had lost all his property drinking and gambling in a Budapest tavern and that she married him regardless. She moved from Budapest with him, leaving her family behind, and began, as well as ended, her life in Trnávka with this man who was said to have been a good man, though he could not build houses.

I found that out the next morning, the first of my necrophiliac mornings. I woke up between unknown walls and into a space screaming at me that it wanted to be fixed, rebuilt, remodeled, and right now. The insecurity pushed me out of the sleeping bag, and while Tania slept, I walked about the house, noticing there was no bathroom, only a sink in the kitchen, and the village toilet was serving its last days. The windows were coming apart so that one couldn't close them, and the floor in the kitchen was rotting. My bare legs sank into it.

I recalled how a long time ago, in primordial times, I'd learned the pipe fitter's trade and thus should have known how to make a water line and plumbing for an ordinary toilet. But I had erased that knowledge from my memory, because it was connected with something I wanted to forget. I wanted to forget the 1970s, because then I had to be a pipe fitter, and my life looked like a foggy November day. Surrounded by fog and stale air, I had taken an interest in myself for lack of better entertainment. I listened to my heart and investigated the possibilities of my body. I read novels, books about the soul, hoping to learn something about myself. However, the world, the State, with all its institutions, constantly distracted me from my concentration and pushed into my hands pipes that I had to weld. With my mate Shanio and three other guys, whose faces I cannot remember, I used to sit in the trailer. I don't want to forget that particular trailer, because it was plastered inside with pictures from *Playboy*, and for hours I would look at a beautiful, nearly life-size blonde and be mired in sadness because such female beauty appeared only in magazines. At nine in the morning Shanio would send me to get beer, and by eleven he and the other three had drunk half a case, while I had spent the time looking at the smiling blonde and chewing a dry roll. Then we climbed up on the tower, and I don't want to forget that either, because for some reason I thought that to tighten up the armature at a height of 250 feet had a different meaning than doing it on the ground. I could not stop looking at the perverse splendor, that spiderweb of pipes. The containers of compressed gas looked like giant peeled onions, and I imagined jumping into the glistening, motionless surface pool of waste oil in which our tower was reflected like in a black mirror. This artificial, absurd landscape, with its odor of garlic instead of air, suited my melancholy, convincing me that the only thing with meaning around there was myself. But Shanio, in his sonorous voice, shouted at me not to sleep. I never saw him breathe through his nose. His mouth was always open, and I am sure that it was because his nose refused to sniff the stink.

He startled me so much once that a size 30 wrench fell out of my hand, hit the railing with a clang, ricocheted from a pipe, and then descended decisively to the ground. With gaping mouths, we followed it as it gathered speed and diminished in size, and were unable to shout a warning to the little figure walking along the sidewalk far below, perhaps to meet with death, if that turned out to be the tool's easiest route. I saw the little figure swerve and turn his white spot of a face upward, and then the sound of metal hitting concrete reached us. The little orange figurine threatened us, gesticulating, and we hid behind the pipes.

"You asshole," Shanio said to me tenderly, with a bashful smile, as if he were humble in the presence of Fate, whose touch he, too, sensed for a moment.

I remembered the odor of iron as it melted under the acetylene flame, the screeching sound of the thread cutter when it held in its teeth a PVC water pipe, and felt sick to my stomach. When I think about metal, I think of the 1970s, and the gray faces of my contemporaries come to me, with their bell-bottom pants and long hair that reflected courage or indifference. We listened to the pathetic songs of Deep Purple and mumbled shaman words in an unknown language. We did not understand the song's words, but it was always better than singing in Slovak. The feeling of awkwardness stayed embedded in my soul, connected to dozens of smells and objects, or to faces that I meet occasionally in the street. We stop to have a chat, but have nothing to say to each other.

Later, when I met Tania, her hair was like the blonde girl's from the trailer, and right away I began to wonder: Is she hiding a similar beauty behind that absurd suit that once belonged to her mother? It happened at a party: the kind given by former professional intellectuals, some of whom had been dispersed to libraries and institutes, and others who were now wielding a shovel. My father used to take me along, and I liked to go with him. These ex-communists, discarded like myself, were learning how to live in the emptiness of the present, and I thought that maybe they'd figured out something.

Tania, however, showed me into her room, brought coffee and canapés, and asked with a polite indifference, "Are you that pipe fitter?"

She did not like me. My hair was falling down on my shoulders, and I had a stone face, a thick neck after the winter training season, and a deep wrinkle in my brow.

"And are you the one who is winning those Russian Olympiads?" I asked.

"Yes, but don't think I'm proud of that."

"I don't think it."

"Still, I guess I am proud a little bit," she answered stubbornly.

I shrugged my shoulders, annoyed. With that gesture I won the first round. Tania cannot handle tension or disagreement. Apparently she was born with this handicap, because I noticed many times afterward that a charge of tension destroys her: it breaks down the primary physiological functions of her body and its coordination. The fingers holding the cup released it, and coffee spilled on her blue-gray skirt.

"Pardon me," she blurted out, and looked unhappily at the black spot instantly absorbed by her thick tweed. "I didn't mean it that way. I've heard a lot about you," she added seemingly nonsensically, but I understood right away. What could she have heard about me?

Only words of praise, or at most of compassion, because who would dare criticize the innocent victims of the perverse State?

So I was walking about our new home while Tania was still sleeping, and I was carefully trying to remember Shanio's hands as he connected the water pipe. But all I could see was his gaping mouth, the tip of his childishly pink tongue sticking out, and his black hair growing down onto his forehead, hidden under an eternal beret. I recalled his mumbled, broken Slovak, spoken through a cigarette in the corner of his mouth, and his long, motionless silences when a problem hypnotized him. Only one part of the picture was escaping me. I was trying to move, by memory, my focus from his face to his hands, in which he was holding a water pipe, but I was not succeeding. It occurred to me that this might not be the fault of my memory. Maybe I never looked at his hands, because I did not want to agree to my hands being sentenced to touch cold metal for the rest of my working life. When he took my place at the apprenticeship examinations, I got him a beer and lit his cigarette off the white-hot weld that breathed on me with burned sulfur. It seemed only right, since I preferred to sit apart and deal with the question of what I was doing there then and what I was about in general rather than learn about water pipes.

Tania's hands interrupted my thread of thought as she embraced me from behind, pressing against me with her body warmed by sleep.

"Why aren't you sleeping?"

"And why aren't you?" she asked, answering with a question.

"I was looking around. Do you want a bathroom?"

"The bathroom can wait. What do you think?"

"It won't wait. Who takes a shower twice a day? Me?"

"We'll take our bath in the Golden Sands. It's only a hop on our bikes."

We were there in a moment, and the lake's beach looked tired after the Sunday onslaught. It was nine in the morning on a Monday in June. The surface of the lake looked like new, and on the shore a dried-up sand castle was collapsing as a last witness to the day before. Water always moves me to tears. I turned to Tania, but she was already sprinting toward the lake, her chin raised up. I stood there for a moment, because it occurred to me that when she had almost died from her ectopic pregnancy, I had found myself, for a moment, in my past, in the timeless loneliness worse than death. But Tania had pulled me to herself, into the present with her life, because she is the only one who has such influence—or at any rate, the only one I know.

When we returned, a wrinkled grandpa who lived next door was sitting on the bench in front of his house. Dressed in overalls and smoking a pipe, he nodded his head and greeted me in a hoarse voice: "Good morning, neighbor!"

I trembled with pride on hearing this title, and when I found out that he was a retired bricklayer—he showed me his cracked hands, damaged by eczema from his allergy to lime—I asked him right away how to make mortar and build bathroom walls.

"How to build them? Well," he smiled unsurely, suspecting me of pulling his leg, "you need some foundation . . . and a plumb. You can't build a straight wall without a plumb." He looked at me anxiously, wondering if I were trying to wreck our neighborly relations right from the outset.

"Hmm," I said, scratching myself behind my ear. "You don't understand me. I need to know how to make mortar. What do you put in it?"

An awkward smile was still stamped on his face, and there was tense concentration in his eyes. He was trying to figure out what I wanted, but then he gave up and stretched his arms in surrender: "I don't understand . . ."

I started to work with an existential feeling that resembled a worm in the stomach. He would chew on the wall to let me know that he was there. I mixed flourlike lime powder with water in a big garbage can and reflected with melancholy sadness that my Tania had been born in her grandparents' villa under the Castle. She had spent her early life in an atmosphere of high ceilings, antique furniture, dusty libraries, and Sunday dinners at the Carlton. I got even more depressed when I remembered how, during one of our walks, she had pointed out the Slovak National Council Building and remarked ironically: "That's where my great grandfather used to live. In 1918 he was made district governor of Bratislava."

The sound of falling pots came from the house and I found Tania kneeling among them.

"I opened the credenza," she said. "Look at this inheritance! Isn't it fantastic?" She picked them up, one by one, and examined the cracked enamel. "Some of them were done by a tinsmith," she drooled.

"Great. Silver service from your grandfather and pots full of holes."

Tania shrugged it off, and a muffled thud reached us from outside. We looked out, and for a moment I was overcome by a dizzy feeling right out of my favorite fairy tale, "The Twelve Little Moons." It's about natural catastrophes—the violation of the laws of nature—and every such catastrophe excites me. The more set in iron a law, the better, and natural law is as firm as handcuffs. If in January the winter disappears for a day and humid, ghostlike warm weather causes the bees to fly out and fall into the snow, I have to go out and jump into the lake. Or if it happens—as it has once in my life—that a May snowfall lands on the green grass, I must run out into the woods in my shorts and, if nobody sees me, barefoot. And now it seemed that such a miracle was happening in June, but it lasted only a moment. The garden was white, and milk was dripping down from the walnut leaves.

"What happened?" asked Tania in astonishment.

"The lime exploded."

"Oh, you poor man," she said, embracing me lovingly.

"Listen. When you make the batter for crepes, what do you start with? Flour or water?"

"First the flour, darling, then the milk."

"I see. I proceeded according to the old natural rules. But the laws rebelled," I said, lost in thought.

"Neighbor! Neighbor!" the old man lamented. Tania kissed me, and there was nothing to be done except go out and face the catastrophe. I pushed my way through the weeds to the garbage can and looked inside. It was hot like a furnace, and the thick mixture bubbled with little craters.

"Watch your eyes, neighbor!" the old man called out from behind the fence, woefully. "I didn't know you were serious," he continued tearfully, "'cause I'm a bricklayer, you see. I can give you a hand . . ."

I was spraying the walnut with a hose, washing the thin milk off its large, firm leaves, when the gate creaked and the first guest entered our new lives. It was Richard. He was wearing a beard again, but still in the same stretched-out T-shirt, loose jeans, and tennis shoes, with the same small bag over his shoulder.

"Hi. What are you up to? Fertilizing?"

Richard, the king of sarcasm, who could utter through his gnashing teeth a line sharper than a dagger, was innocent of it now, because he understood nothing of houses, gardens, or manual work.

"Not really. Our lime exploded," Tania said as she came out.

"How could that happen?"

"Bad luck, I guess," she said.

"Bad luck my foot. I poured the water into the lime and not the other way around. It was a dumb mistake," I joined in.

"Accursed chemistry," Richard mumbled awkwardly.

"And you, you'll burn your little pink feet if you walk outside," I said sharply to Tania.

"I came, really, to apologize," Richard began, as soon as we sat down on the floor in the empty room. I stole a glance at Tania, but she made a face suggesting that everything was in order.

"Let's forget about it," I said.

"Sure," he nodded, "let's forget about that. Something else has happened. I had my place searched, and they took away everything, including some of your books that Tania lent me."

"They're at it again?" asked Tania, fidgeting in her Indian sitting position. The night we were introduced and she spilled her coffee on her tweed skirt, ten men had showed up and searched through the whole house, because you could not allow a cheerful reunion of defeated ex-communists to go off without a hitch. Tania had saved a few of the books in her bed, because she was already in her pajamas, though she could not save her ailing father, who was overtaken a few days later by a heart attack.

"They're always doing it," Richard said, shrugging his shoulders. "In Prague they broke down the door of an apartment and picked up twenty Chartists. Vienna reported that this morning."

"Did they mention you, too?" I asked.

"No," he laughed, as if I had made a silly joke. But he does not know that when the conversation touches the police, I lose all of my sense of humor, of which I don't have much in the first place. It humiliates me when against my will they take on in our conversations an importance they don't deserve and I spend more thought on them than they merit.

As Richard was leaving, Tania observed that he was lost in thought. Then she looked askance at me.

"Yup," I nodded. "He came to see if you were happy with me."

As my days increase, my disgust increases as well, and the older I get, the more reason I can find for it. It was early Wednesday morning, and my imagination projected on the background of my eyes black visions of dozens of bleeding women I would have to lift, though as I was getting up, I felt so weak I could not lift my own body. The day before, I had met Timothy on Michalská Street. He told me that Richard had been found dead in his apartment. As he said it, he had a guilty expression and I understood him. I, too, feel embarrassed for not wanting to live. The stupid thing is that such thoughts don't add any joy to my life.

In our room at the hospital I found Joey the stoker, who would go up there on the sly to phone declarations of love in Hungarian to a barmaid from a neighboring village. He lisped gently into the receiver, but seemed afraid to screw her.

Pista *bacsi* was already taking off his white gown, trying to squeeze into his shabby overcoat. His certainty that I will always show up and be on time upsets me, reminding me of my pettiness.

"How was last night?" I asked out of habit.

"Huh? What do you think? Fucking bad," he answered stoically, and bent under the table, puffing.

"*Puszikam, szeretlek.* I love you, honey," lisped Joey.

"Hold on to your pussy!" Pista roared into the phone good-naturedly, passing a glass of wine to Joey, who cut him with a furious look. "You *bolond*, stupid," Pista muttered, and chewed with his toothless mouth open, sticking out his lightning-quick tongue like a lizard. "What do you have it for, when you don't know how to screw her, huh?" he said, slapping Joey in the crotch with the palm of his hand, interrupting the stoker's beloved Hungarian conversation while his eyes strained from their sockets.

"Don't bother him," I said.

"Why? I only mean well for him!" It was true, because Pista *bacsi*, though resembling an iguana, was as good a man as they come.

"Here you go," he handed me a glass of wine with a shaking hand swollen by alcohol. "Let's drop dead!"

"*Igen. Tudom, puszika.* Yes. I know, honey," said Joey. He was cuddling up deeper in the armchair, not realizing how the wine warmed up his empty stomach.

"How many abortions are there today?" I asked.

"Ugh," Pista *bacsi* shivered. "Let me drop dead. Shall we have another?" When he got it, he added them up. "Eight."

After a second glass that shook me to my foundations, I left them and went upstairs. They were lying in two rooms at the beginning of the corridor, covered up to their ears, and when I entered, they did not show any sign of recognition.

"Good morning," I started politely. I have learned that politeness is the best manner of speaking when I don't know what to say. I never know how to behave toward these women. Each of them had come because she chose death. One of them lifted her head, and her eyes flashed.

"You've had the injection," I said, half-asking, and when she nodded, I approached her. "Then come with me, please."

I led her by her elbow and we walked slowly, as befits a funeral. The sedative made her gait uncertain and infused her face with that insightful expression that accompanies the slowing down of eye movement. An impression forms that the person is thinking. But that did not confuse me.

In the elevator she leaned against the wall and looked ahead. In its own way, her face was perfect. Nature had just completed its work and it had taken eighteen years, but she did not look tired—just the opposite. As a finishing touch, Nature covered her creation with a new skin, all new cells, and I would have sworn that even her elbow, which I held in my hand, was as smooth as the surface of a pebble.

"Will it hurt?" she asked, and her lips suddenly trembled.

"Not you," I answered, because when I drink I have a tendency toward the metaphysical.

I brought her all the way to smiling Ilonka, who led her to the table. The air was thick with ozone, and the instruments looked indifferent, though I knew full well that they were looking forward to their work.

"Come here and lie down, yes, and lift your legs up, and your hands over here," I told her slowly, and she, as though hypnotized, submitted to my words and hands when they placed her into that absurd and otherworldly position. From that moment she tried not to think, or see, or hear, or be, and I would bet that she succeeded, because her eyes remained dry. The day after, she would not recall anything, having forgotten it all, including me, the same as I would gladly forget her. I imagined her brain covered with new cells.

"Good morning," the anesthesiologist sang out. She made a few dozen concentrated moves, the last a gentle pressing of the syringe valve. The girl closed her eyes and sighed deeply, because as far as she was concerned, it was all over.

"Vlado is on duty today and that should guarantee that no one will make a hole through any of them," the anesthesiologist babbled significantly, while the surgeon, who had just appeared, was flattered and smiled.

"Look before you leap, Doctor," he muttered, and put on a white rubber apron. "You've heard the one about the guy from Záhorie who argued with his mother-in-law?"

"Yippee!" Ilonka squealed in anticipation.

He told the joke, which I have forgotten, but meanwhile he was doing things that I will never forget. I had seen them a hundred times, a thousand times, and a question occurred to me: How come I didn't get fed up with it? Was it possible that I—against my will—actually liked it? Aesthetics has no rules. I remember a welder from our team who loved to study the fresh welds. He did it with infinite passion, knocking off the sulfurous waste, smelling their odor like a hunting dog. We were the slowest team of the whole production unit because this welder could not tear himself away from his welds. Unlike Hegel, I don't believe that the classical line of nose and forehead is beautiful. I don't like it. At the same time, I wonder what he would say if he saw how the cervix of the uterus comes out of the female crotch. As I watched, the doctor squeezed it in his sharp pincers and dragged it out from the open cave to the light of the reflector, and I was, as usual, astounded. It is a captivating theater and almost always a premiere. Most of the victims have never lain on that table. The phenomenon is beautiful and repulsive at the same time. It attracts me like a magnet and also provokes me because I cannot name it. It is unique and at the same time resembles much, for example the thick, slimy stigma of a flower, tempting the thought that Nature likes to repeat what works.

The cervix has in the middle of its rosy, shiny garland a little hole, a slit, into which the surgeon slid a nickel-plated needle. After a while he exchanged it for a thicker one, and so it went on until the needle turned into a stick as thick as a thumb. The girl sighed in her sleep, her body tensed, as if wishing to escape from its restraints, but the anesthesiologist lovingly pushed in the valve of the syringe.

The surgeon picked up a pair of pliers with narrow jaws and, concentrating, pushed them inside the hole made ready by the stick. He was feeling his way inside with them, following the picture formed by the books he had studied and by his many years of experience. At that moment he resembled a blind man with perfect knowledge of the standard apartment.

"Are you still collecting livers, Ilonka?" he asked.

"Of course, Doctor. Do you think you'll succeed?" she asked, full of admiration.

Instead of answering, the doctor twisted the pliers and, accompanied by sounds of masticating and bubbling water, pulled out a piece of flesh, dropped it in his apron, looked for something in it, and, when he didn't find what he was looking for, he went back to the hole that had turned to a bloody wound and lost all of its mysterious noblesse. This time he succeeded, because he triumphantly lifted his pliers and dropped what he held in them into an infusion bottle filled with a prepared solution.

"What finesse," said the anesthesiologist, nodding her head respectfully. In the now-pink liquid floated a body as big as a cherry, headless and armless, with stumps for legs; it was transparent, like a jellyfish, so we could clearly see the liver, a black bead embedded in gelatin.

"The people in the lab will be happy," Ilonka rejoiced, and ran upstairs.

"Just don't break your neck," said the anesthesiologist. She turned to the surgeon. "When they see how good you are, they'll make you do the abortions tomorrow."

"Screw it," the surgeon said, and scraped the last remnants out together with the frothy blood. "I didn't manage to eat my breakfast, and now I've lost my appetite. Well, that's it. It's done," he said, turning to me with the last word. I cut short my reflections and watched as the anesthesiologist, nodding her head, slapped the girl's cheeks.

I took the girl in my arms and placed her on the stretcher with the squeaking front wheel. Out of doors peeked women in robes and nightshirts, and I could read in their looks that they knew who I was pushing.

As the day wore on, the wine evaporated from me, and I got so awfully hungry that I felt weak and my knees trembled under the weight of the women. Increasingly tired, I forced myself to place the sleeping bodies back on their beds carefully and softly, but such tenderness took too much strength, and I unloaded the penultimate burden into her bed like a sack. With my eyes closing with fatigue, I searched for the last one. Some of them had already waked up; I heard sobbing. Others, cuddled up with satisfaction in their beds, slept soundly and sweetly.

"Well, let's go," I sighed, addressing myself more than anyone else. This sort of compassion with myself works and they gratefully accept it. She put on her slippers, which had violet pom-poms. I didn't like them, because she had bought them for the occasion, as if she were in a hotel; there may have been a price tag from the House of Shoes stuck to the sole. She hung on to me and stumbled to the elevator in those new cork-heeled slippers in which she couldn't walk.

"Why did you buy new ones? The occasion is not worth it," I said sarcastically, but I embraced her shoulders to prevent her from falling.

"I wanted to . . . ," she started hoarsely, because the sedative had dehydrated her. "I wanted . . ." Again she did not finish. She broke out in sobs and looked for a handkerchief.

"There, there," I said, and went on, more for my own sake, "that will pass. You'll go home tomorrow, the sun will shine, and maybe you'll manage to forget all about it."

She shook her head. "I wanted them . . ." Then she really started to cry. Her tears were flowing down her face, and I saw with surprise that she meant it seriously. "I wanted to . . . throw them away afterwards. But I can't, I can't!"

"You cannot?" I repeated slowly, and tried to turn her gently around. It worked. She turned around, and we walked back. She stumbled along in the slippers she would keep as a reward.

"I want to go home," she muttered, sleepwalking into her room.

"What's the big deal?" a woman in her forties wondered, a veteran of three children and four abortions, lifting herself up on her elbows and quickly sinking back as if sleep had hit her with a big stick.

"That's fine with me," said the surgeon. No one else can say "Time's up" with the gusto of a doctor.

I remained alone with a bloody apron and a pail full of fresh human cells. I leaned against a radiator and reflected helplessly. It was clear to me that the last one had made me somewhat happy. She had won her duel, from a moral point of view, and she had leaned on me to help her do so. But mainly she had saved me additional work.

In a brief, clear moment I understood that I was in it up to my neck. I, who purposefully and maybe out of necessity, moved in a different system of coordinates, or at least hoped I did, had ended up in the gravitational field of normality. Nothing of what I had seen until then had I managed to understand, and yet I had stopped wondering. I didn't even know how it had come about. From some sort of mist appeared a memory that my soul used to have a different state and a different consistency. I didn't know for how long—

perhaps it had been since birth—that I had been covered by a supple foil of banality. It was warm, like a comforter, and even though I knew I should, I would not crawl out from under it.

I went out into the hospital's backyard to check how the December weather was shaping up and stepped back in surprise, because the winter's first snowflakes touched my nose. But I had with me a cloth-covered pail with mysterious contents, and so I crossed the watery mud and poured it all into the garbage container. A cloud of vapor ascended into the moist, cold air. I didn't like the strange, unnamable odor, and so I quickly slapped the tin cover back on.

I did not find Pista *bacsi* in the room; only an empty wine bottle and a full ashtray remained. Joey had left after his telephone call, and on the white sheet covering the armchair where he had been sitting was a burn hole. I sat down in the chair and dialed a number.

"Young Age Publishers," she answered.

"Oh, so this was what you so doggedly concealed? I took you for a psychologist, a sociologist, or even something worse when you didn't want to tell me."

"This is bad enough."

"You're right," I admitted.

"You are calling just like that?"

"Out of curiosity."

"Where from?"

"From work. We just did seven abortions. There was supposed to have been eight, but one decided not to do it. When we consider that we had six births, then it's seven to seven. Nature played to a draw today."

"Do you want to spoil the lunch to which I would like to invite you?"

"Unlike you, I can't leave."

"How about dinner?"

She came in a striped hairy sweater that was as pleasant to touch as a cat's fur. Her black hair was drawn back into a braid, and her big black eyes flew about her face while shining in a peculiar way, as if lit by a studio lamp. She drank a glass of wine in one swallow and, out of breath, placed it in front of her.

"Sorry I'm so late. My calculations were off," she said.

I shrugged my shoulders with a grimace, and before I could open my mouth, she began to laugh.

"You're as polite as a gorilla. I'm ten minutes late, and you look like you've been waiting for me all day."

"I *have* been waiting for you all day. And in this cellar for at least an hour."

She became silent and looked into my eyes with the expression of a professional diagnostician.

"Take those eyes away," I protested. "I'm quite normal, and if I've been waiting for you unnecessarily long, it's none of your business."

She raised her hands. "I'll try to improve. But I can't guarantee anything," she said.

When I heard her jazzy voice, I realized I really had been waiting for her the whole day. It disturbed me for a while, and when I sounded my soul to find the reason for it, I found that it lay too deep, and I had not the time nor will to trace it.

"What are you thinking about?" she asked.

"Your attractiveness disturbs me."

She lowered her eyes and skillfully twirled the glass by its stem. She must have been well over thirty, but you could tell more by the hands than by the face. She played with her short fingers, and in the sharp light of the table lamp I could see on her wrist and the back of the hand traces of the first wrinkles.

"I don't know if I'm attractive, but I do know why it disturbs you," she said thoughtfully.

"My mother has hands like those," I blurted out in astonishment.

"Do you want to know why it disturbs you that you find me attractive?" she repeated mercilessly. But the waiter appeared and politely inquired about our order.

"I feel like having trout," she said ravenously, and I nodded uncertainly.

"You know," I said, leaning against the wicker backrest, "I can't remember the last time I had a good day. This feeling I have—it begins every morning and continues into the night. The girl who decided not to have an abortion today bought herself a pair of slippers with violet pom-poms yesterday. She was going to throw them away afterward. She had bought an offering in the House of Shoes. God knows why she decided not to go through with it. I was so glad she was off my back that I did not even look at her file. I was just glad there would be one less broad to lift, though she did not weigh much more than a hundred pounds. I was glad we would finish fifteen minutes early. It didn't occur to me that in the moment when she turned around under the pressure of my hand on her shoulder, fairy godmothers were standing there muttering incantations. A long time ago I was able to hear their voices and rejoice in their presence; I had a solemn feeling of the presence of destiny; I experienced a sweet shivering in my groin. But today, today I am somehow unable to recognize that moment. Everything runs together, everything is banal. It's like wearing surgical gloves. I have them on constantly and I've forgotten that what I feel is only rubber. I imagine I'm touching wood, a piece of rock, or a female body, but it's really only rubber. So it's only logical that I perceive the whole world as a banality and don't even know it."

She bent toward me, waiting for me to stop, and then she covered my hand with her hand.

"You are too sensitive. I saw it right away. Why are your hands so cold?"

"Because I'm afraid."

"Afraid? Of what?"

"Of you."

"You silly fool. I won't hurt you. You inspire maternal feelings in me, and they are dangerous for me, not for you."

"I don't care what feelings I inspire in you, but you are too attractive, and it seems that you want to provoke me. Your eyes are beautiful, as though you fill them with glycerin."

"You're cute." She did not let go of my hand. "Tell me more."

"What else do you want to hear? I am sitting here with you instead of going home. Tania is waiting for me, worried that the police have picked me up."

"Why would they pick you up?"

"Why wouldn't they?" I countered, and regretted it immediately.

"Have you done something?"

"It depends."

"What does that mean?"

"It means nothing. I just wanted to say that Tania is expecting me, and I have pangs of conscience, because instead of being arrested, I'm sitting here with you."

"But why should you be arrested?"

"I'm not saying I should. But if I don't return home, then for Tania it would be the only natural explanation."

"But why?" she exploded nervously, banging her fist on the table.

"Calm down," I whispered soothingly. "Nothing's going on. It's normal. The police simply don't like me."

"But why?" she whispered in supplication.

I placed my finger on my lips, and she leaned closer. I leaned across the table and took her peachy earlobe into my fingers.

"Because I'm not normal."

"That's no answer." She moved away annoyed.

"I dreamed about you last night."

"Something nice?" She revived.

"I can't tell you about the dream. It was erotic."

"That's a good reason to tell me."

The waiter appeared carrying dead trout on plates. She inspected them spitefully, but I was glad he came, because I could not remember the dream. I suspected that it became erotic only afterward.

"Go ahead, begin," she encouraged me when we were alone.

"Why did you invite me to dinner?"

She frowned in disappointment. "I came to hear about the dream!"

"Let's drop it," I said. "I just want to be with you."

I don't understand, I said to myself. I can't see why I had dinner with her. Why did I call her in the first place? What will Tania say?

I tried to escape that question, recalling rather a funny event that had happened about a year before when we had bought our house. I had to make us a sink. We had no money for kitchen sink installation, but we had to have a place to wash the silverware handed down from Tania's grandfather. Tania loved to cook and decorate the table, and we invited our friends for crepes with chocolate and whipped cream. She took out all the antique silver and the remnants of the family china, and we feasted in the empty room at a low table that I had reduced to knee-height in a fit of avant-gardism. Everyone admired the beautiful waxed floor. Timothy ceremoniously hung his painting on the empty wall, we discussed art, and Tania invited everyone to go to a concert given by some Frenchmen. Tania is an interpreter, and that is why she has an extra brain in her head. This brain only cares about language. It feeds on foreign languages and is always hungry—gluttonous like a sea lion. It once happened that an American came to call, and a week later Tania, who until then had no English, could converse fluently with him in his mother tongue while I stewed in frustration. Anyway, we all went to the Frenchmen's concert, and that, along with the crepes with chocolate and whipped cream, exhausted the evening's entertainment. The guests left, and Tania and I remained alone in a kitchen crammed with dirty silverware that had nowhere to be washed. In a fit of modernism, I had sold the sink as scrap for twenty crowns, which I had then spent on whipped cream for the crepes.

"I have to make a sink," I announced to Tania, who nodded helplessly. A month before, I had found a small tin washtub on a local dump; otherwise I probably wouldn't have given in to that fit of modernism so easily.

A few days later, I was standing in our courtyard in front of an old kitchen table that remembered dozens of hog feasts from the days when, in our rotten woodshed by the fence, the previous owners kept pigs. I looked at the jagged hole in the table and thought back nostalgically to my childhood, when I used to cut teddy bears out of plywood with a pad saw. Where has my childish verve gone? I asked myself. Where has it gone, together with that natural certainty that what I do, I do right? It is not gone, I told myself. It's still here. Everything I do is good, because metaphysically—that is, from the point of view of finality, of death—only good makes sense. If I consider that I have only one life, it would be absurd to sully this absolute value with something so repulsively relative as evil.

That is why, I said to myself, I am at this moment making a sink for my wife, Tania. Tomorrow I'll continue building the bathroom, because it is something that is good and that a man should do. I feel that strongly, because I find it very difficult. In fact I have to force myself. I am not here, after all, to cut holes into old tables. I want to be a writer, a good writer. I don't want to waste the rest of my life installing plumbing! It may be a good thing to do, but can a good thing be demeaning?

With that thought in my mind I cut a hole that was too big, and the sink fell through to the floor with a crash, fragments of cracked enamel flying everywhere. At that moment, the front gate creaked, and a tall man in a black suit pushed through the wild rosebushes with my wife tiptoeing next to him.

They stopped before me, and I felt like a surreal armor-bearer armed with a saw instead of an ax and protected by a shield of sink enamel and a moat of sewerage.

"*C'est mon mari,*" said Tania, radiating happiness and pride. Her breasts were filling up a white silk blouse that had belonged to her Protestant grandmother, whose father had been the district administrator of Bratislava, and around her waist she wore a black skirt from her Jewish great aunt, whose entire family except for Tania's father perished in a concentration camp. Tania's father escaped, not because he wanted to save himself, but because he was fed up with playing tennis and being a successful lawyer in his father's firm. So he rebelled and went to Moscow. Thus he did not escape the fate of the Slovak communist intellectual, though he managed to miraculously avoid imprisonment. When, in his fifties, he lived to see the dawn of the liberal 1960s, he fell in love with an editor of the Tatran publishing house and engendered with her my wife.

"*Et voilà notre maison!*" she said, and pointed somewhere behind my back.

"*Mais c'est mignon!*" said the tall Frenchman as he crossed over the moat and extended to me a slender, cultivated hand that could have belonged to a gynecologist but actually belonged to a pianist. Then he turned around and offered the hand to Tania, who had the presence of mind to accept it.

"Tell him I'm busy. Tell him I have no time," I said, and listened with pleasure to the foreboding tonality of Slovak.

Tania was brought up with the spirit of the aristocracy that had been preserved in her parents. She never received a slap on her behind and remembered only one slap on her face, which she got from her father when, in the Bellevue Hotel in Starý Smokovec, she did not as a five-year-old say good morning to a lady who joined them for breakfast. For everything is forgivable with the exception of impolite behavior.

She turned pale with anger, shook her head, said something energetically to the composer, and set out for the house. I stood and watched her in the excitement that I feel when I witness a major natural event such as a perfect sunset or a river flood.

I was happy and afraid at the same time. I was protected by the consciousness of the honesty and goodness of what I was doing. Our old record player was broadcasting a piano composition through the open window, and I answered with my pick ax. I was digging a ditch across the garden but was soon disturbed by a car that stopped in front of the gate. Two men in suits got out, and so I went to meet them.

"May we come in?" asked one of them with a smile.

"No."

"Would you prefer to come with us?"

"No."

They stood there in puzzlement, their smiles gone, until one of them asked with annoyance, "Why don't you work?"

"What do you mean I don't work?"

"You've been unemployed for two months."

"I am not employed?"

"We mean for some sort of company."

"And who will build my bathroom for me if I work for a company?"

"Don't you need money?"

"I do."

"We'll come back in a week, and you will show us the stamp of your employer on your internal passport."

I shrugged my shoulders.

"As you wish," they said simultaneously, and got in the car.

I returned to my sewerage, but I had lost the mood. I threw the pick into the ditch and sat down on the grass, because a suspicion hit me that I might be wrong. I couldn't tell why I was wrong. It was just a feeling that went through me like electricity and paralyzed my senses. As a test, I rubbed my fingers against my body. I didn't feel a thing; it was as if I were stuffed with straw and my mouth were full of cotton. I suspected that maybe everything I had ever done was wrong. In that terrible moment I realized that I had never had a guarantee of anything. All I had was my feeling that I used to justify by saying that I had it because I was good. An uncertainty flashed in me, and for a fraction of a second I ceased to exist. It was only for a moment. Everything quickly returned to normal, and I was much relieved that my fingers had regained their sense of touch. I picked a blade of grass and chewed it blissfully. I was relieved like the fish caught by the fisherman and thrown back in the water because it was not worth keeping. And like the fish, I did not realize that, having been thrown back, I was no longer the same.

The music stopped, and Tania and her guest came out into the garden. The Frenchman's suntanned face looked thoughtful. He took Tania's hand by the tips of her fingers, kissed the charming delta of blue veins on the back of her hand, bowed to me, said "*Au revoir*," and left.

Tania remained standing by the gate, but I was staring at the handle of the pick, afraid to lift my head, because she was looking at me strangely, more strangely than ever before. "Who am I living with?" she must have been thinking, and I felt that question in the back of my neck. "What if he is a monster?"

Then she turned around and walked back toward the house. Out of the corner of my eye I saw her figure in her white blouse and black skirt. She walked as if drugged, a bit jerkily, and at the same time with artificial suppleness. She actually walked with all of her strength, because she was paralyzed by anger, though she did not understand it. Instinctively, she tried to reach the house and hide there from me. She had never known this kind of anger, and this new feeling completely unsettled her and filled her to the brim with a despair that seemed to have come from outside. She was only an empty vessel for some strange anger and could not do anything but lie down in bed and begin to live again only after it had passed.

I was sitting in the grass, taken aback by my own fear. I was terrified. All for a silly trifle, I thought. She wanted to show off in front of the Frenchman; she wanted to show him her husband, her life, with which she wanted to identify completely. She wanted to show him her happiness. That was her form of coquetry. Instead of make-up, she decorates herself with her smile and her happiness, and I had spoiled it for her. I had stupidly betrayed myself.

I was sitting in the grass, afraid, feeling like I had years before when my parents would go to the movies, leaving me in bed with my eyes staring into the darkness. If she leaves me, I won't survive, I thought suddenly and quite clearly. Tania identifies with me, her meaning of life is in me, and the meaning of my life is in the fact that I give it to her.

I found her lying in bed, as I had imagined, on her back, her eyes wide open.

"The police were here," I said, and remained standing in the door.

"What?" She was startled and shook her head.

"The police were here. I have to find a job. They wanted to pick me up."

There exists a sort of invisible world. Maybe I only imagine it, but I have seen how the matter of Tania's body transforms itself from marble to soft, limp clay, moving to another mode of existence that some would call exhaustion but that I call resurrection.

"Why didn't you tell me right away?" she whispered.

"I didn't want to spoil your joy," I answered, puzzled by my own fantasy. "But perhaps now you understand why I didn't feel like listening to a piano concert."

She breathed in deeply, as if for the first time. "What are we going to do?" she asked.

I sat down by her on the bed and took her hand. "I have an idea. I would like to work in the hospital again, but someplace where they don't die. I would like to work in the maternity ward and be able to watch over you. Because I want us to have a child."

Pity. No one will believe how I felt a clay hand come alive, warm itself up, and invite my hand to confirm that the whole of her body was alive and warm.

As I got up, Tania mumbled something tender from her sleep, and Pepina joyfully wagged her hairy tail. They both like me, I thought in despair. Even in the morning. I don't have enough strength for that. I was dismissing it all in an attempt to banish the idea that there was a whole day ahead of me.

As soon as I entered the hospital I heard someone scream. Pista *bacsi* was pushing an empty stretcher, squinting with his red eyes after a night of drinking, and signing to me with his hand to hurry. In that gesture there was more entreaty than command. He was afraid that he had had too much to drink.

In our room I found an unfinished bottle of gin and a full ashtray on the table. For a second I thought I might have a drink, but my stomach turned, and so instead I mouthed curses through my teeth and quickly took off my clothes and put on the green uniform.

On the table in the procedure room (this term comes from the word *procedure* and is even more sickening than a shot of gin on an empty stomach) writhed a young woman who screamed to the bare tile-covered walls.

"Please, don't shout so much," begged a doctor whom I liked for his somewhat shy and raspy voice and the gentle, harmonious movements of his hands.

"Then do something, for God's sake!" she shouted, and jerked her head from side to side as I tightened up the restraints. Her hair was glued to a face wet from tears, and it obscured her features. "Inject me with something so that it ends, because it hurts so!" She wanted to scream, but something got stuck, and so she just sobbed and bit her lip. "I don't want it anymore. This is the third time. I don't want it. I'll kill him if he does it one more time. I don't want children. Make it so that I won't have them. I'd rather die than to go through this one more time!" She opened her mouth wide, and her eyes opened with terror. Her teeth were bloody from the lip she had bitten.

"I must ask you not to talk like that!" the doctor said, upset. "If you want to die, you came to the wrong address. We have other things to worry about than your stupid talk!"

I looked at him in surprise. He was beside himself with anger.

"Put her to sleep," he added.

As the yellow anesthetic poured into her veins, silence and relief spread through the room. The doctor was ready, and with quick, controlled movements the cervix caught in his pliers crawled out. I experienced that moment of peculiar feeling that Alice had to know in Wonderland, and it disturbed me for the hundredth time. I don't know where this feeling comes from. It is as if it doesn't belong to me, but to something that was here a long time before me. It is an atavistic fear of something unknown emerging from inside. Perhaps a long time ago a tiger with knifelike teeth lunged from a cave at an ancestor of mine and tore open his belly. But by some miracle he survived and now haunts my genes with the experience. Anyway, it was my secret, because everyone else behaved as if nothing unusual was going on.

The doctor picked up a huge syringe with a long needle the size of a knitting needle and, with a fencer's gesture, injected it up to the handle into the depths below the cervix. As he was drawing the valve of the syringe, the glass cylinder filled up with muddy water. He took it out and inspected it against the window.

"There are flakes here. Clear case," he said to two other doctors standing behind him. I just helplessly gnashed my teeth, because I can't stand the vulgar poetry of the medical vocabulary.

"She was right to scream, wasn't she?" I said.

"Pardon?" the doctor asked, turning to me and glancing at me without comprehending. "Oh yes. Take her to the operating theater."

An ectopic pregnancy causes a devastation in the belly like an explosion of a grenade. It looks as if a hysterically angry Nature tried to blow up the witness of its error. Every time I see the torn tissue and black clots of blood that a doctor removes from the belly by the handful, I feel vertigo. That is how death looked when it wanted to tear apart my beautiful Tania years ago. A biological bomb was patiently waiting for someone to light the fuse, and I can't accept that Tania had lovingly chosen me and that I wanted to be chosen. I never wanted anything in the world more than to be chosen by her. But what followed had been terrible.

I know the origin of this vertigo. It originates from my memory of Tania's pale face as she looked with her wide eyes into herself and tried to understand the meaning of that awful pain. I cannot accept that. Tania, face to face with death, did not awaken an atavism. She did not scream because of her politeness, because such was her aristocratic upbringing. Or was she silent because she knew a little more than I?

I was sitting on a stretcher, thinking. Maybe I'm possessed. I am always thinking, though sometimes you can't tell, and always about Tania. She had gotten pregnant three months before, in September. I had taken a holiday, and we left for the mountains. We went there by memory. The sun was still suspended in the sky and aimed directly at the nape of my neck. The old trees extended their branches after me and poured their needles down my neck. Thousands of needles were burrowing into my skin, pushing me up the hill. Then the path finally turned, and we walked on the plateau. The forest came to an end, and the dry mountain grass undulated in the wind. Two does were grazing, but by the time I managed to point them out to Tania and she turned her head, they had elegantly trotted away. That is what usually happens. Tania never manages to do anything in time. Sometimes I suspect that the time in which she lives is different from mine. She does everything slowly. She washes the dishes slowly, dresses slowly, writes slowly; I guess that is why she likes to swim, because the water slows down her movements. When we started packing for the trip, she was wearing a florid bathrobe, holding it closed with her hand because she had lost the drawstring, and using the other hand to pack her rucksack. When slowly, very slowly, she realized that at that rate she would never finish, she decided to use both hands, carelessly freeing the robe to open up, and I helplessly watched her rocking breasts as they swung obediently to her sleepwalking movements. I did not feel sufficiently romantic at that moment, though I knew that Tania would only smile if I approached her. She was always ready for love, though her nakedness was more of a childish mistake than a calculation. She would have smiled and turned her thoughts to me. I suspect her of being so slow because she is always thinking of something important, something that I have never even considered. She got ready for the trip with excruciating slowness, and we made it to the train only at the last minute.

In the middle of a meadow, from a hole covered by rocks, flowed a spring. Tania undressed, and I could see right away that she was doing it with a perfect, smooth assurance and that she was doing something she had thought of a long time before. She walked toward the spring and sat in it. I followed her, and the icy water took my breath away. I sat next to Tania frozen, with my mouth open.

Then we were standing in the middle of the meadow alone, like an absurdly placed statuary. Tania's girlish nipples stabbed me in an imperious way, and when she submissively lowered herself to the grass, I noticed that we were on a different planet. A time warp had taken us to another galaxy, and instead of the sun, a violet-red ball shone on a green sky that extended to the end of the universe, while the edges of the earth were formed by the jagged black wall of the forest, behind which there was nothing.

Actually, not long ago I still thought that children originate in a transcendental manner, that they are the fruit of a gentle, abstract embrace, manifested before the eyes of the Creator, who lovingly answers such petitions from prospective parents. I embraced Tania's cold, dewy body and hid in such a way that an innocent child's eye, seeing us by accident, would not notice. I hid in the soft country, meditated on the essence of pleasure, and then plunged into the hot vault.

A few days later we returned to Bratislava. Our house had been waiting for us, immobile, all that time. Our garden seemed neglected. Through the ripe grapes on the fence the weeds showed; the branches of the trees, heavy with nuts, were bent; and inside myself, there was an uncertain fear of what I had done.

The doctor was silently suturing, stitch by stitch, the hole, which would remain only in my memory, because I'm sure that others have forgotten. It would get lost among the hundreds of similar holes they have seen and have yet to see. Professional memory is merciful and useful. It preserves only what it needs. I envy professionals; I wanted to become one of them. I wanted to be a university scientist with such a useful memory. But I was prevented first by the system, and now I am prevented by my memory. In the meantime, my memory has learned the pleasure of storing items without selection and leaving to accident what will be remembered. It might be directed by the subconscious, my bad, creaking, absurd subconscious, because I remember exactly—as if they happened yesterday—all of the horrors I have seen.

At home I found Tania reading mystical writings. She brought them over from the university library, where she went daily to look through the catalogs.

"What are you actually looking for?" I asked her.

"I don't know, but it is a lot of fun. Searching the catalogs is almost better than reading the books later."

I could guess what she was after. It was her past, her Jewish roots that atheistic propaganda had almost erased. She must rummage through the catalogs and allow the deep currents of her emotions to flow in order to show her the way. The child, who was already about four inches long, was of uncertain origin and Tania wanted to be ready on time. She wanted to find out what the little one would feel while looking at the strange script and how it would react to the quiet mumbling of the Old Testament tongue.

"The coffee is on the stove," she said, lifting her head toward me and offering her fine lips. Her face had become even more beautiful in her pregnancy. There was not a trace of coarseness in her features, and her round breasts drove me crazy.

Outside it was raining, and inside it smelled of coffee and thyme. All seemed to be in harmony. But, I was worried that I did not truly know what was growing in Tania's belly: was it death or life? It seemed that any minute it could all turn into a black mush, and this time we might be too late, and I—I would remain here without her. And only in Tania's eyes was I the person I wanted to be. She loved me; she saw a writer in me. Only with the help of her trusting confidence could I afford to behave like a man who does not depend on money, career, success. She was my career and my success; she was the philosophical system that made me visible. I was reflected, I found myself, in her.

The principle of that system, Tania's starting point, was goodness. The better I was, the more she loved me. I had nothing else to worry about except to be good. Tania related to me with a divine simplicity I took for granted. It was as if she existed only in me, as if her sole meaning was to fulfill herself with my content—my mood, my thoughts. She was happy when I was happy, and that was usually when I managed to be good. Our relationship, with its logic of genius, provided me with the armor that let me laugh at the threats of terror that would otherwise reach every day into the very center of my neurotic soul. The papers full of symbolic lies, the destiny of friends and strangers who were in prison, the anonymous power that was always watching me, and the feeling that I was constantly sinning with my very consciousness against the laws of the State—I remained immune to this fear because I knew how much stronger Tania's love would be if they imprisoned me!

Like every philosophical system, this one, too, had a fault. Actually two: First, it prevented me from knowing its carrier, that is, Tania. I would like to say something about her even now, but she is always escaping into my person. And second, Tania could die. The horrifying mortality of her fragile being persecuted me in apocalyptic visions, and I dreamed a thousand times about that final sigh that I have witnessed so intimately on the lips of others. I would sink into a bottomless abyss, into immaterial space without coordinates and dimensions. I would wake up in a sweat and in darkness, and the feeling of cosmic isolation would remain with me for a few seconds. Beside me, Tania was breathing so quietly that I had to make sure that her shoulder, showing above the comforter, was warm.

Friday, right from the start, I had to rush around at racing speed. I rested only in the elevator. During those short breaks I was accosted by thoughts of my own nobility. Really, I asked myself, who else has so much selfless courage as to do such a job for the salary of a cleaning woman? Pista *bacsi* is an alcoholic, and another orderly wants to study medicine. Nobody but me.

My brain warned me that when one becomes conscious of his selfless nobility, such nobility disappears. I tried to avoid the issue: If, theoretically, I desired some sort of profit, what kind of profit would it be? I couldn't come up with an answer. Maybe my thoughts in the elevator were insufficient, to say nothing about the fact that the curtain of thought was occasionally torn by some doctor who pushed himself inside.

In the afternoon a sleepy peacefulness reigned, and everyone disappeared like an April storm. I lay down on a bed and relaxed all of my muscles to the last one. My jaw fell, my eyelids stopped in the middle, and I could feel how the disks between the vertebrae, one by one, returned to normal after being flattened by tons of female flesh, how they slowly recovered their original shape. I was quite happy. I like physical exertion because it is as clean as a surgical cut. My body works instead of me, while nobody but nobody takes an interest in my well-preserved brain. It is a luxury and a gift to be able to think absolutely and gratuitously what one desires.

An hour later I was awakened by a pounding on the door and screams from the corridor. I stuck out my head and saw Yvette kicking the elevator.

"Shit," she said, looking at me in despair. "It doesn't work."

After I tried it more decisively, the doors opened, and we pushed in a stretcher bearing a tiny woman. The bottom of her dress was wet from fetal water, and she looked at us from below, thoroughly frightened.

Naked on the table, she looked like all the rest. All of them suddenly have thin arms and legs and these flow from their swollen belly. They reminded me of motionless insects turned upside down, the ones I see in summer on the dusty roads outside the city. The aureoles around the nipples turned violet, as if from fear.

"Wait here. I'll go get a doctor," Yvette ordered, and went in the kitchen to light up a cigarette. She was angry because she had seen the narrow hips of poor Mrs. Smid. She was hoping that the booths would remain empty until the end of her shift, but now she would have to make do with a cigarette.

I didn't like Yvette, because she was intelligent and scornful of me. She also had disdain for all those women who ended up in her hands, because those poor vessels were clumsy to open and incredibly stupid and had to learn everything from the beginning. She scorned Nature because she had a distaste for Nature's vulgar technology. She respected only the doctor, because he was the creator, cause, and meaning of everything. With the work of his hands culminated a process, and because Yvette scorned the mysteries, she chose as the meaning and aim of the process the doctor's hands themselves. Yvette's defeat consisted in the fact that she could not be the aim of any doctor, because a woman is not anything more or less than a poor vessel for that process of which the essence, the beginning, and the end Yvette found extremely disgusting.

Yvette knew all that about herself, and her attitude toward her thin body and aging face was as equally scornful as it was toward me. She cared lovingly only for her hands, and I often looked at them thinking how beautiful she would have been had she looked like her hands.

Mrs. Smid's hands were bony and spotted from fear. With her thin fingers, angular like pencils, she grabbed my wrist. She anchored her terrified glance to the ceiling, opened her mouth, and stopped breathing. I placed my free hand on her belly and felt an undulating hardening. Under my hand something rippled. Suddenly everything hardened like rock.

"Please, breathe," I said bashfully, and Mrs. Smid started to breathe like our Pepina, who once followed me into the kitchen and gave birth to a litter of three puppies with her eyes fixed on me. Beads of perspiration appeared on Mrs. Smid's forehead, as if a wave of pain had sprayed her lightly out of its foamy crest. Her cheeks tightened, and her nose became more pointed. She turned to me.

I should have said something to rid her of the horror in her eyes, of the terror from the unknown force that appeared from who knows where. In those few seconds she felt for the first time the attack of a commanding suprapersonal energy within her own body that she knew so intimately, and the experience isolated her with that brutal stranger. In that moment Mrs. Smid knew with her entire being that she was subject to another will, stronger than her own. Her wisdom increased by millennia while I stood by her like some awkward fossil from the Stone Age.

"Please, breathe," I repeated awkwardly, feeling helpless and useless because even participation and compassion were refused to me on account of my lack of imagination. It seized her again, and threw her from side to side as if she were on a flatbed truck as it hurtled down a cobblestone road. Her finger joints went white as she squeezed my hand, and something like a vicious, ravenous jolt of pain forced a scream out of her mouth.

"No, no, no, Mrs. Smid, the whole city does not have to know that you are giving birth," said the deep voice of the head obstetrician from outside the door, and into the booth entered a huge man with the hands of a lumberjack and a belly that could have contained twins. The head obstetrician's attitude toward the world was like the attitude of other people toward puppies or guinea pigs. They like them, because they don't have to be afraid of them. The nurses adored him and ran away from him squealing the minute he appeared in the hallway, because he used to say, "How is the ovulation going, girls?"

Yvette arrived. I wanted to leave, because I had already seen enough, but the doctor detained me with a movement of his hand. Yvette had her double funnel around her neck like a necklace. She put it on top of the mound and bent down, placing her ear on it, listening intently. I liked that picture: two women intimately connected by a brass bridge. I envied Yvette that she could hear the pit-a-pat, pit-a-pat, that she was penetrating to the cosmos and finally connecting with the mystery that would actually vanish with its birth. But I did not find the courage to borrow the funnel from her.

"You will have to hurry, my dear," Yvette said, straightening up coldly. "The baby won't be able to bear such contractions much longer."

"So go for it, mummy!" the doctor said, spreading his legs like a goalkeeper, waiting with his hands ready by the dark slit. Then he entered it with his fingers, feeling the walls of the tunnel while glancing at me with a discontented eye.

Mrs. Smid's body obediently shook in spasms, and her nails jabbed the palm of my hand, transmitting to me the vibrations of the hardened muscles. When the contractions were over, she lay in front of us, helpless and frightened.

"That won't do," the doctor said, startled, as he interrupted his thinking.

"Yvette, honey, put her on a monitor. And we are going to work, mummy," he ordered with a changed voice.

Yvette attached wires to the tight belly, and turned on the switch. From the speaker came the sound of a jazz drummer. The drummer was nervous, and nobody liked his beat. Mrs. Smid pushed with exhaustion against the handles. She pressed her chin against her collarbone and, pursued by the panicky beat of her second heart, launched such a storm inside herself that it could have cost her her life. You could not see much from the outside: She was shivering slightly, and only her face betrayed what was happening inside. She was grimacing like a figure from a Kokoschka painting, showing her teeth and the deep wrinkles of her face arranged into a look of despair. I could not tear myself away from her and stood in awe before this scene of pure existence. Only the body was there or, better still, only the belly and the mouth of the tunnel. Everything else, including thoughts, disappeared in that current of energy and will that obliged her to tear herself in two and push out that other creature even at the price of her own life. I will never understand it, though I've read the medical books, for the mechanics of tissues and hormones does not explain the cruelty of the universe, does not explain why women are gifted with the ability to experience the naturalness of life and death, to experience the touch of the unthinkable, to experience the impersonality of their body. I stood above Mrs. Smid, and in my head were projected my vain attempts to feel what she was experiencing unaided.

Before each race I used to promise myself that this time I would cross the limit of the natural. I knew so well the feeling that came when, during the last three hundred meters, my insides began to turn over. It was not really a feeling of pain, but rather of mortal fear. It was not fatigue, but some monstrous idea that when I'd push my legs into a faster tempo, something inside me would crack and I would throw up my insides and all that would remain of me would be a small, shapeless pile of flesh and bones. Every time I would order my legs to do it, but again and again the fear won, the limit won, though I knew that all I had to do was to cross that limit and I would be a different man.

Mrs. Smid was past the limit. I saw her muddy eyes and the waxlike pallor in her face. The fingers in my hand relaxed and only moved unwittingly when contractions jerked the body. It seemed that this time Nature had miscalculated and distributed the chances blindly and unfairly. The hips were too narrow, or the baby was too big. Maybe the woman was too weak. Contractions shook her as if somebody were slapping her face. The other inside her was trying to escape on its own, to blast its way out, to tear through the tissue at any price. And she tried to help with the remnants of her last strength, strength that issued from another basis than the muscle cell full of sugar.

"That's enough!" said the doctor. He stood up, and his lips were angrily closed. "Yvette, give her a mask, and you," he came up to me and took me by my elbow, "you will push."

He positioned me to the side and placed my arm up to the elbow near the top of the belly right below the breasts.

"Take her by the shirt and push with the entire forearm against me. It's up to you. Is that clear?" he said, returning to Mrs. Smid's crotch.

Yvette turned off the monitor, put a gas mask on the patient's face, attached herself with cool disdain to the universe, and turned her eyes upward.

"It looks bad," she declared.

"Three, four, let's go!" the doctor roared.

I lay down with all my weight against the round belly. Near my ear I heard whimpering sighs, and underneath I felt the shivering of exhausted muscles. They flexed for a moment, but immediately relaxed and arranged themselves under the skin like wrung-out washcloths. I pushed with my forearm against the balloon, but my bashfulness prevented me from pushing it with all my strength, because Mrs. Smid was disappearing below me like a rag doll, as if lifeless, with an oxygen mask for a face, demoted to a poor failed vessel.

"One more time!" ordered the head doctor. "And give it a good push, or else the baby will suffocate."

I threw myself on the body and directed to my forearm all the power collected in myself from the thousands of kilometers I had run and the tons of women I had lifted. It fused there into boundless energy, and I was amazed by its blind brutality and felt a wave of joy rising in me. With the other hand I held on to the opposite edge of the table, preventing Mrs. Smid from sliding forward, and she was helping me, leaning against my arm with her chin, stretching her neck, and pushing her head back. She supported me with all her strength, though she must have felt her insides churning. It incited me to insanity, and I pushed harder, like a predator preparing his victim for the coup de grâce. It started to go dark in front of my eyes and to freeze in the back of my head. There was very little time left. I sensed the approach of a limit. My stomach was angry, and a sharp pressure rose in my chest. Disappointed, I started to brake, my head thundering; I was sick and could not feel my forearm.

"Stop pushing!" the doctor shouted. "Here he comes."

I was reeling. The world was shrouded in a red mist that quickly dispersed so I could see how the doctor's scissors cut the side of the gate. Overflowing with blood, it slowly gave way.

Carefully, with my vertebrae cracking, I straightened myself out and on my weak legs went to stand behind the doctor. From between Mrs. Smid's legs a hairy ball slipped into his hands. Covered by the jelly of congealing blood, it was egg-shaped like a rugby ball, except much, much smaller, touchingly small, with a violet and stonily disinterested face turned toward the ground. The doctor gripped the baby's jaw, and jerked it. The neck stretched like a spring, and a shoulder appeared, then one arm, and then the other. Mrs. Smid gently sighed, and the whole little body flew out: a doll, a bloody little clown with a string attached to his belly.

Yvette picked him up, and the blue parcel hung over her hand while the doctor cut the umbilical cord in two like a chairman of the national council opening a new shopping center. Instead of applause, a few drops of thick blood silently trickled out, and Yvette placed the child in a shiny roasting pan.

I lazily followed her to a young female doctor who was waiting at a changing table lit by the red light of a heater. I didn't want to think about anything, because each thought would start with the realization that once again I'd been suckered into deep feeling. I should have gone to bed, because my brain was seared by the tension. The nape of my neck hurt, and I desperately wanted to hit the sack.

I leaned against the wall and observed the young female doctor. She had no time to resist me, because Yvette placed a blue body in front of her. Her hands had been cultivated for generations to hold a parasol, but in the age of socialism one carries medicine instead. I had heard that half of my classmates from our elite class in the elementary school were studying medicine. I, too, had wanted to become a doctor, but my father dropped out of the elite in 1970, finding a job as a truck driver, and I was shuffled off among completely different classmates. I couldn't decide whether I should feel sorry for myself or for the doctor. I often caught myself looking absentmindedly at her pure face. Her beauty is the fruit of immobility. All of my female classmates, future doctors, behaved in a dignified manner by the eighth grade, like ladies after menopause, and I would bet my life that you won't find a wrinkle on them even on their deathbeds. And I like that. I looked at her hands, which reminded me of childhood, school, and my classmates, with whom I had been in love, one and all. I once belonged there. I vaguely remember the feeling: the world does exist, of course, and I have my own place in it, in our elite class. But since then I have been living in a net of uncertainty that has so many holes that I question whether it is still a net. I have been thrashing about in it for so long that the netting can't take it, and I can climb out of it anytime and do so more and more frequently. I tell everyone that I am already living without one, but occasionally wonder whether I am not knitting another.

With those hands the doctor picked up an oxygen mask, a miniature version of the one worn by the mother, and placed it on the little boy's wrinkled face. She bent her head over him and showed me her shining smooth forehead, which, in a perfect cathedral vaulting, changed into thick, uncolored hair tied with a braid in the back.

"Would you please hold this for me?" she asked, and I took the mask without a word.

She injected a needle into one of two veins imprisoned in the

211

transparent gelatin of the umbilical cord, and as she finished pressing the valve, the boy started to whimper. I took the mask away, and the doctor inserted into his tiny nose a transparent suction tube that missed its mark, because instead of the windpipe, the twisted clot was gathered in the mouth. He opened his mouth and gasped for air, but then quickly closed it. It was as if he had decided to drift into a sweet dream because death was a more logical conclusion to his existence after his mother had expelled him from herself, as if he judged the life outside his mother's body to be merely an absurd spasm.

While I wafted the oxygen wind at him, the doctor took out the tube, listened to his heart with a stethoscope, and pressed his chest with her thumb and index finger. Little Smid broke out into the familiar baby cry, to which all mothers react with a Pavlovian smile. But it always puts me in a mood of disconsolate melancholy, because I cannot help the child. The first experience of the world is murderously gloomy, and though he will try to forget it all his life, one day he will find that it alone was the true one.

"Go ahead and cry, little one. Just clean out your lungs," the doctor said, nodding with satisfaction and making way for Susan, the nurse from the children's ward, who took him in the palm of her hand and put him under a water tap in the sink. He became quiet, but it did not help him. They measured him in a wooden tub, and then the doctor placed him on a felt pillow and jerked it so that the little one's arms flew up, searching for help. She forgot to laugh at this joke and, with a serious expression, noted his reflexes on the first record of his life.

When I passed by Mrs. Smid's booth, she lay in a sort of semiconscious state, and the head obstetrician was bent over a bloody hole that looked like it might have been the result of a grenade fragment. In a bowl next to him was a piece of flesh—about two pounds of red cake embroidered with blue veins, and held together in a transparent membrane. It was ugly, looking like a Medusa pulled out of the water.

Somewhere below, the elevator must have been stuck, and so I walked downstairs, trying to trace the reason for my bad mood. Everything was as it should have been, I told myself. I was helpful during a difficult delivery and even, perhaps, had delivered little Smid by myself. He is alive, and that's the main thing. Had he been stillborn, they would have wrapped him in a diaper and given him to me on a tray. I have been down there a few times, where Joey the stoker always sits by the furnace, as if he were expecting me, smoking his Mars cigarettes and dreaming about his bartender girlfriend. When he notices me, he climbs the iron stairs and, nodding his head like Mephistopheles, takes the tray from me and opens the grate of the furnace. The yellow-red glare of the coke pleasantly vibrates, sticking out its little blue tongues, and Joey's black spittle noiselessly vanishes in it. The diaper catches fire above the surface and drops down as a little black tuft that breaks up almost instantly, but the little body twists. It twists uncomfortably on the red-hot bed until it becomes a ball. I never watch to the end; I leave Joey standing there in silence. His gloomy face is illuminated by the red light, and the smoke rises from the rubber soles of his work boots because a quiet heat is pounding into the steel roof of the boiler on which he stands. I always run away, and I stop breathing, as I rage in frustration that it has to be me.

I went to my room and found her there. She was waiting for me in the armchair like my fate. Her hair was like an Egyptian woman's: it fell on her shoulders heavy and black, and she protected one ear from it with a hair pin. She was smoking a Sparta cigarette.

"May I?" she asked.

"You may everything."

"Don't say that. I came to . . . I wanted to see you," she blurted out, and extinguished her cigarette butt in the tin ashtray. From the edge of a beautiful nail a fragment of pink lacquer broke off.

"Were you busy?"

"I was giving birth."

"I thought women did that."

I shrugged my shoulders because I felt that my secret made me more attractive.

"I don't even know if you have any children," I said.

"Two," she nodded. "But I delivered them myself."

"How was it?"

"Fine. It was easy because, as you might have noticed, I am well built for that."

"I noticed."

I took out of the cabinet a bottle of wine I had planned to drink with Pista *bacsi.*

"A bribe," she said, applauding joyfully.

"It's an expression of gratitude," I said seriously.

The bottle had been brought before lunch by some lady in a fashionable fur coat who was smiling uncertainly. I was supposed to know what it was for. But I remembered only when she was gone, because that fur coat and the lipstick confused me. It was a routine that I never got used to. Each patient had to be made ready for her operation, and with every one of them I found myself on the borderline of my sanity. My victims related to me in different ways: The mature women responded with feigned indifference or even kind understanding; the young girls with hidden hate. The old women treated it like attention from a grandchild, petting my cheeks; the virgins approached the stirrup with mortal terror, as if surrendering to a seven-headed dragon. I reflected gloomily on the vengeance that the gods will send down on my head for this heretical ritual. But I pushed these reflections away with a stream of talk aimed at every woman as she entered the room. I led her by her elbow to the table, accompanying my words with expansive gestures while hiding the razor under my belt.

Like Scheherazade, I occupied their minds with stories they had never heard, so that after a while their eyes absentmindedly wandered about the ceiling. If they did not want to listen, I at least asked them questions, insistently, so that they had to talk. It worked well. They opened up to me as if to a confessor. I was amazed with what relief they surrendered, at how quickly they understood that it was in their power to banish all revulsion and terror. I had to wonder if they would have reacted similarly to a rape. Would they have surrendered voluntarily simply because it was in their nature? Was there a positive principle anchored in them since time immemorial, a sort of existential desire to agree with influences more than with morality?

They would chat about their fear of the next day's operation, about their children (perhaps a son was my age and doing his military service), or about their husband. What would he say, for instance, when she returned shaved, hairless like a girl? They would be carried away to a strange domain of intimacy and breathlessly inundate me with the details of their lives in order not to think that in reality our intimate relationship was based on the ticklish scratching in their crotch, with its humble, prosaic reason.

It would happen that I would finish and they would just go on talking, on their backs with their legs spread apart, and suddenly I had to avert my gaze in confusion, struck by the scene that, after I finished my work, would lose its logic and seem perverse.

At such moments, angry frustration possessed me, because I had been forced to do this by the rules of the professionals, who had ordered and staged it. It would never occur to them that ordinary human souls might be floundering in spasms of the unnatural. It wouldn't occur to them, because they rejected the soul, having gotten rid of its specter the moment they reached into the warm human insides, found them material, and found nothing else besides.

So I would stand indecisively, waiting for the moment when I would be able to do away with this scene and at the same time not disturb the women's monologue. I was searching for the gap between the sentences in which to insert my "Finished!" I never managed to preserve the magic of intimacy; unwillingly I stopped it all. "Oh, thank you," they would say, and that would end it, the story would remain unfinished, because once back on their feet, they had no need to talk and were not in my, Scheherazade's, power anymore. Only a whiff of awkwardness, like after a badly played farce, remained.

"No matter what it is the expression of, it does not change the essence of the wine. I should have brought it myself, but I wanted to be here as soon as possible," said the Egyptian woman.

I didn't know what to say, afraid that each additional word would push me to a threshold. I washed the glasses.

"What do you really think about me?" I heard from behind my back, and was aware that she crossed her legs.

"You like me," I replied.

"That's true all right, but it doesn't say anything about me."

"That's all I know about you."

I brought her a full glass. She took it and looked straight into my eyes. Her eyelids did not move, and her pupils, drawn into tiny little dots, discreetly traversed my face. She stared at me calmly, rudely, upending all the rules of politeness, and with each additional second inspired in me growing confusion. What sort of power resided in her to allow her to behave so shamelessly?

"Are you afraid of me?" she asked.

"Who wouldn't be? You are testing your magic on me. But why me?"

"You're so different. And you like me."

"How can you tell?"

"Don't be naïve. A woman knows."

"I'm not hiding it. But how do you know I'm different?"

"That's my secret."

She continued to stare at me with her wide-open eyes, as if offering to me what her mouth refused to say. I moved closer to them, and they, with their immobility, invited me in, promising they wouldn't budge. In the instant when I touched her unfamiliar lips, her eyes closed.

"That's a bummer," I said, disappointed.

"Hmm," she said, nodding blindly as her hands, searching, slid under my surgical shirt.

"Why do you wear such a wide belt?" she asked.

"I'm protecting my precious waist."

"Could you lift me, too?"

She was wearing a tight-fitting dress, probably of cotton. When I lifted her, she didn't even move, completely surrendering to the sensation of the strange power that carried her off. She just placed one hand on the nape of my neck. The carrying of women was, apart from the poor salary, my only reward. Evanescent moments of intimacy took place like minor miracles. Each woman became languid like a bride carried over the threshold, and I got along best with the white-haired old women because they already knew that reality is deceptive and that one has to believe the momentary illusion.

I was holding her in my hands and slowly realizing that I was letting myself be deceived by habit. Instead of a joyful illusion that disappears on command, I was holding a real woman. She reposed in my embrace with royal confidence, bent back her head, and marched right into my soul, where, except for Tania, no one had ever entered. I don't know what key she had used to unlock it. She simply entered, and I received the right to touch her. I should have wondered about that mythic transformation, but the strangest thing of all was the matter-of-fact way in which I smelled the curve behind her ear and kissed the arch between her neck and her shoulder. She pressed against me as if from fear, as if she didn't know that her breasts would lean against me with a completely different meaning, as if she became afraid at the last minute of her game, the final aim of which was the abolition of rules.

I carried her to the bed and unbuttoned her dress. She shook her clothes off like a butterfly, made a few mind-bending moves of genius, and lay in front of me naked. It hit me like a blow to the head. I was kneeling on the edge of a cosmos that originally was not supposed to be there. I felt the excitement of an explorer who had found the fourth dimension. I penetrated it, intoxicated with freedom, and she understood, embracing me with all her might, as if she wanted to protect me.

"Now you have to tell me all about yourself," I said when my heartbeat slowed down and my head felt empty like a wind-swept sky.

"Why?"

"Because I love you."

"This was quite sufficient."

"No." I brought full glasses, and as I handed one of them to her, she glanced at me thoughtfully.

"All right, then."

She began to talk with a quiet, shrouded voice, smoking a cigarette, and she also stuck one into my mouth. I tried smoking once, a long time ago when I was eighteen and it occurred to me that the time was ripe to sample vice. My coach allowed me to go skiing with two classmates, and the three of us smoked together in the basement of some dormitory. I'll never forget that awesome luxury of togetherness. For a week I was like them. I floated on clouds of collectivism.

Now I filled my lungs with the smoke from her cigarette, listening to a banal story and absorbing it blissfully. Before she arrived in Bratislava to study, she had known only Liptovský Mikuláš and the surrounding mountains. Twice she ran away from her mother, a dynamic woman who taught at the local secondary school and was her home-room teacher. Twice her father, a surgeon at the local hospital, took her back to her mother. At the time of her graduation she weighed eighty-five pounds. It was the result of mental anorexia.

"Were you afraid of your mother?" I asked.

"I was afraid of life. I hated my mother. I wished she would die so I could live with my father. I know," she interrupted me when I started to speak. "I have two semesters of psychology. Then I switched to Slovak."

"Did you want to become a teacher?"

"I wanted to become what I am—an editor and writer."

"I, too, am a writer."

"Everybody is in his own way, more or less. When you pass by the bookstore on the corner of Michalská Street, look in the window and you'll see my book of fairy tales."

"I've read it."

"Did you like it?"

"Socialist realism does not mix with fairy tales. Witches exist, after all. You are the first proof."

She kissed me on my cheek and continued her story. She was married as a virgin and got pregnant right after the wedding.

"I think he never forgave me for it. He married me to get me in bed, and before he taught me anything, we had to stop."

"Did you have to torment him so much?"

"I was a believer."

When she caught my inquisitive look, she added: "Not anymore. Then came the second child, worries about the apartment, a job, the whole insane merry-go-round. I felt that my faith was not helping me. On the contrary, it exhausted and limited me even more."

"Maybe I don't understand, but I'd say a life without faith seemed more attractive to you."

She nervously lit two cigarettes and pushed one between my lips.

"I was twenty-five, with two kids, and had a husband who came home at night from meetings smelling of vodka. Can you imagine?"

"No."

"I wanted to work, write, love, but he would tear up my pages and shout that he wanted meat for his dinner. At night he would dump himself on me like a bag of potatoes and call me a whore. He stank and had a repulsive big hard belly that pressed on me like a tank. I was terrified of the commitment I had agreed to in church. If I wanted to leave him, I had to leave the church as well."

"And together with him, you abandoned sin."

"What do you mean?"

"I don't know."

"So shut up. What do you know about sin? Who can say what's good or evil today?"

"Wait a minute!" I sat up. "Good is what exists. Absolute values in mathematics are always positive. Evil is what approaches zero in value, what suppresses the existing, what aims for annihilation."

"What a goulash. How did you figure that out?"

Offended, I fell down on my back and looked at the ceiling. She was right. She touched my chest with her hand and, as a sign of reconciliation, stabbed me with her pointy nose, the kind Polish actresses usually have.

"I'm happy you don't have a big belly."

"That's because I'm a runner. I got into shape way back in trade school, and if I had been a bit better, I would have won the Republican Championship, and they would have had to accept me at the university. But I never won the big race, because I was afraid."

"You didn't pass the examination?"

"I? I was the best student in the school. For me it's fun to study. When they did not accept me at the secondary school, I studied the subjects I was missing on my own, because I wanted to be educated."

"But why didn't they accept you at the secondary school?"

"Because they took my brother. He is a year older."

"Because they took your brother?"

"Our parents didn't know the ropes. When it was time for me to apply to the university, I took charge of it. I applied in Bohemia and personally took in the application form. I forbade the girls in the office to send me the exam results at home, telling them I lived with a friend. I gave them his address, which was clean. I forbade anyone at home to talk about it. On the contrary, I told them to complain that I did not study. The only person we knew who found out about the results was a distant acquaintance from Prague, because he taught at the faculty that gave me the test. But he didn't know anything about our troubles, and after the exams he happily phoned my parents to tell them that I had been accepted. My father almost had a heart attack, my mother cried, and I smashed the phone. The whole scheme was screwed. And then I learned that it wouldn't have worked anyway, because my friend's address was not so clean. They had played a cat-and-mouse game with me."

"Who?"

"What do you mean, who? The police."

She thoughtfully drew her finger over my body and then said: "You asked how I knew you're different. I could see at first sight that you're paranoid and insane. But I like you."

My face was covered by her heavy hair. She was bending over me, waiting for an answer.

"Because I want to be good," I said. "To be good means to be real, and when you talk about paranoia, then you don't understand. You don't know what it means to live your whole life in a bugged apartment. You don't know what it is to meet daily those nobodies, whose only interest in life is to keep you down. Goodness is the antidote against nothingness, and while I strive for it, I'm safe."

"You won't quit? Goodness is what I like, what I find attractive. I find you attractive. But I don't know how you'll fit into your good that a moment ago you slept with me. What about your wife?"

"Tania? Tania is good," I said, a bit puzzled. "Sometimes it seems that since I've known you, I love her even more. More freely."

"You are kind like a hippopotamus," she threw in darkly, and made a move for the handbag behind her head. She had a deliciously long arm made more slender by its walnut color.

"Sorry," I said.

"That's all right." She took the cap off a little flask, lifted back her head, and dripped some liquid into her eyes. "Serves me right." She looked at me with a sad smile, and her eyes were shining again and in their corners drops gathered.

"I once read a book about Martians who placed masks on their faces according to their moods. When you want to show you are sad, you use drops?"

"I have a condition," she answered coldly. "My eyes dry out. The liquid stopped forming."

"You're kidding. Why should it stop forming? When did it stop?"

"Not long ago. I cried it out."

I was wondering whether to believe that when I was interrupted by a telephone call. I was needed on the fourth floor.

"Please, don't leave. I'll be back in a moment," I said.

She sat up to kiss me, and as I dressed myself, I had to shake my head to free myself of that motionless, erect, self-conscious beauty.

Mrs. Smid lay in a delirious semisleep, with huge black circles under her eyes, and violet-brown lips. She turned her head toward me, attempting a smile.

"I'll move you to your bed," I said in a familiar voice. I realized with relief the force of habit. The fragile body in the hospital shirt reminded me of nothing.

We were waiting for the elevator, and in the meantime I took a peek at the records. Out of ten possible points, little Smid got six. He started life with a handicap. Mrs. Smid and I remained quiet as we moved down the corridors, and only at the moment when she lay in her bed after I had covered her with a comforter smelling of cheap detergent did she look straight into my eyes and say: "Thank you."

I'm good, I thought stubbornly. But she wasn't there anymore. Only the ashtray remained, filled by both of us.

I must have gone mad. The morning rattle of the telephone exchange behind the wall sounded completely different. It moved into my head, filled it with formless arrhythmia, and made me sick. The last time I had felt something similar was in the military. I used to stand guard over some abandoned sealed warehouses. I held an automatic rifle with an empty magazine over my shoulder—the warehouses were so worthless they allowed even me to guard them, though without ammunition—and read Sartre. I took him in doses instead of LSD, and it worked in a tormentingly effective way. I looked hopelessly at an empty bottle dumped in the grass. Its deafening cry filled me up, it shouted into the universe about its mission, its function, its meaning, but there was no one in the whole universe to hear it. Only I existed, lonely like God. It was I who was to bear on his shoulders the burden of the meaning of all the bottles in the world, of each object lying still in the grass, in the stores, in the cities that lost their weight on their journey to the stars. My neurotic brain was supposed to keep together a whole monstrous load of meanings and forms that threatened to burst anytime and discharge into my soul an amorphous diarrhea. My stomach was shaking in spasms, and I was closing my eyes to the limitless nonsense that was descending on me unceasingly, smothering me without so much as touching me. I trembled with a peculiar, tormented pleasure that I was still standing, though I was the last one of all and at the end of my tether, with an empty rifle.

I was leaving the hospital that morning after a night shift that I had miraculously been able to sleep through. Only once did the nurses from the children's ward wake me, when the incubators were running low on oxygen. Little Smid looked good, and nothing in his face reminded me of the struggle of the day before. I changed his bomb.

I was awakened by the rattle of the telephone exchange and felt sick to my stomach. Then Pista *bacsi* arrived as always, stooping, in his old coat, and with his alcoholic depression.

"Oh, you drunken whore," he sighed in disappointment upon discovering the empty bottle.

Joey the stoker came in right after him and slowly and ceremoniously closed the door. He looked us over, gloomily, and walked toward the armchair.

"Here you are," Pista handed me a wrinkled banknote, "Get me some wine or else I'll croak."

I shook my head. "Ask Joey. I gotta go."

"Fuck this life," muttered Pista, because Joey was already dreamily dialing a number.

* * *

Pepina was shaking with excitement, wagging her tail like a fan, carrying a little branch for me in her jaw. In her love she jumped on me, almost pushing me to my knees, and I remained upright only because of the desperate certainty that it was I who decided everything.

I carefully opened the door of the house and smelled the familiar musty smell we never managed to air out completely. There was no unpleasant reaction inside of me, and so I continued. The kitchen was tidy, the stove was still burning from the previous day, and the tap was dripping, because Tania is weak and could not quite turn it off. She was still in bed and called to me with a thin voice. She always woke up like a child, happy the day had begun, and she became a woman only when she was fully conscious.

She took her bare arm out from under the comforter and waved with a gesture that could have been both a greeting and an invitation. With her back to me she was attempting to finish one of her transparent color dreams without a point that she would tell me about at breakfast. I warmed up my hand on her stomach, which was hot from being under the cover, and she acknowledged me by remaining motionless. It was as easy as watching a movie with a familiar plot. She was opening under my hands like a flower in touch with the morning sun, and I was relieved that I still possessed the secret key, that the signs were still valid, even though the world in which they had originated no longer existed.

Or was I mistaken? Could it be that after a while, signs and symbols themselves become real and substitute for the world, functioning in its place? I was excitedly reflecting on the notion of living in a labyrinth governed by my own laws when suddenly someone lifted the roof, and in a blinding light, I found myself watching the labyrinth from a flying helicopter. Tania was experiencing it with me. We flew together at a vertiginous altitude, and I loved her as much as I loved the one who had made me the gift of that light. When later I lay in Tania's embrace, she maternally caressed my hair.

"You left the door open again," I told her at breakfast, reproachfully. "Aren't you afraid that one day somebody else will come in instead of me?"

"Who would come here?"

"I don't know."

"All right, I'll lock the door next time," she promised, as she had many times before. I don't remember ever seeing her afraid. She wasn't even afraid of mice and spiders. Once, when I was working, there was a powerful storm that broke trees like matchsticks and flooded the streets in minutes. I was terrified because I did not trust our little house. I had noticed that the roof was buckling under the rotten joists and that the chimney was crooked and spotted by fist-sized holes made by the aggressive wind. I imagined it collapsing and falling through the roof, breaking through the ceiling, and killing helpless Tania. I hopped into a car borrowed from my father, available because the police had maliciously taken away his driver's license, and forded the flooding water to the other side of the city. The house was still standing, and in the kitchen I found a pot into which water leaking from the ceiling was dripping. Tania was sleeping on an opened book.

"How was work?" she asked, startling me from my recollection.

"We had a difficult delivery, but otherwise nothing unusual."

"What happened? She could not deliver?"

"She had narrow hips, and the baby was large. Why are you asking? It won't happen to you. You don't have to be afraid."

"I'm just asking. I'm not afraid, because I can't imagine it. There's no point in being afraid of something that I don't know. When it comes, you'll tell me what to do."

"You can depend on that."

"I was dreaming that we were on a ship looking at the water as it foamed below us. But it was not a pleasant dream. . . . Oh, I know why now! I wasn't pregnant. It seemed so strange, I wanted to explain it to you, but the wind was blowing and you couldn't hear me."

It was freezing a little before Christmas, but January was like November had been. It often rained so heavily that the puddles looked alive in the storm. I went to run at the stadium because the soil had turned into mud. The track surface was shining darkly, and there were wet crows in the empty stands. I was glad the athletes were training in the hall, because I did not feel like talking to them. They would ask me what I was doing, how my life was, and I wouldn't know how to answer them. It seems to me there are too many people who can reduce the answer to such a question to a single sentence. But maybe they're right. It's only I who am always dissatisfied and want to explain something, while others understand each other without many words. I feel like they are tuned to a station I don't get. They would like to help me, but I have no talent and am always uncomprehending, like a monkey.

I suppose only Paul and Igor would pat me on my back in appreciation. I had known them in trade school. They were sports instructors who brought me from the jungle of pipes into their world, where I found a gymnasium, a sauna, a pool, and tennis courts. They chose me as a colleague because they wanted to make a champion out of me.

"Run morning to night, but don't forget that life is more complicated," Paul once stated.

"It's too complicated," I answered, depressed. "No matter what you do, you always wreck it."

"Foolishness. You're mature, but you behave like a child," Igor laughed, but he meant it. "One of these days your ideals will be the death of you, Milan, and the shame of your innocence will fall on us!"

We were sitting above the deserted pool in the lifeguard's glass booth. One of the regular lifeguards was sick, and I was substituting. A swimming pool without people is a magical space. The transparent water roars into the openings behind the edges, and on the surface the waves vanish, and everything seems otherworldly. The five-meter depth deceives, and an earring at the bottom seems within reach. I would sit on the heated bench by the empty pool for hours, listening to the noise the water made and reveling in the loneliness of the beautiful, artificial space. But it didn't stay like that.

"Check out those babes, you guys," Igor said, digging his fingers into my shoulder, then massaging it gently as his face lit up with inspired joy.

"God, look at that number," he whispered.

She was walking in a distinguished manner, her curly head erect, as if she were bearing on top of her head the precarious burden of her beauty, revealed by her blue swimsuit. She was one of the students of the Faculty of Economics, which rented our pool each Tuesday morning.

Igor peeled away from us like a bull, having preserved from his judo days a thick neck. He dove into the water and swam in a wide arc to the place where she was sticking her painted toenails out of the water and admiring them. Right in front of her he submerged, swam under her, and, breaking back above the surface, made a face at her, smiling childishly and rudely as the water dripped from his hair and his walrus mustache. She just gently pushed him under the water, and he obediently vanished. Soon his wet head showed in the arch of her neck and shoulder, and her red lips beamed with a secret smile.

"He's got her. Quite a guy." Paul said, looking around the pool.

"Your turn now. That blonde over there, sitting in the back, who doesn't want in."

"I don't know how," I objected.

"You've got to try it. Don't be afraid. She's just waiting for you!"

After the fifth kilometer, I got the first signals. The pressure increased in my temples; my hands went cold, because they were the first things affected by the limited amount of blood available. It occurred to me that I wouldn't be able to withstand another five thousand at the same tempo. I shortened my stride, so that I could speed up the rhythm of breathing. I completed each additional lap in the same time at the price of an exactly calculated supply of energy. I saved as much as I could, because I had to pay with suffering. From the time I started using this simple mathematics, I stopped worrying that I didn't belong among the victors. Each victory was only a question of a sacrifice that I was not prepared to make.

In the last lap I stretched myself from the waist up, bent forward against the growing resistance that pushed me back and down to the ground. The last lap is the culmination. It's the moment in which I fleetingly touch the sacrifice. It's the illusion that I am the master of my body, that I can humiliate it and force it to suffer. The more thoroughly does my face twist in a grimace while my stomach turns and the more deafening the fireworks in my head, the colder the cynical judgment of the untouched corner of my brain. It laughs at me because I grin showing my teeth like a neighing horse and because my effort is pointless, as the cynical judge is still there, the only sober part of my crazed "I." Embarrassed by this, I fall into the grass beyond the finish line and while falling know that I'm beginning to feel happy, because I'm done with it. As I return to my cozy melancholy, I am again whole.

The grass was soaked with water like a sponge, but I was wet with rain and sweat and hot like a kettle after its water has boiled away. My tongue was glued to the roof of my mouth, and my lips were covered with white foam. I wiped the foam on the grass. Crows were sitting on the top rail, and as I was leaving, they flew back to the stands. I jogged home drunk with happiness. Suddenly I knew that in simple arithmetic, a multiplication had taken place within me: I loved them both, and my love for each of them was stronger because of the other. And I also knew that happiness cannot be bad, that its presence within me was a guarantee of my own goodness. Happiness and goodness belong together. One without the other would lose its meaning, just like a stadium without runners.

In the elevator of the publishing house, I tried to think about something different. For example, all offices have in common an inability to look like anything but an office. That calmed me down.

I knocked, and her voice from behind the door sounded as if it came through a microphone.

"Come in!"

"I have a manuscript for you," I said, "but it's about love. Do you mind?"

For an instant I looked at her face and felt like an invisible man. It was only a flash before she recognized me, but I had managed to see the bottomless abyss of sadness in those eyes set in her face like two black stones. Suddenly they lit up, and it was I who lent them the light.

"You?" She jumped up so quickly from her chair that the impact hurt her and she groaned in my embrace.

In the Cafe Darling, full of smoke, she lit up and ordered coffees with whipped cream. I was inhaling the smoke from a thin stem of the Sparta cigarette, wondering what pleasure I derived from the light touch of the cigarette between my fingers. I filled my lungs completely, and she was laughing because I smoked like an addict. She had fragile white teeth with a bluish tinge. I was paralyzed with astonishment that my inner self was being invaded by signs that previously only lived in the outside world and thus did not exist. Black hair with a few white strands, earrings, painted lips, long, narrow nails, and on a finger some gold with a red stone. I knew that women wore such signs, but Tania avoided them, and I loved her for the reason that she was able to find her female identity without them. Caught short by the magic of colors and fragrances, I lowered my eyes.

"What manuscript about love did you bring me?" she asked.

"That was only a joke. You are in charge of fairy tales, aren't you?"

It seemed she was put out by that. She brought a piece of whipped cream to her mouth, and when she stopped it at her lips, it was transformed into a white porcelain flower, as if she could transform everything she touched.

"I still don't really know what you are about," she said.

"Neither do I."

"Why do you work when you don't have to?"

"It's good work. I'm often free at the time when the whole nation hustles."

"But at what price? Not even a gravedigger has a dirtier job than you. Aren't you afraid you'll crack up?"

"That already happened a long time ago."

"Listen," she said leaning over and taking me by the hand. "Forget about that and do something normal. I'll help you."

"Normal?" I objected. "You don't understand. Nobody's normal here and there is no normal work."

"What do you mean?"

"Can't you feel it? We're all cuckoo. The nation is nuts. Show me one wise person who can satisfactorily explain what's happening. I don't know any. If there were any, they died out."

"It's only you who are cuckoo, but you think everyone else is. That's why I want to help you."

"I know," I said with humility. "Sometimes I feel that I am mistaken. You are so good that you may be right. Even the police may be right. They always say they want nothing else but to protect me."

"Stop it!"

"But I mean it. Sometimes I am seized with terrible doubts, and I feel like I'm in a Platonic cave. Even worse! That the cave itself isn't real!"

"How can you live like that? I don't understand you."

"Because Tania loves me," I said unhappily. I would gladly have lied, but one needs imagination to lie, and my fairy godmothers refused me that.

"You are a fool."

"I know."

She took her handbag and left without a word. I was afraid to check if she had taken her coat with her, and stared at the Sparta cigarettes that she had left on the table. I know of nothing better than loneliness. Its constant noise does not disturb me, though sometimes, against my will, I turn the volume so high that my eardrums are bursting. But she returned, putting her handbag down on the table, and her eyes were shining.

"Should I get angry with you?" she said. "I would love to."

"Please don't."

"If I find a job for you somewhere in the editorial office, will you take it?"

"You understood nothing that I said."

"Will you?"

"Yes."

It was not until February that we got a decent snowfall. The trolley buses were heroically wading through the slush, which boiled over as if from a miraculous pot. When I arrived for the night shift, Pista *bacsi* was waiting for me in our room, muttering angrily.

"What time were you supposed to be here, you asshole?" he said, without really meaning it. But he did not look into my eyes, because making the obligatory reproach pained him.

"You have three postpartum women upstairs," he added after I magnanimously ignored the reproach. He waited a bit to see if I would invite him to have a drink, but I had brought only a detective novel along. He shuffled off, stooped with disappointment, as if burdened by ten lives.

I was looking down from the fourth-floor window, waiting for the files to be processed. It had stopped snowing, but the night sky preserved its dull gray color. In the east the sky radiated pink from the eternal torches of the Slovnaft, reminding me of my childhood, because from the windows of our old apartment I had often watched the sky for hours on end.

Against the vibrating background, a sulfurous jinn from *A Thousand and One Nights* ascended into eternity with a belly full of precious metals. He had finally found appreciation of his beauty after being dishonored by socialist realism. Only after he had succeeded in ridding us of our optimism did his grand evil manifest itself in all its splendor.

A drop of water landed on my shoulder. The big spot on the ceiling was forming another drop, and I went over to the booths. Judith was washing her well-soaked pink hands. They all suffer from lavomania. Only I resist it, but it's easy for me, because I know I am not going to stay here long. She glanced at me coldly. She is cold and smooth like a cut diamond. That is common to many of them. Nurses tend to be perfectly groomed, as if from spite.

"You can transport them," she told me.

In the first booth was a blonde with long hair that fell over the edge of the bed; her clean shirt was tight because of her drumlike belly.

"Pardon me, I'll come for you after you're done," I told her in confusion, and moved the stretcher out into the corridor. Judith usually told me which booths were ready for me. In the other three there really were exhausted mothers lying, each of them, according to her character, cocooned in her own happiness. I moved them, one by one, down to the third floor, in a good mood, because my pleasant routine fit the natural cycle. I am always relieved when witnessing a law that works.

The nurses from the children's ward were transporting, in double-decker carriages, the babies who had already been fed. They invited me for a night coffee.

"You know I'm shy, girls, don't you?"

"Come now, such a handsome guy as you," said one, and they all laughed capriciously. They still think I'm twenty and apparently know me better than I do. I'm afraid that during those extra seven years I did not get a bit closer to eternity—or whatever you want to call it—for I don't even know what it is I'm supposed to be getting closer to.

I returned with my stretcher to the fourth floor and was parking it in its place by the wall when out of the door burst Susan, holding her mouth and heading down the stairs. I entered the delivery room, and there, on the table, lay the terror. Instead of a face, there was only a gaping hole in the middle of the head, and in it, instead of a tongue, some sort of worm stuck out motionless, as if conscious of its horrifying grandeur.

My beautiful aristocratic doctor stood three feet away from it, pale as wax, biting her lip and holding uncertainly in her hand a mask from which oxygen hissed pointlessly into the air. If it had lungs, it did not breathe with them, and the stumps of what were supposed to have been arms and legs were not moving. We were frozen with horror, unable to take our eyes off it. Behind me two nurses were supporting each other and vomiting into the sink. I felt only that I was shaking with cold. I am always attacked by cold when fear grips me. This alien had arrived here, it seemed to me, to tell us something with its monstrous existence, to speak to us. It was only polite to hear the alien out, but I could not understand it. I could only feel its angry derision at our horror.

Did Satan stick his tongue out, as the worm in the cave suddenly moved? The sunken chest rose, and after minutes of silence and immobility, out of the black hole there issued, somewhat like a siren, a droning sound unlike anything else I've ever heard in my life.

The nurses hysterically plugged their ears and ran away. The young one, Jane, who had arrived a month before, closed her eyes in panic and hit the door post with her head, so that her knees buckled and, as in a dream, she slid along the wall until she found her escape.

The doctor managed to stand another full minute without moving, but she finally gnarled her pretty mouth, licked her lips, approached it, and with a few movements wrapped it in a blanket.

"Please, could you take this to an incubator?" she asked me.

"Do you want it to live?"

"I have no choice," she sighed, and turned away.

It resonated in my hands like a pneumatic hammer. I had to walk very slowly, because each step was forced by reason against instincts I had never even suspected I had. They vibrated inside me, and I felt that if I didn't get to that ward soon enough, instinct would prevail and I would press the thing with all my might until I heard the cracking of its bones and then throw it on the ground with all my might and jump on it to stop that infinitely monstrous voice. Everyone had disappeared from the corridor, but someone had left a door open to the incubators. I placed it inside one on a diaper, closed the Plexiglas firmament over it, and sprinted to the sink.

It seemed to me that the high tone of its scream penetrated the walls, because it reached me even as I was opening the door to my room. She was sitting in Joey the stoker's armchair, wearing a wide pleated skirt and a light blue sweater with large eyelets showing a white blouse. I kneeled by her, placing my head on her lap, and passed my hands over her body, washing off the fear that had settled on them.

"My children are with a friend," she whispered in my ear with moist breath. "I can stay."

"Yes, stay," I begged her. I was resting on the warm, woolen skirt and felt increasingly better as the tension in my fingers relaxed and my body softened as if under a shower. As I got up, my head began to hurt for the first time in my life. I had in it an insistently clean emptiness and a previously unknown feeling of the time being very ripe, but for what I did not know.

"I love you," I said, astonished. She smiled and squinted with delight.

"But now tell me, really tell me, why do you want me?" I asked. "What am I to you?"

"I'll tell you," she nodded. "But promise that you won't leave me."

I sat down in an armchair opposite Nora, leaned my head against the wall, and closed my eyes. The alien had disturbed my natural train of thought, and I felt that it had blown the dust from my brain and from now on everything would be different.

She was a bit hesitant, but otherwise spoke without embarrassment as if she had thought it over a long time ago and only searched for the appropriate words because of me.

"It happened after the divorce. We didn't live together anymore, but he still lodged in our place for half a year, because he had nowhere to go. You can't imagine it."

"No."

"He was even more repulsive than before. He moved into the living room, but otherwise he moved around the apartment as he wished, and when I started to lock myself in my bedroom at night, he would stick matches in the lock. And one night . . ." She shook her head and rummaged in her handbag. "One night he came home drunk and attacked me in my sleep. He held my mouth to prevent me from screaming, but I wouldn't have screamed anyway, because of the children. He was cruel, it hurt, but I could manage even that. The revulsion was something else. Maybe you won't understand this, but it was more than a revulsion. It was hatred, monstrous, inhuman hatred I felt toward him. If I had had a knife, I would have ripped his belly open with pleasure and castrated him. In my helplessness, when he was doing it to me and smothering me on the bed, I thought I would die of hatred." She tipped back her head and put in her eye drops. I sat there paralyzed by supsense, and when she handed me a lit cigarette, I shook with love.

"When my period did not come, I knew I was pregnant. I started to get sick. I felt maddeningly ill. I guess it was more the desperation than the pregnancy. I actually did not sleep for weeks because I cried each night. It was a strange sort of crying. It did not bring any relief, and I could not sleep, because my wet pillow was making me cold, but when I got a new one, it soon got wet as well. I stopped taking water to end the tears, but I would have died of dehydration. I didn't want to die. I couldn't, because of the children. In reality I longed for death, because it alone could have freed me from the necessity to choose one of the hells. You understand?"

"I understand," I said, nodding. "But I think you're wrong. If good exists, then it is present always and everywhere, and there is no dilemma between two evils. Despair is only our inability to relate to that good."

"I know, I know," she said impatiently. She continued, and her voice betrayed an increase of controlled tension, as she placed her words, one after another, with such concentration as if walking along a tightrope.

"I decided to get rid of it. I simply could not imagine delivering and taking care of it. There was too much hate in me, although, on the other hand, I realized it was murder. I felt the proximity of madness, and very little prevented me from succumbing to it. This was when you appeared."

"You can't be serious," I said, worried.

"When it was all over, I understood I didn't want to see another man ever again. Then I met you again at the jazz festival, and if you know that feeling of destiny . . ."

"Again?"

She deeply inhaled the smoke, and as she spoke, clouds flew out of her mouth with her words. "I knew you wouldn't remember. But I will preserve forever each moment of that day whether I like it or not. You were as beautiful as an angel of death. You embraced me around my shoulders and brought me to the threshold of that monstrous room. You were constantly telling me something. I don't know what it was, but it calmed me down, and when you took me in your arms, I felt for the first time in my life a male power that I didn't have to fear and that was there to protect me."

She put out the cigarette in the ashtray and looked at me inquisitively.

"That's absurd," I whispered.

"No," she quickly answered, and leaned over and took my hand. "It isn't. Only you could have relieved me of the hatred, because you are good. I'll never forget how tenderly you carried me to my bed afterward, though I despised myself as the worst criminal."

I aimed a dull stare ahead, and she squatted down right into my field of vision. She placed her hands on my shoulders and tipped her head to one side, making her hair slide girlishly to one side.

"I shouldn't have told you this?" she asked.

I shrugged and dropped my head with sudden fatigue. I couldn't fix on any single idea. Ideas were tumbling unpleasantly in my head in an uncertain chain, as if I were falling sleep. There was only one distinct notion. There is usually a precise reason for such a notion. According to its logic, the notion originates from not fulfilling something, but I was incapable of divining what exactly that something was. I sensed a hopelessly profound and unhappy disappointment.

"It's all right," I said.

"Why did you suddenly become so sad? You don't like me?" she asked, taking my head into her hands, as my mother used to do when I looked pale.

"You're worried, aren't you?" she asked. "You're so beautiful when you worry. Come." She took my hand and led it under her skirt. "You were asking me what you meant to me. Now you know."

Into my hand grew a hot mushroom, and through it, after a moment, I became the master of her body. Her humility touched me, as did her willingness to grant me her royal domain. I am a mystery to myself, I thought during the lovemaking I did not really want, because it did not belong to me. It was as if some strange big stick were angrily pounding the walls of a deep cave.

"You couldn't have enjoyed that," I said afterward, as she passed me a cigarette.

"Why not?" she said, kissing my forehead. "Oh, you don't understand a thing."

"That's true," I nodded, drunk with a sadness pleasant enough to make me faint. "Everything is collapsing. When I was twenty, the concept of good fit in my hand and was as pleasing to the touch as a Ping-Pong ball. Since then it only rises before me, grows, softens, and loses its shape and I feel I can't hold it in my own hands. It makes me sick."

"I like when you take things to heart. But maybe you shouldn't."

"What do you mean I shouldn't? Do you know what horrors crawl all over the place? The country is in ruins, and the nation is degenerating. An hour ago, up on the fourth floor, something was born, something that reminds you of a human being only because it came out of one. When I consider that Tania is pregnant, my heart is in my mouth. There is no other defense but to relate myself to the good. But where has it gone?"

Nice sentences, I thought unwittingly. Nora was silent, and a moment later she slipped out of bed and reached for her handbag. She put in her drops, then lit a cigarette. She did not light one for me. When, slowly and carefully, she started to get dressed, I sensed it was some sort of signal, a sign. I did not understand its significance and patiently waited for her to reveal it. I had to wait until she put her boots on and placed her hat on her head. Then she leaned over and quietly asked me: "Why didn't you tell me she was pregnant?"

"Tania?" I said, thinking about it, and suddenly everything was clear: I knew then that my answer wouldn't change a thing. "You never wanted to know anything about her."

She eyed me attentively from above, mercilessly. She wanted to annihilate me with that stare before her departure. She did not know that though I was lying naked in a defenseless position, I was invulnerable, because from the moment she stopped loving me, she stepped outside my soul, and it hermetically closed behind her.

"I have to admit it," she said, measuring her words. "You've won. In a way, it is not a defeat, because you are a monster. Nobody can win against you."

When I heard the door close behind her in a dignified way, I was relieved. It was as if I were waking up from an exhaustingly long nightmare. Was it really I who had had the nightmare? I wondered. And I was thinking about how many things there were waiting for me to right them.

The snow had melted by morning. In the sewers the water roared, and stockinged women had wet spots on their calves. In the city a mob whirled about, giving me a sensation of pleasant disgust, because it was so strange to me, stranger than any other mob in the world. The mob's atomized indifference is, for a small city like Bratislava, actually a miracle. It was under the windows of Nora's editorial office that the mob was thickest. I escaped from it to the Tempo, where I had bean soup in an effort to ward off my morning mood. It did not help, probably because I had not had enough sleep. The night before, I had had to see the alien five times to change its oxygen. It was yelping with that monstrous falsetto voice until five in the morning. Then it went silent for an hour, and at six it died.

Trnávka welcomed me with its abandoned streets. Everyone had left for work, and our eighty-year-old neighbor, who usually stood guard all day long at his gate, was in bed with pneumonia. I saw Pepina in the distance, tracking some of her acquaintances, and since she was having a jaunt out in the street, Tania was not home. Pepina spotted me and ran toward me; she was a black, hairy ball with a pink tongue that fluttered about like a flying tie.

Our bedroom is much brighter in winter, since the walnut tree is bare. I sat down in an armchair and put my feet up on the tiles of the stove. Pepina lay down on the carpet under the armchair, and we dozed off in a minute.

Tania found us two hours later. She carried a book from the university library.

"Imagine! My grandfather was a writer," she said, still astonished. "I discovered his book, but it's in Hebrew. I didn't know he wrote." Her grandfather had been a well-known lawyer from Prešov who was given an exemption in 1942. So he watched his wife and his daughter get on the train with a group of other relatives, and he saw the platform slowly empty until he remained there alone, in a holiday suit. Then the whistle blew to signal the train's departure, and he made the decision that had marked Tania from birth. He boarded the train, knowing full well its destination.

When his son returned from Moscow after the war, he could not find anyone, and remained alone in the world, without God, whom he had left for communism. I envy Tania the improbability of her existence. It is so high that it almost suggests a certainty that her birth was intentional. One cannot say that about me. Not only was I not supposed to have been born, at least not so soon after my brother, but I should have been a girl! Mother said she was relieved when I was born with a little tail, since I was as ugly as a monkey and ugly boys survive easier.

Tania sat down in the armchair opposite me and joined her fingers on her round belly, which had been growing for a full six months. I realized that her glance had changed. She no longer stared at me, as had been her habit when I was not looking at her or was doing something and could not be disturbed. Now it was as if she constantly turned her eyes inward, no matter where she looked.

"Tania?" I said, and we both froze in surprise. Actually we had never addressed each other by name. Somehow we did not need to, and maybe we unconsciously wanted to prevent limiting our relationship by using our names. Naming means objectifying, and when I say "Tania," I mean only her; at the same time, I am implicitly recognizing the rest of the world and admitting the existence of other women.

I wanted to say in one sentence that it was over and behind us already. I realized my mistake a few sentences later when I saw that I couldn't just cut it off. One word creates the necessity to say another to explain the first. For a while I was floundering with the attempt to stave off an avalanche of inquiries that Tania never launched, since she had found refuge in a catatonic silence. But then I simply began to talk in the way I imagine people speak in the confessional, which I have never entered. My parents did not have me baptized, because they really believed there was no God. I confessed to Tania for more than an hour.

"I can't understand it at all," I concluded. "It gathered over me like a storm, and I guess I was deceived by the peculiar feeling of happiness. Can happiness come from evil? Maybe it can."

Tania was silent for about five minutes, as if waiting for me to remember some more, and then she yawned from excitement. She always yawns before saying something important.

"What do you want to hear from me?"

I shrugged my shoulders uncertainly.

"You know very well I won't leave you. Do you want to hear that I love you? Yes, I still love you, the same as before. Do you want me to understand you? I do understand you, but frankly, I feel it does not concern me at all. I don't even know why you've told me. The whole thing, from beginning to end, is your problem, not mine."

"What do you mean?" I objected. "Am I supposed to live here with a secret?"

"I told you it's your problem."

"Now it's not only mine."

"It is."

I reflected, stunned. She was right. I wanted an absolution she could not give, because I had not hurt her. It was, and would remain, my problem.

*   *   *

Nothing else happened that day. Tania was reading the second volume of a history of the Jews, and I found refuge in a detective novel. By the time we went to bed, it had cleared up outside, and the full moon projected through the window onto the white canvas of the bed a clear rhombus. I fell asleep instantly. I adore sleep, because it postpones life. I almost never dream, but this time I found myself in a train, in an ordinary compartment, where some people stood around me, and I could see that on the outstretched palm of my hand stood a glass.

"Melt that glass," the people urged me.

"With what? With the heat of my hand? It can't be done," I objected, and watched in astonishment as the glass softened and the thin walls rolled down like an accordion and became a delightful, transparent pancake.

Suddenly I stood in a beautiful green meadow, and there were some other people near me.

"We are the last people in the world," they said. "And over there," and they pointed to a group of wooden houses at the edge of the forest, "are the last human dwellings."

The buildings reminded me of a village preserved as a museum. I approached, and one of the log houses had an open door. The single room was lit by the sun, whose rays fell on a table upon which lay a piece of paper in a red frame. I stopped at the threshold.

"Read that poem," someone ordered me, and I craned my neck and focused my eyes. On the white surface unclear lines stood out. They were typed verses, but I couldn't discern them. I squinted at the text and concentrated with all of my will on deciphering the smudged letters. I understood that it was actually very simple. It only was a question of energy. One had only to move the lever of the generator, and the text would be mine. The letters were becoming more distinct, but it was costing me more and more effort. My heart began to pound, and I hesitated for a moment.

"Read!" The command gave me new strength, and the letters were getting sharper. But my heart pounded increasingly furiously, and I realized that this was no fifteen-hundred-meter run. No matter how much energy I had, I feared that I wouldn't be able to withstand the pressure. Someone else pushed the lever of the generator, though the body was mine. It started to throw itself around in spasms, and this was no longer a dream, because I opened my eyes and was filled with the limitless horror that my heart was about to burst. My arms and legs were flying in an insane dance, but the paper did not vanish. It was hanging in the dark, getting closer to me, quite certainly against my will.

"I don't want to!" I shouted silently, because I knew I could communicate even without using my voice.

It withdrew and I sat down, totally exhausted. I went downstairs and turned on the light. I felt that he was there with me, and I said emphatically: "I don't want to. I really don't. I'm afraid. How am I supposed to know who you are?"

I was anguished, knowing that he wouldn't give me an answer, while following me all the while. I didn't want to think about him; my only defense was not to think about him. If I accept him into my thoughts, I'll give myself up to him, because he is infinitely stronger, I told myself. I don't want any mystical experiences. I have enough problems with everyday reality.

I thought about the past few weeks. Nora invested in her clothing her entire female intellect, and I now realized that everything she wore impelled me to remove it. She knew that and incited me. It was unbelievable, but she wanted me. I had never before met such a stubborn will. She necessarily had to have some origin in me, for I was her object and she could have become a key to myself. Pity.

Suddenly I realized that I was deceiving myself. I imagined my life, metaphorically, as the search of my own original, natural, and good existence. I thought I would be happy only when I found it and merged with it. It hovered somewhere around me, and all I had to do was spot it, recognize it, and hide in it. However, I wondered, what if my untrammeled search prevents me from finding it?

Still, it was even simpler. I was not searching for anything. I just pretended to search, to have a reason to frequent the world that tempted me. It was enough to recall my dialogues with Nora. I would have never believed myself capable of such mawkish sentimentality. My brain had gone soft. I had desired a decent job as an editor, yet that wasn't the worst thing. The most embarrassing thing was the pseudophilosophical superstructure of fatality that I invented to give my life meaning, a good meaning. And I had told her I was a writer, because I thought that would protect me from banality. But now, I thought, I have her in the palm of my hand, like that glass, and I can't escape her, because I'm afraid. What if I must pay for my freedom from banality with my life?

I was sitting in my armchair feeling safe, thinking about myself. It was half past two in the morning, and I thought that I might dare to sleep. I carefully closed my eyes, noticing with relief that sleep was beginning to rock me in a good-natured way. Upstairs, Tania sighed in her dream and then sighed again, as if something had awakened her.

"I'm here," I called out, because sometimes she reaches out for me. "I'm here," I said again, when I went up. "Are you sleeping?"

"No," she answered mechanically. She was lying on her back, and her eyes were open to the lunar light. "I'm wet. Something has happened."

I'd actually known all along. But I thought it was fetal water. When I turned on the light I saw that she was lying in blood. I turned it off.

"Just don't move. I'll come get you."

I recognized unmistakably the peculiar, heady odor of disaster that arouses my brain to cold-blooded activity. Only when I am totally engaged am I sufficiently strong to fight a dignified duel with naked existence. I dressed with machinelike, unhurried speed. I ran out into the street and started the car left me by my father. Tania lay motionless, in shock. She'd guessed that life was fleeing from her. I placed a clean towel between her legs and took her into my arms. Pepina at first ran around us excited, but when she smelled the blood that we were leaving behind us, she started to whimper sorrowfully and returned to the door.

I put Tania onto the lowered seat and darted into the empty streets. We came across only a few taxis and a bakery's Avia delivery truck, which desperately honked its horn after skidding on the icy intersection and sliding in my direction. I stepped on the gas until I hit the floor and saw the delivery man jump out. We missed him by two feet. I had known we would make it.

The receptionist opened the door with her mouth open, but she reacted fast and called the elevator.

"Good God, such a thing, such a thing," she repeated over and over, running in front of me and opening the doors, because I carried Tania in my arms.

The stretcher stood, as always, on the fourth floor near the operating room. Judith, who on principle does not sleep during the night shift, met me on my way, and I waited until she took the comforter off the stretcher to put Tania on it.

"I'll call the doctors. Go get changed," she ordered me namelessly. I was skipping the stairs on my way down, and on the third floor I met one of the doctors as he hurried toward me, tightening his belt on the way, squinting, with his red eyes set deeply into his wrinkled face.

"What's going on?"

"I brought my wife. It's probably the placenta," I shouted after him, since I had disappeared behind the corner of the staircase. In the room Pista *bacsi* was lying asleep across the bed, and one of his legs was hanging down to the floor. I'll never understand how instincts work. In his hand he firmly held a bottle of gin like a candle, and never, never did I see him spill a drop of liquor. He babbled some chewed-up words and snored with his mouth open.

They were already gathering in the operating room. Otilka, in her sterile gown, was watching me from behind her mask as if she wanted to tell me something.

"Good morning," I mumbled awkwardly, and Otilka barked back.

The anesthesiologists were already there. The aristocratic woman doctor greeted me with a nod; the head obstetrician arrived and scrubbed himself, frowning, because when he could not joke, he was quiet. They displayed that fatal cold-bloodedness and calm for which they had trained for years, and I adjusted myself to them.

I moved Tania to the table and attached her arms to the restraints, which proved too large for her weak, slender wrists. She could never open a mason jar or a can, and I always felt that the world must seem to her built to the wrong size. She did not notice me; again she had that strange, inward-looking stare. It even seemed to me that her eyes went dead, as a sort of self-defense, sooner than the yellow arrow of liquid could fly through the transparent tube into her forearm and disappear into her vein.

When the doctor inserted the intubation, I forgot to turn away, watching uncomfortably the red tube that was sticking out of Tania's mouth like a vulgar cigar. I was relieved when it vanished under the flood of white sheets. Only her toes were sticking out, childlike, as if boneless, with rings of puffy flesh around her tiny nails. Her feet were smaller than my hands, and I liked to take them in my hands, though I had to be careful, for sometimes she would laugh fitfully and then kick wildly.

On the hill of her belly appeared a square of bare skin. Around it gathered three doctors in surgical gowns. The head obstetrician raised his scalpel like a baton and waited for the sign.

"Go ahead," said the anesthesiologist.

I knew the cesarean section ritual by heart. But I liked to take part in it repeatedly, because the opening of the secret passage with which man fooled Nature had a magic effect.

The head obsetrician drew with a scalpel a line that came alive on the white square like a Jackson Pollock streak, widening as if it wanted to leave the picture, its flat, yellow sides colored motley red. When I realized that under that scalpel was Tania's body, it was too late.

As a child, before going to sleep I would play a game to stop my heart. I stopped breathing and waited for the moment when the valves pushed the blood out. Before they managed to open again, I would stop them, taking off on a ride like the ones in Vidam Park in Budapest, descending into the vertiginous abyss until my courage failed, and then I would shoot upward, like in a high-speed elevator.

I don't know what it was I expected, but under the unbearable weight of evidence that Tania was made of the same tissue and re-acted to the scalpel the same way as any other person, that she was equally mortal, my heart stopped beating. I lost my balance and only recovered when I hit the back of my head. I fell back, but the wall stopped me. No one noticed a thing except Otilka, who wagged a warning finger at me.

The doctor was cutting one membrane after another, cutting them in a cross, clipping the slack corners, and pulling them away from each other, so that after a while he was at the deep-red strip of abdominal muscle. He cut that, too, and inserted chromium jaws into the hole, extended them, and secured the opening with a screw. I could already see a piece of the big ball of the uterus, wrapped in other membranes, but the scissors cut them easily and a violet-gray balloon appeared, looking like a surrealist globe. Along its wet, shiny surface ran thousands of tiny, dark blue and violet rivers. The doctor's hand lightly descended to the surface, and the blade scratched it gently, as if accidentally. Sometimes that causes an explosion of fluid. Pure fetal water often squirts up at us. The doctor used his fingers to make his way in while thick blood was spilling from the edges.

He inserted his hand up to his wrist, and in a moment a little head came out from there; it burst out like the rubber devil in the jack-in-the-box that my father brought home from Germany. He took the child out and lifted it high; the assistant clipped the umbilical cord and cut it. Judith was already waiting and took him next door.

I followed her. The aristocratic doctor was waiting at the table, and I was a bit embarrassed that it had to be she who would see my child. In their sixth month babies paradoxically look older than in their ninth. They are thin and shrunken like old ladies. It was a girl.

The doctor did everything that one can do when there is trouble. She suctioned off the blood from the mouth; pressed the mask to her sunken little face; let Susan hold her and gave her a big injection of clear fluid into her umbilical cord. She massaged her; listened to her heart with a stethoscope; exercised her arms, lifting one and attentively watching how it fell back to the table. She again massaged the bony chest covered by yellow skin and spotted with drying blood, repeating the procedure faster and harder, until finally she lifted her by her legs upside down and rubbed her back with her hand, so that the whole body twisted like a rain worm. Then she put her down and observed with a frown how the artery on the belly moved only faintly. It would soon stop because the lungs did not inhale, and anyway it was already too late. I recalled how enthusiastically the nurses applauded at the athletic medical checks when I proudly raised the cylinder measuring the volume of breath and the doctor nodded in appreciation. But this little girl had inherited her lungs from Tania and her distaste for life from me.

I returned to the operating room. The head obstetrician was suturing the uterus that had shrunk to a tough, flexible ball. He finished, pushed it back inside the belly, and membrane by membrane he darned the wrung-out wound. Into the extended hand dripped blood from a misty bottle on a stand. I placed myself behind the anesthesiologist and waited until she measured the pressure. But she just shook her head and tenderly pushed me away.

"Go away," she whispered. "It's low, but she'll be all right."

So what? I thought involuntarily. I changed the comforter and put a new sheet on the stretcher. The doctor was already suturing the outer walls, and I watched with relief how Tania's belly was definitely closing. His big fingers flashed like a professional cardsharp's, and Otilka was the only instrument nurse who could keep pace with him.

"Forty minutes, twenty seconds," she announced in admiration.

Tania had violet lips and a marked face. As I carried her to the stretcher, she shook with cold. She had lost a lot of blood, and the IV was as cold as ice cream. We covered her with two comforters in her room, but they slowed down the shaking more by weight than warmth. I wanted to warm her hand in my hands, but I suddenly noticed that they were icy and wet. I bent down and breathed on her fingers, and a nurse put a hot-water bottle in her bed. Tania's index finger moved and found my lips. She moved her finger, and I leaned over her. She opened her mouth, and I could see her tongue move in a vain effort to articulate. She did not produce any sound, but when I put my ear closer, she concentrated all her energy and punched through the fog of anesthetic to whisper to me the words: "She is in heaven."

It was strange. Despite the drugs circulating in her, I felt that she was looking at me with her atropinized eyes, with the huge black holes of her pupils, seriously and wisely. I did not notice whether that sentence ended with a period or a question mark. Maybe she physically did not have enough strength to stress the last syllable. To make sure, I just nodded uncertainly and brushed the hair from her forehead. I was a little offended that she fell asleep so easily and that I did not know whether she was calmed by my hand or by the secure embrace of her faith.

I went out into the hall and tried to think which particular thread from the evil ball of threads I should grab to fall asleep. I desired nothing more than to lie down and dream about something pleasant and mainly not to think about the moment when I would have to wake again. I could recall the hours of transparent time when I used to run in the pine forest of Záhorie. It almost always works.

The nurses were moving the wrapped and crying babies in the long, double-decker carriages. I watched them, though I knew I should not, thus unwittingly picking from the ball the worst thread. On the other hand, I was moved by curiosity, by my desire to find out what it was that disturbed me as I watched them. When I found out, I moved mechanically back a step, but it did not help me. I was flooded by a wave. Chemically, it could have been a charge of adrenaline, but it does not make any difference. I darted down the shiny hall, and in the following moments I was just careful enough not to break my head by not making the turn to the stairwell and not to break my ankle while jumping down five steps at a time, hoping not to find in my way one of the fat cooks who go to the storage room for jars of stewed fruit.

Joey always locks himself in. That is why I didn't try the door handle; I kicked the door in. I fell inside with the momentum and stopped at the rail on the three steps leading to the iron platform above the boilers. For a fraction of a second I saw him. His face was lit by the red light coming from the open grate of the furnace. He was looking inside, and when he noticed the noise from the door, he slowly turned to me. We stared at each other for a long time. His frowning, uncomprehending look detached itself from me only when he started to lift his feet like a bear dancing in a country fair, because smoke had begun to rise from his boots. I felt sick. Someone turned my insides upside down.

I was sitting in the armchair, leaning my head against the wall. With all of my power I tried not to think but to relax, to close my eyes. My jaw dropped, and my eyelids were slowly falling down. Then Pista *bacsi* woke up as the telephone exchange started to rattle. He carefully sat up, cleared his throat, and happily checked the contents of the half-full bottle of gin he was still holding in his hand.

"You came early today?" he wondered. "Or did I sleep in? Fuck." He touched his head and groaned, "What a night."

I dissolved in tears. Salty water was flowing from me in an incredible stream. It sprayed from my eyes and flowed down my face and neck, soaking my shirt and chilling me. I began to shake in a pleasant, relaxing trance.

Pista *bacsi* looked at me, scared, and lifted his arm as if he wanted to stop me with this gesture.

"What are you doing? You *bolond* crazy?"

I was mooing like a cow and crying more and more intensely, because the beautiful, fantastic absurdity of my flowing tears painfully moved me and forced me into more intoxicating bursts of crying.

"Fucking stop it," he said. "Here, take it." He pushed the bottle into my mouth full of salty water. That drove me to insanity, and I gulped down the gin while Pista *bacsi* happily chuckled and petted my hair. "That's it. Just help yourself, but leave something for me, you drunken whore."

I remembered Nora. No, I won't cry my eyes out, I told myself. I sobered up. I didn't want to use eye drops for the rest of my life because of all that tearing.

"Brrr," I said, shaking with cold, and my tears stopped flowing. "That's a nice swill! How can you drink it?"

Pista *bacsi* smacked his toothless gums in offense. "Then leave it, you fine mug."

I washed my face in the sink and looked at myself in the mirror with my red eyes. I hadn't changed. Maybe I was a little swollen; my wrinkles were a bit deeper. My hair had not turned white. So what? I thought. Reality is annoying, like a swarm of flies, but the State has turned me to steel. You have to find a heavier-caliber weapon.

I suspended myself on a heating pipe and swung for a while to relax my joints. It was not easy without a mirror; I can't think in the second person. I was having trouble making a turn when I remembered that it was about time for Tania to regain consciousness. I started toward her.